Praise for *Dead Don't Lie*

"Lean, evocative prose, tight plotting, a great love story and truly scary moments make *Dead Don't Lie* a sure winner. I guarantee you'll be up past your bedtime, sweating bullets. L. R. Nicolello is a wonderful new voice to watch. I can't wait for more."

—*New York Times* bestselling author J. T. Ellison

Praise for *Dead No More*

"Don't miss this exciting mix of hot romance and black ops."

—*New York Times* bestselling author Catherine Coulter

"Incredibly intense, beautifully written and drop-dead sexy, L. R. Nicolello's *Dead No More* is a top-notch romantic thriller. It grabs you by the throat on the first page and doesn't let go until the very last line. Nicolello's storytelling gets better and better. You won't want to miss this one."

—*New York Times* bestselling author J. T. Ellison

Also by L. R. Nicolello

Dead Don't Lie

DEAD
NO MORE

L. R. NICOLELLO

HQN™

ISBN-13: 978-0-373-77954-3

Dead No More

Copyright © 2015 by Lynell Nicolello

Recycling programs
for this product may
not exist in your area.

This edition published by arrangement with Harlequin Books S.A.

For questions and comments about the quality of this book, please contact us at CustomerService@Harlequin.com.

® and TM are trademarks of Harlequin Enterprises Limited or its corporate affiliates. Trademarks indicated with ® are registered in the United States Patent and Trademark Office, the Canadian Intellectual Property Office and in other countries.

www.HQNBooks.com

Printed in U.S.A.

To my best friend, partner in crime,
and absolute love of my life, Drew.
Loving you is so easy.

CHAPTER ONE

One Year Ago
Wednesday, August 15, 10:00 p.m.

POUNDING FOOTSTEPS ECHOED off the walls in the empty back alley. The sleeper cell's leader turned, saw her closing in and blindly fired. Lily Andrews dodged to her left, sidestepping the bullet as it whizzed by her. *Amateur.* She took a deep breath, pushed herself harder and closed the distance between her and Amed.

"Stay on him, Andrews. We can't lose that briefcase." Jackson's smooth voice crackled in her earpiece.

"I got it. Driving him toward you now."

Amed rounded the corner and raced across the busy New York City street. Lily shadowed his movement, car horns screaming at her as vehicles skidded to a halt. She jumped and slid over the hood of a Honda, her feet hitting the ground lightly before she fell back into stride. Amed tore down the alley hugging the Grand Hotel. There was no way out.

We've got you, asshole.

"He's in the alley adjacent to the hotel," she relayed to her partner. "Tell me that door is unlocked."

"Affirmative. Coming into the front lobby now."

Amed froze, cast a spooked glance over his shoulder and fired. The panicked shot went wide, hitting the brick wall to her left. He lunged for the hotel's emergency exit and vanished. Lily followed, racing up the stairs. She peered around the landing wall. Amed thrust his open palm into the door on the next floor. The door didn't budge. He cursed, turned and raced up the next flight of stairs, taking the steps two at a time.

She sprinted after him, closing the gap.

"There's nowhere for you to go, Amed," she yelled up the stairs. Her heart raced, pumping in time with each footstep. Adrenaline and excitement coursed through her veins. "Let me help you."

Another bullet flew past her. This one closer. *Shit.*

"I take it that's a no."

At the next landing, he slammed into the exit door. It flew open—as Lily had known it would.

She stopped at the exit, hugged the wall and slowly pushed the door open. If her intel was correct, this guy was a rabbit, not a shark, so he'd rush to find a place to hide, not wait to blow her head off. *Let's hope they're right.* With a deep breath, she threw herself through the door, rolled and ended in a crouch, gun raised. Head intact, she smiled. *Thank you, Intel.*

A crash echoed down the empty hall. She pushed herself close to the wall. No one was supposed to be on this floor. And there was no way Jackson could have beaten them to the rendezvous location.

"Where are you?" she whispered.

"Coming up the front steps." Jackson's deep voice popped in her earpiece.

Lily's eyes flicked to the end of the hall and back. "Proceed with caution. Our location may be compromised."

"How? Wait for me."

"Negative. We can't lose that file."

"Wait for me, Andrews. That's an order."

Another crash reverberated down the hallway.

"Yeah, that's not going to happen." She got up and ran.

The hotel room door was propped open and Lily paused just outside, listened. Only silence met her ears. She crept in, softly breathing, back pressed against the wall as she made her way into the room. The mirror was smashed. Tiny, razor-sharp shards littered the carpet. A lamp was broken.

Her instincts screamed at her to get out.

Now.

She inched back toward the open door, but it banged shut. Her brain registered the soft pop of a gun silencer behind her. She dove for the chair, grabbed it and brought it down on its side as two more slugs zinged past her head.

Where was Jackson? Where was her backup?

The door opened and slammed again. The only sound in the room was her own thundering heart. She took a moment to gather herself and organize her thoughts. This mission was going to hell. And fast.

Flattened against the wall, gun up, she took a deep breath and peeked around the chair. Amed was sprawled out at the foot of the bed, his lifeless eyes staring back at her. The case he'd been carrying? Gone.

Then, in the broken mirror, she caught a glimpse of a fractured reflection—one she knew intimately. *What the hell?* Her throat constricted.

"Jackson?"

"Of course you would disobey my order," Jackson

said, his tone hard, clipped. "Are you going to show yourself, or do I have to talk to a chair?"

"That depends." Her bewilderment boiled over to a hot rage. "Are you going to shoot at me again?"

He chuckled. Funny, how that deep sound used to make her smile. Now her skin crawled with apprehension.

"Lily, sweetheart. Why would I shoot my partner? My lover?" he continued in a voice as smooth as velvet.

A wave of nausea hit her. Not the I-want-to-puke sensation due to a simple stomach bug, but the debilitating sickness you couldn't escape after riding the roller coaster one too many times. She trusted this man with her heart, with her life. The room spun, and she reached out her hand to steady herself. Had Jackson turned? Her mind tumbled over itself, fought against the inevitable. No. It wasn't possible…was it?

Lily reached for the second gun strapped to her ankle. Her fingers brushed the cold metal, and she drew it out of its holster, simultaneously peering under the chair. She held her breath and flicked off the safety. The soft click echoed in her ears like a canon.

"Is that what this has come to?" he asked.

"Don't give me that shit, Jackson."

How were they having this conversation? Better yet, how had she not seen this coming? She'd sensed his distance and moodiness, sure, but chalked it up to the grueling hours on this assignment. Her mind raced, landing on sure tells that something had been amiss: the late-night calls, last-minute cancellations, occasional disappearances. She shook her head.

Son of a…

She should have seen those signs for what they were.

But those damn green eyes of his got her every time, dulling her well-honed instincts.

Their romance was against Unit 67's strict protocol. She knew it, Jackson knew it, hell, even the director of their top-secret government agency knew it. But when he'd hauled her into his office, she'd argued with him, promised to keep her romance with Jackson under wraps. Swore it wouldn't impede her judgment.

When the director—who also happened to be her godfather—started searching for a new partner for Lily, she'd thrown the I-have-no-one-else card at him, which, no doubt, had been a slap in his face. Kennedy finally relented, agreed not to interfere with Lily's relationship with Jackson, but threatened to bench her if she couldn't separate work from play. She'd laughed, promised she had it under control.

Clearly, she'd been wrong.

"Stand up, Lily, or I'll kill you," Jackson said in a do-not-fuck-with-me tone.

Lily knew that tone, had heard it before, and he'd been good on his word. *Shit.* She checked both guns, took a deep breath and slowly stood.

Jackson leaned against the far wall, his weapon trained on her forehead. The kill shot he'd all but perfected. Her gaze landed on the silencer, and her heart seized.

She kept one hand hidden, raised the other arm, pointed her .45 at her partner—her fiancé—and prayed she wouldn't have to pull the trigger.

"Why are you doing this?"

"Because I'm tired of putting my ass on the line for nothing but a pat on the back and a medal that's taken away right after a classified ceremony." He picked up the briefcase and took a step toward her. "Do you know what this formula is going for on the black market?"

"Give me the case." She scanned the room with her peripheral vision, searching for an exit. The door was closed, and the window was shut—probably sealed tight. She was trapped. *Just perfect.* Choosing the closer of the two limited options, she edged toward the window and held up both guns. "You don't have to do this."

"Oh, but I do. The man I'm in bed with now will kill me, and slowly, if I don't deliver this. Besides, I'm looking forward to an early retirement." Something that resembled hope flashed across his face as he took a tentative step toward her, reaching out his free hand. "Join me?"

She'd heard that tone before, the quiet plea blanketed in bravado, when he'd all but begged Lily to say yes, to throw caution—and protocol—to the wind and accept his marriage proposal. And just like then, it about damn near split Lily's heart in two. Then she'd agreed. Now…she hesitated, caught up in the past, in the promise of more.

He stopped, tilted his head and locked eyes with Lily. She tried to see past the darkness dancing in his green eyes, to the man she'd loved from the minute she'd been paired with him for her first mission.

On the streets of Paris, they'd played the part of lovers perfectly, and she'd fallen for him.

She'd soaked up his woodsy smell as he'd tucked her into his side. They'd meandered down the Seine, their target in sight. The feel of his blond curls running through her fingers. The stubble on his strong jawline scratching her as he pressed his face into her neck sent fire racing down her spine. Everything about Jackson drew Lily to his side—his rebellious spirit spoke to hers on so many levels.

That connection followed them from that first mission in France, to the next and the next, until there was no separation between the cover of the mission and their reality behind closed doors.

She blinked hard. *No.* The man before her wasn't the man who'd been her partner for the past three years, and definitely wasn't the man she'd pledged her love to and was set to marry next month. It was supposed to be small and intimate, just the two of them and a couple witnesses, but that was all she'd ever wanted. Now it looked like that would never happen. A tremor ran down her arm.

How could she have been so wrong?

"You know I can't," she said in a broken whisper, barely recognizable to her own ears.

A dull, blank shadow descended over his face, turning his handsome, model-like features into something grotesque, evil even, and he stepped back. "Or won't."

"I'm not going to play this semantics game with you, Jackson." She leveled both weapons, aimed them at his heart, and put more pressure on the .45's trigger. "I don't want to shoot you. Just give me the case."

Scorching fury burned out any nostalgia she'd had left for her fiancé. If he'd turned, he was the enemy.

End of story.

"You won't shoot me." He smirked at her. "You can't."

In another lifetime, he would have been right—she couldn't have pulled the trigger. But time blew by at a blistering speed, and she was no longer the agent racing after a known terrorist hell-bent on destroying her country. She was staring at a skilled, narcissistic traitor, a sociopath who had no problem whatsoever betraying his partner *or* the cause he'd held dear.

And for what? Self-preservation?

She'd promised to defend her country against all enemies foreign *and* domestic.

The bullet flew past his head, nicking his right ear. Jackson's hand shot up reflexively to the wound. Pulling his hand away, he glanced at his bloodstained fingers, stunned. Seizing that brief moment of dropped guard, Lily sprang and tackled him.

He recovered quickly and went on the defensive, flipping her over his shoulder. The .45 sailed from her hand. Landing hard against the scratchy carpet, his body tumbling down onto hers, Lily thrust her open palm into his throat, hoping to crush his larynx. She was off by a fraction. Nevertheless, he gasped and stumbled backward, struggling for air.

Pushing to her feet, Lily searched for an escape. Jackson had recovered from her attack and now stood blocking the door. She glanced at the window, weighing her options. *Where was her freaking backup?*

That moment of inattention was her undoing. With a roar, Jackson charged. She snapped to attention, sidestepping his assault. He spun and jabbed out his arm, his fist connecting with her jaw. Light exploded behind her eyes. As she blinked back the pain and squared off again, his other fist made contact with her lower back, just below her kidneys. Lily swallowed the cry in her throat, swung again. He deflected her fist and drove his into her stomach.

Lily tried to stumble away, doubled over in agony. But Jackson was faster, grabbing her by the shirt and lifting her off her feet. With a snarl, he slammed her into the window. It shattered. Knifelike shards of glass bit into her back. Pain ripped through her. A shadow crossed Jackson's face—was it regret?—but quickly disappeared. She clutched his wrists. He pushed her hard until half her body dangled out the window.

"You should have said yes."

"Don't do this." Cold panic encased every cell in her body. *Dear God, he's going to drop me.* The blood in her veins crystalized. She tightened her grip. "Jackson, please. Don't do this."

"Sorry, Lil." He twisted his arms, dislodging her hold, and let go.

CHAPTER TWO

Five Days Later
Monday, August 20, 3:00 p.m.

SOFT BEEPING PULLED at Lily from the dark recesses of her mind. Where was she? She shifted slightly, then gasped as pain ripped through her back. She groaned and forced her eyes open. Bright light blinded her. Where were her reflexes? Why was she taking so long to move? She concentrated, tightening her focus on the room around her.

Ben's tanned, weathered face hovered over her. Worry shone in his brown eyes, pulling his crow's-feet even deeper. She wasn't surprised he was here— wherever here was. In some serendipitous moment just before her parents had been killed in action, he'd sworn that if the unimaginable happened, he'd step in.

He'd been there ever since.

"Easy, Lil." He leaned over and stroked her hair.

"Where am I? How long have I been out?"

He hesitated.

"How long?" The words came out in a pathetic squeak.

"Five days."

"What?" How the hell had she been unconscious for five days?

"You've been in a coma. Intel screwed the pooch. Your backup ended up in the wrong place, on the other side of the damn city. When they finally found you, you were in seriously bad shape. You'd fallen from a three-story window, Lil. They had to shock your heart twice in transit." He shook his head and looked away. "Jackson didn't make it."

"Didn't make—" She choked on the words. Why did Ben think Jackson was dead? She clenched her fists. The bastard wasn't dead. He'd betrayed them and slipped off into the dark.

"They found blood—Jackson's, yours, Amed's—on the scene. The team worked around the clock to piece it together. The mission was compromised. They knew you were coming. Killed their mule, tried to kill you. From the looks of it, Jackson put up quite a fight." Ben rubbed his hands over his buzz cut, got up and paced. "They took him and the case. We tried activating his tracker, but they found and disabled it. The trail went cold. There was nothing we could do. I'm so sorry, Lil. We lost him."

"I didn't fall," she whispered.

He turned and his eyes narrowed, the warrior he'd once been pushing to the surface. If Lily hadn't known Ben since she was old enough to walk, she'd be terrified at the fierceness staring her down. "What do you mean, you didn't fall?"

Why was her throat so parched? And why the hell was he staring at her as if she'd sprouted two heads in the past five minutes? Hadn't he heard what she'd just said?

She reached for the IV in her arm and yanked at the tubes, desperate to get out of her sterile prison. She'd been down too long—she had to find Jackson. "I didn't fall. Jackson threw me out that window."

"You sure?"

Lily laughed and then cringed, the soft movement shooting daggers into her side. Damn, she hurt. "Believe me. I'm sure. I looked into his eyes as he dropped me."

"He dropped you?" Ben's face darkened, his voice stone cold.

"He said, 'Sorry, Lil' and let me go." She pushed herself up and grit her teeth as pain poured over her, followed by a wave of nausea. She clawed at the tubes sticking out of her arm. "The case. Jackson had the case. Where is it?"

"Easy." Ben caught her hands in his larger, calloused ones and held tight. "Are you absolutely sure it was Jackson who pushed you?" He frowned. "Your injuries were pretty severe. The doctors said they could have adverse effects on your memory."

"My damn memory is fine." Her voice rose, and she struggled against his strong hold. Why didn't Ben believe her? She remembered everything, down to the tiny specks of brown that had shimmered in Jackson's green eyes before he'd let her go.

Before he'd tried to kill her.

"Ben. Where is the damn case?"

"It disappeared. And until this moment, I thought—" He shook his head. "*We* thought that Jackson was dead. If he isn't, then he's gone to the wind, with the case."

She stopped fighting. Jackson had betrayed them, betrayed her. He was a traitor, and she'd let him get away.

She'd failed.

The heaviness of guilt crushed her until she could barely breathe. She'd never been unsuccessful on an assignment before. Lily closed her eyes and slipped back into the welcoming darkness.

Jackson hadn't died. He'd gotten away.

And she'd let him.

SEETHING, LILY PACED beside the director's long window overlooking the city below.

"Let me get this straight. You want me to stand there, lie through my teeth to the team and pretend Jackson died a heroic death, when he actually betrayed this agency and our country?" *That wasn't the only thing he'd betrayed.* She clenched her fists. She'd trusted Jackson with her life.

Worse yet, she'd loved him.

"You do remember he threw me out of a three-story window, right? He tried to kill me. I was in a coma for five days." She stopped her march and stared out into the dark night. There was no way in hell she'd honor that man for betraying her country. No matter what the director wanted. "I'm sorry, sir, but I can't do it. I won't go to Jackson's funeral."

"It's not a request, Andrews." The director spoke slowly, quietly. "It's an order."

She spun around. "Are you kidding me?"

"No, I'm not. You'll stand beside his grave, and you'll mourn your partner. End of story."

"With all due respect, sir, I—"

He lifted his hand and cut her off.

"Do you know what it would do to this place if people found out that our top operative turned? That we had a traitor within our midst and didn't know it?"

Lily didn't need to be reminded. Only the elite of the elite within the intelligence community made it through Unit 67's doors, and only after being hand-selected, black-hooded and whisked away in the middle of the night.

There was no application, no interview process.

On paper, 67's operatives embedded themselves among the rest of the alphabet agencies, but that was *not* their true directive. The small group of men and women Lily shared a building with had one common goal—to flawlessly execute their missions and allow the other government agencies to safely accomplish their jobs. Unit 67 was called in whenever the CIA didn't want to get their hands dirty, paving the way for them to ride in on their white horses and step into the spotlight.

Their mission success didn't make the news because humanity couldn't handle the hidden darkness walking among them. Which suited 67 just fine. They were ghosts, even among the other spooks. Unit 67 didn't exist to the world. And they didn't make mistakes.

Ever.

Having a traitor working within their ranks highlighted a security breach, and they needed to know, needed to step up their individual games. Be more alert. Lily opened her mouth to argue again.

"No, Lily," the director said firmly, shaking his head. "We wouldn't survive it. To keep morale high, the others need to think he died in the line of duty."

"He didn't—"

Director Stephen Kennedy pushed to his feet, his face flush with anger. "Enough! That isn't the point here, Lily. This place—your team—needs to see you shed tears for your partner. So that's exactly what you'll do. Consider it your greatest assignment yet."

A perfect storm of emotions swirled in her head. She couldn't let Jackson's betrayal go, yet disobeying a direct order from her boss—godfather or not—wasn't an option, unless…

A wave of regret hit her as she stared at Kennedy, but it soon passed as an ironclad resolve settled into her mind.

"Fine." She walked to the door and reached for the knob. "But, sir, it'll also be my last."

CHAPTER THREE

Thirteen Months Later
Monday, September 15, 4:00 p.m.

LILY FELT CAPTIVE in her own skin. The longer it took her to find Jackson, the worse the sensation became. It had been thirteen months to the day since she'd dangled three stories above the pavement and stared into his face before he let her go. She'd kept her word to the director and walked—and had hunted Jackson ever since. To end that horrible chapter and get her old life back at Unit 67. The life she loved and missed every second of every single day.

She couldn't escape the mental imprisonment she found herself in, no matter what she did to combat it. So, on a daily basis, she took to the wide dirt path along the Missouri River snaking through Omaha and ran until her lungs gave out.

To clear her mind, her thoughts, her mood.

Endless months of searching had resulted in nothing but dead ends. Frustration and anger ripped through her veins as one foot after the other pounded against the well-traveled trail. Jackson couldn't have just disappeared. People didn't vanish into thin air. They always left a trace. Always. She just had to find it.

Her legs screamed at her to stop and her breath came

in soft gasps as Lily eyed her fellow joggers. On cue, they moved left or right, as though somewhere deep within their subconscious, a tiny voice screamed not to have any contact with her, to get away from the impending danger.

A man approached from behind and ran next to her. She stumbled, regained her footing and picked up her pace. He matched it. Stride for stride.

Lily stole a quick glance at him. Dark stubble peppered his strong jawline. Short brown hair clung to his perspiring forehead and defined muscles pressed through his damp shirt. Everything female about her perked up. *Damn. He's sexy.*

He also blocked her only escape route...unless she wanted to take a swim in the Missouri River to her left. Which she didn't.

She picked up speed again.

So did he.

"Thought you could use a running buddy."

"Not interested."

"You know, they say women shouldn't run alone."

She snorted. This man had no idea what she was capable of. "Go away."

"Not going to happen. I need to talk to you."

Lily slowed to a stop and shoved her hands to her hips, glaring at him. "Look, I appreciate the Midwest friendliness, really, I do. But I don't take to strangers interrupting my life, and especially my runs. Now. Go. Away."

"I'm not a stranger."

"Like hell you aren't."

She turned to leave.

"I *do* know you, Lily Andrews." His voice sliced

through the dusk air. He pushed his sunglasses up on top of his head and pinned her with piercing blue eyes that made the clearest Caribbean water look dull. "Your reputation precedes you. I know you were 67's *best* black-ops agent before you went quiet. I know that you moved to Nebraska to escape…"

As the stranger rattled off classified information, the irritation drained out of her, replaced by a white-hot rage. *Who was this guy?* Another 67 agent? How else would he know so much about her? She'd never seen him at Langley, so he had to be embedded in another agency. DEA? FBI? She refused to believe the alternative—that she'd been burned—and focused on searing his image in her memory.

Lily backed into the tree line, scanned the running path. Reaching behind her, her fingertips brushed the petite gun tucked against the small of her back.

The man mirrored her movement, almost as if he could read her mind, knew her playbook, and stepped closer. "I wouldn't do that, if I were you."

She gripped the butt of the gun. All her senses were on high alert. Why would 67 come after her now? A year after she'd walked? Did Kennedy honestly think the raging fire in her belly would have snuffed out? A soft crunching behind her pulled at her ears, and her muscles coiled. She cast an uneasy glance over her shoulder, calculating the impending risk.

Nothing but a bunch of young high school kids.

"Get your hand off that gun, Lily." He stopped talking and let a group of joggers run past. "A Mexican standoff in public all but guarantees you'll blow your safe haven to hell."

He had a point. She tipped her chin toward him, carefully watching his movements. "You first."

A grin spread across his face, and a deep dimple appeared. He raised his arms in surrender.

She stepped back and put distance between herself and the handsome stranger. "I don't know who you think you are, but stay away from me. I won't ask again."

"Just hear me out."

"Hell will freeze over first." She pulled the gun out and let it hang by her side. It was an extreme gesture, but he'd rattled her.

His eyes widened, but so did his grin.

Lily cocked the hammer back. "Run. You have five minutes to be out of my sight. Or I'm coming after you."

"As tempting as *that* thought is…"

She increased the pressure on her trigger. "I told you to run."

"And I told you that a standoff wasn't necessary."

Before she could respond, he sprang and tackled her onto the ground, straddling her. She reacted instinctively, bringing her gun up to aim. He hit her at the wrist joint and sent the weapon tumbling into the tall ornamental grass planted along the running path, hiding it from view. Grabbing her arms, he pinned Lily beneath the bulk of his body. She gasped and struggled against his ironclad hold.

He moved his mouth to her ear. "Don't make a bigger scene than you already have. We have an audience. Follow my lead or we're both going to spend some time behind bars."

Follow his lead, my ass. She fought hard, desperate

to put some space between herself and this brute of a man. He cocked his head and grinned down at her.

"Don't forget I asked nicely."

Asked nice—

The stranger lowered his head and brought his lips to hers.

Lily froze. Every nerve ending in her body fired spontaneously—and without her consent—as he deepened the kiss, pulling a sensual reaction from her that she hadn't experienced since Jackson. It hummed within every fiber of her being. *What the hell?* She tried to twist away, but he pressed down harder, the heat of his body seeping into her coiled muscles, coaxing them to relax, to let go.

To trust.

Not able to break his iron grip, Lily did the only thing she could think of.

She bit him. Hard.

With a surprised yelp, the stranger jerked back and stared down at her as if she'd lost her mind. Maybe she had—she'd drawn blood.

"Is everything okay here?" an older woman asked, eyeing them suspiciously. Her male running companion reached for his phone.

Lily's eyes flickered between the couple and the man on top of her. He licked away the drops of blood on his lip and gently increased the pressure against her wrists as he spoke softly in her ear. "Damn it, Lily. Sell it. Make them believe I'm your lover."

Of course. That was why he'd kissed her. It was the perfect cover with so many public, prying eyes. She forced her muscles to relax, hating that this stranger invading her personal space was right.

"Lovers' spat," Lily muttered, glaring up at him.

The man straddling her pressed his lips to hers again, looked up and shrugged, feigning sheepishness.

Lily wanted to kill him.

The older woman shook her head, muttered something that sounded like "stupid young people" and walked off. The man with her laughed as he pocketed his phone, put his earbuds back in and followed his companion.

Lily wrestled against the stranger's strong, but gentle, hold. "Get off me."

"Are you going to behave?"

She glared up at him.

Chuckling, he rolled off her and stood.

Scrambling to her feet, Lily dug around in the tall grass until her fingers landed on cold metal. She scooped up her gun, letting it hang by her side. Her heart hammered against her ribs. Who was this guy? A shudder swept through her, followed closely by fiery heat that sucked the air out of her lungs.

"I see today isn't a good day to chat." He took a step back, put on his sunglasses and flashed her a grin, sending her heart into overdrive. "I'm out."

Before she could respond, he turned and joined a passing group of runners, melting into their small pack.

SHE BIT ME.

After seven years of covertly working as a black ops agent for Unit 67, Derek Moretti could safely say that no one had ever bitten him—until today. *That* was one for the books.

When she'd turned on him, he'd all but forgotten to breathe. She wasn't as tall as some of the other female agents he'd worked with, but she'd held her ground as she glared up at him, the wind whipping strands of brown hair around her delicate face. Her hazel eyes flashed as she'd shoved her hands onto her slim hips. He couldn't tell if it was anger or the sun that had kissed the tops of her cheeks, coloring her olive skin to a rosy pink, but he didn't care.

She was drop-dead gorgeous...and hell-bent on killing him, a fact Derek couldn't ignore.

Curiosity curled in his stomach like a warm fire when he'd taken the now-familiar running path along the river. *Lily Andrews in the flesh.* What would she say? How would she respond? After months of reconnaissance work, watching her, studying her, he'd conjured up a handful of scenarios. But her biting him?

Yeah, he hadn't seen *that* coming.

But then again, none of Derek's scenarios had involved tackling Lily to the ground, pinning her beneath him—at least not this time around. *That* was a different fantasy, for another time...maybe.

He chuckled to himself briefly, then stopped as the searing memory of her body beneath his flashed through his mind. Her body had been hard, yet soft in all the right places. Just the sheer awareness of her underneath him, at his mercy, left him momentarily frozen, wanting more. He doubted she'd felt the same—in fact, he was pretty positive that he'd seen fire flash when she'd turned those hazel eyes on him.

The woman was a freakin' tigress.

No doubt she'd meant to deter him, but her feistiness did exactly the opposite—it entranced him.

Clearly the kiss had taken it too far. But how could he resist? The woman was a knockout of epic proportions. Derek reached up, touched his fingers lightly to his still-throbbing lip and smiled. Yeah, that was *definitely* not the response he'd hoped for.

Veering off from the running path, he headed west, making his way back to his place. He needed time and space to regroup before he approached Lily again with a proposal she wouldn't be able to resist.

CHAPTER FOUR

Monday, September 15, 5:00 p.m.

LILY STALKED INTO the downstairs lobby of her penthouse loft. Despite another hour of pounding the running trail, she couldn't shake the image of that strange man smiling down at her...or the memory of his body pressing against hers. He was all male, all alpha—and taking up *way* too much real estate in her mind.

George, her doorman and longtime family friend, looked up from behind the concierge's desk. He frowned. "You okay, Lil?"

Of course he'd sense something was off. "I've had better runs."

Wasn't that the understatement of the year. How had that stranger known where to find her? Better yet, how had he known so much *about* her?

She headed to the elevator, having no intention of starting *that* powder keg of a conversation with George. No doubt the giant man would quietly corner her, demanding full disclosure of whatever had spooked her—because she *was* spooked.

"Lily," George's low baritone voice interrupted her mental tirade. "There's a note for you."

She stopped midstride and turned slowly back toward George. He held out a cream-colored envelope and watched her warily, his bushy black eyebrows fur-rowed. "A man came in a few minutes ago. Says he owes you an apology."

She clenched both hands into tight fists, her nails digging into the softness of her palms. "Toss it."

"That's what he said you would say, and I was tempted." He tilted his bald head to the side and searched her face with his deep brown eyes. "Why does he owe you an apology?"

She shrugged, reached across the desk and snatched the envelope. "It's a long story."

"Time is all I've got these days." George crossed his log-like arms across his barrel of a chest and didn't move. Despite his concierge uniform, he looked men-acing and huge, and every bit like the Senegalese war-rior he was. For all Lily could tell, he didn't even blink before he slowly spoke, his voice dark. "I'd appreci-ate an answer."

Lily swallowed down the frustration seeping up. He'd been tasked to do one thing and one thing alone: watch her six. Which was one hell of an assignment, given the independent, stubborn streak she was known for. Disappearing into the wind in Omaha had been a godsend, and she was grateful for the shelter her safe house gave her, but at thirty-one years old, Lily didn't need yet another set of eyes watching her back.

But here George was.

Her parents had seen to that, even from their graves—between him and Ben, she'd never been alone or with-out protection. He was merely doing his job, but being constantly watched, even by someone she considered family, still pissed her off.

"If you must know, that man interrupted my run

today and knew way too much about me." She hesitated, then scrunched up her nose, not wanting to see his reaction to her next three words. "The old me."

"Shit, Lil." George's eyes grew wide and the vein in his forehead bulged. "Does he know yet?"

Lily cringed. Of course George would bring up Ben. Every warrior needed a wingman, right? Well, she'd been blessed—or cursed, depending on the day—with two.

"He's my next call." She held up the envelope. "Especially with this awesome little love note."

"Lily, this isn't something to joke about."

Walking over to the elevator, she pushed the up button and glanced over her shoulder. "Believe me, I'm not laughing."

LILY CLOSED HER front door, tossed the envelope on the counter and reached for her cell, pressing one on her speed dial. As she rubbed the back of her neck, she tucked the phone between her ear and shoulder and quickly moved to her bedroom.

Ben answered on the second ring.

"What's up, Lil?" His familiar voice cut through the quiet and instantly soothed her frayed nerves.

She faltered. Never in a million years did she think she'd utter the words that hung on the tip of her tongue.

"Lil…"

"I've been compromised."

"What? Who?"

"Not sure. But, Ben, I think he's from 67."

"Why is that?"

Lily heard the unspoken question veiled within those three words—*Are you burned?*—and her head spun. No, that wasn't possible. Was it? Destroying all passports and 67-issued equipment, she'd gone dark, covering her tracks and doubling back multiple times to ensure she wasn't being tracked before heading to Omaha.

The only people on the planet who even *knew* she was in Omaha were Ben and George, and only because they were the only family she had left.

"How else would he know so much about me? The alternative is one I refuse to consider. I can't go there, Ben."

Lily shut her bedroom door, turned the lock and moved to her closet. To the casual observer, it appeared to be a massive walk-in closet for a woman who was obsessed with shoes, clothes and jewelry. But she wasn't that woman. They were all props. Lily didn't care about any of that stuff. She only cared about what it concealed.

"I want to know who he is, and why the hell 67 sent him after me."

"You and me both," Ben grumbled, his voice hard as steel.

"Well…" She stopped in front of the tall dresser, flipped up the jewelry tray and pressed her hand to the cool, smooth surface underneath. A screen—doubling as a smaller mirror hanging on the wall—appeared and scanned her palm. "Let's find out. Shall we?"

The display lit up, and she quickly keyed in her code and started scanning through the lobby's video feed.

"Yes. Let's."

Despite the agitation rapidly firing from one nerve to the next, Lily grinned. She could almost see Ben's face growing as stormy as the Pacific Northwest in the winter.

Within minutes, she'd found her running buddy. Apparently he'd managed to slip in a shower before invading her personal space. *Fantastic.*

Despite her best efforts to be pissed off at this stranger, she couldn't help a twinge of admiration. He was tall—six-two, or maybe six-three—defined and, even in his casual attire of jeans and T-shirt, damn right beautiful. His black T-shirt was snug, but not obnoxiously so, and she could see muscle definition beneath the dark fabric. No doubt the result of rigorous training. She rolled her eyes. She didn't need to be imagining *anything* about this guy.

He looked directly up at the camera, mischief in his blue eyes, and winked. Lily snorted. Nothing subtle there—the guy had balls of steel.

Lily tapped the screen. *Got you now.*

She froze the image and took a screen shot. "Sending over a picture. Can you check him out?"

"I'll get my IC people on it."

Lily couldn't help but smile. Ben's people were *her* people, or at least they had been. On the books, they were all part of the United States Intelligence Community, or IC, which was led by the Director of National Intelligence, and each had their own cover story. To those outside of Unit 67, Lily Andrews was a CIA computer analyst, the best hacker to come through Langley's doors in a decade. Off the books was a whole other ball game, and one she missed desperately. Unit 67 fell under a separate director, one that reported directly to the president himself, and was unknown by any of the other sixteen separate government agencies.

Though she'd gone dark, Lily still had allies within the intelligence community—all Ben had to do was mention her name, and they'd have the intel on this joker, 67 agent or not. No one within 67 tolerated a breach in protocol, and showing up unannounced to another agent, potentially blowing their deep cover, was a serious one.

"You want me to come get you?" Ben's voice grew serious.

"No. I don't take people flushing me out lightly." She eyed the photo. Her mind pulled images of him straddling her, and heat surged through her body, which royally pissed her off. *Not a chance, buddy.* "This is *my* home. I've been doing just fine here for a year. I'm not leaving."

"Lil."

"No. I'm staying. Besides…" She moved over and tugged at the massive mirror hanging on the far end of the closet. It swung open on cleverly concealed hinges, revealing row after row of firearms and ammo lined up on hidden shelves. She reached for her favorite Glock and pulled it from its bracket. "You and I both know this place is my own personal Fort Knox. If he gets past George, which is very doubtful, he'll regret it."

"I still don't like it," Ben grumbled.

"Me neither." She closed the mirror-door. "But I'm not leaving. End of story. I'll meet you tomorrow, and we'll go over what we've both scrounged up tonight."

"Call me if you need anything. And no heroic shit. We don't know who this guy is."

"Promise." She hung up.

Oh, she'd keep her word to Ben, but she'd track this mysterious man until she knew the type of toothpaste he used. She didn't appreciate her life being interrupted or her anonymity being blown.

Lily shook her head. Who was she kidding? She was spooked this stranger had not only found her and snuck up on her like a freaking ghost, but he'd also caught her attention…more than she cared to admit.

She reached for the .32 sitting on the dresser, tucked it into the small of her back and grabbed her tablet. Whistling for Dakota, her three-year-old malamute—the only good thing Jackson had left her with—Lily walked into her bedroom and sat cross-legged on the edge of her bed. Dakota lazily sauntered in, jumped onto the bed and curled up against her back. Lily reached over and ran her hand over his heavy coat. She loved that dog, had since the moment Jackson presented her with him as a puppy, complete with a blue ribbon tied around his neck.

She pointed the tablet at the seventy-two-inch flat screen and pressed another button. The screen blinked to life and divided into four separate displays—each one granting her access to a different ABC government agency.

"Not sure who you think you are, buddy, but you messed with the wrong woman."

Lily keyed in her search requirements and, for the first time in thirteen months, felt alive. Like the woman she'd been *before* Jackson dropped her from that window. Bringing that bastard in would be her life's mission, but she couldn't deny that she missed this—the researching, the tracking…the hunting. Worse yet, she was bored, and a bored agent eventually became a threat to themselves, or worse…

They ended up dead.

CHAPTER FIVE

Tuesday, September 16, 6:00 a.m.

LILY BURST INTO Keystone Café and glanced around the coffee bar that could have been plucked from Tuscany itself. The tension in her shoulders evaporated. Everything about the small shop invited her in, calmed her nerves: the tan walls peppered with shots of the Italian coastline; the dark, hand-scraped wooden floors; the fireplace nestled into the farthest corner, its flames softly flickering. The whole ambience of the café beckoned her to sit, relax.

Ben looked up from behind the tall, black granite coffee bar and greeted her with a weary smile.

"Mornin', Lil. Here you go." The big man reached over and handed Lily her usual latte in her favorite burnt-orange mug.

"Thanks, B." She grabbed a wooden chair at the farthest table facing the door and sat, positioning herself to watch those who came and went through the tiny café. Ben joined her and also angled his seat to have an eye on the whole place. She grinned. *Once an agent, always an agent.*

She noticed the file in his hands and sighed—it was just as tiny as hers. "What did you get?"

"Not much." He tossed it on the table. "At least nothing that anyone with a computer, internet access and a normal IQ couldn't have stumbled upon. My guys are still working on it, but they need to be careful. You?"

Lily wasn't surprised. Gaining information about this guy had been trickier than she'd imagined. Which begged the question: *Who was he?* She pulled out the small file she'd scrounged together, handed it to Ben. "I couldn't risk back-channeling into 67's computer mainframe yet—"

"Smart."

"—but my facial-recognition software got a hit early this morning. Our pretty boy is one Derek Moretti, retired Air Force pilot, now supposedly working as an FBI forensic psychologist for BAU. Interesting cover story, but I, for the record, would have gone with something a little more…" Lily took a sip of her latte and set the mug down, searching for the appropriate word. Finally, she looked up and smiled. "Badass."

"Badass?" Ben deadpanned back, a single eyebrow raised.

Lily swirled the liquid heaven around in her mug, her mind drifting back to Derek. *Obnoxious. Ballsy. Gorgeous. Arrogant.* They all suited him, or what Lily knew of him, anyway, but to define Derek Moretti in a single, neat little package? Yeah, there was only one word in the English language that summed him up.

She raised the mug to her lips, took a sip and met Ben's gaze over its orange rim. "Badass."

Ben shook his head and flipped open the file. "What do you think he wanted?"

She pursed her lips, then shrugged. "Not sure."

"Do you think Director Kennedy sent him as a cleaner?"

Lily doubted Kennedy wanted her dead. The director was just as determined to get her back into his court as she was to ignore him. But if for some reason she'd fallen completely out of grace with her former boss, and Kennedy wanted her eliminated, she'd be withering away in some undisclosed location or sinking to the bottom of the ocean with a bullet in her head, not drinking a latte.

"No..." She let her voice trail off as she studied the printout of Derek staring into the surveillance camera on the table.

Black Ops? Definitely. Part of 67? Probably. Sent by the director? She didn't know, which bothered her. But a simple FBI profiler? Yeah, right. And she was the queen of freakin' England.

Ben peered over the edge of the file, his brown eyes searching her face. "Think this guy will approach you again?"

"Yes, but on his own terms, in his own time." She took another sip of her steaming drink. "Until then, have your guys stay on it to see what they come up with, and I'll work on burrowing down on Derek."

"Be careful not to trip any internal security measures."

"Ben—"

"I know." He held up his hands in mock defense. "I know who I'm talking to, but sometimes even the best need to be reminded they aren't invincible."

Lily winced. No one needed to remind her of that—the nightly reoccurring dream of her free fall did that *just* fine.

Ben looked at his watch, pushed back from the table and rose. "Need to finish this conversation later, my regulars will be here any moment." Rounding the counter, he started prepping a new pot of drip coffee. "Just be careful, Lil. He already got the drop on you once."

"Don't I know it." Lily rubbed her shoulder. She'd been out of the game for far too long. "Apparently I'm a little rusty."

Ben glanced up, his face solemn. "Or he's just that good."

"I'd rather think I'm rusty." Considering he was that good made her feel as if a million ants scurried over her. No one got the drop on her. Or at least they never had before.

She needed time to figure out her mystery man's next move *before* he made it. And to clarify the raging thoughts sparring in her head. She'd woken up still annoyed that he'd found her, yet *wanting* him to find her again so she could differentiate the truth from the bullshit...and get a second look at him, if she were being truly honest with herself.

"Mind if I jump behind the counter after I'm done with this?" She raised her latte. "I could use the mindless—"

Ben shot her a glare. "It's not mindless."

"Come on, B. Compared to what we've been trained to do? This *is* mindless. I'm not knocking it. But really?" She enjoyed teasing the tall ex-ranger, even if it was as dangerous as poking a sleeping, cranky lion. She couldn't resist—putting a smile on that hard, windswept face was a challenge she'd been tackling since she was five.

"It's not mindless," he muttered.

In Lily's opinion, the day the doctors delivered their devastating news to Ben was the day Unit 67 lost their greatest asset. A piece of shrapnel from his last encounter in the sandbox lodged too close to his heart for the doctors to safely remove. One misplaced jostle, and Ben was a goner. Given their line of work, he'd had no choice but to hang up his guns. If not for that news, Lily was positive he'd still be out in the field, or at least training the next up-and-coming agents.

She took a small sip of the molten liquid. She loved him. He was family. She'd do anything for him. And how could she not? He'd saddled up when most people had stepped out.

Lily got it. Many people didn't know how to deal with grief, couldn't handle the searing heartbreak of tragedy. Most reverted to awkward conversations, eye avoidance and painful silence. Or simply vanished.

Not that she could blame them.

Death was a bitch.

But Lily would be forever indebted to that big, bald and way-too-serious man who'd stepped in when she'd lost everything…and stayed.

ONCE SHE'D DOWNED her drink, Lily set up behind the coffee bar and took orders. As she handed a skinny vanilla latte to a young girl, the door chime dinged and Derek Moretti walked in, flashing a grin her way. A strange sensation fluttered in Lily's stomach as he walked up to the counter, flipped open the menu and perused it.

She flicked her gaze to the seating area and searched for Ben. He'd want to know that their *profiler* had found her. *Again.*

Ben leaned against the back wall, looking warm and approachable in his navy cable-knit sweater and worn jeans, chatting it up with some of his regulars. They were nodding their heads in agreement with something he'd said. Lily sighed. There was no way to get his attention. *Great. So much for that idea.*

"What are you doing here? What do you want?"

Derek looked up from the menu and set it down. An easy grin curved his lips up, deep dimples forming in both cheeks. "Easy. You."

"Oh, yeah?" Lily propped her hip against the counter, crossed her arms and couldn't help but smile back. His sheer proximity was chipping away at her resolve, despite her best intentions to remain aloof.

He reached out his hand. "Derek Moretti. But you already know that, don't you?"

She studied Derek, then sighed. *No use being rude.* Leaning forward, she reached out her hand. He wrapped his fingers around hers and gently squeezed. Her breath caught in her throat. She hadn't been touched in… well, she couldn't remember the last time anyone had touched her, other than George and Ben, who *clearly* didn't count.

Derek's hand was large and covered hers completely. Calluses rubbed against the soft skin of her palm. His touch was possessive, yet gentle, and a wave of security washed over her. She'd all but forgotten the warm feeling that seeped through her body at the simplest human touch—*a man's touch*. The flutter in her stomach returned with a vengeance.

Don't squirm. Don't squirm.

Without letting go, he cocked his head to the side and quietly studied her. Lily blinked, trying—and failing—to break the pull he had on her. What was hiding behind those blue eyes? And why couldn't she resist their draw?

Hell no. Human touch or not, she couldn't go there. Not ever again.

The last man she'd let in tried to kill her.

Lily extracted her hand from his grasp. The flutter died out, followed closely on its heels by a dull, empty ache. "I'm not interested."

"You don't even know what I'm going to propose."

"Doesn't matter."

But it did matter. And she was interested, very interested. In the man silently studying her, in the way every cell in her body sizzled whenever he was near *and* in whatever he was after.

"Well, maybe you'd reconsider—" He reached behind him, and she tensed automatically. Derek quickly held up his hands. "Whoa. Relax. I'm just reaching for my wallet."

"Course," she muttered as a flush burned her cheeks.

Derek pointed at his wallet. "May I?"

"Of course, sorry about that."

He pulled out a business card, placed it on the counter and slid it across. "When you're ready to listen, call me." He smiled softly, turned and headed for the exit. Without looking back, he waved as he left the café.

Lily picked up the card and spun it between her fingers. *What are you after, Derek Moretti?* She chewed on her lip and watched him through the front windows, unable to deny the effect he had on her. Everything about him, down to his swagger, made her squirm like a hormonal teenager.

"He want to read you in on a case?" Ben approached her, hands pushed into his sweater's front pockets.

Lily quickly shoved the card into her back pocket

and shrugged before reaching for a rag to rub down the counter. "Even if he is, I'm not sure I'm interested."

"Why?"

"Come on, B." Lily glanced over at the old couple and lowered her voice. "The last guy I worked with tried to kill me. Remember?"

"I know, Lil." He went to the espresso machine. "But not everyone is Jackson."

Ben was right. Not every man on the planet was a traitor, and there was no trying to skirt him—he knew her better than she probably knew herself at this point. Lily blew out a sigh. She was interested. She just didn't know enough about the man who'd just blown into her life to do anything about it.

Yet.

LATER THAT AFTERNOON, Lily sat in the corner of Ben's café and enjoyed another tall latte. A shadow passed behind her closed eyes and Lily slowly opened them, expecting to see Ben towering over her. Derek smiled down instead. For the second time that day, Lily found herself drowning in the endless sea of blue staring down at her. It stole the air from her lungs.

She set down her mug. "Oh, for the love of God."

"Hello again."

"Apparently you have a death wish."

"Just doing what's necessary." A slight smirk crossed his face as he dragged out the chair across from her and sank into it, leaning onto his elbows. "And you and I both know you won't draw a gun on me."

"After your little stunt yesterday? And just showing up here? Twice?" Lily eyed the man sitting in front of her. "I'd consider it."

"You loved it, and no, you won't."

He had her there—she had never pulled the trigger based on emotion, nor would she ever. The heat of his lips flashed through her mind, as did the searing memory of his body pressed against hers, and she felt a tingle up her spine. If he'd left that kind of impression when he'd hijacked her, what would he do if she willingly went into his arms?

She shifted in her seat, ignoring the bizarre and *very* vivid mental picture. "How do you know so much about me?"

"You know the answer to that." He pushed his chair onto two legs, laced his fingers together and propped his head back.

"I told you I wasn't interested, so why are you back?"

"Yes. You did." He grinned and let the chair drop to all fours. He leaned forward. "But here's the deal. Your reputation precedes you, even after going to ground. Believe it or not, you're still 67's best asset, and I need your unmatched ability…to become someone else."

Her eyebrows arched. "Really."

"I'd gather the information myself, but I can't risk blowing my cover. So my hands are tied." He shrugged, laced his fingers again and returned to his casual pose. "We need the intel to crack open a case, and I need to protect my asset. As much as I'd like to think I'm invincible, I know my limits."

What? You're not superhuman? Lily opened her mouth to let her internal monologue out to play, but Derek held up his hand, sending her a dry look. "Let me finish before you shoot me down."

She clamped her mouth shut.

"As I was saying," Derek said, a hint of laughter in

his voice. "My client is too high a government asset to roll the dice and play Lone Ranger on this. So here I am. All but begging for your help. Which, for the record, I don't do. Ever."

"I'm not working for 67 anymore. Does Kennedy even know you're here talking to me?"

"Did the director know every asset you pulled in while working an op?" Derek countered without missing a beat.

Lily studied the man in front of her. "Fair enough. But why not pull in someone else who's still on 67's payroll?"

"Easy. I don't need anyone else." He settled into his chair and drilled her with his steely gaze. "I need you."

She squirmed in her seat. Wow, she needed a life. Or a boyfriend. Or both. She knew he meant her skills, not her body. But still...

"Well?"

She cleared her throat, banishing the sexy thoughts romping through her brain. "I'm done—"

He reached across the table, grabbed her hands and grinned at her appealingly. "Please. Don't make me beg."

The same jolt that rushed through her the last time he'd touched her surged again. She slowly withdrew her fingers from his grip, but couldn't help noticing the thrill of the game rush through her. He'd piqued her interest, captured her attention and drawn her in.

How had this stranger managed—in less than twenty-four hours, no less—to do exactly what Director Kennedy hadn't been able to do over the past thirteen months?

"What do you want me to do?" She sat back. "If…
I'm interested. Which I'm not saying I am."

Yeah, right. Who was she kidding? Clearly not the
man sitting across from her, who was doing his best—
and failing miserably—to conceal the grin that spread
across his face. A deep dimple appeared as his smile
grew. She bit the inside of her cheek to keep her own
grin from escaping onto her lips.

"I want you to do what you do better than anyone—
get close to my client's partner, Rowland James."

"That's it?" She tipped her head to the side and
eyed him. "Why do I get the feeling there's more to
this story?"

"Because there is."

His transparent, candid nature both fascinated and
shocked her.

Derek glanced around. "But I can't go into details
here."

And there it was: the tight-lipped, possessive behavior she'd grown tired of before walking away from the
agency. "Why not?"

"First, you haven't agreed to anything yet. Sec-
ond, and more important, there are too many ears."
He crossed his arms and cocked his head to the side.
"Would you go into details now, in this place?"

He'd nailed her. She'd never talk a case here—not
with so many unknown people. And she wouldn't share
everything with him, even if they worked together. She
wouldn't do that again.

Not after last time.

"Fair enough. But at least throw me a bone."

"We've intercepted some chatter that might or might
not involve a national security breach. I can't get close

enough to Rowland to confirm or refute the chatter. My IC team is working around the clock, but they continue to come up empty. He's a bit of a ladies' man, and I figured…"

"You figured what? That I'd whore myself out to get information?" Lily's face—and temper—flamed, all thoughts of Derek's charm and sexiness gone. "Clearly you don't know me as well as you think you do."

She got up, knocking the wooden chair against the desert sand-colored wall. Her whole body trembled with anger as she glared down at him. "Forget you found me. If you don't, I promise you, you'll regret it. I mean it, Derek. Don't underestimate me. I'm not the same woman that you've read about in my file."

Without another word, she stalked toward the door and slammed it on her way out.

CHAPTER SIX

Tuesday, September 16, 3:00 p.m.

WELL, THAT WENT WELL. Derek rubbed the back of his neck and watched Lily through the glass window until she got to the streetlight and rounded the corner, disappearing from his line of sight. He chuckled. She was going to make him work for her involvement, but he was up for the challenge. That brunette bombshell was totally worth it.

The file he'd pulled on Lily didn't do her an ounce of justice. Not in her capacity. Not in her looks. Not in her feistiness. He'd enjoy working with this one—if he could get past that barrier she'd constructed around herself.

He reached for his phone and dialed.

"Is she in?" Director Kennedy asked without preamble.

Typical. Derek ran his hand over the back of his neck. "I wouldn't say that, no."

"What happened?"

Throwing out the "ladies man" card with her was a jackass move. Derek should've known it would rub Lily the wrong way. Nothing in her file indicated that she'd ever used sex to complete a mission. At first he'd scoffed at that. What agent didn't use sex as a weapon, even as a last resort? But after watching her over the past few months and building his *own* jacket on her, he imagined that aspect of her to be true.

He pinched the bridge of his nose and closed his eyes. "She might or might not have walked out on me."

"I told you she wouldn't be easy to bridle," the director snapped. "The girl's got more sass in her little finger than most people have in their entire bodies. She can't—make that *won't*—be manhandled."

"I definitely misjudged the sass quotient," Derek muttered. Which was the understatement of the century. Lily Andrews was a firecracker of epic proportions. He'd never seen anyone—aside from his feisty Irish mother—go from calm to boiling in a single breath. If Lily wasn't such a vital part of his case, he would have laughed at her explosion…and enjoyed the view as she left.

But he needed her. Without her, this mission would go to hell and he'd be screwed.

"Don't underestimate her," the director said. "She's your equal. Treat her as such, and she's yours. Don't, and she's as good as gone."

"Yes, I gathered that."

Kennedy sighed into the phone. "Hate to tell you this, but if Lily walked on you, you might have lost her for good."

Derek wasn't about to let her off the hook *that* easily. He just needed to regroup. "I haven't lost her."

"What's your next move?"

"Circle around. Come at her from another angle."

"Good luck, and keep me posted."

The line went dead.

Derek tossed the phone on the table. His 67 cover

within the intelligence community as a profiler with
the BAU wasn't his first choice, but he'd learned how
to read people better than anyone he knew—and Derek
had picked up on the tightness in Kennedy's voice.
Why? What was eating at him?

Derek scrubbed his hands over his face. He craved
movement, a shift, anything that would get him closer
to completing his mission and moving the hell on.
After his recent experience in Seattle, Omaha lacked
the adventure he thrived on.

But Director Kennedy had specifically asked for
him.

Turning down a "request" like that wasn't an option, not as a 67 agent. So here he was, landlocked in
the middle of the country, spinning his wheels like a
freaking hamster on a wheel, going nowhere fast. And
it was getting old.

His mission in Omaha was a bit more complicated
than what he'd just revealed to Lily. And when she'd
asked if Kennedy knew Derek was speaking to her,
he thought he'd blown it. The fifteen seconds she took
to contemplate his response were the longest seconds
in his life. He wasn't there to gather intel on Rowland James alone—the director had specifically asked
Derek to keep an eye on Lily—to ensure she didn't inadvertently stumble into the crosshairs of a killer—is-
suing a gag order on that latter half of Derek's happy
little assignment from hell.

Simple enough, right?

Hardly.

Nothing was simple when it came to Lily Andrews.
He knew what haunted her long into the evenings.
What pushed her to pace in front of the tall windows

of her loft late into the night. And he couldn't blame her. Losing a partner to treason, and having no answers to the million questions whirling around, would shake even the toughest, most seasoned agent.

He'd tracked and memorized her mundane routine within a week: Keystone Café, running trail, shooting range, home. She'd switch up the order occasionally, especially after burning the candle into the early morning hours, but never the activities.

Which Derek appreciated.

It simplified his objective: keep watch over Lily.

The only problem? The more he watched, the harder he fell. Which was trouble. *Lily was trouble.* Without knowing it, she'd gotten to him, settled into his bones and turned his world upside down.

He looked up, caught Ben's steady gaze and nodded in his direction. The tall, bald man didn't return the gesture. *Great.* How was it possible that he'd pissed off both of them? Derek could engage with a tree. He knew no stranger. It was part of what made him so good at his job, yet here he was grasping at straws.

Time to do some serious damage control, because he'd just crashed and burned. Twice. Derek rose from his chair and made his way over to the counter.

Ben didn't move.

Derek knew exactly who was staring him down, and Unit 67's infamous Benjamin Tinsdale was *not* the man you wanted to go up against in a brawl. Of any sort. Derek swallowed his grin. Now was not the time to go toe-to-toe with this alpha.

"Good work on the shop." Derek glanced around. "I like it in here."

Ben crossed his arms over his barrel chest, tucked

his hands under his armpits, didn't smile. "What can I get you?"

Fantastic. He'd significantly angered this mountain of a man when he'd ticked Lily off. "Doppio macchiato."

Ben turned toward the espresso machine, glanced into the mirror behind the coffee bar and watched Derek as he pulled the caramel-colored shots. "Be careful with that one." He spoke in a low, deliberate tone.

What the hell? Derek caught that underlying threat. He hadn't expected Ben to go there. This guy wasn't messing around. Derek filed that away and switched gears. "It was just a friendly conversation."

"Yeah, and I'm the fucking Dalai Lama." Ben passed Derek his coffee. "I'd advise you to find someone else to have a friendly conversation with."

Derek handed Ben a five-dollar bill. "Keep the change."

"That wasn't a suggestion, Moretti."

The hair bristled on the back of Derek's neck. Legend or not, Ben was no longer active and had no say in what Derek did or did not do on a case. Derek took a deep breath, toned down the internal sarcasm before he answered the man glowering at him. He needed Ben on his side, not as an enemy. Might as well learn to play nice. "I'll take that into consideration."

Like hell he would. With the undercurrent at ARME Industries rapidly shifting and the tension between his boss and Rowland James heating up, Derek really needed to read Lily in on this case. And sooner rather than later.

CHAPTER SEVEN

Tuesday, September 16, 8:00 p.m.

WHAT A NIGHTMARE. Every time Lily closed her eyes, she could see the blue of Derek's. She could feel the warmth of his hands, his lips. Her heart raced at the sheer *memory* of his touch. She sat at the baby grand, her fingers flying over the smooth ivory. Her form of therapy. When everything around her seemed to fall apart, she'd lose herself in the soft melodies of Chopin. As her fingers raced, her mind flew to the past.

To who she had been.

She was 67's best agent. And how could she not be? Both her parents had served Unit 67 before their untimely—and classified—deaths. Though it had snatched Lily's family from her, she'd never given leaving this life a second thought—she'd been part of the black-ops world since her birth. It was part of her, entangled in the deepest recesses of her DNA. Had she been studied by psychologists, she would have blown the whole nature versus nurture argument straight to hell, because she wasn't just one, she was *both*. She knew it well, becoming another person. Transforming to learn vital information, in order to protect and to serve.

Lily had loved every second of it.

Until Jackson.

The lonely melody of the piano matched her mood.

She let the last note slip quietly into the night, then reached for the goblet of Merlot and let the tart liquid wash over her tongue. She closed her eyes and opened her heart to remember her father's calm voice. *Once an agent, always an agent, sweetheart.*

Lily swirled the crimson liquid in her glass. She wished things were different. But they weren't. She wished *she* were different.

She wasn't.

Dakota leaped to his feet, growled and rushed the front door. Setting the wine down, Lily grabbed the .45 sitting on the edge of the piano and flipped the safety. Gun drawn, she moved to the wall monitor and peered into the screen. George's face stared back at her. Strange. Why hadn't he just called up? She lowered the gun and pulled open the door. "George, what's up?"

He held out his hand. "Another note from our friendly little stalker."

"Don't be a smart-ass." She took the note, her curiosity sparked. "What did he say this time? Another apology?"

"He walked in with roses—"

"Roses?" Lily managed to choke out.

"I pitched them." He smiled, his dazzling white teeth a stark contrast to his deep brown skin, and winked. "Didn't figure you'd want them."

She snorted. "You figured right."

He grew serious. "He wanted to see you. I told him you weren't available. The guy simply nodded, handed me the flowers and asked that I make sure you got them."

"Ballsy."

"I talked to Ben."

Lily's eyes narrowed. Of course they'd talked. They were both former 67, but the lifetime commitment that most agents made ran true in both men. Unit 67 trained them to be lone rangers, to think on their own and for their own, but every so often, a tight-knit group of lone rangers banded together—and Lily had found herself in the middle of one such phenomenon.

George—giant, scary-as-shit George—decided Ben Tinsdale, his newest trainee, was part of the family when the twenty-something, pissed-off ex-ranger had shown up at Unit 67, hell-bent on avenging the death of his unit. Ben had been looking for a fight, but instead, George introduced the young warrior to Lily's parents, and just like that, a family of misfits had formed. It wasn't unusual for them to check in with each other, especially when it came to her.

"Oh, yeah?"

"Yeah. And I don't like it, or this Moretti guy, for that matter. This place—" George gestured into her loft "—has been off the radar far too long for some maverick to come along and jeopardize life as you know it."

Resisting the urge to roll her eyes, Lily leaned against the door frame and let him talk. The man was worse than a Sidewinder missile when he'd locked on to something. Which, by the determined look in his eyes, was now.

"George, I know."

"Your father would be livid to know his daughter's safe house had been compromised."

Oh, dear lord, how long was he going to go on about

this? She'd figured Derek dropping in on her would rattle George just as much as it had her, but she was a grown woman...and a trained operative. "I get it. And I haven't agreed to anything yet."

He crossed his arms over his chest. "Well, are you going to?"

"I don't know." And that was the honest answer. She didn't. "But it beats the alternative."

"Which is?"

"Sitting on my ass for the rest of my life. I loved my life, loved everything about it, and though I will be forever grateful for you and Ben, I can't sit back and do nothing. Jackson may have boxed me into this corner, but maybe this thing with Derek is my ticket back into the game."

"Do you trust him?"

She considered that for a moment. "Kennedy may be on my personal shit list for making me stand over Jackson's fake grave, but I still trust him. If he sent Derek here, then he trusts him, and one thing I know about Kennedy is that he knows how to read people."

"Except Jackson."

She cringed. That would always be the one black mark in *all* their files. "We all fell for Jackson. I can't fault the director for that, not when I fell for it, as well."

"I still don't like it."

Lily pushed off the door frame, stood on her tiptoes and kissed George on the cheek. "I hear you."

He nodded and grunted an acknowledgment, turned and walked away.

She shut the door, then reached for the tiny note tucked in the envelope. Tugging it out of its hiding place, she read the smooth, controlled handwriting.

For the second time in just as many days, I apologize. I didn't mean to insult your character or your intelligence. If you aren't interested, I understand. But if for some strange reason you are, you know where to find me.
Derek

Lily flopped down onto her oversize white sofa, let its soft, brushed microsuede envelop her. As angry as she was for the disruption in her quiet—granted, ridiculously mundane and yawn-inducing—life, a feeling that had been a stranger to her for the past year reemerged.

Excitement.

Suddenly feeling energized, she stalked to her room, threw the note onto her bed and went to work on her computer.

She spent several long hours back-channeling into 67's computer mainframe, researching and vetting Derek Moretti, filling the recesses of her mind with every detail she could find as her eyelids grew steadily heavier. She finally signed off her computer, padded to the bathroom and flicked on the lights, and stared at her reflection in the mirror.

"You took an oath to serve and protect." She dared the soft hazel eyes returning her gaze to disagree. "Who are you kidding? This is your chance to get back to the life, and work, you love...without having to crawl back to the director with your tail between your legs. You'd be an idiot not to take it."

DEREK WAITED UNTIL the lights in Lily's loft went off before moving from his perch. He yawned and stretched, then checked his watch. Two-thirty. *Damn, woman. No rest for the weary, eh?* She had no doubt spent the past several hours drilling down into his file as far as she could go—which, knowing her, was down to whether he wore boxers or briefs.

Rubbing his hands over his face, Derek walked into the kitchen, searched for a glass and, once finding a clean one, filled it with water. His computer had pinged every time she'd broken through the next level of his encrypted files. It had only taken her four hours to track down just about everything. He downed the water and set the glass on the counter.

He hoped she liked what she saw. If she didn't, his mission was dead in the water.

CHAPTER EIGHT

Wednesday, September 17, 10:00 a.m.

LILY STUDIED HER MARK from the trees along the running path, hidden within their shadows. Dakota sat obediently on her right side. She reached down and stroked the soft fur on the top of his head. He pushed her hand with his wet nose. Her eyes wandered behind her dark, oversize, oval sunglasses, traveling down Derek's powerful back to his defined legs. With every stride, his quads tightened and straightened. The muscles in his back strained against the running shirt, which was dark from sweat.

She had to admit, she enjoyed the view.

Derek turned and ran toward her. Dakota got up as Derek stopped in front of Lily.

"Morning, sunshine." He smiled at her, then bent down and rubbed Dakota behind the ears. "Hey there, handsome."

Dakota nuzzled Derek's neck and Lily's mouth dropped open. *What the...?* She'd never seen Dakota take to another person like he'd taken to Derek, not even Jackson. She trusted her dog's intuition more so than her own...*he'd* never gotten into bed with the enemy. Dakota nuzzled Derek's neck again and she cleared her throat. "I'm here to talk to you about your proposition, Derek."

Looking up, he grinned. "I was hoping you'd say that." Straightening, Derek ran his hand through his short brown hair and tipped his head toward the water. "Walk with me?"

They veered off the running path and headed toward the river walk, making their way to the farthest bench overlooking the river. Lily peeked up at her companion. At five-nine, she wasn't short for a woman, but his large build dwarfed her and—yep, damn it—he was still as smoking hot up close as she'd remembered. Sinking down onto the worn wooden bench, she turned slightly to keep her line of sight open.

"I see you haven't lost your instincts."

"No, I haven't, which is the only reason I'm willing to listen." She crossed her legs and bounced her right foot. It was a bad habit she had when she focused, one she'd never been able to break, no matter how much she'd tried. "There are no ears here, so start talking."

"No, there are not." Laughter played in Derek's eyes. He hooked his hands together and leaned his head back. "I work directly for John Elsworth, CEO of ARME Industries—"

Lily stopped bouncing her foot and whistled. Nearly every advance in modern warfare and weaponry during the twenty-first century had its genesis within ARME's walls.

Derek glanced at her. "Heard of him?"

"Not him, no." She shook her head. "But I wouldn't know my stuff if I didn't know that ARME is our leading weapons manufacturer."

He lifted his face toward the sun. "Exactly. ARME

and John are one and the same. When one is threatened, the other is, and vice versa. I've been working
this case undercover for almost a year now as Elsworth's security adviser."

"Unit 67 has you working as a glorified security
guard." Lily smirked and went back to bouncing her
foot.

"Easy, tiger." Derek gave her a sideways glare. "Not
all assignments are the glamorous kind."

"Ain't that the truth. But I can't help it—just calling
it how it is." She shrugged and winked at him.

He did a double take, his eyes growing wider at her
unexpectedly playful response. Seeing him caught off
guard only made Lily want to laugh that much more—
served him right. He caught her eye and they stared at
each other for a moment. The wind fluttered, whipping her dark hair around her jaw, and he smiled, his
expression softening. Lily sat back. *Wow. Time to rein
it in, Andrews.*

"Sorry, please continue," she said, smiling wryly.

"There's been chatter that his COO, Rowland James,
is working behind the scenes on certain business deals
that could put the company, and subsequently the family, in harm's way. My objective has been twofold—
protect Elsworth and his family, and gather as much
intel on Rowland James as possible to put him away
and neutralize any possible national security threat."

"Wait." Lily's brows pinched together. "Couldn't the
local cops take care of protecting his family? It seems a
bit extreme to bring in black ops for babysitting duty."

Derek hesitated.

The muscles in Lily's shoulders constricted. She
didn't have time, or the mental energy, to walk into

anything with less than complete transparency. Fair? Hardly. But *he'd* come after *her*. The ball was squarely in her court, and she wasn't waiting around to see if Derek would play nice. Not this time. She jumped up.

"Lily. Wait a minute. Where are you going?"

"If you won't be honest with me, then this partnership—or whatever you want to call it—is over." She turned to leave.

He reached for her hand, wrapped his fingers around her wrist. She jerked away and glared at him.

"Read me in. Now. Or I'm gone."

"Damn, woman. You're impatient."

She was running on a short fuse, no doubt. She tilted her head to the side, stared him down.

He sighed. "Rowland James is a known associate of multiple enemies of the state—"

"What?" She paced, her mind crunching Derek's information. She glanced over her shoulder and frowned. "Then why in the world is he allowed anywhere near ARME?"

"He hasn't broken any laws. Until he trips up and does something quantifiably targeting the United States, our hands are tied."

"Why can't John fire him?"

"It's not that simple. Over the last two years, Rowland has been quietly buying up stock and currently owns 30 percent of ARME's stocks. The board would have to have a majority vote to oust him from his position, but he could still use his controlling interest in the company to get some of his own people on the board."

She shook her head. That made sense, but damn, she hated political bullshit. "Unbelievable. And the rest of this happy equation?"

"As you already know, ARME is one of our government's leading suppliers for all things military and its top research facility. If John was out of the picture, Rowland James would be the most likely candidate to replace him."

"Which is a huge problem."

"Exactly. He'd have complete access to all of our top-secret projects."

Now everything made sense. Lily sat.

"Obviously, that's something the US government would like to prevent—at all costs. That's where you come in." He motioned toward her. "Not to whore yourself out, which is crude, by the way..."

Lily cringed, her cheeks growing warm. Though it had saved her on more than one occasion, her Spanish feistiness also got her in just as much trouble. Case in point? Yesterday.

"But with the way you've been trained...get inside his inner circle, find the evidence we need and put him away. Permanently."

"If this Rowland James character is so hard to get near, how do you propose I do it without raising his suspicion?" Lily reached for Dakota and stroked the soft hair on his ears. Without giving Derek a second to respond, she continued slowly. "Because he will be suspicious."

"All we have to do is find the right opportunity for you to be in the same room with him, and *he* will come to *you*." Derek turned, pinning Lily with those damn eyes of his. She all but forgot to breathe. "Guaranteed."

Bouncing her foot, she tried her best to push back the flutter in her stomach. Her nerves tingled in anticipation. "And when will such an opportunity arise?"

"Saturday night. There's a black-tie event at the Jos-lyn Art Museum for the who's who of Omaha. Row-land will be attending." Derek stared straight ahead. "How's your calendar looking Saturday?"

Her calendar was wide-open—had been for months—but she shook her head. "I can't just waltz into this event and saunter up to someone like Rowland. It'll raise too many red flags…if I can even get close enough to him."

"I know. That's why I'm going with you as your date."

"Wait. What? You're going…" The bouncing halted. Lily glanced over at Derek, who silently stared out over the river. She tried to play it cool, but the idea of spending an entire evening with Derek was surprisingly appealing.

"John has a previous engagement and asked me to go in his place." Derek looked over at her. "Care to join me?" he asked softly.

This was exactly the type of mission she lived for, craved…missed desperately. And having Derek as her partner for the evening wouldn't be so bad, either. Lily prayed she could maintain a poker face. No need to give him the satisfaction of knowing he'd roped her into this mission hook, line and sinker.

"It's in three days. That's not a lot of time to prep." She shook her head and began to rattle off the imperative information she needed. "Bodyguards, arrival times, accessibility…"

"So I take it you're in?"

Her second chance looked back at her, his gentle eyes burning away all her defenses. Lily looked out over the river and tucked a strand of hair behind her ear. This was the opportunity she'd hoped for—after not knowing, not acting, and walking away.

Redemption.

With one word, her entire life would change. She just didn't know whether it was a good change or not.

Only one way to find out.

"Yes."

CHAPTER NINE

Wednesday, September 17, 6:00 p.m.

LILY HAD BALKED at meeting at Derek's place, which had been a relief. He'd rolled the dice by dropping in on her at the river and gotten lucky. Very lucky. Taking up shop just across the street from her was a different matter entirely. He hadn't quite figured out how he would have explained *that* one away if she'd accepted his veiled offer.

Somehow, he doubted Lady Luck would have been on his side twice.

As he juggled the large file box, Derek pushed open the tall glass door to Lily's building and headed into the grand foyer, the white marble floor reflecting his shadow, and glanced around. He'd spotted the cameras, both seen and unseen, the first time he'd walked in.

Today, their locations were different. He couldn't help but smile. *Nice job.*

The doorman stared at Derek, his black eyes hard and searching, reminding him of an enormous Maasai warrior he'd once met on one of his 67 trips to Africa.

"I'm here to see Lily Andrews, penthouse."

The old man glared at him. "Yes. I'm aware of that."

Though the information wasn't in Lily's file—which irritated the shit out of him—it hadn't taken

Derek long to piece together that both George and Ben had a background similar to his own. Ben Tinsdale was a no-brainer. The man was a legend within Unit 67.

George, on the other hand, was a bit of a mystery.

Derek had watched the massive black man until he was certain. There was no denying it, in the way George moved, and with his access to Lily and Ben. It screamed that something was missing in the papers that chronicled Lily's short life—he definitely played some role in her life in Omaha, and quite possibly even before.

He quickly read the situation. The big man staring him down had gone from DEFCON 5 to DEFCON 1 overnight. Time to diffuse *that* ticking time bomb.

Derek dropped the file box on the counter and reached out his hand. "Let me get straight to the point here, George. I'm not the enemy."

"Maybe. Maybe not. Jury's still out on that one." George grabbed Derek's hand and squeezed, hard. "But let me get straight to the point, too. I'm watching you."

Derek locked eyes with the man trying to crush his hand bones and smiled. "No doubt."

George let go and tipped his head toward the elevators. Derek silently made his way to his waiting ride and resisted the urge to shake his hand until *after* the elevator doors closed.

Damn, that old man had the grip of Godzilla.

LILY'S FRONT DOOR swung open before Derek could knock. Impressive. Cameras downstairs. Monitor upstairs. What other surprises did this woman have up her sleeve? He was sure there were plenty, and he hoped to uncover every single one of them.

"Hey." Her brown hair was pulled back into a high, messy ponytail. She wore a black tank and matching yoga pants. There wasn't a spot of makeup on her olive skin.

She was beautiful.

His stomach tightened. *Focus, Moretti.*

She glanced at the box of case files in his arms and grimaced. "This is the part I could've lived without."

Stepping back, she let him through the door, then closed it tightly behind them.

"You and me both. But there's no getting around it. We have less than three days to bring you up to speed, and we need to put together your file. Rowland will vet you, so we need your identity to be airtight."

"I thought you might say that," Lily said, grinning. "I'll be right back."

She disappeared into her bedroom for less than sixty seconds, then reemerged, balancing her open laptop. "Already started."

Of course she had.

And that, ladies and gentlemen, was exactly why he wanted—needed, really—Lily on this case. She knew the outer workings of this game just as well, if not better, than he did, and a solid, unbreakable file was crucial to the success of their mission—and essential to keeping her alive.

She set the computer down on the island and turned it to face him. "Take a look. Rowland is your guy, so feel free to add whatever information you feel is pertinent."

Derek set his box of files next to the computer and silently scanned through her backstory, checking for any inconsistencies. He found none. "Impressive."

She leaned against the counter, an embarrassed smile lighting her face, and shrugged. "Thanks."

"Now we bring in the big guns." He reached for his phone and punched in his security code.

"Wait, what? What are you doing?"

"Testing to make sure this thing holds." He punched in a number he knew by heart, held the phone to his ear and waited, grinning at the sight of Lily's scrunched forehead.

A soft, feminine voice answered on the third ring. "Hey, D."

Derek smiled at his baby sister's nickname. Alexis didn't call any of her brothers by their given name, hadn't since she was old enough to talk.

"Hey, sweetheart."

Confusion swept Lily's face, and her brows arched in a silent question. He threw her a wink. She turned away, color rushing her cheeks. Derek turned his attention back to the other woman in his life. "You have a second?"

"For you? Always."

"Great. I need red." Red was their term to go secure on any line. His genius baby sister had figured out a way to scramble their calls without needing a special phone. It had saved all the Moretti brothers at one point or another.

"Go ahead," she said, her voice high with excitement.

"I just sent you a file. I need you to run a background check on it, see if you can find any holes or discrepancies."

"Easy peasy." Her tech skills were legendary and highly sought-after. She'd been able to hack into the

FBI database without leaving any type of footprint since she was fifteen. Vetting Lily's cover story *would* be child's play for Alexis. "When do you need it done?"

"Yesterday."

"How about thirty minutes?" she countered.

"Sounds perfect. I'll wait for the call." He hung up and pocketed his phone.

"Okay, I'll bite," Lily said. "Who was that?"

"My baby sister, Alexis."

Lily's mouth popped open. "You sent my encrypted file to your *sister*?"

"Easy, tiger. There's no one else on this planet that I'd want to make sure your file is bulletproof. Trust me."

"Okay, but we're going to need something stronger than water tonight." Lily headed to the kitchen and called over her shoulder, "What do you want, Merlot or Guinness?"

Derek followed her movement with his eyes. What he wanted to drink didn't matter, not when he was in the same room with Lily. *Especially* not with her walking around with that tight black getup hugging her curves just so, no matter how he looked at her.

She stood on her tiptoes and reached for a glass on the top shelf, her shirt riding up, exposing her soft yet tight stomach. *Oh, shit.* "Guinness."

Lily obliged and rejoined him at the island, handing him his chilled beer and staring down at the overflowing box. He took a sip of the frothy liquid and watched as she grabbed half the case files and, bypassing the table, plopped herself on the floor. Without a word she spread the files out, arranging them and rearranging them, and finally made herself at home on the floor among the information.

As she caught her lower lip between her teeth, he couldn't help but stare. She flipped through Rowland's folder, stopped, turned back a page and frowned. Tossing the file aside, she bent forward and stretched for a file just beyond her reach. The neckline of her tank fell open slightly, revealing a sexy, black lace bra. Derek did a double take, staring at the soft feminine form playing peekaboo with his libido.

He scrubbed his hands over his face and swallowed hard, unable to focus. He couldn't believe he was in the same room with Lily instead of watching her through a scope. He cringed inwardly. *That sounded creepy.* He took a swig of his beer. It was the truth, though, wasn't it?

What had started as a simple mission directive— *keep an eye on Lily Andrews*—from Director Kennedy months ago had turned into something more. Much more. At least for Derek. He'd have to be a dead man not to notice her sex appeal, her strength and dogged determination, or how—despite the shit life had handed her—she attacked each new day with a fresh vigor, which surprised even Derek.

But he wasn't dead.

He was alive and kicking…and every cell in his body went on full alert whenever she was near.

Now he wanted to know everything about Lily—not just what he could see through a scope. He wanted to know what made her *tick*. What went on behind those mesmerizing hazel eyes when they locked on to a target. It was almost as if a nebulous star had exploded within them: a rich chocolate hue warmed to a honeyed gold before giving way to an exotic teal green. He glanced over at her and was surprised to see her quietly studying him. For a moment, he got lost in the vibrancy of her gaze.

Color kissed the tops of her mile-high cheekbones as she looked away.

Yeah, he wanted to know everything about her, all right. He took a swig of his beer. But was the feeling mutual? How much would she let him in? Would she be honest with him about George? Ben? *Jackson?*

"Tell me about your doorman."

Lily's head snapped up, and she slowly set down the file in her hand. "George? Why?"

She reached for her glass and took a sip.

"Because he's one of us." Derek kept his tone casual, curious to see what tale she'd weave. He could easily go to the director and gain access to both men's files, as it pertained to the case, *especially* now that Lily was part of it, but Derek posed the question to see how much of the internal wall she'd constructed he'd be able to dismantle. He wanted—needed, really— Lily to share, let him in. To trust. So he pushed harder. "So is Ben."

She choked on her wine. Carefully placing the glass down, a nervous laugh escaped her lips. "You don't miss much, do you?"

"Part of what makes me so good at my job." He winked at her, then grew serious. "But what I don't understand is how they ended up here. As a doorman. And a coffee-shop owner."

Lily traced her finger around the top of her wineglass. "Would you drop it if I said they were family friends?"

"Not a chance. Start talking, babycakes." Derek froze. *Shit*. He hadn't meant to call her that. It had just slipped out.

A tiny smile twitched at her lips. Derek caught the twinkle in her eyes and his hopes rose slightly. Maybe his slip of the tongue was *exactly* what he needed to break down her invisible barrier.

Her brow arched and she drilled him with her eyes, the playful smile widening. "Babycakes?"

"Let's just circle back to George and Ben," Derek muttered into his beer.

She laughed, the sound light and airy, then brought the wineglass back to her mouth, taking a small sip. Setting the glass down again, she let out a sigh. "Can't you just ask them yourself?"

"And miss out on watching you squirm? Nah. I'd prefer this approach." He tipped his head up in a quick nod. "Start with George."

"Not everything is going to be unlocked to you. I know that might shock that handsome little brain of yours, but some things are outside your clearance."

My clearance? "You're kidding—"

She lifted her hand in the air, and he swallowed his comeback. "No, I'm not. And I'm not trying to be a bitch about it, either. There are just some files buried so deep it would take you a million lifetimes to cut through the red tape and secrecy wrapped around them. Better to leave some things alone."

"But you know."

She looked away.

Gotcha, babycakes. He winced a bit. Damn it. He needed to get that, whatever *that* was, under control. If the director even suspected that Derek had a thing for the irresistible brunette sprawled out on the floor, he'd be jerked from the case so fast his head would spin.

Unit 67 didn't tolerate relationships, end of story.

"Red tape and secrecy aside, George hasn't lost that touch. I know he's one of us." Derek locked his gaze with hers and refused to blink. They sat in silence. Neither moved. Neither breathed. He bit back a laugh, then smirked at her. *I can do this all day, babyc—shit. Knock it off, Moretti.*

Lily jumped up and stalked to the kitchen. He followed and leaned against the counter, watching her. What trigger had he just pushed? She reached for the bottle of Merlot and poured herself another large glass. As she swirled the crimson liquid, she stared off into space. Derek studied her closely, fascinated. *Where have you gone?*

"I didn't just stumble into this line of work," she said in a quiet voice. "I was born into it. Literally."

Derek's eyebrows arched. That wasn't what he'd expected to hear. Recruited? Yes. Born into it? No. What was this? The mob?

"I know that sounds dramatic and all, but it's not. Both my parents were black ops."

Derek nearly choked on his beer. *Her parents were black ops.* Well, wasn't this pretty little story getting stranger by the second? Derek took a deep breath. No wonder he hadn't been able to gather any intel on her earlier years; her mere existence was against protocol.

She leaned against the opposite counter and took another sip. "George trained them. He's been around a long time. He's family. End of story."

Bullshit. The more Derek tugged at the thin golden

string that was Lily Andrews, the stranger her story unraveled. "Not likely. Keep talking."

She wrinkled her nose. "Not sure what more there is to say. He's like the grandfather I never knew, never had."

"Go on."

"My folks being together was frowned upon, just as it is now."

He grimaced. Wasn't *that* the truth.

"Envision everyone's surprise when they not only got married, but then had me."

"I can only imagine." Derek crossed his arms over his chest and shook his head, dumbfounded. When had that ever happened in the history of 67? Oh, that's right, never…or at least that's what they'd all been led to believe.

Her lips curved as she peered at him over her glass. It took all of Derek's willpower not to close the space between them and kiss her. Talk about being frowned upon. She'd probably punch him. The director would definitely track him down and shoot him.

Derek reached for his beer instead. "So, where does Ben fit in?"

Lily's face softened.

"He and my folks did a long-term undercover op together when I was about five, and shortly after they returned, he became my guardian whenever my folks were out of the country on business." She walked to the sofa, sat and tucked her feet underneath her. "When I turned eighteen, he read me in."

"He read you in. Just like that?" Why would a sea-soned black-ops agent read in a teenager? He eyed her as she tapped a fingernail against the side of her wineglass.

"I blame my folks for that one."

Derek frowned, waited for the smile to follow her words. Silence blanketed the room. "Not following."

"They were gone a lot. I kept busy learning all things computer-related…and the art form of watching. I hated being left alone all the time. Hated even more when they lied to my face about where they were *really* going the week of my birthday. And I got mad." She shrugged. "So I hacked into their computer."

Derek choked on his Guinness. "You broke into a classified computer."

"Yes."

"Lil…"

"And then I relentlessly peppered Ben with a million-and-one questions about my folks until I pushed him to the point of breaking. He couldn't lie to my face when I had hard evidence to support the questions." She looked up and smiled. *Damn, she was beautiful.* She shrugged. "I can be persuasive at times."

"No doubt," Derek replied, laughing.

Lily wrinkled her nose again. "So like I said, I didn't just stumble into this line of work. Ben and George made a vow to my parents. If anything happened to them, they'd watch out for me."

She looked up and the floor just about fell out from under Derek. Tears pooled at the edge of her eyelids. Raw emotion ripped across her face as a sad smile that never made it to her eyes tugged at her lips. "Just after my eighteen birthday, something did."

Her bottom lip trembled and she looked down. Without hesitating, Derek moved next to her. When she didn't move, he reached down and rested his hand on top of hers. "Hey. Sorry for pushing. You don't—"

"No, no. It's fine." She withdrew her hand and wiped her face. "Wow. Sorry. It's been over ten years. I thought I'd locked that away."

"Hey." Derek tipped her chin up. "You never get over it, Lil. It's what keeps us human."

Lily's bottom lip trembled and she caught it in between her teeth, looking away. Derek recognized her need to shut down the emotions. It was the only way to stay sane. He would know—he'd done it himself more times than he'd care to admit. He moved back, giving her space.

She took a deep breath. "The official report is that they lost control of their car while on the autobahn in Germany, which we both know is a load of crap. No matter how much digging I do, I can't unlock the classified file, but I know it was a mission that went south. Ben and George, well, they kept their word, even though I was technically an adult by then, and they've watched out for me ever since."

"As a doorman and a coffee-shop owner?"

"Ben once told me coffee beans smelled better than blood." She raised her eyes to Derek's. Golden flecks danced within a sea of green and brown. A sad smile pulled at her lips. "How can you argue that?"

He reached out and gently stroked her cheek, wiping away a tear. "You can't."

And he couldn't. Combat was shit. Necessary, but shit nonetheless, and the aftermath of it was lasting. Derek would never change the path he'd walked, but it took a long time—if ever—to get the smell of blood out of his nostrils.

It never escaped his mind.

She stared at him for what felt like an eternity, searching. For what, Derek didn't know. But as far as he was concerned, she could search for as long as she wanted—he had nothing to hide.

Well…Derek swallowed hard.

Her lips curved slightly as a small, sad laugh escaped. "No, you can't. So you smile and support it, especially after they've given up so much to support you."

"But how did you get here?" Derek gestured to the open space. They could have plucked her penthouse loft straight from a designer magazine. It was spectacular, with its dark espresso hardwood, floor-to-ceiling white sheers draping the windows of walls and the black baby grand piano sitting in the corner.

The gourmet kitchen opened up to the main living area and the granite that made up the kitchen island, with its deep veins of gray and specks of blue, looked as though it had been flown in from Italy. Instead of the typical backsplash, old exposed brick covered most of the kitchen wall, only adding to the "industrial meets glamour" look Lily's place boasted. The various apartments of fellow agents he'd seen—including his own—had nothing on this place. It was huge and perfectly designed.

"This place…" she motioned around her "…has been our family's safe house for as long as I can remember."

"Remarkable."

He was sure the things he couldn't see far outweighed the things he could. He scanned the walls and the room, looking for anything he could use as a tell—a painting hung too far from the wall, a misplaced seam, a piece of the wooden floor that gave too much—to pinpoint where she kept her gear, because he knew she had it. Somewhere.

He got nothing. *Impressive.*

"Okay. Better question. How have you managed the prolonged flight under the radar? You don't just walk away from 67."

She got up and paced.

"How did you do it?"

Lily took another sip of wine. What was she trying to hide? It was a simple question, so why had it spun her up? Operatives retired all the time for multiple reasons. Age. Mental health. But to just up and leave? No way in hell.

"Lily…"

She chewed on her lip, then let out a long, exasperated breath, pushing a stray hair off her face. "The director is my godfather."

Derek whistled. *Holy shit.* Another vital piece of information conveniently left out of her file—whoever put that thing together needed to be booted from the Unit.

"So you're the one everyone whispers about. I honestly thought that was 67 folklore."

She tipped her head and frowned. "Not following."

"You're company royalty."

A nervous laugh escaped her lips. "Hardly."

"Says the woman who all but flipped them off, quit and is still breathing."

"I didn't quit." Spots of pink kissed her cheeks.

"Easy." He held up his hands. "Sorry. You didn't quit. Why did you go to ground? Why'd you go quiet?"

"I had my reasons."

"I read your file, Lily. Afghanistan. Korea. Iran. Shit, you've been in more countries in the past twelve years than most agents see in a lifetime. You speak seven different languages. Someone like you doesn't just turn her back on the very thing that makes her tick." A shadow passed across her face. "No matter how much shit hits the fan."

"I walked because I couldn't get past the last case, okay?" Her voice caught as she shook her head. "Still can't. And no matter how much I might've loved the job, or been the best, or whatever the hell people say about me, I'm stuck in that moment."

"Lil—"

"No one wants an operative with that mind-set." She locked eyes with Derek, almost daring him to disagree. "That's when people get killed."

"Fair enough. But—" The shrill sound of his phone interrupted him. Pulling it out of his pocket, he glanced at the number and frowned. *Alexis.* She was late. She was never late. Every muscle fiber in his shoulders knotted as he answered on the second ring. "Well?"

"It'll hold," Alexis reported, all business now. "It'll better than hold—I couldn't crack it, no matter how many different approaches I took, and I tried them all. Hence why I'm late—which, for the record, I hate."

"Excellent." The tension evaporated. "Thanks, sweetheart. That's exactly what I was hoping to hear."

"Whoever put that file together is a genius, like, my kind of genius. I'm impressed."

Derek looked over at Lily and smiled.

Yes, so was he.

CHAPTER TEN

Saturday, September 20, 4:30 p.m.

LILY FIELDSTRIPPED HER GLOCK. Her mind wandered as she removed the magazine and racked the slide to eject the round from the chamber. Saying yes to this mission was ludicrous. As much as she wanted to dismiss that ugly fact, it was unchanging: this mission was unsanctioned until Lily called the director. She checked the chamber, pointed the gun toward the exposed brick on the far side of her loft and dry fired.

Hell would freeze over before she did that.

Not until she was good and ready. And she wasn't. Thirteen months later, and she was still too angry—or, if she was being honest, proud—to call him.

Disassembling the gun into its four main component parts quieted her. Lily took a deep breath and glanced at the box of files Derek had left behind. Her heart hammered against her rib cage.

Derek.

Sweet-talking, unwavering, solid-as-rock and hotter-than-hell Derek.

She grabbed the barrel and pushed the cleaning rod into the breech end of it. She knew she walked a tightrope with him. Agreeing to work with him was one thing, but there was no way she'd go to his place to prep, no matter how much she trusted him.

She grabbed the slide and vigorously scrubbed the slide rail cuts. In the few days they'd spent together, she'd started to trust him. His probing, though direct and persistent, was never hard. Curious? Yes. Demanding? No.

That alone eased the tension permanently residing in her back. They'd easily, and almost instantaneously, fallen into a natural rhythm that coaxed her further and further from her hiding place.

But it was his eyes that chipped away at her suspicious guard, made her trust.

Jackson's eyes had been calculating. She'd been mesmerized by what they saw and computed, but she'd always felt their shrewd stare on *her*.

Watching. Evaluating. Assessing.

Derek's eyes were gentle, yet alert. Try as she might to fight it, they drew her in with their softness and away from her self-made shelter.

Bottom line, her bullshit meter hadn't pinged once, and Lily had to trust that. If she couldn't, if she'd lost confidence in herself, she'd lost it all.

Still…she wasn't the naive agent she'd been. Lily insisted on always meeting here, at her home, on her ground. When she'd moved in, she'd updated and installed cameras, audio and heat sensors in the lobby and the landing right outside her door.

This was her castle.

Here, she was queen.

She reassembled the gun, did a function check and smiled. Perfect. Lily quickly thumbed bullets into her magazine, switched the safety on and tucked the gun into the small of her back.

Lily glanced at her watch and stood. Her two hours were up. Derek had called earlier, informing her that he'd be over at five o'clock. One thing she'd figured out about him—he was always early.

Here they were again.

Round two.

She stared at the monitor. Partly because she was curious about how George would respond to Derek "invading her space," as he'd ranted earlier. And partly because she enjoyed the view—it was the only time she could stare at his impressive physique without getting caught.

He stopped at the concierge's desk and chatted with George. Her mouth dropped open in surprise. Since when had those two become buddy-buddy? Derek smiled at something George said, looked up into the camera and winked. If George approved, maybe, just maybe, her bullshit meter was still intact after all.

Rowland was her one and only focus tonight, no matter how sexy Derek looked in his tux. And he did— damn right delicious. Deep down, Lily knew tonight was only a mission, but still…her gaze swept over Derek's wide back and traveled south as he walked toward the elevator, and heat rushed to her cheeks.

He stepped into the elevator and tossed his head in a quick nod toward the corner camera as the doors closed. She switched the monitor to the thermal view. The outline of a gun hung just below his right armpit.

Packing heat, are you, pretty boy?

Lily bit back a laugh. That was okay. So did she. She opened the door before he could knock.

"Hey." He smiled down at her.

She stepped aside as he strolled in, a black garment bag thrown over his arm. Her heart kicked up a gear, as it seemed to do every time he was near, and despite her best attempts, her gaze traveled south down his back and rested on his ass.

"Looking good, Moretti."

Derek held out the garment bag on two fingers. "For you."

She eyed the bag, curious to see what he'd brought. They'd both agreed to let Derek take charge of her wardrobe, but Lily wasn't entirely confident that his idea of appropriate evening attire matched her own.

An easy grin spread across his face. Her stomach fluttered. Again. *Give it a rest, Andrews. Don't forget what happened last time.* The fluttering stuttered, then disappeared entirely.

He gave the bag a little shake. "I can help with the zipper if you need…"

She snorted, snatching the bag from his outstretched hand. Their fingers briefly brushed, sending sparks down her spine. For a brief moment, she wondered if her eyes mirrored the want burning in his.

Wouldn't *that* be one hell of a way to derail their op before it even started?

She turned and walked toward her bedroom. Derek followed after her. She glanced over her shoulder and rolled her eyes. "You. Stay put."

Lily kicked the door shut with her foot, silencing his deep laugh, and tossed the bag onto her bed. Unzipping the bag, she pulled out two dresses.

Thousands of tiny black sequins covered the first gown. Soft chiffon, satin and lace made up the second.

Each ink-black dress was exquisite. She'd been out-
fitted on other missions with her fair share of amazing clothes, but those were burlap compared to these
gowns. She whistled softly. "Wowzah."

Lily carefully laid each out and examined them.
Yanking her tank top over her head, she dropped it to
the floor. She stepped out of her jeans, kicked them
over to join her shirt and held out the first sequined
dress. The neckline swooped down gracefully between
two tiny spaghetti straps. She twirled the dress.

The back plunged in a deep V.

"Well, that won't do." She frowned and tossed the
dress over the side of the chair tucked in the corner.
A twinge flickered in her stomach. "Not ever again."

Turning her body slightly, she glanced over her
shoulder into the tall mirror leaning against the wall.
Angry purple scars peppered her back. The pang in
her stomach twisted.

Jackson's treacherous actions had damaged not only
her confidence, but also her body. She'd hoped to one
day be able to move past the emotional barriers that
day had erected.

But she'd never escape the physical evidence of his
betrayal.

They—and subsequently Jackson—would be with
her forever. Whether she liked it or not.

She rubbed her eyes with the back of her hand.
She didn't have time to deal with *that* shit. Hands on
her hips, she glanced at the second dress option. It reminded her of something she'd seen some Hollywood
star wear on the red carpet. "Guess you'll have to do."

Slipping the dress over her head, she let its soft fabric envelop her. The smooth material perfectly hugged

her curves, fit her like a glove. Lily stared at her reflection in the mirror.

The front plunged low in a deep V and barely covered her belly button or her breasts. A delicate strip of black lace connected the two sides of the V, concealing just enough to keep the gown from being entirely indecent. When she moved, her thigh peeked out the top of a mile-high slit.

The dress was daring. Flawless. Exquisite.

She loved it.

Turning, she peered into the mirror again. The high back concealed everything it needed to.

Well played, Derek. The dress couldn't have been more perfect if it had been hand-tailored to her.

Game on. Time to go to work. She hitched her leg up, let the seam fall open and reached for her .32, then stopped. Normally, she'd be strapping on her thigh holster.

Not this time.

Tonight, they'd agreed she'd go in unarmed. Not her preference, but there was nothing she could do about it.

She left the bedroom and silently studied the man who'd blown into her life, turning it upside down. Derek stood with his back to her, gazing out the window overlooking the city. One hand was shoved in his pocket, while the other rested on Dakota's neck as the dog sat by his side. The perfect pair, as if they belonged together in this place. *With her.* Lily froze. Where the hell had that come from? She shook her head. That would never happen, no matter how inviting a picture the two of them made.

"So?"

He turned and did a double take, desire sparking in

his eyes. Lily recognized it immediately, and her stomach tightened. Derek whistled. "You look incredible."

Warmth spread through every inch of her body, pooling in her stomach at his open approval. She couldn't deny the pull Derek had on her, had from the very moment he'd tackled her to the ground. Yes, she'd been pissed and fought it—still tried to fight it, if she was being honest—but the urgency to push him away diminished with every second he was near.

"You think he'll take the bait?"

Derek's eyes traveled down her body. He ran his hand over his head and scratched the back of his neck, then nodded.

"Oh, yeah, he'll take the bait."

CHAPTER ELEVEN

Saturday, September 20, 7:00 p.m.

COBALT BLUE GAVE WAY to the blackness of night as
the sun finally relinquished control. Tiny stars pushed
through the inkiness, twinkling in the autumn twilight
sky. Lily glanced around, taking in every inch of her
surroundings. She had to admit—she was impressed.

The statuesque, all-stone building rose from the
ground, elegant and majestic. A long, thin, rectangu-
lar reflection pool stretched off and to the right of the
main entrance. Two tall stone pillars, straight from the
ancient Aztec civilization, jetted up through the still-
as-glass-water, their ageless and stoic beauty highlighted in the soft glow of a single spotlight.

On another occasion, Lily would have loved to ex-
plore the gems hidden within the stone fortress jetting
up from the ground.

This was her first mission since...Lily paused midstep as another wave of self-doubt pummeled her. *Stop!*
She took a deep breath to silence the demons torturing
her mind, to lock them away. Jackson hadn't stopped
her then; she wasn't about to let the ghost of him stop
her now.

Derek pressed his hand against the small of her
back. "You okay?"

"Yeah, I'm good. Let's go get our guy." Lily straightened her shoulders, gathered the material swirling around her ankles into her right hand and climbed the grand staircase of Joslyn Art Museum with the grace and ease of an A-lister, immediately spotting the five armed guards stationed between each of the four imposing columns holding up the museum's heavy stone ceiling.

She tipped her head toward the five men. "Impressive show of force, isn't it?"

"Our host wouldn't have it any other way," Derek muttered.

"Duly noted."

The man stationed between the second and third column held up his hand, halting them. "Invitation."

Derek handed him their satin envelope, compliments of John Elsworth. The guard took the invitation, scanned it briefly and passed it back. His eyes roamed Lily's body and landed on the deep V playing hide-and-seek with her navel. She cocked her head, and a coy smile played on her lips.

He swallowed hard, then stepped to the side. "Have a good evening."

"Thank you." She gathered the flowing material in her hand and walked into the grandiose building.

Derek lowered his lips to her ear. "Nicely played."

They walked through the east foyer and, following the soft piano melody, continued past another stone archway before the ceiling opened up into a majestic room, showcasing Joslyn's infamous two-story Storz Fountain Court.

"Wow," Lily breathed into the striking room.

"Beautiful, isn't it?" Derek leaned close and whispered into her ear, his soft breath tickling her skin.

Beautiful was an understatement.

Every inch of the room was overlaid in perfectly sculpted tiles, reminding Lily of a Roman bathhouse she'd once visited while in Rome, down to the minute details of the mosaic columns on the second-floor balcony level overlooking the foyer below. A gold-plated stainless-steel sculpture, resembling a sunburst, rose elegantly from the middle of a mosaic fountain situated front and center in the room.

The massive two-story room, already stunning in its own right, had been turned into a dazzling ballroom, and couples swirled by in time with the piano's hypnotic tune.

"Shall we dance?"

Lily turned her attention back to her handsome companion and nodded. He gently put his hand on the small of her back and led her deeper into the room toward the dance floor. The crowd parted, conversation ceased, curious faces turned toward them. *What are they staring at?* She glanced around and stopped short.

Shit. No wonder the guard had given her a once-over. She was going to kill Derek. He had to have known the conservative tilt of this crowd. Among the high-society matrons in their demure, elegant ball gowns, Lily's daring dress, with its plunging front and thigh-high slit, positively screamed for attention.

She swallowed a sigh. There was no way she'd go unnoticed by her mark tonight.

Derek swirled her onto the dance floor and either oblivious to the blatant stares of their fellow dancers or enjoying the attention—Lily couldn't tell—closed the distance between them. He laid one hand lightly on the lowest part of her hip and entwined their fingers, bringing her hand up to his chest. Lily tensed at the intimate gesture, then all thoughts of Rowland disappeared as her muscles relaxed and she molded into Derek's embrace. He tucked her closer and bent his head, his soft breath against her ear as they swirled to the music.

They followed the soft melody around the marble floor. As the tune changed, Derek looked down and smiled. "Game on, babycakes."

She scanned the crowd again. Yes. Game on. *Where are you, Rowland?* Almost as if he'd heard her mental musing, the most elusive and intriguing man in the room turned and caught her in his piercing gaze.

Rowland James.

The man commanding her attention was more distinguished than she'd imagined from the photograph Derek had given her to study. Rowland's tux framed his tall, strong physique with detailed perfection. His raven-colored hair gave way to salt-and-pepper layers, and his cheekbones hinted at an exotic heritage.

But it was his eyes that gripped her. They were a dark emerald, and hard, almost as if they could drill holes into her soul, and they'd locked on to Lily, holding her gaze in their hypnotic grasp. Her heart skipped a beat and she glanced away, shaken at his intense magnetism.

"Well." Derek tightened his grip on her hip, the rhythmic thumping of his heart kicking up. "He noticed you."

Lily's breath caught. *Was Derek jealous?*

She tugged her gaze from Derek and turned it toward Rowland. Sure enough, he followed their movement around the dance floor, never taking his eyes off Lily. As they twirled past Rowland again, his eyes narrowed and the muscle in his jaw tightened. Lily looked between Rowland and Derek. Well, there was definitely no love lost between *these* two men. *Why?*

She could circle back to that later. Now, maybe, just maybe, she could use Rowland's distain for Derek to pull Rowland in? She peered into the mirror Derek swirled her past and caught Rowland's stormy reflection.

Yep, that might just work.

Lily glanced up at Derek, wishing she could stay tucked close to his side, knowing she couldn't. She breathed in deeply, tried to sear this feeling of being tucked close to him permanently into her memory. A soft smile pulled at his mouth, and she almost lost her nerve. Almost.

"Sorry about this."

Derek cocked his head to the side as she drew back and slapped him. Hard.

"How dare you!"

His eyes widened and he dropped his hand from her waist, stepping back from her as if she were a snake ready to strike. Cool air rushed to fill the space his body had just warmed. She had a job to do—and falling for the man staring back at her with a horrified and bewildered expression was not it.

Lily gathered the flowing material of her dress from around her ankles and rushed from the dance floor. Grabbing a flute of champagne as it floated by on a server's silver tray, she brought it to her lips and scanned the area. *Where are you, Rowland?* She spotted him animatedly speaking to a brute of a man and pointing toward Derek. She grimaced. *I owe him. Big time.*

Bringing the flute to her lips, she tipped her head back and downed the rest of the sparkling liquid. Would Rowland make the first move? And if not, could she?

DEREK RUBBED HIS JAW. Lily had all but slugged him. Would that woman ever cease to surprise him?

Probably not.

Rowland stormed up to him, fire dancing in his eyes. Two tall men with earpieces and heavy holsters—mercenaries, no doubt—flanked him.

"Why am I not surprised that you'd be the center of attention tonight, Derek?"

Derek shoved his hands in his front pockets. "It was nothing more than a friendly little dispute with some woman I barely know and, quite frankly, none of your business."

Rowland leaned close. "My party. My business."

Derek inwardly cursed and hoped John wouldn't fire him, because in order for this whole scheme to work, Derek needed to be thrown out of this party, not merely put in his place.

He squared his shoulders and looked Rowland in the eyes. "Isn't this ARME's party? Which would make it Mr. Els—"

"Enough." Rowland's face flushed. He tugged at his tux, smoothing the ruffled edges, and he lowered his voice to a quiet but deadly tone. "John may put up with you, but I will not, not tonight."

Rowland snapped his fingers at the man to his left

and the tall brute grabbed Derek by the bicep, jerking him toward the door. Derek dug in his heels and looked over his shoulder, trying to locate Lily. He finally spotted her in a corner of the room, sipping champagne, looking put out and very alone, and he bit his lip to keep from grinning—she was playing right into Rowland's ego.

Atta girl, babycakes. Go get him.

ROWLAND MADE HIS WAY toward Lily, never breaking eye contact with her. *You're not the only hunter here, Rowland dear.* She smiled tremulously—though hopefully without losing her dignity—and prayed it would be enough to draw the predator locked on to her into her own lair.

Rowland crossed the distance between them.

"My apologies for the despicable behavior of my guest." A strange mixture of fire and ice floated over his soft English accent.

Lily feathered her fingers against the base of her neck and bent her head slightly. "No apology necessary." She spoke with a soft Southern twang, assuming the persona she had devised for Rowland's benefit.

He cocked his head to the side, his gaze traveling down her body. She caught the pulse quickening in his neck, but nothing else. She couldn't read him, couldn't get past the veiled expression blanketing his handsome face. Then he frowned slightly, and her shoulders knotted.

Maybe this wasn't her ticket back into the game, after all.

"Do I know you?"

"No, I don't think so," Lily responded innocently. "I'm new to town."

Stepping closer, he swept her hand up in his and bowed slightly. "While it's unusual for me not to know everyone on my guest list…"

She checked for the closest exit.

"I'm pleasantly surprised at my oversight. Let me introduce myself."

Lily blinked. The tension released, and her heart settled back into a normal rhythm. Swallowing a triumphant expression, she focused her attention on the tall man in front of her, who was eyeing her as if she was a piece of candy he *had* to have.

Yep…she still had it.

"My name is Rowland James. I'm the COO and vice president of ARME Industries. And this—" he gestured with his free hand "—is my party. Welcome."

Lily smiled. *Well done, Derek.* He'd nailed his research on Rowland. Maybe she wouldn't kill him after all.

"Well, that's quite the introduction, Mr. James."

"Please," he said charmingly. "Call me Rowland."

"Rowland it is, then."

"And you, besides being one of the most beautiful women in the room, are…?"

Lily swallowed a laugh. Though the soft fabric hugged her curves in all the right places and played up her athletic build, she was hardly the most beautiful woman in the room. At five-nine, and with her three-inch heels, she towered over most of the other women that milled about, yet she still needed to tilt her head up to meet Rowland's gaze.

She'd been told more than once they gave her an intoxicating, exotic look, taken from her mixed Spanish and Cherokee Indian heritage, perhaps. So, although not a supermodel in any sense, Lily knew how to flaunt what she had.

"How incredibly rude of me." She feigned embarrassment. "My name is Addison. Addison Moore."

"Ah, a Southern belle."

"Born and raised in Alabama," she said, the drawl in her voice curling.

"And what brings you to these parts, so far from the warmth of the South? If you don't mind me asking."

The man who held her hand in a commanding yet gentle grip unnerved Lily slightly. She blinked and focused. "The warmth doesn't suit everyone. Some enjoy a crisp fall."

She didn't move, barely dared to breathe as his eyes searched her face. Time seemed to slow to an agonizing crawl. What was he thinking? He reminded Lily of a falcon. Calculated, cunning and deliberate. Did he see her as prey? Or an equal? She waited, heart racing. *Take the bait. Come on, Rowland. Don't let that mortifying scene on the dance floor be for nothing. Take. The. Bait.*

Finally he smiled, and the muscles in her back relaxed.

"Well, whatever brings you to our great city, I hope you'll accept my invitation of hospitality, Ms. Moore." He tucked her hand into the crook of his arm and Lily swallowed down her surprise at the gallant gesture. "Let me introduce you to the people of Omaha."

CHAPTER TWELVE

Saturday, September 20, 7:45 p.m.

A SET OF green eyes kept a watchful eye on the statuesque brunette that had caught Rowland's eye. Close enough to see the kiss of color on her cheeks as Rowland swirled her past, far enough to maneuver around her unseen. Elegant and regal in her daring gown, the woman had stolen the attention of the entire room when she'd entered earlier escorted by ARME's head of security.

Angelica Dupree made her way toward Rowland and Lily.

Well...this should be interesting.

All of Omaha knew that Angelica had her sights set on Rowland—and his endless bank account. The eyes of the crowd, bright with curiosity, followed Angelica's movements as she waltzed up to the stately pair and interrupted their intimate conversation.

Angelica said something, and Rowland's eyebrows arched. His companion smiled softly, but didn't move from her position by Rowland's side, staring Angelica down until the woman's face flamed and she made a hasty exit stage left.

Rowland gazed down at the woman beside him with

clear admiration and swept her hand up in his, bringing it to his lips before he moved again to the sweet melody swirling in the air.

THREE HOURS LATER, Lily desperately needed to get home and take off her damn heels. She didn't know which ached more: her feet or her head. Rowland had introduced her to seemingly the whole town—or, at least, presumably those in his pocket—and her mind was swimming with faces and names, and the champagne that had continuously filled her glass.

He didn't seem to worry that the woman on his arm was a complete stranger to their world. Nor did his other guests.

It was obvious in the time she'd shadowed him that he was revered by many—and feared by more.

In between the introductions, the endless new faces and incalculable stories, she'd gathered enough information for a dozen or so case files. She scrambled to make sense of all the players, and what team they were each playing for.

And why John Elsworth would be in any sort of danger.

She'd made the ten undercover bodyguards hovering nearby in the first minute of being on Rowland's arm. They stayed within lunging distance in case Rowland so much as yelped.

Which she doubted ever happened. The man she clung to, though disarmingly charming and captivating, was cold as ice.

She'd rubbed shoulders with her fair share of dangerous, vicious and deadly people. But something about Rowland sent her head spinning, almost as if somewhere in the depths of her subconscious, a warning bell rang like a lighthouse bell clanging on a foggy night to proceed with caution.

On more than one occasion, she'd been swept away by his magnetism as his velvety voice purred in her ear and his strong arms encircled her waist, and she'd forgotten whom she clung to. Then just as quickly, his unspoken brutality would peek through his allure, chilling her to her very bones, and she knew, without a doubt, that given the right motivation, he wouldn't hesitate to kill her.

Lily needed space, some time to clear her head. To get away from the enchanting spell he cast over her.

"Would you excuse me for just a moment?"

Rowland looked down at her, raised an eyebrow and released her arm. "Of course."

She managed to send him a coy smile as she made her way down the grand staircase and followed the long hallway to the restroom. Once there, she checked under the stall doors to ensure that she was alone, then pulled out her phone and dialed Derek. The call went straight to voice mail. She hit redial. The call went straight to voice mail again. *Strange.* "Where are you? Why aren't you answering?"

She sighed and hung up.

Lily freshened her lipstick, then began to make her way back down the long corridor toward the ballroom. She stopped suddenly, a feeling of unease prickling up her spine. Someone was in the hallway with her. She could sense it. Her muscles coiled as she looked over her shoulder. The corridor behind her sat empty. Lily picked up her pace, ducked into the next alcove and waited. What wouldn't she give to have her .32 right now.

A waiter walked by, his tray held high, obscuring his face.

Back pressed into the ornate stonewall, she watched him move, frowning slightly as something about him tickled the deepest recesses of her mind. *Waiter, my ass.* She moved to follow him and came face-to-face with Rowland. She stopped short in surprise but quickly recovered, smiling up at him as she snuck a glance over his shoulder. Her heart sank. The waiter—or whoever he truly was—was gone.

"There you are," Rowland said, reaching for her. "I was concerned something happened to you."

So you came looking for me? "You know how these big old buildings can be. I got turned around."

He rested his hand on her waist and looked down at her, heat and a mixture of something else, something dark, lingering in his eyes. "Can I get you anything?"

Once again, Lily found herself swept up by the genuine concern resonating in his velvety voice, and she hesitated, frozen by his allure. *Careful, Andrews.* Blinking, she broke their connection and quickly laughed to cover her slip. "Only if you can make a town car appear. I'm mortified to admit it, but this Southern belle is exhausted and I came with—"

"Of course. Let me call my car."

Damn it. The last thing Lily needed was this strange, dangerous man knowing where she lived—she had to keep Lily Andrews and Addison Moore separated.

Her home had already been compromised once with

Derek blowing into her life. She had no intention of letting that happen again.

"That's not necessary. I can arrange for another town car to pick me up."

The bone-chilling coldness returned to his eyes. "I insist."

Of course you do.

ROWLAND HAD BACKED Lily into a corner, but he hadn't outmaneuvered her.

The car drove up to Hotel Deco, one of Omaha's finest. Fortunately, Lily had briefly stayed there while she'd done some revamping of her "closet." Otherwise she'd have no idea where to direct Rowland's driver.

"I see you've experienced the finer joys of hotel living," Rowland said drily as he peered out the window.

"It's not bad at all. Until I've settled in and discovered the perfect area for me, this is home." She gathered up her small purse. "And it's been lovely so far."

As she reached for the car door, Rowland put his hand on hers. "I have a prior engagement tomorrow, but let me take you to dinner Monday night."

Lily swallowed her triumph—*gotcha, pretty boy*—before looking back over her shoulder with a small smile. "Dinner with you sounds delightful."

"Excellent." He released her hand and settled back into the plush leather seats of his town car, the hungry glint in his eyes returning. "Seven o'clock Monday, then?"

"Seven o'clock Monday. It's a date."

She stepped from the car and let the slit of her dress fall open over the top of her thigh. She could feel his gaze drift over her body, burning into her. Once outside of the car, she bent low to bid him farewell, giving him a generous view of the front of her dress once more.

"Rowland, thank you for your generous hospitality. It wasn't expected, but it's most appreciated."

Her instincts screamed to proceed with caution as Lily willed herself to walk calmly to the hotel entrance. The doorman held open the large, glass doors. Lily walked into the lobby and headed straight toward the restrooms. She pulled out her phone and did a search for cab companies. She scanned the list that popped up and spied a company on the other side of the city. Might as well give plenty of time and space between her cab and Rowland's departure. She punched in the number.

"Cornhusker Cab."

"Yes, I'd like a cab to pick me up at Hotel Deco, the servers' entrance."

"Um…" The man on the other end of the line hesitated. "Ma'am, that will be at least a half hour."

"That's perfect."

LILY ENTERED HER LOFT, slammed the door and threw her purse onto the counter. She kicked off one shoe, then the other, and rubbed her right foot. She'd forgotten how much she hated heels.

Her phone rang. Grabbing her purse, she dumped its contents out onto the counter and snatched up the phone on its third ring.

"Hello."

"Home so soon?" Derek's deep voice cut through the quiet.

She flipped off the lights, her heart skipping a beat, and went to the wall of windows, pushed back the sheer curtains and peered into the black night. "Do you have me under surveillance?"

"How'd it go?"

"It seemed strange, the Elsworths not being there. I think I met every member of Omaha's high society tonight." Lily frowned, let the curtains fall from her fingers. "Come to think of it, I didn't see you the rest of the evening, either. Did you leave?"

"I didn't have a choice in the matter," Derek grumbled. "After your little show, I was escorted out by Rowland's goons."

Lily pressed her lips together to keep from laughing. She hadn't meant to hit him *that* hard. "Sorry about that, Derek. I didn't know..." She stopped and frowned. "Wait, what did he say?"

"I think the exact words he used were 'John may put up with you, but I won't. Not tonight.'"

Walking toward her bedroom, Lily tucked the phone between her shoulder and ear and reached behind her, fingers grasping for the zipper. She needed out of this dress, pronto. Her fingers landed on the zipper and she tugged. "Your reaction was priceless."

"I'd say you hit like a girl," he deadpanned back, "but that's not true at all."

"It worked, though." The dress fell from her shoulders, the soft material pooling around her ankles, and Lily stepped away as she reached for the crystal hairpins folded into her hair and yanked. Soft curls fell around her shoulders. Raking her fingers through her hair, she massaged the places on her scalp that the hairpins had bitten into all night. "I'm in, but can we debrief tomorrow? I'm exhausted and still need to write out my reports."

"Nope. We debrief tonight."

"What?" She stopped short. "Absolutely not."

"I'm not asking. I'll be there in ten."

She stared at the dead phone, annoyed. But after dancing in his arms across the marble floors of the museum earlier—even ever so briefly—Lily had to admit that she was looking forward to seeing him again.

She shook her head violently to clear those thoughts and went to hunt up something to wear. *Don't go there, Andrews. He's nothing but trouble.*

CHAPTER THIRTEEN

Saturday, September 20, 11:15 p.m.

DEREK CHECKED HIS WATCH. He imagined Lily would be furious if he showed up before his ten-minute warning. Walking across the street would take him all of fifteen seconds. So he settled in and went back to surveying her building.

When the cab had pulled up in front of Lily's building and she'd stepped out, Derek damn near had a heart attack. Four hours after they'd headed out to meet Rowland, and she still sizzled in that shimmering black gown. He'd worked with some gorgeous women in the past, but Lily surpassed them all. She radiated class and beauty. A deadly combination.

Peering through his binoculars, he frowned. Everything about her screamed that she was on edge—her staccato steps, the subtle glances over her shoulder, the beeline to the door.

Why? Did something go wrong with Rowland? He scanned the street. It was empty, except for the two of them.

Lily threw another look behind her, then walked through the front doors and out of his line of sight.

Derek looked out his window and studied the penthouse. She'd drawn the sheer curtains across the wall of windows. He could see her soft silhouette. Not the best protection from prying eyes, but good enough.

Focus, Moretti.

Derek rubbed his hands over his face. That was the problem, though, wasn't it? He couldn't get his focus *off* her. He checked his watched. Again. *Screw the ten minutes.* He got out of the car and made his way toward Lily.

LILY SWUNG OPEN the door before he knocked. It was a pattern she'd established since their first rendezvous. *Pattern?* He grinned down at her. Her hair was up in a sloppy bun, and she'd slipped into her uniform of black yoga pants and black tank top.

"It hasn't been ten minutes."

"Who's keeping track?"

Rolling her eyes, she stepped back. "Did we really have to do this tonight? I'm exhausted."

Dakota barked and bounded toward the door, skidding to a halt in front of Derek. He knelt and ruffled the soft hair behind Dakota's ears. "That's exactly why. We need every detail to be perfect."

"I wouldn't have forgotten anything." She shut the door behind him. "This is ridiculous."

He couldn't argue with that. Why was he acting like a freaking teenager? Lily walked by Derek and he caught the soft scent of jasmine. *She's why.* Ridiculous or not, he was here. But he needed to keep his distance. If he so much as touched her, all bets were off.

"When do you meet with Rowland again?"

"Monday night." She sank onto the sofa. Dakota jumped up and curled around her.

Whistling, Derek plopped down in the chair opposite her. "Nice work."

"Did you expect anything less?" She folded her leg under her and threw him a smirk.

"From you? Not really."

"So…" Lily fidgeted and tucked a piece of hair behind her ear. "I think I might drop by his office on Monday afternoon."

"You sure that's the best move?" *That* was definitely not what he expected, nor what he'd do. "It might be a bit aggressive."

"I showed up at a conservative black-tie ball in *that* gown." She shot him a look. "No thanks to you."

Derek choked back a laugh. Now was not the time to push any of her buttons. No matter how much he would enjoy it. "It got the job done, didn't it?"

Fire flashed in her eyes. "I didn't need the help, thank you very much, but yes, it did. So, while dropping in on him is a bit aggressive, I think he might expect it."

"It's risky."

"So was bringing me on."

"Touché." He laughed and tipped his head toward Lily. "So a drop-in tomorrow it is. Then let's go over the key players again."

She let her head fall back against the back of the sofa and groaned. "Derek."

"It's happening. Do you have anything stronger than water?"

He wasn't about to let her walk into the lion's den without *him* being completely confident that she was ready. If that meant he'd be here all night, so be it. A primal urge to protect her ripped through him, motivating every action he took.

Even if that meant protecting her from herself. Derek wouldn't apologize for that. Not when her life was on the line.

And with Rowland in the picture, it certainly was.

"There's Merlot on the counter. Or Guinness in the fridge." She gestured to the kitchen. "But you know that. So make yourself at home."

He pushed to his feet and headed for the kitchen.

Oh, he planned on it.

CHAPTER FOURTEEN

Monday, September 22, 1:00 p.m.

LILY GAWKED AT the impressive structure before her. Pristine white marble walls soared up from an immaculate emerald lawn. Sunbeams danced on the building's glass facade.

ARME Industries was stunning. And monstrous.

Straightening her dress, she concentrated on walking in the Dolce & Gabbana stilettos. *Whoever invented high heels should be taken out and shot.*

She focused on the microscopic chip nestled between her forefinger and thumb and smiled suggestively at the men leaving the building, who were drooling like Wile E. Coyote as they ogled her body-hugging charcoal dress. Rolling her eyes behind the dark, oversize oval glasses perched on her face, she tried not to laugh.

Hopefully Rowland would have the same reaction.

Lily pushed the tall glass doors open and made her way to the front desk. She'd come prepared, and the older, elegant-looking woman behind the counter, with her silver hair and perfectly tailored, champagne-colored suit, was her first target.

"May I borrow a pen?"

Lily didn't wait for the woman to answer. She leaned

down, reached for a pen and knocked over the woman's coffee cup. The hot contents flooded the receptionist's lap and she yelped, jumping up.

"Oh, my goodness. I'm so, so sorry. How embarrassing." Lily reached down to assist her. "Here, let me help."

"That's not necessary. Please stay here." The woman grimaced. "I'll be right back."

Racing across the marble floor, the woman disappeared into the women's restroom. Lily glanced around quickly before pressing the microscopic chip onto the underside of the woman's computer. It contained a malware that would, once connected with the computer's surface, take complete control over the system— including downloading and uploading files, tracking web history, adding infected software installations and even controlling the keyboard so she could type commands.

Everything the receptionist saw and heard on her computer, Lily would be able to tap into.

The bathroom door swung open and the receptionist made her way back toward the desk. The woman didn't speak until she sat. Lily waited, her hands clasped in front of her. No need to further piss her off. Bug in place, it was time to turn up the charm. This woman staring Lily down was the gatekeeper.

"Now," the receptionist asked, her tone icy. "How can I help you?"

Lily couldn't blame her. She'd probably just ruined the woman's expensive-looking outfit. Discreetly, she checked the nameplate sitting on top of the desk.

"I'm so sorry about your suit…Helen," Lily gushed, opening her designer bag and rummaging through it.

"Please allow me to cover the cost of replacing it, or at the very least, to get it dry-cleaned."

The fire in the woman's eyes died a little. "Thank you for the offer. That's very kind, but not necessary. Do you have an appointment with someone?"

Lily hitched the bag onto her shoulder again. "I'm here to see Mr. Rowland James."

"Your name?"

"Addison. Addison Moore." Her Southern twang came out in a soft drawl.

At the sound of her name, the woman jolted as if struck by lightning, then smiled welcomingly. "Ms. Moore, so nice to meet you. Mr. James is expecting your visit."

Lily was slightly startled by the woman's remarkable transformation, but gratified to see that she hadn't lost her intuition or her charm. Thank goodness she'd listened to her gut this time.

The woman reached for her phone. "I'll call a security guard to escort you up."

"No need, Helen. We're headed that way," a voice said from behind them. "We can take her up."

Lily turned and came nose to nose with the voice. She took a step back. Disdain and curiosity flickered in the man's dark brown eyes. He flashed a reserved smile. She glanced over his shoulder. Derek flanked him, just behind and off to his right. Their eyes locked, and it felt as if Derek reached inside her with his steady, heated gaze. She jerked her focus back to John Elsworth.

His appearance in the flesh shocked her, just as it had in his picture. She would have assumed that the man who dominated the controlling percentage of

ARME Industries, the largest weapons manufacture in the Northern Hemisphere, would be more of an alpha male, with a quiet, but take-no-shit strength.

She still couldn't get her head around the fact that Elsworth more closely resembled a basement accountant.

"Thank you, Mr..." She held out her hand and cocked her head to the side in an assumed manner of polite confusion, giving him time to respond to her unspoken question.

"John. John Elsworth." He took her hand and shook it with more force than she'd anticipated. Without letting go, he asked, "And you are?"

"Pardon me. Addison Moore." She gracefully withdrew her hand from his and tried not to wince. The man had an iron grip. "Nice to meet you, Mr. Elsworth."

"You said you were here to see Rowland?" The crispness in his voice made Lily reconsider the man in front of her. Surely one had to have a steel spine to stand his ground against the likes of Rowland James.

"Yes, I am."

He nodded. "Follow me. We'll take you up."

"Thank you. That would be most kind." Her words come out in the slight drawl she'd mastered.

The express elevator took them straight to the executive level on the third floor. Derek's hot gaze pressed on her back, and she resisted the urge to squirm the short ride up. The door opened, exposing an expansive lobby. Massive doors flanked the grand space on opposing ends. A handful of desks peppered the area in between.

Lily stepped out, then looked back at Derek. A tight

smile rested on his face. Her heart flip-flopped. What was *wrong* with her?

She'd been annoyed when he'd shown up on her doorstep last night, but only because it wasn't on her terms. He was ballsy, stubborn as hell and he gently pressed until he got what he wanted. But truth be told, she enjoyed Derek's company. Though she'd never admit it to him.

John disappeared into his office, and Derek followed. Only then did the assistant, with her flawlessly styled, black-as-night hair and doe-like brown eyes, swing her attention from Derek's vanishing backside to Lily. "May I help you?"

"Mr. James, please."

She looked Lily up and down. "And who may I tell him is asking?"

"Addison Moore." Lily struggled to keep the Southern drawl audible. She wanted to reach across the desk and smack the snotty expression off the young assistant's face.

Her name did it for her.

The woman blanched, her brown eyes widening even further than Lily thought humanly possible. Pushing back from her desk with trembling hands, she stood. "My apologies, Ms. Moore. Mr. James is expecting you. Please, follow me."

What the hell was going on here? Lily figured Rowland kept a tight ship, but the hypersensitivity was beyond bizarre. She glanced at the woman's nameplate. "Thank you, Ms. Montgomery. I sure do appreciate it."

"Please, call me Alyssa." She flashed a tight smile, then walked Lily to the wooden doors. They appeared ancient, as if flown in from some castle in Europe, and they were a work of art, as was nearly everything that had to do with ARME.

Alyssa pushed the door open and stood aside, ushering Lily into a small, cozy sitting area. "Mr. James is finishing up a call in his office. He'll be with you shortly."

"Thank you, Alyssa."

The lovely young woman nodded and pulled the doors closed behind her, leaving Lily alone. Wrapped in a cocoon of silence, she stood still, glancing around.

Then she spied the photos. Curious, she walked over to take a closer look.

Frame after frame of the top leaders in the world sat neatly displayed on a long side table overlooking the expansive courtyard below. The average citizen would have been stunned, grappling with the picture of Rowland with his arm casually thrown around Saudi's youngest prince, Shaled bin Daad.

If the average Joe even knew who was in the photo.

If not for her previous training—and firsthand encounters with many of them—she would have been amongst the many awed at Rowland's powerful connections with the world's leading international businessmen, princes and leaders. And she would have missed the true significance of the photos.

But Lily saw them for what they were.

"Holy shit," she breathed into the quiet room.

She'd filed, memorized and burned their smug faces into her memory. They weren't just businessmen, but some of the top players in the international terrorism circle.

One particular photo caught her eye, and she reached for it. The man Rowland embraced was none other than the Afghan warlord she'd been sent to track on a recon mission two years ago. Her blood ran cold.

Violent, vivid images she'd tried hard to forget flashed through her mind. She squeezed her eyes shut and pushed the old, aching pain down. She'd lost many friends at that brutal man's order.

If he could, this one man alone would happily take out the entire United States government and the life and freedom Americans knew.

Lily scanned the many faces on display, and the hair on the back of her neck stood on end. He was but one of a dozen framed photos of equally evil and dangerous men that Rowland triumphantly exhibited.

You cocky son of a bitch.

She couldn't believe Rowland's arrogance. To openly flaunt his connections to some of the most powerful and deadly men of the twenty-first century was loathsome. Her mind raced. Why not have those photos in his office? Why showcase them in his sitting area? Was he trying to intimidate his visitors?

She softly gasped. *Holy shit.* He was. It was the perfect, ultimate mind game. Of course someone who knew enough to be visiting Rowland at ARME would know some, if not all, of those men he showcased. At least they should, especially if they were in the weapons manufacturing industry.

"Addison. Welcome to ARME."

Lily cringed inwardly. In her preoccupation with the photos, she hadn't heard him approach. She put down the frame and turned, throwing him a sultry smile. "I hope you don't mind me dropping in like this, but—" she took a step closer "—it seemed as though you were expecting me."

Rowland leaned against the door frame between his office and sitting room. His crisp white shirt, hinting to a well-defined chest, was tucked neatly into his perfectly pressed sharkskin suit pants. Lily would have to be dead not to be affected by his enigmatic charm and good looks.

Why were sociopathic animals frequently so damn beautiful?

"Coming to my office uninvited is rather assertive, but yes, I expected it." He lifted a crystal tumbler to his mouth and searched her face. He stepped aside, waved her past him. "Please, join me in my office. It's more comfortable."

She obeyed, following him into the immense room. A sleek conference table sat to the left, eight black, stoic-looking leather chairs neatly tucked against it. At the far end of the room sat an ornately carved mahogany desk, one that Lily could only imagine came out of some Italian chateau, anchoring the perfectly designed space. Behind the desk, a vintage-looking world map, covering every inch of the far wall, stretched wide. To the right, along the floor-to-ceiling windows, two dark leather chairs, mirroring their counterparts across the room, and a matching sofa encircled a coffee table, all overlooking the grounds below.

The space fit Rowland—beautiful, yet cold.

He sat on the edge of his lavish desk and swirled the Scotch in his glass. "After arriving at my gala in that daring albeit stunning gown last night, I'd have severely misjudged you had you not shown up today, which—" he sent her a wolfish grin that sent electricity buzzing down her spine "—would have been a disappointment."

She shifted uncomfortably at the intensity of his stare and, tilting her head to the side, forced a soft smile onto her lips. "A disappointment? Why is that?"

"I'm drawn to the confident, although slightly brash, way you carry yourself. It's refreshing among the tittering, insecure women I'm accustomed to." His cold, green eyes roamed her body. "You're enchanting and, quite frankly, you fascinate me."

A chill ran over her skin. She didn't want to intrigue him, didn't want him to look at her as if he wanted to consume her. But it didn't matter what she wanted. The mission was her main objective, and if having Rowland look at her as though he wanted to bed her right now was the way to achieve her ends, so be it. She shut down the shudder and crossed her legs, letting the hem of her skirt ride up.

"I must admit, the feeling is mutual."

He took another sip from his glass and captured her with his icy, sensual stare.

Lily didn't move. She didn't want to undermine her position. He'd accepted her, deemed her worthy of his presence. She wasn't prey. She was a huntress, damn it. Just like him. If she hesitated or showed any sign of weakness, it would be over before it had even begun.

This man responded to power.

The assumption of anything less could be deadly.

She pushed a smile to her lips and prayed it made its way to her eyes. "May I persuade you into a late lunch with me, then?"

"Unfortunately, no." He put down his tumbler and pushed off from his desk. "I have an unexpected appointment I cannot miss."

"Oh?" Lily's heart sank. Had she pressed him too far? "That's rather disappointing."

He walked to her and reached for her hand. She let him entwine their fingers together and pull her to her feet, tugging her closer to his chest. He looked down at her and, without a word, ran the back of his fingers down her cheek. The touch was light, but unexpectedly sensual, leaving Lily breathless.

"It is for me as well, *mi amor*," he said, his voice dark, husky. "But sometimes business trumps pleasure. And as much as I'd rather be dining with you tonight—" he let his hand slide down her hip and settle on the small of her back as he guided her toward his office door "—dinner will also have to wait for another time."

And just like that, he ushered her out and gently closed the door in her face.

CHAPTER FIFTEEN

Monday, September 22, 5:00 p.m.

LILY FLICKED THE worn yellow card between her fingers.
She reached for the phone but then hesitated. Leaning
against the windows flanking her western wall, she
tapped the card against her thigh and stared into the
darkness below. How someone who openly flaunted
his relationship with known enemies of state stood
within one breath of owning and running the largest
weapons manufacturer in the northern hemisphere as-
tounded and infuriated Lily.

She looked at the tattered card and sighed. Calling
Director Kennedy was ridiculous. What would she say?

*Hello, sir. I know I basically told you to go to hell
when I walked out and have ignored all your attempts
to contact me, but I agreed to undertake a mission with
another one of your operatives, and my mark had photos taken with a dozen or more known enemies of state.
I don't have anything more than a promise of dinner,
but I thought you should know.*

"Don't be ridiculous," she murmured, mortified just
thinking about it. Calling Director Kennedy was *not*
an option.

The house intercom chirped. Lily tucked the card

into her back pocket, walked over to the kitchen and picked up the phone. "Yes?"

"Derek is coming up to see you."

Lily's eyes flipped to the monitor. Derek's face flashed across the screen as he stepped out of the elevator. Damn it. She was a hot mess. She hadn't bothered to change out of her running gear. "Next time, a little heads-up would be appreciated, George."

"I called, didn't I?" He chuckled and hung up.

She yanked the door open before Derek could knock. The corner of his lip twitched into a slight smile. How he managed to make a simple T-shirt and black leather jacket look sexy was beyond her. She didn't want to feel like the floor was tumbling out from her whenever he turned his blue eyes on her, but she couldn't prevent her body from responding to Derek. It had a mind of its own.

And it wanted him.

"What are you doing here?"

She shut the door and headed into the kitchen, putting some much needed space between them. At some point during their escapade at Rowland's party, Derek had effectively chipped away at her internal resolve and the pendulum had swung wildly.

In his favor.

"I wanted to catch you before you headed off to dinner with Rowland." He leaned against the counter, his gaze sweeping her body.

Flushing, she wrapped her arms around her waist.

Derek raised an eyebrow. "Although judging by the looks of it, that's not happening?"

"He postponed—'business before pleasure.'" She shrugged, ignoring the flash of heat she felt as she recalled Rowland running his fingers down her face, and opened the fridge, reached in and pulled out a bowl of grapes. "Said an unexpected appointment came up. End of story."

Lily grabbed a grape and popped it into her mouth. She wasn't hungry, but she snatched another grape, anyway, anything to keep her focus off the man standing in her kitchen, openly evaluating her…and the rush of terror and excitement Derek evoked.

"When's your next contact?"

"Whenever he summons me." She wrinkled her nose. "Which, for the record, I hate."

"So no dinner tonight, and no idea when he'll call next?"

Pursing her lips, she nodded. "Correct."

"Great." Derek pushed off from the counter and rubbed his hands together. "Let's have dinner."

Lily nearly choked on the half-chewed grape in her mouth. Her heart slammed against her rib cage. Dinner sounded lovely and dangerous, all at the same time. This was getting too comfortable. She was growing more and more accustomed to having Derek here, in her home, with her. Missed him when he wasn't around.

Ever since that damn party, it was as if her body came alive whenever he was near. And that was bad news. If history had taught her anything, it was that nothing good could come out of whatever was starting to spark between her and Derek.

He shrugged off his jacket and threw it onto the sofa. Lily stared as the muscles in his back strained against his shirt, and her hands grew clammy, aching to reach out and touch. *Oh, shit...*

"I don't think—"

He cut her off. "More chatter came through."

Images of his muscles beneath her fingers vanished and she perked up. "Why didn't you say that to begin with?"

"I figured that would get your attention." He shook his head and laughed. "Did it work?"

He tossed a grape into his mouth and smirked.

Oh, yeah, he was trouble, all right. But more chatter meant they could be one step closer to wrapping this case. And shutting down whatever *this* was between them. Lily swallowed the disappointment creeping up her throat. "Start talking, and I'll start cooking."

Derek dragged out a stool, straddled it and settled in. He pulled the bowl of grapes closer and popped a few into his mouth. "Intel is still trying to decipher the bullshit from the rest of it. But from what they've gathered, this just ramped up our timetable."

Her heart sank. A shorter timetable meant less time with Derek. *No. This is for the better.* "What did they gather?"

"Portable weapon of mass destruction."

She frowned. "Nothing new with that."

"True. But see that?" He pointed to her Coach hand-bag. She nodded, opened the fridge and pulled out a steak. Derek grabbed another grape. "It could fit in that. And it's undetectable."

"What?" Lily peeked around the door and shook her head. "Not possible. There has to be some sort of fingerprint. Something."

"That's what we thought, too. Until ARME created a WMD that is undetectable."

"ARME created this weapon?" She set salsa and chips in front of Derek, then grabbed a knife from the knife block.

"Yep." He scooped the salsa high on a chip and tossed the combination into his mouth.

"If we already know that ARME has this technology, why are we even discussing it?" Lily stopped cutting the steak into strips and looked at him. "Lock it down."

"We can't just lock it down. Chatter indicates that the technology got smuggled out—"

"Smuggled out? What the he—"

He held up his hand.

"Sorry. Go on."

"Like I was saying, the tech was smuggled out—we suspect it's an inside job—and a bidding war is currently underway. The shitty thing?" Derek waved a chip in the air. "We don't know who the players are. And we need that intel. So our hands are tied. We watch and wait."

"So let me get this straight." Lily fought to keep the sarcasm out of her voice, but it had a mind of its own and oozed out with every word. "There's chatter about a bidding war happening for a portable WMD, and we're not doing anything about it."

"Yep."

"You're kidding, right?"

"Nope. This could be the catch of a century—nail the buyer, the seller and the leak. Higher-ups want to bring in a big kill on their watch. So our directive is to let it play out long enough to guarantee a big win before we tighten the noose."

Lily bristled. Nothing about that scenario was a win. It was the same shit as Jackson: identical storyline, different players. What had happened to the country she so loved and believed in? When would this type of political bullshit stop? She bit her tongue. Tonight was not the time to jump on her soapbox.

She opened the fridge. "Guinness?"

He nodded and she handed him a bottle and an opener. "This why you want me to get in with Rowland?"

Derek popped the top and took a deep swig before answering. "We think it's the tip of the iceberg. From what we can ascertain, Rowland is gunning for John's position. With him out of the way, Rowland will be able to do business with whomever the hell he wants, whenever he wants. Unchecked."

Steam rose from the frying pan. The steak cracked and sizzled. "What about the wife? Wouldn't the company go to her?"

He laughed, a deep belly laugh. "She's nothing more than a trophy wife."

"Trophy wife?" Lily threw him a look. "What is this, Sexism 101?"

His lips twitched into that grin again. "Have you seen her?"

"No, but still…" Lily shot him another look.

He shrugged. "She isn't in the picture. Even if she were, Rowland would eat her alive."

Lily set the fajita fixings in front of them, pulled the stool around and sat facing Derek. "Bon appétit."

"This looks incredible." Derek reached for a tortilla,

piled it high with fajita fixings. "We need to figure out his next move. Scratch that. *You*—" he gestured at Lily with the serving fork "—need to figure out his next move."

"Oh, I do?"

"Yes. You." He tipped the utensil toward his chest. "Because I've got nothing."

Lily laughed and opened her mouth to respond when the shrill ring of a cell phone interrupted them. Jumping up, she grabbed it.

"Addison." Rowland's velvety voice echoed in her ear.

She spun around, snapped her fingers, pointed to the phone and mouthed, "Rowland."

Derek slowly put down his fajita, all clowning around vanished.

"Rowland, how are you?"

"Ask him to meet," Derek mouthed from across the counter. "Ask him to meet."

Lily frowned, waved him off and turned away from him. What did Derek think she was? An amateur? She had this. He moved around the counter and stood in front of her. Lily pressed an open palm into Derek's chest and pushed. He held up his hands in surrender and took a step back.

"My apologies for having to cancel today, but it was unavoidable," Rowland said, his voice like butter, delectable but dangerous. "I'd like to take you to an early dinner tomorrow."

"There's no need to apologize, and dinner tomorrow sounds lovely."

Derek pumped his fist in the air and grinned. Lily

bit back a small laugh, turned her back on him. The man was insufferable.

"I'm in closed-door meetings tomorrow from six to three. Would meeting at ARME at four o'clock be too much of an inconvenience? If it is, I'll send a car."

A driver showing up at her home was the last thing Lily needed.

"That's not an inconvenience at all. I can meet you at ARME." She glanced over her shoulder and threw Derek a sassy look. "I look forward to it."

He crossed his arms and leaned against the counter, sending Lily's heart into a wild stampede.

"Four o'clock it is."

She hung up and grinned at Derek. He grabbed her, twirled them in a circle. "Atta girl!"

Lily instinctively threw her arms around his neck and laughed. Then Derek set her down and pulled back, worry etched in his face. "That wasn't your personal cell phone, was it?"

She slipped out of his arms, rolling her eyes. "This isn't my first rodeo, cowboy. It's a burner."

Derek sent her a wide grin and her knees buckled. No matter how hard she pushed against the rogue emotions Derek evoked, they surged through her veins whenever he was close, burning her from the inside out.

Every. Single. Freakin'. Time.

"Figured as much." He tipped her chin up with his fingers and grinned down at her. "I just like pushing your buttons."

She couldn't move, could barely breathe. "Oh, you do, do you?"

"I do." Derek lowered his lips to hers, pressed lightly.

Lily froze, but only for a split second. His heart hammered against her chest, matching her heart's own wild thumping. She leaned into him, his warmth seeping into her skin. Every inch of her wanted him. Now.

Her body melted into his, and the internal barrier she'd scrambled to build crumbled. Unthinkingly, Lily threw her hands around Derek's neck and pulled him closer. His hands slid down her waist, sending fire into her veins, until they stopped at her hips and hoisted her up. A tiny cry of surprise escaped her mouth as her legs wrapped around his waist. He leaned in, set her on the counter and deepened the kiss. A small, contented sigh escaped her lips.

Demanding yet soft. Salty yet sweet. Gentle yet intoxicating.

And inviting…so very inviting.

Then warning bells exploded inside her mind. Panic gripped her. Lily felt suspended in the air all over again, falling, grasping at nothing. Because there was nothing. That's where her heart had landed her the last time she'd let a man in—in a Dumpster, barely alive. Her back stiffened. *What the hell am I doing?*

She jerked back and stared up at Derek. Wiping the back of her hand across her lips, she shook her head in dismay. "I'm sorry. I can't."

He raised his hands and backed up. An emptiness filled the spot his warm body had just occupied. Disappointment crashed into her.

"It's just, we're on this case together. And I don't think this—" she pointed between the two of them "—is a good idea."

Why was she justifying her actions? Better yet, why was she babbling on like an idiot?

A small, playful smile tugged at the corner of his lips. "Now or ever?"

Hope filled her mind as it transported her back to the party, to being tucked close to his side, to feeling protected. And then defeating fear gripped her and squeezed. She swallowed down the ache in her throat.

"I think it's best if you leave now."

CHAPTER SIXTEEN

Tuesday, September 23, 5:30 a.m.

LILY CROUCHED IN THE bushes outside Rowland's estate, waiting. Derek would kill her if he knew her plan—which was exactly why she *hadn't* told him. But they needed more intel, and if that meant breaking into Rowland's estate in broad daylight, then that's exactly what she was going to do.

The elaborate iron gates, shielding its inhabitants from intruders, receded into themselves. A black Bentley pulled out, turned right and quickly picked up speed. Drumming her fingers along her thigh, Lily glanced between the gates and the retreating car, waiting, anxious to get moving. *Come on. Come on.* The second the bold car took another right and pulled away from sight, she got up, sprinted toward the gate and dove, rolling under the gates as they shut tight.

She pushed her spine up against the stone wall, gun up, and quickly scanned the perimeter, searching for guards. Silence greeted her. Once clear, and keeping her head low, she twisted out of her backpack, unzipped it and checked her equipment, ensuring it was intact.

Eyes up. Ears open. Shallow breaths in and out.

She crept along the outskirts of the border of the

stone wall, making her way toward the back entrance. Pulling out the alarm decoder, she gingerly pressed it to the side of the mansion's security system panel. Everything went into hyperdrive as she waited, anticipating the soft ping of the decipherer telling her she'd gained access.

Twenty seconds later, the gentle chime sounded and she reached for the doorknob.

She crept through the quiet house, then froze as soft Spanish music wafted down the long hallway. Lily stepped into the first open door she saw and pulled it partially closed, watching through the crack as a plump Spanish woman with graying hair pinned up in a tight bun walked by, mop in hand.

Lily looked over her shoulder and did a double take. Well, wasn't that providence—Rowland's home office. "Gotcha now," she whispered into the quiet room and went to work.

Nothing he said and did in this room would be a secret any longer.

LILY TWIRLED IN her desk chair, quite pleased with herself. It had taken her less than twenty minutes to get in and out of Rowland's home office, which included installing two separate camera feeds.

She took a sip of her latte and glanced at her computer. At least something had gone right in the past twenty-four hours. Her face flushed as another wave of desire surged through her. Derek. She'd almost thrown caution to the wind when he'd kissed her.

Almost.

Shaking her head, Lily tried to focus. Good grief.

She needed to be drilling down into Helen's system, not imagining Derek's lips.

With the malware chip she'd installed on Helen's computer, she could piggyback into ARME's server practically undetected and search for hidden files. She clapped her hands together once and twirled in her chair.

Hunting time.

Her fingers raced across the keys and the screen flickered to life. Unbelievable. Did they think ARME was invincible? Or was this weakened firewall intentional? She made a mental note to ask Derek to look into that, typed in a simple command and overrode the system. Pressed Enter. Lily let the computer scrub through the many layers as she eyed the files racing past.

Nothing.

She changed the parameters of her search and hit Enter again.

Still nothing.

"Come on, baby. Work with me."

She stretched her neck to the side and refocused the search, then watched as the computer scanned. *There*. Lily stopped and leaned in. Nestled amongst mundane files was one labeled in Czech.

"Got you now."

She highlighted it and hit Copy.

There was no telling what was in that file. But it was the only one that arrested her attention, pulled at her gut. She had to trust her intuition. Lily strummed her fingers against her desk as the download percentage inched toward eighty.

"Come on. Come on."

Fear prickled at her skin. The longer she stayed logged into Helen's computer remotely, the higher the risk that Lily would trip a firewall. The percentage stalled at ninety.

The muscles in her shoulders tensed. She held her breath. *Please. Come to Momma.*

One hundred percent.

She dragged the copied file to her remote hard drive, ejected it and cleared out of Helen's computer, sagging back in her chair as the tension in her body released.

Glancing at the clock, she groaned. It was already eleven. That left her only five hours to scrub the file and get to ARME for dinner with Rowland.

Setting her alarm, Lily grabbed her backup laptop and plugged in the hard drive. She crossed her leg and bounced her foot as she waited, praying the file wasn't bogus, but would contain viable information that could shut Rowland down.

Her screen exploded with multiple folders. She clicked on the first one. Black–and–white weapon schematics peppered her view. She clicked out and moved to the next file. Past travel documents popped up.

So far, this file was a dud.

She dug deeper, spied another folder tucked within the clutter and labeled "DH." *What the hell?* She dragged the cursor over it and double-clicked.

A handful of additional files popped up. What was this? A freaking wormhole?

She clicked on the first file.

Photos of badly burned naked bodies populated her screen. Men, women and children with twisted limbs and faces unmoving in their torment stared up at her. The gruesome photos reminded Lily of old WWII concentration camps. Only these were worse. Far worse. And in full color.

Lily had seen her fair share of death. But she hadn't been prepared to see the tortured, mangled bodies or the faces frozen in agony.

What had she stumbled on? Better yet, what did it have to do with Rowland?

Closing that file, Lily moved to the next and double-clicked again. An Excel spreadsheet full of names populated the monitor. The first name sparked a memory.

She opened a tab in Safari, typed in Zagor Horvat and hit Enter. Multiple links popped up. He was head of the Croatian mafia. She grabbed a pen and notebook and scribbled down his name. He was a major kingpin in the Afghan heroin trafficking, human trafficking and money laundering. Killed by a swarm of bees that had been placed in the front seat of his Maserati.

She frowned, marked him deceased on her paper, then scanned the second article. The ME report stated that he was deathly allergic to bee stings. His car's locks had malfunctioned. He'd been trapped.

Lily shuddered. *Malfunctioned, my ass.*

Someone had murdered that man.

Next was Abu Zadran. He was connected to Al-Qaeda. Burned alive. Lily swallowed the bile that rose in her throat and moved on to the next name, the next target.

Twenty-seven names later, twenty-seven searches later, she stopped, her head swimming with the dark, murderous images. A number of unopened folders still remained, so Lily tried to regain her focus, clicking on one and scanning through its contents. As she read, she grew more and more dismayed.

The tattered pieces of information came together in Lily's mind, shaping into the image of an organization that resembled a world-domination terrorism ring. She'd never heard of them, not even a scared whisper within the back confines of the black market. So what was all this information doing on Rowland's hard drive? What did it have to do with him? Better yet…

What the hell was Dům Hrůzy?

CHAPTER SEVENTEEN

Tuesday, September 23, 6:00 p.m.

DEREK SKIMMED OVER the spilled contents of Lily's case file scattered across the immaculate mahogany surface of his desk. John quietly powered through his own paperwork in the adjourning office, oblivious to the shit storm Derek was staring down at. He stopped, reached for the stack of files on the edge of his desk and riffled through them, landing on the last file.

"Son of a bitch. Babycakes, you did it."

Not that he was surprised.

Growing frustrated at the lack of intel after weeks of searching within ARME's systems, Derek had—with more help from his computer-genius sister than he cared to admit—remotely hacked into Lily's system and waited. His computer alerted him to Lily's movement within ARME's system, and he'd followed her electronic breadcrumb trail straight to the file marked "DH," the file he'd failed to locate.

Until now.

He rummaged through the contents of the case file and shook his head. She'd remotely piggybacked right into ARME's system and singlehandedly cracked his case wide-open. Lily most likely didn't even know what she'd stumbled across yet.

Derek knew of only one other person who had the skills to accomplish such a feat—his baby sister, Alexis. Heaven help him if the two women ever got together.

He got up, shut his office door and reached for his secure cell. This was definitely not a call he wanted to make, not while Lily was at dinner with Rowland. The director answered on the second ring.

"Lily hacked into ARME's computer system—"

"She did *what*?"

"You heard right. I'm sending you the encrypted file now." Derek could almost see the vein on the side of the director's face bulging. He'd seen it happen a hundred times before. Derek hit the send button and turned his focus back to the scattered pages in front of him. "Take a look for yourself."

Derek folded his arms and settled back, waiting for the reaction he knew would come.

It didn't take long.

"Tell me I'm not reading this correctly."

"No, sir, you are. I triple-checked the intel myself before I called." Derek pinched the bridge of his nose and took a deep breath. The director hadn't seen *anything* yet. Gotta love being the bearer of bad news. The director was going to shit himself. "Sir, Rowland James is part of the original world-domination terrorism ring, an organization known as Dům Hrůzy. It's Czech, and literally translates to 'House of Horror.'"

Stony silence rang loudly in Derek's ear. He flipped through photo after grisly photo of murder scenes, pressed on.

"Rowland is the only remaining founding father. The photos in the file are evidence of Rowland's modus operandi. Every other member either mysteriously disappeared or died a violent death. Rowland now single-handedly controls this organization."

"How is this even fucking possible?" Kennedy demanded. "How is it that my division of the world's best operatives can't zero in on this one guy?"

"That's the million-dollar question, sir, and at the present time, I only have one answer for you. And you're not going to like it. But I believe it's because they haven't been Lily."

"Oh, come on, Derek. Don't give me that bullshit. That's all you've got?"

Derek cradled the phone between his shoulder and ear and reached for a black-and-white photo of Rowland and Lily from the gala event the other night. He hated seeing them together. Acid rolled in his stomach and he tossed the photo down in disgust.

"Rowland is a coldhearted, sociopathic bastard whose single apparent weakness is beautiful women, and Lily is already playing to that. And something about Lily's direct, forthright manner is drawing him in. I've seen it with my own eyes. It's almost like he's found an equal player, and it's become his Achilles' heel."

"I don't like it. Pull her."

Derek sat back as if he'd been punched. Why the hell would they pull Lily now, when she'd just gotten close to Rowland?

"Sir?"

"Pull her."

"There are questions that she can—"

"I don't want more questions, damn it." Kennedy's voice rose an octave. "I want answers."

Derek lurked forward in his chair. "Then pulling her is ludicrous. Sir, with all due respect, you asked me to bring in the best, and I did. She's just getting started. Give her time."

The director sighed. "Fine. But when I tell you to pull her, you do it. No questions asked."

The muscles in Derek's neck relaxed. Thank God they'd dodged *that* bullet. Where was this reaction coming from? He knew that Lily held a special place in Kennedy's heart—she was his goddaughter after all—but come on. Pull her? Derek had never seen Kennedy try to yank an agent while on a mission.

It was impulsive. It was emotional. And it was fucking dangerous.

How would Lily respond to this monkey wrench? Doing recon on someone from the watch list was one thing. Getting up close and personal with a known terrorist was quite the other.

And that was just the tip of this screwed-up iceberg.

Derek wanted to punch something. He hated playing things so close to his chest, detested keeping Jackson's whereabouts from Lily. He knew she searched for him, for closure. But orders were orders. Derek hoped she never found out, that he'd never be tied back to this bullshit. If Lily ever found out that her ex-partner might be working with Rowland, she might never forgive Derek for roping her into this case, for pulling her closer to the man who'd betrayed her.

Who'd tried to kill her.

Watching Jackson had been the third and final of Derek's objectives. He'd been sent to see how far Jackson took the sale of the formula after he'd gone dark, after he'd tried to kill Lily. Did Derek want to know the extent that Jackson was involved? Probably not. Still...

"How deep do you think Jackson is involved with this, sir? Is he part of Dům Hrůzy? Could he be the reason Rowland has been able to elude us and get past us so far?"

The director hesitated.

"Sir?"

"We aren't certain. That's part of your assignment. To ascertain that information, without tipping your hand to any of them. Jackson, Rowland or Lily."

A high shriek shattered the silence. Derek jumped up from his chair. "Sir, I have to go."

"Keep me posted," Kennedy demanded and hung up.

Derek pocketed his phone and, reaching for his .45, threw open John's door. His boss sat perched on the edge of his seat, coiled to spring and wearily looked up at him.

"What is going on, Derek?"

"Not sure. But I'm about to find out."

Another scream pierced the air. John's face drained of all color and his eyes widened. Derek looked toward the outer door connecting them to the hall. He pointed to his boss. "Stay here. Lock the door behind me."

He yanked the door closed, waiting for the soft click of the lock and quickly moved to the outer door connecting them from whatever had pulled those screams from Alyssa, John's assistant. He slowly opened the door and peered out. She sat frozen at her desk, white as a ghost and trembling. Derek cleared the room, then moved quickly to her side. "Alyssa, what in the world is going on?"

"It's Helen." Alyssa pointed to the screen on her desk that monitored the foyer. "Something's wrong with her."

He took one look at the screen and sprinted for the emergency exit. Slamming his open hand into the door, he tore down the steps, taking them two at a time.

He burst out of the emergency door and raced toward Helen, waving his hands at the bystanders gawking at their coworker convulsing on the floor. "Get back! Get back! And someone call 9-1-1."

Derek skidded to a halt and dropped to his knees, reaching for Helen's neck, desperate to protect her head from bouncing off the white marble floors any more than it already had. He took one look at her and his heart sank. Pink foam bubbled at the corners of her mouth. Blood streamed from her nose and ears. Her eyes, wide with fright and pain, rolled back into her head and her blue irises vanished.

The circle of ARME employees tightened around him and Helen, and righteous anger burned at him. Did these people have no souls? "Get the hell back. Now. Or do you want to be next?"

They crowd scampered backward, horror flashing across most of their faces. Derek looked back down at Helen, trying his best to stabilize her flailing body when a soft, scared voice broke through the chaos.

"Derek?"

He glanced up and into the ashen face of Gina Elsworth. *Oh, shit.* What was she doing here? "Ma'am, what are you doing here?"

"I'm early for a dinner date with John. I thought…" Her voice shook, and she cast a quick look at Helen, tears filling her eyes. Her hand fluttered at her throat. "I thought I'd surprise him."

Derek hung his head. *Of course she did.* Sweet, innocent Gina. Always looking to please her older husband, be the perfect wife and mother.

Movement to his left caught his attention. A thin man with glasses, clutching his leather briefcase to his chest moved toward the glass double doors. Derek jumped to his feet, whipped out his gun and pointed it at the man.

"Stop. Now. No one leaves."

The thin man froze midstep, his glasses sliding down his nose and his face turning pale. *Good. Serves him right.* He shoved his glasses back up his nose and shuffled back to the small group, head down.

"Mrs. Elsworth." Derek looked over his shoulder. Arms limp at her side, Gina stood above Helen's still-shaking body, her face blank. "Gina! Look at me."

She jerked as if he'd slapped her and raised dazed eyes to him. "I… What…?"

"Gina. Listen to me," he commanded in a low, calm voice. "I need you to call 9-1-1."

She nodded, reaching for her small handbag and digging out her phone. With trembling fingers, she typed in the number and held the phone to her ear.

"Please. Hurry," Gina glanced over her shoulder at Helen. "We need an ambulance…"

Derek shoved his gun back into his holster, knelt next to Helen and, stabilizing her neck, bent close to her ear, careful to avoid getting any of her blood on him. "Hang on, Helen. It's going to be okay. I got you. It's going to be okay."

For a brief second in time, Helen came to. She

looked directly at Derek, her eyes pleading with him to save her. His blood ran cold. *She knew.* Then the moment of clarity vanished as another convulsion wracked her body.

He knew it, too—Helen was as good as dead.

LILY'S PHONE VIBRATED ANGRILY. She glanced down, recognized the number and hit decline. Again.

"Is everything all right?"

"Of course." Lily pressed the linen napkin to her lips, folded it and tucked it next to her plate. The vibrations started again. She looked up and shrugged one shoulder. "Rowland, my apologies, would you mind if I take this call?"

He smiled, though light never reached his eyes, and waved his hand. "Not at all. Hopefully there isn't some sort of emergency."

Lily grabbed her phone and pushed back from the table. *It better be a freakin' emergency.* "I'm sure it's nothing like that. I'll be right back."

She made a beeline toward the softly illuminated sign in the back of the elegant restaurant. Pushing her way into the restroom, she waited until the door shut behind her, cocooning her in silence, before reaching for her phone.

"There better be a good—"

"It's Helen," Derek said, without so much as an acknowledgment. "She's dead."

"What?" Lily slumped against the bathroom counter. That was the last thing she'd expected to hear. "When?"

"About an hour ago. When I got to her, she was

curled up in the fetal position, convulsing and foaming at the mouth."

"Do they know what caused it?"

"No, but John made a few calls and they're rushing the autopsy. We have to make sure there wasn't a breach in security. And if there was, what steps we need to take to manage it."

Lily straightened. "Are you still at ARME?"

"We're all in lockdown—John, myself, Gina, a small group of employees—until the autopsy results come in."

Lockdown? Lily's stomach dropped. How was it that ten seconds ago she'd wanted to kill Derek for hounding her, and now all she wanted to do was throw her arms around him *just* to make sure he was all right?

"Lil?"

"Yes. Sorry. I'm here." The bathroom door opened, and an elderly woman walked in. The two women exchanged polite nods as the woman disappeared into the first stall. Lily walked into the stall farthest from the woman, shut and locked the door, then brought her hand up to her mouth and lowered her voice. "What do you want me to do?"

"There's nothing you can do. No doubt John is calling Rowland and giving your current dinner date the heads-up. I thought it best to keep you informed…stay on your toes tonight and end the evening as early as possible, got it?"

"You don't have to tell me twice."

"I'll meet you at your place as soon as I can get out of here."

Lily pressed her eyes shut and slumped against the stall door. *That sounded divine.* She didn't completely understand it, but she knew one thing for sure. For the first time in a long time, something other than darkness consumed her. Derek did that to her, he made her feel alive—and if he ever tried to kiss her again, she wouldn't stop him.

But it most likely wouldn't ever happen again… thanks to her. Lily cleared her throat and shook her head. No use chasing *that* rabbit.

"Keep me posted and be careful, okay?"

"Yeah. You, too."

Lily flushed the toilet—no use causing anyone to give her a second glance—and quickly washed her hands before tucking her phone safely inside her clutch and weaving her way through the crowded restaurant back to their table. When she came closer, Rowland stood and helped her back into her chair. She looked up and smiled. *Well, aren't you a gentleman…and a monster.*

He sat and cocked his head to the side, drilling her with his soulless eyes. Lily fought to remain still. "No emergencies, I hope?"

"No, and I'm so—"

A shrill ring sounded. Grateful for the interruption, Lily sat back. Rowland scowled, fished in his front coat pocket, pulled out his phone and held it to his ear. "Yes, what is it?"

Lily strained to hear the other side of the conversation. *Nothing.* He sat silent for a moment and then nodded. "I see. That's rather…unfortunate."

He listened to the other end of the line for a minute more before hanging up and pocketing his phone. He casually reached for his wine and took a sip before looking up. "Well, tonight seems to be the night for eventful phone calls."

"Oh?" Lily sat forward. *Helen.* "Is everything all right?"

"It's our receptionist." He pressed his lips together until they formed a thin white line and casually shrugged one shoulder. "She unfortunately passed away tonight."

"Oh, Rowland." Lily reached out her hand. "I am so sorry. Do you need to go?"

"No." He grasped her hand and entwined his fingers with hers. "I'm here with you. The dead can wait."

He pressed his lips to the top of her hand, never taking his eyes off Lily. His callous response didn't really surprise her. Everything about the man studying her from across the table was cold, calculated.

With his free hand, Rowland brought his wineglass to his lips. She blinked. *Had he just smiled?* Lily's blood ran cold. Did he know? Had he figured out she'd piggybacked into Helen's computer? Lily's mind tumbled over itself as she recounted her every move. No, she'd been a ghost—slipping in, slipping out. There was no way anyone could have known that she'd bugged Helen's computer.

Pulling back her hand, Lily reached for her spoon, took a small piece of the lavender soufflé and brought it to her mouth, tasting nothing. *Had Rowland killed Helen?* There was no way, was there? He'd been sitting here eyeing Lily the whole evening.

She locked eyes with the monster occupying her table and wanted to scream.

He'd asked *her* to dinner.

His perfect alibi.

CHAPTER EIGHTEEN

Tuesday, September 23, 9:30 p.m.

DINNER WITH ROWLAND had been excruciating and long. Derek had sent a text that the autopsy results were inconclusive. *Inconclusive, my ass.* Lily had all but sprinted past George when she'd finally gotten home, taken Dakota for the world's shortest run and raced back to her computer, turning it on.

Quickly, and without hesitation, she hacked into the city morgue's system and went to work. An hour later, Lily reached for her phone.

Derek answered on the first ring. "Lil, what's up? You okay?"

The sound of his rich, deep voice instantly made her tight muscles relax. "Yeah. But we have a problem— those autopsy reports the medical examiner sent you were tampered with."

"I'm not following. Tampered with how?"

"Derek, I worked backward and found the original cause of death. I've never heard of it and was only able to find a few articles on it, and they were mostly blacked out, but Helen died from something called Malattia."

"Wait. What did you say?"

"There were traces of a biological toxin called

Malattia in her system. From the limited research I could find, it's pretty rare, and has an immediate onset of symptoms once exposed—muscle convulsion due to the toxin attacking the nervous system being the first to represent itself," she explained. Derek remained silent on the other end, and fear prickled her skin. "Why?"

"Lily." Derek paused, and she squeezed her eyes shut, pushing back the raw anger bubbling up in her throat. Her gut knew what he was going to say, but she still prayed that she was wrong. Derek took a deep breath on the other end of the line. "If you're correct, and I think you are, ARME is the only manufacturer authorized to produce Malattia, and it's still in its developmental stages."

Lily dropped her head and pinched the bridge of her nose. "What category will CDC label it once complete?"

"Cat A," Derek said. "It'll be right up there with Anthrax."

Category A. Of course. Easily transmitted from person to person. High mortality rate. Major health impact. Not to mention the public panic and social disruption. Lily didn't expect anything less from Rowland.

"Wait." Her head snapped up. "How did none of you get infected?"

"Clearly it still needs some tweaking," Derek said drily. "Because once fully vetted, it will make Anthrax look like child's play, and will be for the military's exclusive use. It's supposed to be kept under lock and key."

Lily wanted to scream. Rowland was evil incarnate,

and he needed to be put down. Permanently. "Yeah, well. Someone got to it, and used it to kill Helen."

"I know, and I promise we will find them."

Lily had no doubt that they would, especially since she already knew who the murderer was—Rowland James. And he'd used her to keep his name unsullied. Bastard.

"Hey, you still there?"

Lily blinked, focused on the conversation at hand. "Yeah, sorry. What were you saying?"

"CDC cleared us to leave. Want me to come over?"

She did, but something still gnawed at her. She wanted to get back to those files, dig a little deeper. "Can I take a rain check?"

"Sure thing, babycakes."

Lily smiled at the nickname. "Meet me at Keystone in the morning? Around seven?"

"It's a date," Derek said and hung up.

She brought her fingers to her lips as warmth surged through her body. Yeah, a breakfast date with Derek was exactly what she needed. It sounded divine. She glanced over at the computer and the warmth faded. *Helen was dead.* Lily jumped up and paced her room, letting her mind tumble over the current information, no matter how scattered and fragmented.

Rowland killed Helen and covered it up within a day of Lily hacking into Helen's system. How was that even possible? Lily hadn't even found the exact files until less than eight hours ago.

Stalking to the kitchen, she opened a cabinet, grabbed her favorite mug and slid it under the Keurig coffeemaker. A few moments later, cradling the cup of scalding hot liquid, she whistled for Dakota and went back to her room, settling at her desk.

She set down her coffee and went to click on the first unmarked file when her computer chimed.

Spinning in her chair, she turned her attention to the screen monitoring Rowland's office and smiled as Rowland sank into his large leather chair.

"Gotcha now, handsome."

He yanked open the top drawer and pulled out a frame. The angle of her camera picked up the faded faces of two smiling dark-haired beauties, and judging by the similarities between them, they were mother and daughter. He gently rubbed his thumb over the picture safely hidden behind the glass.

"I will punish them, *mi amor*, I swear to you. I will avenge you and our daughter."

Lily's mouth dropped open. *Rowland had a wife? A daughter?* Somehow she doubted Derek was privileged to *that* tidbit of information. She zoomed in on the frame as far as she could and leaned forward to get a better look.

They were standing with their backs to the ocean, purple, red and orange hues spread across the sky behind them. Black hair framed the woman's large dark eyes, which sparkled even through the faded photograph. She'd thrown her arms around the little girl's tiny body and hugged her close to her chest as they both grinned at the camera, not a care in the world.

Lily glanced at Rowland's face and her chest constricted. If she hadn't seen it with her own eyes, she would have never believed that the coldhearted monster *had* emotions, let alone that he could cry—but sure enough, tears rimmed the edge of his bloodshot eyes.

For a split second, a resonating pain attacked Lily, and her heart ached for him, felt his loss.

He reached for the crystal glass, his hand shaking. *What the hell had happened to Rowland's family?* She watched, fascinated, as he tipped his head back and downed the caramel-colored liquid.

Gone was the swagger, the charisma, the magnetism.

Lily stared at the face of a heartbroken husband, a crushed father.

Never letting go of the frame, he poured another full glass of Scotch and took a swig before setting the glass down. Dumbfounded, Lily watched as Rowland stared at the photo, face drawn.

Without taking her eyes off the screen she reached for a pen and scribbled "He has a family?" on the first piece of paper she could find.

His cell phone rang and he swore, set down the frame and snatched up his mobile. "This better be good."

He silently listened to whoever was on the other end of the line, and then his face grew hard and he slammed the crystal glass down. "That is *not* something you need to concern yourself—"

He stopped midsentence. Lily's pen hung suspended above her scribbles, and she stared at the monitor. *Who had the balls to interrupt him?*

What she wouldn't give to hear both sides of this conversation. *Damn it.* She needed to get a tap on Rowland's phone. Pronto.

"No. You listen to me, you son of a bitch." His face darkened and he leaned forward. "I've been systematically positioning my people amongst world leaders for years, and they answer only to me." He thumped his fist into his chest. "I'm the puppet master. When the time is right, *I* will pull the strings."

Dům Hrůzy.

Was Rowland at the helm of Dům Hrůzy? Lily scribbled notes as fast as she could, her mind tripping over itself. Had he really infiltrated the world's top governments, and if so, how high up did his people go?

"Do *not* call me again. Wait for my call." Rowland chucked the phone across the room and it hit the far wall, shattering into pieces. Pushing back from his desk, he got up and walked out of sight of her cameras.

Lily leaned back in her chair and whistled, long and low. She'd expected to gather vital intel from her little rendezvous with Rowland's office, but she hadn't expected it so quickly, or for it to be such a game-changer.

Rowland had a family, and he was quite possibly the head of the deadliest terrorist group she'd even encountered, silently positioning *his* people within *her* government.

Head spinning, she went back to the folder marked "DH," clicked on one of the two unmarked files. A photograph of a complex, handwritten equation popped up.

To the average person, the scribbles would look like the scrawlings of a mad scientist, but Lily had seen something like this during an old mission with a defecting Russian nuclear physicist. It wasn't just random scribbles, but a complex chemical equation.

Was that the chemical formula to weaponize the WMD?

Enlarging the photo to give her tired eyes some relief, she studied the multifaceted and intricate equation. It had been a few years, but maybe that part of her—very fatigued, mind you—brain would kick in. She read through it, stopped, started from the beginning and then paused midway. *What the...?*

It was incomplete.

Useless.

Pushing back from her desk, she left her room and paced along the wall of windows, staring at the twinkling lights of downtown. The traffic light at the corner switched from green to yellow to red and back to green without a single car passing. The city was still, quiet. She leaned her head against the glass, enjoying the cold seeping through the hard surface, and closed her eyes. Nothing was quiet in her brain. The further she dug into these files, the stranger things became.

Settling back in front of her computer, she clicked on another unmarked file and numbers flooded the monitor. Lily leaned forward and studied them again, her eyes flipping between the numbers.

"You aren't random now, are you," she whispered into the stillness surrounding her.

Rubbing the palms of her hands across her eyes, she blinked twice and turned back to the screen, letting her mind roam over the numbers, deciphering their meaning. She sucked in a breath.

They were coordinates.

Snatching up her laptop, she moved into the main living space and set the computer down on the kitchen island, then rushed to the closet and pulled out an old paper map of the United States. Spreading it flat across the kitchen island, she weighted down the edges.

She looked at the first two coordinates and, shoving

a pen between her teeth, Lily drew her fingers down, found the first coordinate on the map. She pulled the pen from her mouth and circled the location.

St. Louis.

She repeated the process and circled the next spot.

San Francisco.

She continued mapping out each set of numbers— Boston, Chicago, New York—until eighteen locations were circled. Stepping back, she stared down at the map, perplexed.

"Why are these so important to you?"

Sinking onto the closest bar stool, she reached for her laptop, plugged all the cities together into her search engine and hit Enter. Waited. Nothing. She chewed on her bottom lip, rearranged the cities, left some out and tried again. Still nothing. On a whim she typed in the first twelve cities.

"Well, I'll be damned."

Twelve of the eighteen cities housed a branch of the Federal Reserve.

Was Rowland planning to bomb the banks? Taking them out would cripple the economy, cause mass panic, quite possibly throw the United States into a second Great Depression, yes, but somehow Lily didn't think that was his endgame.

Bombing the banks, or even the cities that housed them, didn't have enough flair for Rowland, and nothing was *that* easy with him. The man was cold, calculated and—the photo of his family flashed in her mind—very, very…complicated.

And what about the other locations? She tapped her pen against the list she'd scribbled. There were no coincidences with him, everything had a purpose, so what did Omaha, Raven Rock Mountain, Colorado Springs, Berryville, Culpeper and White Sulphur Springs mean to him?

Updating her search engine with the last six locations, she pressed Enter and waited. She scanned the first article that popped up and her eyes hit on one disturbing sentence. *All part of the government's doomsday plan...*

Each of the remaining six cities listed housed alternative command posts for use in the event of a nuclear emergency, ensuring the continuity of the US government. Take out all six while they were occupied, and you'd cripple the most powerful government in the world.

Was Rowland planning on launching a nuclear war on the United States? She flipped between the two lists of cities—what did a list of eighteen cities mean? Frustrated, she settled back on the bar stool and sipped her coffee. Without more evidence, a solid plan of attack, something, it was all just circumstantial.

Dakota curled under her feet, resting his head on her ankle. Smiling, she reached down and ran her hand over his ear. Her eyes traveled over the documents and landed on an unmarked folder buried within the numbers.

"What have we got here?" Lily opened it, and a detailed time line popped up. She studied it for a minute, then sat back, stunned.

The twelve cities housing the Federal Banks aligned with one date, the other six corresponded with a second—three days apart, and both set to happen in less than three weeks.

The world fell out from underneath her. The bastard

was planning a two-prong attack. Against her country. Against her people.

She hung her head and pinched the bridge of her nose. But with a formula that wasn't complete, it wouldn't work. What was she missing? What the hell was going on? Damn, her brain needed a reprieve.

Reaching for her phone, she dialed Derek's number, cradling the phone between her shoulder and chin as she stared at her computer screen until her eyes crossed, blurring the screen.

"You okay?" Derek asked in a drowsy voice after the first ring.

She blinked twice to focus her eyes and glanced at the clock, cringed. The green numbers shone back at her—4:00 a.m. "Sorry. Yes. I didn't realize it was so early. It can wait."

"What's up?" Derek pressed, all grogginess gone.

Lily hesitated. What if she was wrong? What if…

She stopped. *Screw what-if.* If she didn't say anything and those locations were attacked, she'd never forgive herself.

She'd already questioned her instinct once, before Jackson had ultimately betrayed her. She'd played the what-if game and lost everything.

Her love. Her job. Her confidence.

She sure as hell wasn't about to do it again. Lily took a deep breath. "I stumbled across something that I think we need to discuss. And quickly. This isn't just about a bidding war."

"Talk to me."

She sent the documents to the printer. "Can you meet me at Keystone in an hour?"

"I can come over now."

"No. Call Ben. Let him know we're coming over. I need an hour." She hung up, tapped her foot as the printer spit out paper and prayed she was wrong.

CHAPTER NINETEEN

Wednesday, September 24, 5:00 a.m.

LILY HAD CIRCLED dates and names before sprinting over to Keystone. Papers lay scattered across the long coffee bar. Derek and Ben hovered over the pages. Quiet.

She paced as she spoke. "It's complicated, and quite frankly, my brain is still trying to work out the truth from the lies. I stumbled across something called Dům Hrůzy—"

Derek sank into a chair, rubbing his neck and looking ill at ease. "I know."

"Rowland is at the helm, isn't he?" Lily didn't need to ask—Derek's reaction confirmed it. But if he already knew, why hadn't he read her in?

Derek ran his hands over his face, then glanced up at Lily, suddenly looking very tired. "Yes, he leads it."

"When were you going to share that vital piece of information with the class, Derek? Better yet, if you knew that Rowland leads Dům Hrůzy, then why the hell was he allowed to strut across ARME's threshold?"

"We didn't know." Derek pinched the bridge of his nose and let out a long sigh. "We only just figured that out."

"Okay, you two." Ben glanced between Lily and

Derek. "I'm not following. What the fuck is Dům Hrůzy?"

"Dům Hrůzy is a world-domination terrorism ring." Derek pointed at Lily. "Yours truly stumbled across a file documenting all its past members and international movements that Langley didn't even know existed. Until yesterday. Until *she* triggered it with her little hacking escapade inside ARME's system."

"Why doesn't that surprise me at all?" Ben chuckled and threw Lily an impressed grin.

Lily closed her eyes and took a deep breath. So Rowland James was the head of Dům Hrůzy. Fantastic. That just made the rest of the intel she'd stumbled across that much shittier.

"There's more."

"Of course there is," Derek muttered.

"There's a time line and a formula." Both men snapped to attention as she reached for the map and laid it flat. Weighing down the edges, she continued. "The time line has two dates on it—both within the next three weeks—that are three days apart, and I believe the numbers are coordinates for these cities."

She stepped back to let both men examine the map for themselves, to wrap their heads around the situation, because hers was still reeling. Side by side, they leaned over the map, studied it. Ben's favorite navy cable-knit sweater pulled across his strong back, Derek's go-to black T-shirt hugged his shoulders and, despite the hurricane in her brain, Lily couldn't help but smile.

There was always a silver lining within even the darkest of clouds, always—the sheer presence of both these men proved that, didn't it?

"Most of those cities hold a Federal Reserve bank," Ben mumbled, running his fingers over the worn map. He stopped and looked up, his face ashen. "The other six cities are part of our doomsday plan."

"That's not possible." Derek straightened, ran his hands over his face. "Those sites are impenetrable."

From her perch against the counter, she nodded, spoke slowly. "From the outside, yes, but not from within."

"What are you saying?" Derek looked at her as if she'd lost her mind. "That Rowland has plants within every nuclear bunker our government has set up?"

"I heard Rowland say that he'd strategically positioned his key people, that he was the puppet master, and when the time came, he'd pull the strings." Derek paced the kitchen like an African lion caged within a zoo enclosure, his hands shoved deep into his pockets, lost in thought. Lily watched him closely as she continued. "If that's truly the case, and those coordinates are accurate and what we think they are, then, yes, he could already have people set in place within each of those bunkers."

"Son of a—" Derek stopped midsentence, frowned. "What do you mean, you *heard*? How? Where?"

She hopped onto the countertop and crossed her legs, her right foot tapping the air. "I may or may not have broken into his home office and installed two cameras. I overheard a phone call tonight—that's when I learned about his involvement in Dům Hrůzy."

The smiling faces of his wife and child flashed in Lily's mind's eye again, and her heart ached. That wasn't the only thing she'd learned.

"It pisses me off that you went in alone." Derek

stared at her for a long moment, his face hard. She resisted the urge to squirm. She'd done the right, the only thing...

But then his eyes softened, and he grinned. "But damn, woman, you're incredible."

That smile, those dimples. They lit Lily up from the inside out. She wished she could turn back time, that they'd had last night to themselves before this proverbial shit hit the fan. But she'd taken a rain check.

Stupid, stupid woman.

Ben cleared his throat, glanced between them. "Mind if we get back to the business at hand?"

Lily threw Ben a cheeky grin, then nodded. "Sorry. Okay, according to these documents on Dům Hrůzy—" she jumped down from her perch and pointed to the printouts scattered across the large table "—Rowland's taken out all his competitors, presumed or otherwise. Why should we expect anything less now?"

Ben took a sip of his coffee, put down his mug. "Who's his direct competition?"

"John Elsworth," Lily and Derek answered in unison.

"Which brings me to the next part of this convoluted puzzle...I don't think there's a bidding war happening for ARME's WMD."

"Lily." Derek's brows arched. "My guys vetted that—"

"Yes, but nothing else." She threw herself into the chair across from Derek, leaning forward. "Doesn't that strike you as strange? No chatter? No movement? If something as huge as an undetectable nuclear bomb had hit the black market, it would have sent all the who's who of terrorism scrambling to get their hands on it."

"She's right," Ben said, his face hard.

Derek sighed and tipped his chair back on its hind legs. "Go on."

"I think it's to keep your guys busy, and to set the stage for John Elsworth to take the fall when the attacks happen."

"So you think Rowland's placed his people to set off these WMDs?" Ben asked, setting down the pictures Lily had printed. "First the economy, then all our top governmental officials… It would cripple us."

Derek let his chair fall back on all fours. "I see where you're going, but why the charade?"

"Where is the first place we always look when there's an internal leak of this magnitude?" Lily tapped a photo. "The head honcho. John Elsworth. I believe Rowland leaked this information and set up this whole game so he could pin the attacks on John. John goes down, Rowland steps into ARME's helm."

Pushing back from the table, Ben walked to the coffeepot and poured another cup. "He'd swoop in, play savior, help the government back to their feet after the attack, help them regroup, with him conveniently leading the charge. He'd be unstoppable."

"Yes, he would, expect for one thing." She pursed her lips and glanced between the two men. "And this is where it gets bizarre—the formula for the bomb's chemical compound is incomplete."

Derek's jaw twitched. "You know how much I respect you, so don't shoot the messenger here, but I have to call bullshit. How could you possibly know that?"

Lily resisted the urge to smile. If the tables were turned, she would have called bullshit, too. "I once worked with a Russian nuclear physicist who'd defected."

"Of course you did. Another case *not* in your file. I'm beginning to question why they even bothered with a file in the first place," Derek grumbled.

"I didn't have a choice but to learn his language—both literally, and figuratively—in order to complete the…transaction. I'd still want to get an expert in on this, but from what I can decipher here, this formula won't work. Someone's trying to set Rowland up."

Ben walked back and handed Lily a mug of coffee, then sat and studied the files in front of him. "Sabotage a sociopath? Sounds dangerous."

She took a sip of the steaming liquid. "I did some digging and, besides stumbling across the fact that Gina's family—not John's—started ARME, I also discovered that Gina has her PhD in nuclear chemistry."

Derek's expression darkened. "You're kidding me."

"She graduated at the top of her class at Harvard before dear ol' Daddy married her off."

"Of course," Derek said, shaking his head.

"I know you think she's nothing more than a simple trophy wife." Lily shrugged. "And maybe she is. Maybe I'm wrong. But if I'm not, then this 'trophy wife' also happens to be a brilliant chemist, who I think is secretly working for ARME's labs. COO or not, I don't think the Elsworths trust Rowland with their most valuable weapon. An incomplete formula ensures its safety, and Gina is the perfect cover—give the least suspecting person the greatest asset you own."

Derek ran his hands over his face. The soft rustle of skin and stubble made her heart kick. He looked up and caught her with his irresistible sapphire eyes. "I don't know. I can't imagine it. But maybe."

"'Maybe' is not exactly what I'd hoped to hear," Ben said drily. "According to that time line, we have less than two weeks to figure this out, and we're running around with a lot of assumptions."

Lily understood Ben's concern. She shared it. But wasn't that what they only ever had—assumptions? The black-ops game was the biggest game of craps in the history of mankind.

Roll the dice. Hope you get lucky.

Lily shrugged. "It's all we have at this point."

Chugging the last of his coffee, Ben set the mug on the counter. "So, what's next?"

"Get back into Rowland's house," Lily answered at the same time as Derek said, "Get Lily close to Gina."

"I need to get back into Rowland's house." Lily kept talking, didn't give either of the men a second to interrupt her. "I need to reposition one of the cameras and go through his files. I didn't have time last time. I need to get into his house."

"No," the two men replied in stereo.

Lily sank into her chair. What the hell was with the double-teaming? She'd known her idea would get pushback. But really? From both of them?

"You've already played Russian roulette with him once." Derek glared at her. "Let's go with something other than messing with a psychotic sociopath on his stomping ground, okay?" A slow smirk spread across Derek's lips. Lily crossed her leg and bounced her foot. What was he up to now? "If Gina is the missing link, we get you close to her."

Lily swallowed a groan. There was a reason she

so easily fit into the male-dominated world of black ops. She hated all the drama and gossip most women thrived on, and she avoided interaction with her own gender at all cost. She didn't have any girlfriends growing up. Didn't have any now.

Which suited her just fine.

"I like," Ben said, nodding.

Lily threw him a look. *Traitor.* She was outnumbered, and she knew it. "Fine. Rowland invited me to this party on Friday—"

Derek frowned. "You didn't tell me about that."

"Yeah, well, we've all been a little preoccupied."

He rolled his eyes. "That we have." Looking off into space, he sat quiet, thinking, then grinned. "Yes, the party is the perfect place. Gina will most *definitely* be there."

"I doubt Gina's going to be buddy-buddy with me."

Derek laughed. "If you can lasso Rowland, you can rope in Gina. It'll be a piece of cake."

Somehow Lily doubted that.

CHAPTER TWENTY

Wednesday, September 24, 7:00 p.m.

THE ELEVATOR DOOR OPENED and Lily stepped out. Glancing up, George frowned, his large forehead crinkled. "Going for a run *now*?"

"Yep."

After leaving Keystone, she'd locked herself away and pored over the files. Twelve hours later, she'd gotten nowhere fast. The strain on her eyes had triggered a killer headache, and her muscles screamed for a release. Lily needed a break, something to get her mind off the chaos lying in front of her.

"Where's Dakota? Should you be going by yourself?"

"Dakota is racked out, and I'm not going alone." She pulled the .32 from the small of her back and grinned. "I have company that's much more effective."

"Lil—"

She stood on her tiptoes and kissed George on the cheek. "Relax. I'm not ten anymore. I won't be gone long."

George grumbled, pulled the door open and stepped aside.

"I'll be fine. I just need to clear my head."

Nothing was what it seemed. She was sure of it.

The question now was what the hell was she going to do about it. The once-simple mission of "get close to Rowland" had spiraled into a web of shadows and deception.

Lily lengthened her stride, the cold air rushing her lungs. Despite the grueling hours of research, the intricacy of the mission thrilled her. She was fully engaged, alive.

The urgency to find Jackson faded as the case consumed her more and more. She'd circle around to him. Eventually. She needed to shut that chapter of her life for good and put it behind her, but Jackson would have to wait until she'd nailed Rowland.

She ran, her mind tumbling over itself.

The hair on her neck prickled, signaling impending danger. In the sandbox, her team always kept one wary eye on her and her strange sixth sense. If Lily hit the ground, they followed. No questions asked. It had saved them more times than Lily cared to remember.

And that same sensation now screamed at her in warning.

Lily slowed and glanced over her shoulder. The running path lay empty, desolate. She didn't buy the lonely scene. Someone was following her.

Lily paused her music but kept her earbuds in, not wanting to warn whoever lurked in the dark. She ran on, senses fully alert.

Slowing her breath, she focused on the noises around her. She filtered out the rush of the river and… *there*! Whoever was behind wasn't in sync with her footsteps. The crunching of gravel under her stalker's feet gave that away.

She stopped and squatted to tie her shoe. Glancing

over her shoulder, she spied the outline of a figure in the distance. Irritation ripped through her. She didn't have the energy to deal with some mugger tonight. She sighed, stood and looked toward the figure.

I see you.

She reached behind her and flipped off the safety of her gun, wanting to be ready.

Heading off the trail, Lily made her way downtown, toward people. The stockyards would be hopping tonight. Safety in numbers. It also meant that whoever followed her could disappear.

It was a gamble she was willing to take.

She slowed and walked down Allen Street—careful not to turn her ankle on the uneven bricks that lined the street—made a left and stopped in front of a hair salon. She glanced through the window and into a stylist's beveled mirror. The angle gave her the perfect view behind her.

She spotted him, but couldn't make out his face. A baseball cap pulled low obstructed her view. Lily moved further into the crowd and picked up her pace.

So did her shadow.

Dodging between two massive men, she turned right onto Woodbridge. Lily ducked in between two buildings, flattened herself against the brick wall and waited. Her pursuer stopped short and searched the area.

Lily pressed herself further into the dark. She caught his profile for a moment—strong jawline, Roman nose, white scar on the edge of his mouth.

Jackson?

The world fell out from under her. She struggled to breathe. He walked past, and her mind refused to process the signals her eyes sent. No way in hell he was here—in her city, of all places. It couldn't be that simple, could it?

Only one way to find out.

She stepped out from the shadows and fell in behind him.

He pulled out a cell, spoke into it, then shoved it into his back pocket. She studied the man in front of her. His gait. The way he hunched his shoulders and thrust his hands deep into his pockets.

Her blood hammered in her ears. Her hands fisted, fingers digging into the flesh of her palms. *Son of a bitch.* There was no mistake. Lily could pick out her ex-fiancé anywhere.

She slowed her pace, lengthening the gap between them, but kept Jackson locked in her sights. Her mind spun. What the hell was he doing here? In her city? That couldn't be a coincidence…could it?

No. She didn't believe in coincidences. If her old life had taught her anything, it was that nothing happened by chance. Nothing. That bastard was in her city. She'd never once mentioned Omaha to him. Why was he here?

He turned right, hugged the building facades and peered into the stores doubling as fishbowls.

He has no idea I'm behind him. I've got you now. Two can play at this game. The thrill of the hunt surged through her veins. She'd forgotten just how much she loved this, lived for this.

She was the huntress. He was her prey.

Should she engage? She could. She was armed.

He took a quick left and disappeared.

Lily sidestepped an older couple who were ambling slower than molasses and followed Jackson into the dark alley. Her senses jumped to DEFCON 1. She slammed to a halt, reached for her gun and pressed herself close to the bricks. *Shit.*

Her brain registered movement to her left. She pivoted and raised her gun.

"Jackson."

He mimicked her response and trained his gun on her chest. The last time she'd been in this situation, the man staring her down had tried to kill her. Lily glanced at his weapon and her heart stopped. It was the same gun he'd used to shoot her. With difficulty, she pulled her eyes away from the Glock. *Focus, Lil.*

"Everyone at 67 thinks you're dead. Imagine their surprise when I tell them you're here. In my city."

Jackson shrugged. "Guess I'm dead no more. Am I, Lily girl?"

The once-intimate nickname rolled off his tongue and made Lily's skin crawl. How she had ever loved this man was beyond her. She suppressed a shudder. "Don't call me that. Why are you here?"

"Why do you care?" Jackson tilted his head and studied her. "Miss me?"

A familiar, all-consuming ache reared up and held her heart in a vice. A mixture of rage and bone-aching grief swirled in her brain. Pushing against the inexplicable emotions, she glared at the man she'd once loved.

"Not even for a second."

"Why are you following me?"

"I could ask you the same question." She glared at him, put pressure on the trigger of her .32.

He cocked his gun. His face hardened. "I wouldn't do that if I were you, Lil."

The familiar standoff chilled Lily to her bones.

He laughed, though there was nothing light about the sound bouncing off the alleyway. It was dark, and menacing. "I see you're as feisty as ever. Answer my question. Why are you following me?"

"I wanted to see who was following *me* on the trail. Imagine my surprise when it turned out to be my ex-lover. You know, the partner who betrayed me."

Her emotions spun out of control. In one breath, she wanted to reach up and snap his neck, and yet, a strange pang in her chest threatened to undermine the past thirteen months of black hatred.

The muscles in his jaw twitched. Lily frowned. She'd known him long enough to know his tells—and *that* was one of them. "Why are you upset, Jackson?"

"You didn't see me," Jackson said, his tone cold as steel. "As far as you're concerned, I'm a ghost. Leave now, and don't try to find me. Ever."

She shook her head. "You know I can't do that."

"Why are you always trying to play the fucking hero, Lily? Just for once, can you let a dead cat lie?"

"Sorry, Jackson." She increased the pressure on her trigger finger.

"So am I." In a single, fluid motion, his boot connected with her arm.

Her gun went flying, and she lost her balance. Lily scrambled to regain her footing and backed up until her shoulders hit the brick wall. He'd hemmed her in, outmaneuvered her. He pressed the muzzle of his gun between her breasts.

She didn't move, barely breathed.

"Which has always been your Achilles' heel, hasn't it, Lily?" He shook his head, pushed the hard metal deeper into her soft flesh. She resisted the urge to flinch. He leaned his face close to hers. "Why do you always have to be the hero?"

"At least I'm not a traitor."

Jackson pulled back as if she'd struck him. His jaw twitched. Again. *What the hell was wrong with him?* Just as quickly, the flicker of humanity disappeared.

Grabbing the front of her throat, he jammed his thumb into the carotid artery on one side of her neck and pressed his ring finger into the other. Lily clawed at his hands and fought. She had ten seconds, tops. Her head grew light, drifting, as she pushed against the advancing darkness she knew was coming for her.

Jackson tightened his grip, leaned close. "I'm a ghost."

Her vision tunneled and went black.

CHAPTER TWENTY-ONE

Wednesday, September 24, 9:00 p.m.

THE WORLD WAS tilted sideways. Lily blinked, then struggled into a sitting position. How was she alive? Why hadn't Jackson killed her?

Jackson.

She scanned the alley. Of course he was gone. And damn it, so was her gun.

Reaching up, she gingerly touched her throbbing head where her hairline met her forehead and winced. The tips of her fingers were slick. Fabulous.

Lily stood, gave herself a minute to find her balance and made her way back into the crowd, heading toward the one place she knew would be safe.

Ten minutes later, she walked through Ben's back door.

"I saw him."

The conversation between Derek, Ben and George ceased. All three men stared at her. Lily stopped short. What was Derek doing here? Better yet, what was George doing here? She shook her head. Not important. What was critical was Jackson. And the fact that he was here.

In her city.

"I saw him," she said. "I saw Jackson."

Derek leaped to his feet and rushed to her side. His fingers brushed the hair back from her forehead. Despite her current state of panic, her insides tightened at his soft touch.

"Damn it, Lily, what happened?"

"I'm fine." Lily waved him off. And she was. The egg-shaped knot throbbed in time with each heartbeat and she needed to get it cleaned, but she'd experienced worse.

Much worse.

Lily couldn't get her mind off of one fact: Jackson was in her city.

Derek held up his hands in surrender and backed off. The space between them felt cold. Empty. And she hated it. But not as much as she loathed the fact that Jackson had swooped down and screwed with her mind. Again.

"The bastard is here. In Omaha."

None of the men reacted.

Scanning their faces, Lily recognized the set looks and quickly put the pieces together. *They knew.* Her blood started to boil. "But you already knew that."

George didn't move. Ben nodded.

"Ben. When?"

"This morning. We were read in after you left."

Lily took a deep breath, trying to calm down, and looked at George. "Is that why you didn't want me running alone tonight?"

George said nothing, just nodded.

Ben pointed to the chair in front of her. "Sit down and let me see to that."

"No." She crossed her arms and tilted her chin up. She didn't know what she was more furious about:

Jackson being in her city, or the two—no, make that three—men in her life not telling her. She understood Derek not reading her in on everything. She'd known from day one that he held his cards close to the vest, as did she. But Ben? George? They should've told her the moment Derek read them in. That she hadn't seen it coming stung.

"Lily, sit down," Ben said in his don't-argue-with-me commander's voice as he grabbed his suture kit.

Lily couldn't ignore that directive, or the throbbing in her head.

She sat.

"Did anyone think it a crucial piece of information that might or might not help with this case, or better yet, keep me breathing? Did anyone think it wise to inform me that my traitorous ex-partner was in town?" Her voice rose an octave. "You know, the man who tried to kill me a year ago? Anyone?"

She swiveled around in her chair, cast an incredulous look toward George. Why was he being so quiet? He averted his eyes and hung his head. *Serves him right.* He was supposed to be protecting her. Keeping vital information from her was definitely *not* helping that cause.

"Hold still." Ben dabbed at her forehead with an alcohol-soaked cotton ball. She sucked air between her teeth as he passed the soft ball of torture too close to the open skin.

"Sorry," Ben whispered before placing the butterfly bandage against her small but nasty cut.

"Why is Jackson here?" Lily asked, looking up. Ben opened his mouth, then shut it. What were they hiding? "Why is he here, and why now?"

Ben pressed his calloused finger against the bandage, securing it against her skin. She winced, then focused on how pissed off she was in an attempt to ignore the pounding in her head. But damn, she needed an aspirin.

"Does it have something to do with the situation at ARME?" Without moving, she threw Derek a searing glare. He was silent. "Is this mission even legit?"

"It's legit," Ben said. "I called Director Kennedy myself."

She pulled back and winced at the sudden movement. Her eyes narrowed. "The director already knows about this?"

"He knows that Jackson is in Omaha, yes."

Lily pinned Ben with her gaze. "I'll ask again. Did no one think it prudent to tell me Jackson was here? It's my ass on the line. No one else's."

Derek crossed his arms.

Yeah, you better be on the defensive, buddy.

"It was a need-to-know basis," he said.

"It was a need-to—" Lily choked on the words. Hadn't they gotten past that bureaucratic garbage? Clearly not. A deep ache twisted in her gut. "Don't give me that shit, Derek."

Silently, George leaned across the table and tapped the thick manila files spread across its flat surface. Lily followed the staccato movements of his finger. The big red letters screamed at her. *Classified.*

She reached over, ignoring the fire that the subtle movement sent through her head, and grabbed a file, holding it up. "Someone talk. Now."

Derek cleared his throat. "Jackson contacted ARME about sixteen months ago."

Her mind rushed to keep up with the information. Sixteen months? She'd been on Derek's radar for sixteen freakin' months? She sank back into her chair.

"And that's our cue." Ben gathered his first-aid kit. George rose. "We've already been briefed. Time for these old men to turn in."

George walked over and, careful to not touch her newly dressed cut, pressed his lips to Lily's forehead. She stiffened. How long had he kept this secret from her? He knelt in front of her, forcing her to look at him.

"Don't be mad. I would never keep something from you if it meant putting your life at stake. I'd die before I let anyone hurt you. You know that."

Lily stared into the safe, warm face she'd seen day in, day out for the last year, and her entire body relaxed. She knew he'd never purposely keep anything from her or hurt her. She glanced over at Ben and forced a tight smile onto her lips. *Yeah, she knew it.*

She cradled her hand to George's cheek. "I know, G. Sorry for freaking out."

He stood and pressed his lips to her forehead again. "You're our priority, Lil. Always have been. Always will be. Don't forget that."

Lily nodded. George shook hands with both men and left. She waited until Ben disappeared down the hallway and pulled his door shut tight behind him, before turning to Derek. He threw her a cautious smile. She knew George and Ben had her best interests at heart; they'd had her back since she was a toddler.

But Derek? He'd kept Jackson's whereabouts from her from the beginning. And she was furious about it—rightfully so. And no doubt the man quietly examining her knew it.

Lily chewed her lip and quietly moved through her limited options. Trust him, or don't. Her bullshit meter hadn't pinged once with him. And *that* she could trust.

But now, it was time for the cards to be put on the table.

All of them.

"Start talking."

CHAPTER TWENTY-TWO

DEREK PULLED OUT a chair and straddled it. *I need to get this shit off my chest.* He stared at the woman who'd captured him completely, and a sick feeling stirred in the pit of his stomach. She was a trained operative, so keeping vital intel under wraps wasn't a new concept. But withholding vital intel about her ex-partner—the man who'd betrayed his country and tried to kill her— yeah, that *might* have pushed the boundaries of what was *understandable*.

He scrubbed his hands over his face and took a deep breath. Here's hoping that Lady Luck was on his side. "Like I was saying, Jackson contacted ARME about sixteen months ago."

Lily nodded, and then her mouth dropped open as she put the pieces together. "The formula…"

"Exactly. From what we can piece together—and it's shaky, at best—Jackson spoke with Rowland and pitched a hypothetical to him. Rowland promptly locked him down. But only on face value."

Lily slowly nodded. "Smart. No way he'd show any interest over the phone. Too many potential ears."

Derek's lips curved in silent approval. She was handling this information barrage like a pro, but that didn't surprise him at all—watching the wheels turn in that pretty little head of hers was always fascinating.

"Rowland keeps his hands clean, as in squeaky clean. That call triggered Langley and alerted us to ARME and Rowland for the first time."

"Unbelievable." She sank into a chair and stared at something just above Derek's head. "What are the chances that all roads could lead back to Jackson?"

Derek heard the raw pain in her voice and felt like an ass, but he continued, eager to lay it all on the table. "I was put on him immediately after that call was logged."

"You were put on—" Lily frowned. "I don't understand."

"He didn't have the formula and, at that point, had only pitched a hypothetical, so our hands were tied. But he'd made his intentions known. I was ordered to watch until Jackson made his move."

"Then that means I—"

Realization flashed over Lily's face, and Derek inwardly cringed. *Shit*. If they could make it past this moment, if Lily didn't kick him out for not reading her in on the whole case when he'd promised he would, then maybe, just maybe, Lady Luck loved him and he hadn't completely screwed the pooch with Lily.

He swallowed hard and locked eyes with her, didn't blink. "You've been on my radar for sixteen months, Lily."

She chewed on her bottom lip, nodding. "So, the running path."

"I knew you'd be there."

"Makes sense." She lapped the kitchen again, then stopped. "Sixteen months, huh. How closely?"

Derek reached up and rubbed the back of his neck. Okay, scratch that. *This* was the proverbial hurdle they had to get over. He sighed. "Close enough."

"How close, Derek?"

"I was at Arlington," he said in a soft voice.

Her eyebrows shot up and she slumped into the nearest chair. "The fake funeral? You were there?"

"I was there."

SHE'D KNOWN THE DAY he got the drop on her at the running path that Derek was good. And maybe, if she were honest with herself, she'd known all along that their chance meeting hadn't happened by chance at all. But damn, she hadn't imagined he was *this* good. She couldn't figure out if she was angry again, or in awe of the man calmly staring back at her.

"How'd I do?"

He pursed his lips and nodded. "I was impressed."

She snorted. "You didn't even see the half of it."

"Oh, no, I saw it all."

He smiled and rubbed the back of his neck again before looking up at her. Was that a tinge of pink on his cheeks? There was never a dull moment with this guy. The spinning in her head kicked up a gear, as did the systematic throbbing against her butterfly stitch.

"I stayed the whole time, Lil. I'd been read in on the incident. All the intel pointed to Jackson showing up—we didn't think he'd be able to stay away." Derek shrugged and grimaced. "We were wrong."

"Clearly." Suddenly feeling like a trapped rabbit, she got up and paced the kitchen. She lapped it three times before finally stopping again. She pressed her fingers into the corners of her eyes and took a deep breath. "You can't use your profiling voodoo on him, Derek. He's smart and vicious."

"So am I."

Her eyes flipped to his face. Saw the strength, the dominance flash in his eyes, and her whole body hummed—and it wasn't coming from the small cut on her head.

Derek was every bit as alpha as Jackson, and then some. It was no wonder she'd been drawn to Derek from the second she'd laid eyes on him. He was dynamic, and sexy as hell.

"And it's not voodoo. It's science," he said in a matter-of-fact tone.

Lily couldn't help but smile. "Let's just agree to disagree on that one."

"Fair enough."

The whole conversation was beyond bizarre. In the past two hours, she'd come face-to-face with her ex-fiancé…and learned that Derek had known not only that Jackson was alive this whole time, but also exactly where he was.

She was irritated that Derek had withheld so much vital information from her, but she was also begrudgingly impressed. Aside from Jackson, she'd never met another operative who matched her in wit, intelligence and spunk. When most backed down, Derek went toe-to-toe with her.

She loved it.

He reached for his beer and took a long swig. "As I was saying, when we knew he wouldn't show, my team left. I couldn't."

Her gaze snapped to his face. "Couldn't?"

"I couldn't tear my eyes away from you, Lil."

Vivid memories of their kitchen escapade flashed in her mind. Yeah, she definitely shouldn't have stopped that kiss. She resisted the urge to lick her lips.

"You intrigued me. *I* knew he wasn't dead. And I knew that *you* knew he wasn't dead. You were remarkable." He flashed Lily a smile, the dimple in his cheek deepening. "If I hadn't known the play myself, I would have thought it was real when you threw yourself on that coffin."

"It was real," she said in a soft voice. "It wasn't theatrics."

The pain of that moment crashed into her. Jackson had shattered her that day. For better or for worse, she'd walked away from his bogus grave a different woman. No longer the young, naive agent who believed justice always won out.

In the real world, bastards like Jackson got away with murder, the good guys didn't win and innocence was stolen. Lily swallowed the memories and shrugged. "I was cussing him out and crying over my broken heart."

"Makes sense," Derek said, nodding. "He was your partner."

"He wasn't just my partner, Derek." Lily paused for a moment, confused, and stared at the man she was beginning to fall for. *He didn't know. Holy shit. How could he not know?*

She took a deep breath. "Jackson was my fiancé."

DEREK WENT RIGID. Jackson was her *fiancé*? Derek hadn't thought this case could get any more complicated. He'd been wrong.

"Oh, God." Her hazel eyes widened, and she clamped her hand over her mouth. "You really didn't know?"

No, he hadn't known. What a nightmare. Derek's mind went into overdrive. If Jackson had been her fiancé, maybe he'd set up this whole elaborate scheme to get her away from the case, from Rowland—that's what Derek would have done, maybe. He grit his teeth. *No.* The director suspected Jackson had gone dark, sent Derek to keep an eye on him, to monitor his movement within ARME.

"No, I didn't," Derek said slowly. "Jackson being your fiancé was something Kennedy failed to mention… that is, if he even knew." Derek glanced up. "Did he?"

"Ex-fiancé," she corrected, eyes still wide. "And yes, Kennedy knew."

"Of course he did. Fantastic."

"I'm sorry."

"Nothing to be sorry about." Derek's mind reeled from the bomb she'd just dropped on him. He didn't want to focus on Jackson any more than he had to, but Derek was beginning to really hate the bastard.

Lily sighed and picked at the staple holding the classified file together. "That assignment broke me. Jackson broke me. Not only did he betray me, he betrayed our country. I think *that* shattered me more than the personal betrayal. I've seen enough shit in the world to know that humans can be evil. But my idealistic logic that the good guys always win was blown to kingdom come."

"Lil—"

"No, Derek, the good guys don't always win. We both know it. If Ben hadn't been there, I wouldn't have been able to walk away that day." Lily paused. "I'm sure you saw him cart me off."

Yeah, he'd seen, all right. When she'd collapsed over the closed coffin, it took every ounce of willpower he'd had not to blow his cover, to make sure she was okay. Even then, she'd left him mesmerized, wanting more. But it wasn't his place then, so he'd stayed rooted.

Derek pressed his lips together and nodded.

"That wasn't to add to the dramatic effect." Lily flicked the staple across the table. "Jackson's betrayal devastated me. I couldn't even put one foot in front of the other."

She attacked the next staple with a vengeance. "To add insult to injury, I let the sting of his betrayal, and the bureaucratic bullshit that followed, force my hand into giving up the very thing that I loved most—my job."

Pushing back from the table, she went to the kitchen and poured herself a glass of water.

His mind raced. Jackson was her fiancé? Ex-fiancé, he reminded himself, and still a traitor.

"You know, I've prayed for a second chance to get back into the game every day since. For someone to toss me a lifeline and rescue me from the pit I'd pitched myself into. I hated that I'd walked, but I didn't know how to rectify it." She leaned against the counter and locked eyes with Derek. "Then you came along."

Derek lost himself in the endless depths of her exotic eyes. The warm sensation returned, stronger this time. And judging by the way Lily quickly looked away, her face coloring, she felt it, too. He couldn't help but smile.

Yes, definitely ex-*fiancé.*

Derek cleared his throat. "I didn't rescue you. From where I'm sitting, you rescued yourself. An opportunity came along and, instead of tucking tail and running, you seized it. No matter how bizarre or unclear the case, you're the one who stepped in. No one else. I don't see a broken woman. I see a woman I'd gladly have on my six any time, anywhere, any day."

She studied him quietly—oh, to get inside that pretty little head of hers—and then walked across the kitchen, parking on the table just inches in front of Derek. It was a bold gesture, and it invaded his personal space, but apparently she didn't care.

"Full disclosure, Derek."

"Come on, Lil." He shook his head and he sagged back in his chair. "You know I can't promise that."

"Yes, you can." Lily put her hands on either side of his chair and leaned forward, the edge of her tank falling open. An urge to close the gap between them and press his lips to hers hit him. Hard. They were warm and inviting, and oh so close. But judging by the glint in Lily's eyes, she wanted answers right now, not sex.

She straightened. "Full disclosure, Derek. Nothing less. You owe me that much. I'm not backing down."

"Yes, I can see that." Damn, this woman was like a dog with a bone right now. There was no way he'd be able to redirect her focus, not this time. "Fine. Full disclosure. I'll read you in on everything I have. But are you sure you want to do this?"

She nodded.

He reached around her, grabbed a thick file and held it up. "Can you honestly handle what's in this file? Because you're going to need to compartmentalize whatever emotions it conjures up—and I guarantee you, it will evoke some."

She took a deep breath and slowly blew it out. "Yes. Jackson is in my city. He's connected to ARME, which, by default, means he's connected to Rowland. We flush Jackson out, unlock and verify the files I found on Rowland today and nail them both." She smiled, the thrill of the game flashing across her face. "Why not kill two birds with one stone?"

"And the stone being?" Derek looked up at Lily, and his chest tightened. He didn't like that ferocious, calculated glint in her eyes.

She scooted off the table and threw Derek a wicked smile. "Me."

"Yeah, I was afraid you were going to say that."

CHAPTER TWENTY-THREE

Friday, September 26, 7:00 p.m.

EXCITED ANTICIPATION HUNG heavy in the air. ARME had transformed one of their two-story labs into a grandiose stage for the unveiling of their newest addition in a long line of state-of-the-art weaponry. Lily was perched high above the mingling throng in a private balcony reserved for ARME's honored guests, and she searched the crowd, eyes trained for one person: Jackson.

She knew he was there. Could feel him.

Derek walked up next to her and stared straight ahead. "You looking for Jackson?"

Lily scanned the crowd below. "I know he's here."

"Probably." Derek shoved his hands in his pockets. "You doing okay?"

She took a sip of her champagne and nodded. He didn't respond, just stood next to her. Heat radiated off him, and the strain in her neck faded. The pressure in her chest eased. His silent presence not only calmed her, but also solidified her resolve to nail Rowland and Jackson.

She could get used to being on his six.

And much, much more.

A commotion to her left captured her attention. Lily

turned slightly. A tall, blonde bombshell wrapped in a tight sequined dress entered the room. Her sheer presence demanded the attention of those around her, including Lily. "Whoa."

Derek chuckled. "I see you've spotted Mrs. Elsworth."

"*That's* Gina Elsworth?" She was everything Lily had expected. Tall. Exquisite. Walking perfection. The woman looked like she belonged on a runway.

"Don't let her looks fool you."

Lily frowned.

"Remember. Trophy wife."

"I'd hate to hear what you have to say about me." Lily smirked into her champagne.

"What? That you're feisty, stubborn and a genius? Or that you can run circles around any of the operatives I've ever worked with? And I've worked with the best, mind you. Or that you're the sexiest woman I've ever met, the woman I can't keep my mind off of?"

Lily choked on the sparkling wine. Trying to appear nonchalant, she swirled the golden liquid and looked over at Derek. "I said I'd *hate* to hear. That wasn't an open invitation to let your inner monologue out to play."

He leaned in and his breath tickled across her neck. "Wasn't it, though?"

She shook her head, suppressing the urge to turn and press her lips to his. "Don't you have somewhere to be? Someone to protect?"

"Play nice." He laughed, then walked away.

Lily stared after Derek. The longer this case lingered on, the faster her resolve to keep her heart closed to him faded. Past logic and the hopeful future battled within her. She grasped at the unraveling fringes of her determination, but she knew it was futile.

Every inch of her body wanted to finish what they'd started in the kitchen.

She was losing the battle against logic very quickly.

Lily swung her gaze toward Gina, intrigued by the tall beauty who owned the room and captivated its occupants. Could she really be capable of setting Rowland up? Or was she truly the way Derek had often described her? A trophy wife?

Gina greeted an older couple with a dazzling smile and nodded her head softly before moving on to the next person. As Lily studied her, a peculiar thought scurried across Lily's mind.

Could Gina be *involved* with Rowland?

Lily wouldn't put it past him to have charmed his way into Gina's bed. Despite his savage background, he was gorgeous, his personality hypnotic.

Making a mental note to ask Derek, Lily turned her attention to the swirl of people below her. The air was electrified. She spotted Rowland mingling with the guests and raised her glass in acknowledgment.

He saw her and made his way up the curved staircase to her right to join her, wrapping his arm around her waist and tucking her into his side.

The intimate gesture caught her off guard. "Don't you look handsome tonight."

"Are you all right?"

"Of course." She frowned and did a mental check of the past five minutes. What could she have possibly done to warrant that question? "Why do you ask?"

"Just making sure the help is minding his place," Rowland answered, his voice hard as steel.

Lily's blood ran cold. *Derek*. The last thing she wanted was for him to be the focus of Rowland's psychotic attention. Whatever was happening between her and Derek needed to stop, before it got them both killed.

She glanced up at Rowland and forced a smiled to her lips. "He was just answering a question I had about the facility."

"I see." The green in Rowland's eyes turned black, and his hand tightened on her waist. "In the future, let me be the one to answer your questions."

"Of course. The excitement of the evening must have gone to my head."

He tilted her chin up and looked down at her. "Meet me tomorrow, and I'll take you on a private tour of the facility."

It wasn't an invitation. Lily's heart hammered against her chest. "That would be lovely."

He bent his head low, crushing his lips to hers. There was nothing gentle or loving about his kiss. It was demanding. Dangerous. Possessive. Pulling back, he gave her a measured look, then turned on his heel and left her.

Lily grabbed her flute of champagne and brought the sparkling liquid to her lips. A small tremor caused the bubbles to dance wildly within the crystal flute. She quickly lowered her hand, rested the trembling glass against the railing. Her heart skipped and fluttered.

He'd just claimed her.

Lily commanded her heart to calm, and spied Gina making her way toward the balcony where Lily was perched.

"I see Rowland has you under his spell."

"Mrs. Elsworth." Lily smiled. "You look exquisite tonight."

"Thank you. Please, call me Gina." Her lips curled, but the smile never reached her stunning emerald eyes. "You look beautiful, as well."

If the woman standing in front of Lily, openly assessing her, only knew what lay beneath her mile-high makeup. It had taken *forever* to cover the gash on her forehead, compliments of Jackson, and she'd finally resorted to styling her hair in such a way as to hide the remnants. Lily tipped her head down, then fingered the diamonds floating around her neck. "I hope it's not too much."

"It's not. It's perfect. You must have quite the stylist."

Lily combed the room for Derek and smiled inwardly when she found him. *Yes, I do.* He'd blown into her loft again with another assortment of stunning, expensive gowns. All of which had high backs. When she'd questioned him, he'd shrugged and said he noticed she liked that style.

"Oh." Gina turned and faced the stage below them. "Here we go."

Rowland and John walked onto the platform together and stood shoulder to shoulder in front of the podium. Weariness etched around John's eyes, the strain pulling at his handsome features catching Lily by surprise. A smile was fastened to his face, but the edge illuminated in his eyes betrayed him.

"Ladies and gentlemen." Rowland's deep, velvety words rolled through the quiet crowd.

Lily glanced at Gina. Why was Rowland addressing the crowd instead of John? The blonde woman stared straight ahead, lifted her champagne to her lips, calmly took a sip.

"Fine people of Omaha, thank you for honoring us with your presence tonight. A night that will prove to be the grandest moment in ARME's long and glorious history."

Deafening applause urged Rowland to continue.

He glanced up and caught Lily's eye. She nodded at him and smiled.

"Tonight—with the backing of our own government—we unveil the first long-distance, multitarget missile *ever* to be produced in this majestic world."

Lily stiffened. She had a hard time swallowing the fact that some bureaucratic talking head, who had most likely never seen a day of combat, had actually signed off on the development of this missile. It was insane.

Rowland glanced over at John. "Anything you would like to add?"

John and Rowland eyed each other like two peacocks competing for a mate. Neither moved. Neither blinked. Finally, John plucked the microphone from Rowland's hands.

"Thank you, Rowland. I believe I do have something to add. People of Omaha and the world, I promise you this." John scanned the crowd. "We at ARME Industries are committed to building weapons that protect humanity from any evil—foreign or domestic—that might arise to threaten our way of life, our survival."

Support resounded throughout the crowd.

Gina's back straightened just a fraction. A tight smile tugged at her lips.

"We're committed to truth and equality. We build

weapons not to arm those who wish to bring harm to us or our partners, but to aid our brave defenders all over the world with the equipment they need to accomplish the task at hand—freedom for every man, woman and child…"

Another roar of approval swept through the throngs of people below them. Lily studied Rowland closely. He'd perfected his poker face. She got nothing. Again. *Damn that man.*

"And if we ever veer from that commitment, I promise you this." John glanced up to the balcony. Gina stared down at him until he looked away. "We will close our doors for good."

Silence blanketed the crowd. Lily peeked at Gina and caught the slight tick in her jaw. *What the hell was that about?*

Rowland stepped up and put his hand on John's shoulder. "Always the champion of the people. John Elsworth, ladies and gentlemen, president and CEO of ARME Industries."

Rowland clapped his hands together. The stunned crowd followed his lead. Lily glanced over at Gina. She gripped her glass hard, her knuckles slowly turning white. The tops of her ears were pink. Lily frowned.

Who was Gina so pissed at? Rowland or John?

"And without further ado," Rowland said, "the first long-distance, multitarget missile."

The thick red fabric was pulled away from the display, revealing a small warhead perched on a bed of black velvet. The missile was smaller than Lily had imagined it would be, but she didn't doubt its destructive ability.

Gina stepped closer to Lily and leaned in. "Rowland is quite the man, isn't he, Addison?" Her tone was venomous.

Lily blinked back her surprise. Was Gina jealous? Angry? Lily hesitated, searching for the correct words before answering. "He is. I'm quite fond of him. And I'm very intrigued by the work that goes on here."

Gina's eyes flashed, and she jerked her chin slightly. "Are you now?"

"Yes. Rowland is giving me a tour tomorrow."

Gina's eyebrows arched. "He is, is he?"

Lily suppressed the sarcasm itching to be released and calmly answered Gina. "I'm looking forward to it."

"I'm sure you are." The tall, green-eyed beauty lifted her flute to her lips, took a sip and turned to leave. Pausing, she looked over her shoulder. "Enjoy your evening, Addison."

Lily couldn't have been more stunned if Gina had slapped her across the face. Lily watched the retreating woman. Any doubt that Gina and Rowland could be working together vanished. The men called her a trophy wife. *Yeah, right.* That woman definitely had some brains to go along with her beauty.

Lily had recognized Gina Elsworth for what she truly was the moment she'd made her appearance into the room. She portrayed herself as a beautiful trophy wife, but that woman wanted—all but demanded—the spotlight, and she didn't want to share it with anyone.

Including Rowland James.

Derek casually joined Lily. "What was that all about?"

Her heart tripped over itself, and her blood ran cold. She scanned the crowd below for Rowland. She raised her champagne flute to her mouth, desperate to hide their conversation.

"You shouldn't be here. Rowland has me under a tighter microscope than I anticipated. It's dangerous for you to be speaking with me."

"Let me be concerned with that."

Lily cast him a sideways glare. Why couldn't he just listen to her for once? "Stop being stubborn."

He kept his eyes glued on the crowd mingling below them and smiled. "Right back at you, babycakes. Now, what was that all about?"

Lily sighed. The man infuriated her, but there was no use fighting him. She knew when she'd met her match. "I have no idea. But I doubt she and I will be BFFs."

Derek laughed quietly.

"I'm not kidding, Derek. I'm not sure I'm welcome here," Lily murmured. "But I'll keep working on her."

He looked down at her. The warmth in his eyes seeped into her, pooling in the pit of her stomach. "You've got this."

Lily lifted the champagne to her lips.

Somehow, she wasn't convinced.

CHAPTER TWENTY-FOUR

Saturday, September 27, 7:30 a.m.

THE COMPUTER CHIMED, signaling movement in Rowland's office.

"Crap." Lily shoved the last bite of a toasted bagel into her mouth and sprinted toward her room, throwing herself into her chair.

On the screen, Rowland sat at his desk, steepling his fingers and staring at his companion. "We need to speed up the process."

"You can't just speed it up," the man argued, his face obstructed from view, his voice garbled. "There are things that need to be in place first."

Had she damaged her equipment diving through the front gates? She sighed, made a mental note to get back in and reposition that camera, check its receptors. She had ears, barely, but her viewpoint was handicapped, or at least partially so, and that drove her crazy—she needed full access to that office; an obstructed view wouldn't do.

"Don't tell me what I can and can't do," Rowland said, his voice clipped, face dark. "A group of men wearing black masks broke into my home looking for me, and found my wife and daughter instead. They tortured my wife to find out where I was. The medical examiner told me she bled out, slowly and painfully. My daughter woke up and walked in on them brutalizing my wife. They killed my little girl in front of my wife as she lay dying. She was only six."

Their smiling faces flashed through Lily's mind. *Dear God, who'd murdered Rowland's family?*

"I understand your desire to speed up the——"

Rowland slammed his fist down on the mahogany desk. Lily flinched, despite knowing he couldn't touch her. He leaned forward, murder flashing in his cold eyes. "You understand nothing. The men who tortured and killed my family were CIA. They brought this on themselves, on their people. I've waited too long to exact my revenge."

Lily felt as though she'd just been hit by a brick. In the face. *Her* people had done that, killed that beautiful little girl? *No.* She couldn't believe it, wouldn't believe it.

"I've made it my mission to bring this country to its knees, and if it's the last thing I do…" Rowland paused, his tone acid "…so be it."

The man pushed back from his chair, stood. "If we speed up the process, Rowland, it *will* be the last thing you do."

Rowland watched the man go, then picked up his Scotch glass and hurled it against the office wall, shattering the crystal into a million tiny shards. Cradling his head in his hands, a mournful moan ripped through the silence.

Lily reached for her phone and punched in the numbers she now knew by heart.

"I think you'd better get over here, and bring Ben,"

she said and hung up, her eyes never leaving the sorrowful scene filling her computer screen.

LILY'S LOFT HAD transformed into their command center. Despite her best protests that they were *all* safer in her tall tower, George stood guard downstairs. Derek and Ben sat next to each other, quietly discussing Lily's latest information download on Rowland, and what the hell to do about him.

Despite the shit storm they'd walked in to, Lily smiled. She trusted Ben with her life, and how could she not? He'd essentially taken on a father role since her own had died, and seeing Derek and Ben getting along as if they were lifelong friends and teammates eased the strain of this case.

Ben rested his hands on the table and smiled wearily up at her. "Well, as fun as this brainstorming session has been, there really isn't anything else I can do at this point, and I need to head by the shop." He got up, stretched. "Jury is still out on the newbie."

He walked around the table and drew Lily into a massive bear hug. "We've got this, Lily girl." He released her and turned to Derek. "You sticking around?"

Derek checked his watch and stood. "Can't."

"Wait." Lily's heart sank. "Where are you going?"

Derek gathered up his files and stuffed them into his shoulder bag. "I need to catch a flight for a last-minute meeting in DC."

"Fair enough. Safe travels, then." Ben nodded, opened the door and left, leaving them alone.

Lily eyed Derek. Why was he going to Washington this late? "DC? On a Saturday?"

"You and I both know Kennedy works weekends."

"How long will you be gone?"

"Why?" He stopped cramming the papers into his bag, looked up and gave her a knowing smile.

Her heart sped up as he took a step toward her. Lily backed up until she hit the kitchen's granite island. He closed the distance between them and leaned close, bringing his mouth within an inch of hers. The urge to stand on her tiptoes and close the gap between their mouths coursed through her.

"Will you miss me?"

Every muscle in her body tightened. Oh, yeah, she'd miss him all right. She put both her palms into his chest and gently pushed him away. "Don't be an idiot. I was just curious."

"Keep telling yourself that, babycakes." He laughed and squatted to pet Dakota. "It's a quick turnaround trip. I should be back tomorrow morning, early afternoon at the latest."

So many words, yet no information. "Is there something I should know?"

He shook his head. "You know how it goes. When Kennedy calls, I answer. It's just a quick trip."

She moved to the door and pursed her lips. Maybe she'd go see Rowland tonight. He'd canceled their private tour earlier, blaming an unexpected weekend business meeting. *Yeah, right.* Lily knew when she was getting the runaround. It was a bit reckless, yes, but she'd do anything at this point to move this case along from its current painstakingly slow speed.

Derek looked at her and narrowed his eyes. "Whatever is going on in that pretty little head of yours, don't even think about it."

"I have no idea what you're talking about." *How*

does he do that? She'd never met someone who could read her so accurately. Even Jackson hadn't been able to get inside her head. Yet Derek had managed to unlock her thinking within days. *Unbelievable.*

Throwing up both hands, she gave him an innocent grin. "I swear."

"Uh-huh," he muttered. "I'm not kidding, Lily. We'll get to the bottom of this case *together.* No heroic shit."

She held the door open. "Promise."

He was shaking his head as he left.

She'd promised, yes. But they needed answers. And they needed them *now.* They didn't have time to do it by the book, not with Rowland speeding things up, not when they were already one step behind.

One thing was certain. Time was no longer on their side.

DEREK HATED WALKING AWAY from Lily, especially with that dangerous glint flashing in her hazel eyes, making the swirl of colors dance even more wildly than usual. Somehow he knew that his no-heroics shit had gone in one ear and out the other—she was up to something, and he knew it.

The elevator doors slid open, and Derek reluctantly walked in. Turning, he punched the lobby button and leaned against the wall, staring at Lily's front door, unable to shake the growing sense of unease, until the doors closed. He rested his head against the wall and closed his eyes. If it were up to him, he'd be staying put. But the director had called, wanting him on the next plane to DC to debrief the Dům Hrůzy situation with the team.

Derek had suggested he teleconference in. The director had hung up on him.

So, despite Derek's better judgment, he was off to DC. He just hoped that Lily wouldn't do anything rash while he was gone.

CHAPTER TWENTY-FIVE

Saturday, September 27, 9:00 p.m.

LILY PULLED UP to the elaborate gates sheltering Rowland's estate and took a deep breath to still her racing heart. They needed answers. And she knew of at least one surefire way to get them. She pressed the house intercom located just outside the gate.

"Addison Moore to see Rowland James."

The gates opened, granting her access.

She slowly pulled her Maserati into the circular drive, parked and got out, tugging down the skintight red dress she'd thrown on. Bottle in hand, she made her way to the front door. It opened before she could knock and JB, Rowland's ever-present bodyguard, stared at her, his eyes cold, detached.

"Mr. James is in his study."

Lily let JB show her the way. He opened the door, ushered her in and shut it behind her, never saying a word. Rowland sat in one of the two chairs facing the large fireplace in the back corner of his office.

"Addison, darling. This is quite the surprise." Rowland rose to his feet, searching her face.

"Rowland, darling, I know it's late, but I took the liberty of bringing along a bottle of Screaming Eagle." She held up the Napa Valley Cabernet Sauvignon that had cost her nearly two grand. It was a shame to waste such a brilliant bottle of wine, but…

She let her lips curve up suggestively. "I thought we could celebrate ARME's new technology on our own."

"I like the way you think." He smiled and walked over to his bar, pulled out two red wine goblets. "Celebrating with you sounds…invigorating."

Oh, you have no idea.

"As long as we have privacy tonight, it will be."

Fire danced in his eyes, and a cruel smile crossed his face. He handed her the glasses. "Excuse me for a moment while I make sure that happens."

She watched him walk out the door—*well, that was easy*—then quickly uncorked the wine, poured the crimson liquid and let three droplets of gamma hydroxybutyrate drip into Rowland's glass. GHB had no color, smell or taste, but it would knock him out for several hours at least. Rowland would have no idea what hit him. It was a powerful and dangerous drug, and Lily prayed it worked fast, because she sure as hell had no intention of sleeping with him.

He came back in and she handed him the doctored wine. They toasted, and she tipped her head back, letting the tart liquid flow down her throat. *Damn, this wine is good. Worth every penny.* He mimicked her movements, quietly watching her. She took another sip, and he followed her pattern.

"I must say, Rowland," she said, stepping closer to him. "My luck changed the night you blew into my world."

"Not luck, my dear. Fate."

"To fate, then." She raised her glass.

"To fate."

He downed the last of his wine, took her glass from her hand, set it down and pulled her to him, kissing her hard.

"Come with me." He took her hand and led her out of the office.

Please kick in. Please kick in. The last thing she wanted was to have to sleep with this monster. She allowed a soft laugh to escape her lips as she stumbled after him. He stopped, pushed her up against the wall and kissed her, pushing his hand under her dress. She laughed, wiggled away and danced backward, curling her pointer finger in a come-hither motion.

He followed, pushing her through his bedroom door and shutting it behind them. Again he shoved her up against the hard surface of the closed door. She allowed him to kiss her, knowing that there was nothing she could do about it. Not until the drug kicked in. He pulled her dress over her head, his eyes burning into her.

"So beautiful," he murmured, kissing her neck.

He reached behind her, unfastened her bra and slid her straps off her shoulders, one at a time. She raked her fingers through his hair, anything to buy her more time. Time for the damn drug to kick in.

Rowland stepped back and unbuttoned his shirt, never taking his eyes from her body. His face showed no sign of the drug she'd given him. Lily's throat tightened. She was going to have to sleep with him, or her cover—and their mission—would be shot to hell.

Might as well take control of this nightmare.

She grabbed his hands. "Let me."

In another life, one where she didn't know that the man hell-bent on taking her to bed was a sociopathic psycho who'd murdered hundreds of people, she could have easily been captivated by the handsome man, fallen under his enchanting spell. But she knew exactly what he was, and his barely leashed brutality scared the shit out of her.

Putting her hands on his chest, she guided him toward the bed, careful to keep her scars hidden from view. When he bumped into the mattress, she pushed him down, made him sit, then took her time unfastening every button of his shirt. Pushing it down off his shoulders, she dragged her fingers across his strong chest. Judging by the heat in his eyes, he took it as foreplay.

She took it as a lifeline.

"Take off your panties," he ordered, his voice husky.

She obliged, but slowly, every cell in her body regretting coming to this house of horror as he reached out, ran his fingers over her bare skin. His arms encircled her waist, pulled her naked body between his legs.

"Darling, Addison…" Then he blinked in confusion, his eyes rolling into the back his head as he slumped against her.

It's about damn time.

Unfastening his belt, Lily pulled off his pants and boxers, throwing them on the floor in a heap. She tugged back the covers, entangling his body in them, as if they'd just enjoyed their romp in bed.

Grabbing Rowland's button-down, she shoved her arm through one sleeve, then the other, fastening a few buttons. If, and that was a big *if*, someone else was still here—that damn bodyguard, a maid—and saw her walking around, she'd appear to be a slightly intoxicated guest…or at least that was Lily's hope.

Glancing over her shoulder to see that he was still out, she headed straight for Rowland's office. She closed the door behind her, then made her way to his desk. She sank into his chair and tried the top drawer. Locked. She pulled at the next one. Locked. Frustrated, she flipped on the small table lamp and thumbed through the papers on his desk.

Bills, old receipts, a handful of business cards. Nothing incriminating.

She hung her head and pinched the bridge of her nose. *Please don't let this be for nothing.* Turning her attention to his home computer, she keyed in a simple command that should have unlocked a back channel.

Nothing. She tried another command.

Still nothing.

"Damn it," she whispered

She glanced at the clock, cringed. She needed to get back, couldn't afford to get caught. Wiping down the keyboard, she flipped off the desk lamp, let her eyes adjust to the darkness swirling around her and headed back to Rowland's bedroom.

Creeping back in, she slid under his covers, pushed her naked body close to his and stared at the ceiling, fighting the heaviness threatening to pull her into a deep slumber.

She should have listened to Derek.

LILY WOKE TO faint sunlight streaming in the window and the weight of Rowland's arm draped over her bare stomach. She didn't move, barely breathed. How was she going to get out of this mess, especially if he wanted an encore? He stirred, lifting his head and reaching under the sheet to caress her.

"Good morning, handsome."

"Addison, darling." He cupped his hand around her breast, hard. A startled gasp popped out of her mouth and Lily froze. He released his hold and pressed his lips to hers. "I missed you last night."

"What do you mean?" She turned on her side and pulled the sheet up to cover her nakedness. "I was here."

Rowland stretched and reached over the side of the bed. Lily followed his movement with her eyes and then tensed, coiled to jump. *Too late.* With lightning speed, he grabbed her, flipped her onto her back and straddled her. He gripped her throat with one hand and shoved a blade against her belly with the other.

Her head spun. How had he found out? What had she done to trigger this reaction? Lily commanded her breath to settle, her heart to slow.

He pressed down on the blade and searched her face. "Who are you, and why are you really here?"

She clawed at his hand, fought to breathe. He released his hold a fraction, just enough to allow her to speak.

"I don't…what are you talking about? I'm Addison Moore, from Alabama." She gasped for air. "I'm sure you've already done your research on me. You know I'm telling you the truth."

"But you didn't come up to Omaha for the autumn foliage. And as much as I like to think you're warming my bed because you find me irresistible, I'm not an idiot. Imagine my surprise last night when I woke to find you gone."

He woke up? Shit. She was good as dead. Her mind

tumbled over itself, scrambling for an excuse, any reason, to give her more time.

"Wine doesn't always sit with me." She stumbled over the words. "I went to the kitchen to get something to settle my stomach."

"Don't bullshit me, Addison." The tip of the blade bit into her flesh. Panic tore through her as he glared down at her. "Who are you?"

Lily clambered to find a reasonable explanation.

"You're right," she blurted out. The pressure against her belly subsided. Barely. But it gave her enough of a reprieve to lie with conviction. "I represent a very motivated buyer who's interested in ARME and is willing to invest heavily in the company."

A motivated buyer? For the love of God, was that the best she could come up with? She swallowed the bile in her throat.

"Due to his rather questionable connections, he flies off the radar." Lily knew she was rambling, but she couldn't help it. Not when it meant the difference between life and death. "He sent me to vet you, to vet the company before he approached."

Rowland's eyes narrowed. Lily's heart bucked against her chest.

"I swear to you…" Fearful tears that were not at all contrived rolled down her cheeks. "It was purely a business transaction. I hadn't planned to end up in your bed, Rowland."

Which was true. She'd expected the drug to kick in long before it had. The intimacy of last night, and their nakedness now, made her skin crawl.

Rowland eased off the pressure on the knife. He brought the blade to her face, traced it down her cheek, her ribs, and rested the tip back on her stomach. The muscles in her abdomen tightened, pulling away from the cool metal.

"Set up a meeting with this client of yours." He leaned his mouth close to her ear. "Immediately."

He brought the knife to her face again. Lily flinched, but after a moment he removed it, wiping the blade on her pillow. She didn't move, barely breathed. How was she still alive? He rolled off her and walked toward the bathroom. Scrambling out of bed, she pressed her hand to the wound, assessing the damage.

Nothing more than a shallow cut.

He stopped at the bathroom door and turned. "Do *not* underestimate me, Addison. If I find out you've fucked with me, I'll kill you. I'll take my time doing it, and I will enjoy every agonizing second until you beg me to end you. And then I'll track down everyone you've ever loved and do the same to them."

She reached for the sheet, wrapped herself in it and pressed her back into the corner. Lily didn't doubt he'd make good on his word. What the hell was she going to do?

"And, Addison…" A cruel smile spread across his face. "I own you. I expect you to warm my bed tonight."

She swallowed hard and nodded.

"Now. Get the fuck out."

CHAPTER TWENTY-SIX

Sunday, September 28, 9:00 a.m.

LILY PULLED HER jacket tight. Her head swam. The cut in her belly, though shallow, pulsed with a dull ache. She took a deep breath, hoped the café would be empty of prying eyes and stepped into Keystone. Derek and Ben glanced in her direction.

"I've been made."

Ben slowly put down his coffee mug. "What do you mean, you've been made?"

Derek didn't speak. He eyed her, glancing between her face and the hand shoved into her jacket. She refused to look at him and prayed he wouldn't see past her makeshift bravado.

"Rowland knows something's off." She lowered herself into the closest chair.

"Lil." Derek's eyes narrowed. "What happened?"

She shifted uncomfortably, refusing to meet his eyes.

"How did Rowland make you since I saw you last night?" Ben's brows scrunched.

Lily cleared her throat, continuing to avoid Derek's gaze, and locked on to Ben's confused face. "This morning—"

"This morning." Derek jerked back as if he'd been

struck. "You were with Rowland this morning? Is that why you broke contact last night?"

Heat burned her cheeks. She gnawed the inside of her lip. Partially to keep the tears at bay, because she hurt like hell, but also to keep her mind off Derek's tone. He sounded hurt, confused and royally pissed.

Derek glanced at the clock.

It was barely past nine in the morning.

Lily cringed. It wouldn't take a rocket scientist to figure out she'd been at Rowland's last night. And it wouldn't be a far leap to envision what might have happened between last night and this morning.

Why did it matter if Derek knew she'd been with Rowland? He looked over at her, veiled pain swimming in his eyes, and the bravado she'd been struggling to maintain crashed and burned. She hung her head.

It mattered to her because *Derek* mattered to her.

The only sheets she wanted to warm were his.

She'd fallen for him, and fast, which was the last thing she'd expected. Or wanted, for that matter. But now she'd gone and screwed it up before they ever even had a chance.

"I went to his house last night and apparently miscalculated the sleeping agent I'd slipped into the wine. I didn't have a choice. Nothing happened," she clarified quickly, but the dull look on Derek's face slashed her heart to pieces. "I slipped out when he finally dozed off to riffle through his office."

"Damn it, Lily." Derek slammed his hand on the table. She jumped, and a pain-filled moan escaped her. "We decided to leave that monster be."

"I know, I know," she said. "But you were gone. My night was free."

She stopped short and winced. *Her night was free?* Ben's eyebrows arched.

Lily heard herself running at the mouth, understood that she was babbling like an idiot, but she couldn't stop. "It seemed like a good idea at the time. The kicker is, I didn't even find anything. I couldn't slip out in the night like some hooker, so I went back to his room."

What was going on behind Derek's guarded eyes? Lily felt as if she was going to throw up or cry…or both.

"This morning, Rowland went a little crazy." Her voice trembled.

Derek's attention snapped to her face. "Define *crazy*."

"Crazy like he had a knife to my stomach?"

"Shit, Lily." Ben groaned.

Derek's eyes narrowed and his gaze went from her face to the hand tucked into her jacket, then back to her face. His eyes hardened. "Did he hurt you?"

"'Course not."

He got up, silently walked over and squatted in front of her. Without a word, he reached for her hidden hand, gently coaxed it away from its hiding place, revealing a small crimson stain. His face darkened.

"I'm going to fucking kill him," he said in a quiet, deadly tone.

Lily looked down at him pleadingly. "It's really nothing. Just a small cut. It barely hurts."

Which was true. The cut in her stomach paled in comparison to the way her heart ached at Derek's hooded expression.

"It's Rowland's way of leaving me with a constant reminder of his brutality."

"Ben, got that suture kit handy?"

Derek scooped Lily up into his arms and headed for the back room. She instinctively looped an arm around his neck—being close to him was as natural as breathing—and laid her head against his shoulder.

Why, oh, why did she have to go to Rowland's last night?

Derek gently set her on Ben's desk and, without a word, peeled open her jacket, lifted her shirt again. He shook his head and looked up at her. "This isn't as bad as I'd imagined, but, Lily, what were you thinking?"

Lily tried to say something, anything, but nothing came out. She pressed her lips together tightly. Derek had asked her not to do anything heroic, and she'd gone ahead and done just that. She leaned her head against the wall and closed her eyes.

Stupid, stupid woman.

"I told you no heroic shit." His tone was soft, gentle even. Nothing like the tongue-lashing she expected.

"I know." There was nothing else she could say, not when she wished she could turn back the hands of time.

Silence greeted her.

Lily peeked out from under half-closed lids. Derek had moved away from her and now leaned against the opposite wall. *Perfect. Could this morning get any worse?*

Ben walked in and knelt down in front of her. "Sorry, Lil, there isn't a numbing agent in this kit."

Yep, it could.

"Do it." She gripped the chair. "It's not that bad, and I'm not going to the hospital. Too many questions. We don't have time."

"Lily girl."

"Do it."

Ben swabbed the edge of the small wound. "What possessed you to go to Rowland last night?"

"We needed answers."

"We needed—" Derek choked on the words. "Are you kidding me? We discussed this. Right before I walked out. Or did you forget that little conversation?"

And there it was. The tongue-lashing she'd expected. Her heart sank. She wanted the floor to open up and swallow her whole. "I know."

"Lil—"

"Derek, I get it. It was the wrong move."

Ben pushed the torn skin together and pressed down on the butterfly bandage. She bit her cheek and focused on that dull pain rather than the searing ache in her chest. Ben didn't say anything. Which Lily appreciated. She could only handle one lecture at a time.

Lily glanced over at Derek. He hadn't moved from his perch against the wall. She couldn't read him, and that aggravated her and scared her all at once. If she'd known last night would have ended up in this disaster, she might have reconsidered taking the chance.

Maybe.

Derek pushed off from the wall. "Wait. How are you alive?"

And there, ladies and gentlemen, was the million-dollar question. Given everything they'd uncovered about Rowland, she should be laying in a pool of blood on his floor, not currently getting her ass chewed out by the man she was rapidly falling for.

Was this Rowland's sick, twisted game of cat and mouse?

"Lil?"

She scrunched her nose up. "I made up some wild

story about a motivated buyer who sent me to vet Rowland and the company."

His eyebrows arched. "And he bought that?"

She nodded. "He demanded I set up a meeting with my client. Immediately."

Ben whistled. "Well, I'll be damned…"

"Unbelievable," Derek muttered.

Lily couldn't look at him. If there had ever been anything between them, she'd gone and blown that to smithereens. Why'd she have to give in to her heart? She should have listened to reason and stayed away from Derek. She rested her head against the wall and closed her eyes. *Stupid libido.*

"Who do we know that we can read in on this case?" Ben swabbed around the butterfly stitch and gently pressed a clean bandage over it. "Derek, do you have access to anyone with the skill set to pull off something like this…without getting Lily killed?"

"Yeah." Derek rubbed the back of his head. "I've got someone in mind."

"How quickly can they be read in?" Ben put his kit back together and stood.

"I'll see if they can be here this afternoon." Derek threw Lily a stern look. Her heart nearly broke in two. "Is there anything else we need to know?"

Heat rushed into her cheeks. She squeezed her eyes tight, shutting out the world. Maybe then the room would stop spinning and she could get her footing back.

"Lily."

She opened her eyes. Ben's face was blank. She took a deep breath. "Rowland wants me back tonight."

"You're shitting me, right?" A dumbfounded look crumpled Ben's features.

The light blue of Derek's eyes darkened to a deep sapphire. A muscle in his jaw jumped. "No. Fucking. Way."

Lily sat up, the hair on her neck bristling with indignation. "I couldn't agree with you more, Derek. But what the hell am I supposed to do?"

"It's simple. I'm not putting your life on the line for this bastard." Derek crossed his arms. His face was set. "You're done."

She jerked back as if he'd sucker punched her. "Take me off the case now, and we blow this mission. We'll figure something out."

Ben had been strangely quiet. Lily glanced over at him. Surely he didn't agree with Derek's reasoning.

"She's got a point, Derek." Ben finally spoke up. "She's been backed into a corner. We all know—"

"You." Derek pointed a finger at Ben. "Stay out of this."

Ben threw up his hands and walked out.

Lily chewed her lip, waited for Derek to continue with his rant. When he didn't, she spoke softly. "This isn't your decision, Derek. It's mine. I'm staying on this case."

"It's not my—" Derek broke off, looking livid. "This is my case, babycakes. *I* brought *you* on. Not the other way around."

"And for good reason." Lily straightened her back as much as she could without pulling apart her newly stitched wound. He wasn't the only warrior in the room, damn it.

"I could order you off this case."

Lily's mouth dropped open. Had he really pulled that card? The fall from partner to grunt had been short and fast. She took a deep breath. "But you won't."

His eyebrow arched. "Oh, no?"

"No. I agree. Going back tonight isn't happening. But pulling me off this case is the wrong call."

Derek glared at Lily. She refused to move. She wasn't backing down, not this time. "It's the wrong call, Derek."

"This is bullshit." Derek kicked at a chair and sent it flying across the room. Lily jumped. He walked to the door, jerked it open, walked through and slammed it behind him.

Emptiness swept through the room and wrapped its cold hand around her throat, squeezing hard. Whatever moment they'd shared, whatever they'd once had, was gone.

Lily was sure of it.

DEREK HAD NEVER met another human being who pulled such opposing emotions from him.

He paced on the brick sidewalk outside Keystone Café, hands shoved into his pockets, shoulders hunched against the morning cold. He couldn't decide if he wanted to kill Lily himself for deliberately disobeying a direct order, or applaud her brilliance for getting out of Rowland's home alive.

He massaged his temples wearily. That damn woman was going to be the end of him.

Pulling out his phone, he dialed the only person he trusted enough to help get her out of this mess.

"What's wrong?" Marcus Moretti, Derek's brother, demanded.

"Can't a man call his brother?"

"Not at seven-thirty in the damn morning," Marcus grumbled. "Not unless it's an emergency. Which leads me back to my first question. What's wrong?"

"Shit." Derek glanced at his watch. He'd totally spaced on the two-hour time difference between Omaha and San Diego. "Sorry about that."

"No worries." A toddler's giggles in the background pulled a smile to Derek's face. "I've been up with Liam for an hour. Talk to me."

Derek paced. "I'm in deep, man. My asset—"

"You mean the woman you've not stopped talking about since you landed in Omaha?"

"Yeah, that'd be the one." Derek ran his hand over his head. "She's been made."

"Shit."

"My thoughts exactly. But she gave our target some crazy-ass story about representing a motivated buyer wanting to invest in ARME, and now we need to set up a meet with this client immed—"

"Say no more. We'll be on the next plane out."

"Thanks, brother. I owe you." Derek hung up, relief washing over him.

Maybe, just maybe, they'd all get out of this alive.

CHAPTER TWENTY-SEVEN

Sunday, September 28, 7:00 p.m.

THE AIR HUNG THICK with tension. Derek stalked from one end of the wall of windows to the other, hands grasped behind him, head down. Silent. At this rate, Lily would have to refinish her hardwood floors soon. Ten minutes after slamming the door on her, he'd burst back into the office at Keystone and insisted on taking her home.

Ben hadn't stepped in. She'd argued. And lost.

Without a word, Derek carted her past George, ushered her into *her* home and bolted the door.

Then he stayed, waiting for his contact to show.

Lily wasn't sure why he bothered to stay with her. His reaction this morning…she'd never seen such disappointment rip across someone's face before. Her stomach rolled just remembering it. She wished he would just leave. She didn't need to be freaking babysat—especially by someone who refused to speak to her.

The house phone chirped. Derek snatched it up, turned his back and spoke quietly. Lily bristled. Why was he treating her like a prisoner in her own home?

He hung up. "They're on their way up."

Two minutes later, a knock sounded at the door.

Derek stalked from his silent post in the kitchen to open the door for a dark-haired woman.

"Hey, D."

Derek pulled the tall, gorgeous woman into a tight embrace, whispered something into her ear, then kissed her on the cheek before letting her go. Lily grit her teeth. *That* was Derek's contact? What the hell? She'd told Rowland her client was a man, not a freaking supermodel.

The woman tucked a strand of silky black hair behind her ear and glanced over Derek's shoulder. She searched Lily's face with lovely blue eyes that gave Derek's a run for his money. The woman's face lit up and a soft smile pulled at her lips.

No use being rude. Lily got up from the sofa and moved closer to the stunning woman. Dakota jumped down from the sofa and stuck close to her side.

Derek put his hand on the small of the woman's back. "Lily, this is Evelyn. She's a former homicide detective with Seattle PD, and now consults with the BAU. Best profiler I've ever met. Want to delve into the mind of a sociopath?" He smiled at Evelyn. "She's who you call."

Lily flinched. Yeah, she was definitely jealous. *Great.*

"Evelyn, Lily Andrews and Dakota."

Lily held out her hand. "Thank you for coming on such short notice."

"It's so nice to meet you." Evelyn reached her long arms around Lily and drew her into a hug.

Lily tensed. Why did *this* woman have to be Derek's contact? Better yet, why was she *hugging* her? Lily tried to figure out the relationship between the two of them. Co-workers? Friends? Lovers?

"Ev, you got the file I sent over this morning?"

Evelyn released Lily and nodded. "It was definitely one of the most interesting reads I've had in a while."

Derek snorted. "I'd hardly call Rowland James *interesting*."

Lily retreated to the sofa and Dakota followed, curling up at the end of the sofa, stoically eyeing them.

Evelyn sank into the armchair across from Lily, an easy smile pulling across her delicate features. "What *isn't* interesting about Rowland James? He's sophisticated, smart, a psychotic sociopath and ruthless. That combination is deadly, at best."

"Tell me something I don't already know," Derek said in a dry tone.

"Don't be a smart-ass."

Lily swallowed a laugh. Whatever their relationship was, she couldn't help but like this woman, if for nothing else than going toe-to-toe with Derek. It served him right, having someone put him in his place.

Evelyn tilted her head. "It might seem obvious to you, but those characteristics are the very things we can use against him."

"Sorry, Ev." Derek shook his head. "I'm not on my game."

"Yes." Evelyn glanced over at Lily and raised one eyebrow. "I see that."

Derek flushed. "It's complicated."

"Always is. That's why we're here, though. But we definitely have our work cut out for us."

We? Us? Lily glanced at Evelyn's hand. A thin diamond band glistened on her wedding finger. The muscles in Lily's neck tensed still further. Why did she care if this supermodel, superspy—or whatever the hell Evelyn was—had a thing with Derek?

Damn it. Because her heart was his. If she hadn't known it before, she definitely did now.

"You okay?" Derek asked softly, his gaze concerned.

Lily blinked hard. No use prolonging the agony. She willed a cool facade onto her face. "Of course. Why wouldn't I be?"

His lips pressed into a thin line and turned his attention back to Evelyn. "Where's Marcus?"

"On his way up. He stopped to speak with the doorman." Evelyn smirked at Lily. "Who isn't just any old doorman, is he?"

Derek laughed, got up and moved into the kitchen. "No, he's former black ops."

"Impressive. Especially given his age."

Lily smiled. "It is—"

Loud knocking interrupted them. Dakota leaped to his feet and growled. Derek opened the door and a tall, handsome man walked in.

"Marcus."

"Brother, it's good to see you." The two men bear-hugged.

Turning, Derek smiled at Lily—the first smile he'd given her since barricading her in her own home—and slapped his hand against the tall man's back. "Lily. This is my brother, Marcus. He heads up a special task force for the FBI. Between the two of them, you're in great hands."

Brother? Lily glanced between Marcus and Evelyn and caught the way the woman looked at Marcus.

Wait? They're married? Lily gingerly sank back onto the sofa.

Oh, this was just getting better and better by the second.

THEY SAT AROUND Lily's table and reviewed the file Derek had gathered on Rowland. After scrubbing through the documents and studying the extensive, and impressive, profile Evelyn put together, they settled on a game plan—and it was a hell of a strategy.

Hours after their arrival, Lily's head still spun. Aside from Ben and George, she'd never seen such unwavering devotion. Never once did Marcus or Evelyn question Derek or Lily.

They were all in.

Lily studied Evelyn. The woman bent over the file exhibited unshakable confidence and poise that everyone drew strength from. A faint scar snaked itself from underneath Evelyn's ear to her chin. Lily frowned.

What's your story?

Clearly, now was not the time to ask. Come to think of it, Lily hadn't been able to ask *anything* of these two. They'd blown into her home, her life and this case without a moment's hesitation and taken over.

And Derek had let them.

If he trusted these two, then she'd trust them. No questions asked.

Still, worry clawed at Lily's brain. Rowland was brutal and savvy. Their plan was for Lily to introduce Marcus to Rowland tomorrow night, but they had to play out this meeting with him with surgical precision.

One misspoken word, one misstep, and the whole operation would go south.

Fast.

"Tell me again what Rowland did this morning?" Evelyn asked, a thoughtful look flickering across her composed face.

"He pulled the typical alpha-male strut, threatened me, my entire family and everyone I've ever loved, threw in a little—okay, a lot of—physical pain."

Derek's face darkened, and Lily resisted the urge to roll her eyes. She got that he was still angry, but he needed to realize that she was every bit the well-trained operative that he was, and that she'd taken a calculated risk—albeit one that didn't work out the way she'd hoped.

"Rowland told me he owned me, that he expected me back tonight—"

"Which isn't a fucking option." Derek got up and went to the kitchen.

"Yes. I heard you the first time," Lily countered as she watched him storm around the kitchen for a second before turning her attention back to Evelyn. "Then he kicked me out."

"Yes." Evelyn twirled a piece of hair around her finger and nodded. "Yes. This phone call should most definitely work."

Without a word, Derek passed Lily a glass of water. She accepted the water gratefully, took a long swig. The icy liquid cooled her parched mouth.

"Time to get this over with." Derek handed Lily her burner phone, his fingers brushing hers. His feathery touch sent her heart into a wild gallop.

Rowland picked up on the second ring. "Addison?"

Lily pressed a button and cradled the phone in her palm, praying that Rowland wouldn't pick up on the fact that she had him on speaker. "I'm not coming, Rowland."

She flicked her eyes up. Derek sat on the piano bench, his elbows perched on his knees and his chin resting on his fisted hands.

"I'm surprised you—"

"Believe it or not, Rowland, there are men in this world more brutal than even you." Lily glanced at Marcus. "My client is one of them."

Derek got up and paced the long wall of windows.

"That's quite the gamble," Rowland said, his voice hard as ice.

Evelyn pressed her lips together and nodded, almost as if silently encouraging Lily onward. She pulled from the woman's quiet, unwavering strength and pressed on with the lines they'd rehearsed over and over until Lily nailed them.

She took a deep breath. "I'll take my chances, Rowland. I've set up the meeting just as you requested for tomorrow night at five o'clock with my client. He will meet you at the Boiler Room off Jones Street. I reserved the corner room to ensure the utmost discretion."

"I'm interested to meet this...client of yours."

"As is he. Good night, Rowland." Lily hung up.

"That was perfect," Evelyn said in a soft, kind voice.

Lily bit her lip until she tasted copper and forced a smile to her lips. Nothing about this mess she'd made was perfect. And now these incredible people were putting *their* asses on the line to help her get out of the shit storm *she'd* created.

What a disaster—she hadn't made this massive of a mistake since her rookie year.

Evelyn cleared her throat and shot Marcus a quick look. He stood.

"We're going to head out. It's been a long night, and tomorrow is a huge day. More so now than ever."

"You're more than welcome to stay here. I can sleep on the sofa." Lily patted the seat next to her. She didn't want to come out and say it, but she didn't want to be alone tonight. Rowland had done a number on her head.

Marcus draped his arm over Evelyn's shoulder. "We're going to stay at Derek's. You need to sleep in your own bed tonight."

"That's not necessary." She glanced between Marcus and Evelyn. *Please don't make me beg you to stay.*

"It is, though." Evelyn gathered her bag. "We'll be back in the morning."

Marcus went to the door and held it for Evelyn. She kissed Derek on the cheek.

Lily straightened up. Derek wasn't staying, was he?

Evelyn whispered into Derek's ear. He scowled and shook his head. Walking over to Lily, she bent down and folded her arms around her. Evelyn smelled like lavender.

"We've got this. You're not alone." Evelyn let go and stood up straight. "It's going to be okay. Promise."

Was it?

CHAPTER TWENTY-EIGHT

Sunday, September 28, 11:45 p.m.

THE SILENCE WAS DEAFENING. Derek had moved to the kitchen when Marcus and Evelyn left. He'd busied himself with the dishes. Hadn't said a word to Lily. This was ridiculous. What were they? Five?

Lily finally gave up. "Are we going to talk about this morning?"

"Not sure there's anything to talk about," he said, with his back still turned.

"Derek, I saw your face."

He stopped washing the glass he held, set it down and turned to her, frowning. "What exactly do you think you saw?"

"Anger. Frustration. Disappointment." *Disgust.*

She walked into the kitchen. He wasn't going to stand around and make her feel unwanted. This was her house, damn it, and if he couldn't at least be civil to her, she'd make him—

He laughed, cutting off her inner torrent of emotions. "Not even close."

She bristled. "You have no right to be disgu—"

He tossed the kitchen towel into the sink. "Wrong again."

The man standing in her kitchen, glaring at her,

was infuriating and stirred up the strangest emotions in her. He could reduce her to an emotional mess faster than any human being on the planet. Yet also spark a flame in her that no one else had—not even Jackson.

Lily shoved her hands onto her hips. "If you'd *just* let me finish my—"

"I was jealous, okay?"

Her heart skipped. *Jealous?* Her arms fell to her sides.

Derek scrubbed his hands over his face. "The mental picture of another man putting his hands on you makes me insane, specifically a man like Rowland, especially since I know what he's done."

Lily reached for the counter to steady herself. She was sure her head was about to explode. She'd been walking around the whole day thinking that Derek was disgusted with her, wanted nothing to do with her anymore. She'd never dreamed that he was jealous of Rowland for taking her to bed.

Clearly, her instincts were completely unreliable when it came to this man.

Every cell in her body wanted to go to him, but she couldn't move. Fear froze her in place. Not after Jackson. She'd trusted him, let him into her life and barely survived.

Derek moved toward her. "Look, I know I don't have a right to—"

She took a step back. Her throat closed as cold panic reached up and gripped her. *Shut down whatever is going on here, Lily. Nothing good can come out of this.*

"You're right." Tears sprung to her eyes. "You don't. This conversation is over."

She all but raced to her room and shut the door behind her. She leaned against the frame. The blood hammered in her ears and her head swam.

The man she loved, who'd thrown her a lifeline, who'd brought her into his inner circle of trust and put *his family* on the line for her, was jealous.

Derek wanted her. And she'd just shut the door on him.

Perfect.

She crawled into bed, pulled the covers over her head and cried.

DEREK SPRAWLED ON the sofa. Wide-awake. There was no possible way he could sleep, not with Lily in the next room. That woman both exasperated and excited him all at once. He'd never met anyone like her. He couldn't get her off his mind, despite the fact that she'd made it clear she wasn't interested.

Nice, Moretti.

His phone vibrated and he grabbed it, checking the ID. It was too late for this to be good news. "Marcus, what's up?"

"You alone?"

"Yeah." Derek sat up, fully alert. "What's going on?"

"We've been over every inch of Jackson's file, just like you asked."

"And?"

"We can't put a finger on it yet, but something feels off about this whole thing." Marcus hesitated. "I hate to be the bearer of bad news, brother, but neither Evelyn nor I are convinced Jackson went rogue."

Derek's heart sank. Yeah, he'd already made that short leap into crazy town when the fiancé bomb had been dropped in his lap. He'd dismissed it then, thinking it was ludicrous, but if both Evelyn *and* Marcus jumped to the same conclusion...

Derek cradled his head in his hands.

"Have you considered Jackson might be on an off-the-books but sanctioned mission?"

Leave it up to his brother to bring it home. Hard. Fast.

"I have." Derek got up, moved farther from Lily's bedroom.

"You have? You going to tell her?"

Derek looked back at her closed door. "Not sure. What the hell am I supposed to say? 'Hey, Lil, you know the man who tried to kill you and went underground? You know, your partner, your fucking ex-fiancé? Well, that's all a lie. He's one of us. Well... maybe.'"

"She needs to know if there's even a slight possibility."

"Have Evelyn speak with her tomorrow." Derek walked into the kitchen, reached for a glass and shoved it against the refrigerator's water dispenser. "She's much better with that psychological stuff."

Derek knew he was being a jackass, but he couldn't do it. He couldn't give Lily the hope that the man she'd been engaged to might be a hero, not a traitor. Not when it could be false...and although it was selfish, he didn't want to give her that hope when he wanted her so badly for himself.

Marcus sighed into the phone. "She needs to hear it from you."

"Why?"

"She trusts you. You're the lead on this, man. She needs to hear it from you."

Derek set down the glass too hard and water sloshed over the rim. "Sorry, man, I won't do it until I know for sure."

"Derek."

"I won't say anything to her until I've verified it myself. You didn't see her crumpled over his casket, Marcus. I did. I've watched her try to piece her life back together ever since. He doesn't deserve her, even if he is on a sanctioned mission. That bastard shattered her. That's a game-ender."

"Bastard or not, she needs to know. And, it needs to be by the books, man. You can't be swayed by anything else."

"What are you trying to say?"

"Did you honestly think we'd miss the way you looked at her tonight?"

Of course they hadn't. Nothing got past the two of them.

It was why Derek had called them in the first place when the shit hit the fan this morning. Fatigue washed over him. Had it really only been this morning? It felt like a million years ago.

Derek glanced at the closed door and sighed. Somehow, he'd have to find a way to tell her what they all suspected about Jackson's true motives.

Whether he liked it or not.

CHAPTER TWENTY-NINE

Monday, September 29, 2:00 p.m.

MARCUS AND LILY had role-played until noon, until all hesitation vanished, until they'd mastered it. Exhaustion gripped Lily in a tight vise. She'd slept for all of an hour the night before. She couldn't get her mind off the sexy, stubborn man sleeping in the next room, couldn't get her mind to settle.

Derek was jealous. He wanted her. She wanted him. And she'd said no.

Clearly, she was an idiot.

Last night, curled up in bed, she'd recognized that Jackson still had a hold on her, a hold that needed severing if Lily ever wanted to find happiness again. And she did. With Derek. She snuck a peek at him. He leaned against the windows, arms crossed, face set. Regret blanketed her, and she had to force herself to shake it off—there was nothing she could do about *that* right now.

Now she needed to focus on the task at hand: Rowland James.

"Stay behind Marcus," Evelyn said from her perch on the kitchen counter. "Keep your eyes on the ground. Rowland needs to believe Marcus is just as aggressive as he is, and that Marcus is furious with you."

"No problem there," Lily muttered.

Marcus chuckled, then picked up where Evelyn left off. "Introduce me, then let Rowland do all the talking. The fewer people in this dialogue, the better."

"Head down, eyes on ground, no talking. Got it." Lily was feeling more than a bit low about her plummet from prized agent to silent sidekick, but it couldn't be helped. This was the role she had to play to get them out of this mess, and she was determined to do her part.

"If he buys it—and for all our sakes, let's hope he does—Marcus will schedule a follow-up meeting with him in a few days." Evelyn smiled. "That'll give us some time to figure out the next step."

Marcus nodded. "It's not ideal, but it'll do."

Evelyn jumped down from the counter, flopped next to Marcus on the sofa and tucked her feet under her. "We make the most of the situation. Bottom line—if you hadn't come up with this story, you'd be dead, and we'd be back to square one, or worse."

Silently, Derek moved to the piano bench and sat, face still set.

"It was a mistake," Lily said softly, refusing to look at him. "I shouldn't have gone in the first place."

Marcus looked up sharply. "Stop right there, Lily."

Startled, Lily glanced up. Marcus had been nothing but kind and calm since he'd arrived, but this tone was different. It commanded her attention.

"That kind of second-guessing yourself isn't going to do you or any of us any good. I read your file and asked around. If you weren't the best, Derek would have never brought you on board. Stop doubting your abilities and start thinking like the great agent we all know you are."

Evelyn smiled at Lily. "I don't know a lot of agents who would've had the balls to go in the first place, let alone be able to come up with a story that would stick—and while a knife was shoved into their stomachs, no less. Don't doubt your ability to do your job. None of us do."

Damn, they tag-teamed well. Lily was beginning to understand why Derek had called them in when things started going downhill. Family or not, they were amazing at what they did.

"Thanks."

Derek had been quiet through their final instructions. Lily didn't blame him. It was easier this way. Once this case was over, and they'd delivered Rowland on a silver platter, she'd be back in the game. And on a one-track mission: to find Jackson. He might want to become a ghost, but she wasn't going to let him slip into oblivion.

If it took her from here until eternity, she would find him.

She glanced at Derek. There'd be no room for *this*. Whatever *this* could have been. She'd done what was best and shut him down.

Why, then, did her heart feel as if it had shattered all over again?

CHAPTER THIRTY

Monday, September 29, 5:00 p.m.

MARCUS AND LILY stood in the back room of the Boiler Room, wrapped in silence. He glanced down at Lily and grinned. She could see the family resemblance between him and Derek. The Moretti men definitely had some great genes.

"He's here." Her earpiece crackled to life with Derek's deep voice.

Lily fidgeted with her scarlet dress. The soft fabric draped her body perfectly and hid the .32 strapped to the inside of her thigh. She wasn't going in unarmed. Not today.

The ruching across her stomach also allowed breathing room for the bandage beneath. One move in the wrong direction and the throbbing flared. She'd pulled the bloodred dress from the back of her closet on purpose. She wasn't planning on ruining another outfit. She shifted her weight from one leg to the other. Her feet already screamed. She hated heels.

"Cute dress, Andréws," Evelyn whispered through Lily's earpiece. "Relax, you've got this."

This woman could read her like a book. "That obvious?"

"That obvious."

Marcus winked. "Rowland will most definitely have a hard time focusing on me tonight. You're smoking hot, Andrews."

"Marcus," Derek said in an almost growl.

Lily's heart kicked. There was that tone again. Was Derek still jealous? Her cheeks flushed.

"Easy, brother. Have you seen my wife lately?"

Lily wasn't used to the family banter, especially with her at the center of it.

"Boys, focus." Lily could almost see Evelyn's smile through her earpiece.

Marcus wrapped his arm around Lily's waist and gently tucked her to his side. He leaned his mouth close to her ear. "Ready to kick some ass?"

Lily pushed her shoulders back and smiled. "Game on."

"Marcus…" Derek's voice, low and cold, came on again.

"Hands off, lover boy." Evelyn's soft laughter echoed in their ears. "Your brother's getting antsy up here."

Dropping his arm, Marcus grinned down at Lily. She bit her lip to keep her amusement at bay. Now was not the time to piss Derek off any more than she already had.

Marcus folded himself into the back corner booth. Lily stood next to him, steady, confident. What was it with the Moretti men's ability to put her at ease?

Lily glanced at her watch just as Rowland James strutted into Boiler Room's darkened private room. JB, his thug from the other night, smirked at Lily.

She pointed at the door. "Guard dogs stay outside."

Rowland's eyes narrowed, and he glanced at Marcus, who didn't move. He held Rowland's gaze, face blank. Lily swallowed her smirk. Whatever the outcome, she was enjoying Rowland's present discomfort.

"Wait outside." Rowland tipped his head toward the door. "Don't come in until I call for you."

JB left, and Lily felt vindicated, albeit briefly. She flicked her gaze to Rowland. Time to start this happy little party.

"Rowland." Lily stepped to the right and motioned with her hand. "This is my client, Desmund De Luca."

Marcus's lip twitched. She had come up with that one, and immediately Evelyn jumped on board with the name. Lily wished she could see Derek's face now. He'd griped about it being too metrosexual, but finally came over from the dark side. Not that he had much of a choice. They sure as hell weren't going to give that sociopath Marcus's real name.

Playing the role of submissive eye candy, Lily rested her hand on Marcus's shoulder. "Mr. De Luca, allow me to introduce Rowland James."

"It's good to finally put a face to the name." Marcus remained seated, cast a short glance up toward Lily. She dropped her hand quickly and clasped both together in front of her. "Addison's told me all about you, Mr. James. Please, join me." Marcus nodded to the empty seat across from him.

Rowland lowered himself into the booth. "The pleasure is all mine, Mr. De Luca."

"My time is most valuable, Mr. James, so let me get straight to the point." Marcus leaned forward. "I'm very interested in ARME and the potential items you might be able to supply my buyers."

"That *is* very direct." The vein in Rowland's neck

kicked. "But I respect your candor. I assure you, depending on the price, I can supply you with anything you want."

"That's quite the claim." Marcus steepled his fingers together. "How do I know this isn't some sort of entrapment?"

Marcus was killing that alpha-male role. What a freaking genius.

"Addison mentioned you sent her to vet my company, to vet me. I'm assuming that process ran smoothly, and to your liking, or you wouldn't be sitting here."

Rowland shot Lily a searing look.

Her shoulders tensed. The last time she'd seen that look, he'd pressed a cold blade into her. She tipped her chin up. This man would not best her again.

Rowland flipped his gaze back to Marcus. "Am I correct in my assumption?"

"Ms. Moore's involvement in this business exchange stopped the moment she slipped between your sheets, Mr. James."

Lily cringed. She knew Marcus was just playing his role, but still…that hurt. Marcus put his hand on her hip and tucked her to his side. "She's here to facilitate this introduction, and nothing more."

Rowland glanced between Lily and Marcus, face hardening.

"Someone doesn't like you playing with his sparkly toy, Marcus. Well done, babe." Evelyn laughed in Lily's ear. Lily's face grew warm.

Marcus kept his hand on her hip. Despite the present hell they were in, his touch was soft and comforting. "She's no longer part of this discussion, Mr. James, or the picture. I'm here to talk to you about ARME assets, not Ms. Moore's."

Rowland cleared his throat and shot Lily a shielded glare. Her skin crawled. He cocked his head and studied Marcus.

"Point taken." Rowland reached for his glass of water. He took a sip and then set it down. Hard. "Well, then, let *me* get straight to the point, Mr. De Luca. You want guns. I can get you guns. You want missiles. I can get you missiles. You want bombs. I can get you bombs. ARME Industries is at my disposal. There's nothing outside my reach."

Lily tensed. *You cocky little bastard.* Marcus tightened his hold on her hip and drew her closer. She took a deep breath and forced her body to relax.

Marcus loosened his grip.

"My buyers are eager to find something…compact, with the greatest impact."

A cruel smile spread across Rowland's face. "I already have something in mind."

Of course you do, you asshole.

"Excellent." Marcus dropped his hand from Lily's hip and pressed his fingertips together. "My buyers will be most pleased. How many do you have available?"

"For the right price, I can get you as many as you'd like."

CHAPTER THIRTY-ONE

Monday, September 29, 7:30 p.m.

LILY UNSTRAPPED HER thigh holster, checked the safety and set the gun down on the counter. She headed to her bedroom, unzipping her dress as she went. At this point, she didn't care about modesty or who saw what part of her *assets*. Marcus had knocked it out of the ballpark with Rowland, but really? Did he have to hold her like that? More people had touched her—and rather intimately—in the past seventy-two hours than had touched her in over a year.

The only person who hadn't?

Derek.

The universe hated her.

Lily pulled her bedroom door shut, stepped out of her dress, kicked it aside and slipped into her yoga pants. She tugged a black tank over her head and sat down on her bed.

She was exhausted, mind and body.

And this charade had just begun.

She fell back onto her soft comforter and closed her eyes. Dakota jumped onto her bed, licked her face and nuzzled her arm. Lily slowly opened one eye. "Slave driver."

He licked her face again. Sighing, she pushed herself up, grabbed a hair tie and threw her hair into a bun that tilted to one side before joining the Morettis back in the living room.

When she entered the room, Derek did a double take. His reaction warmed Lily's cheeks. Maybe there *was* hope after all, and she hadn't completely screwed up. *A girl could dream, right?*

"So, how do you think it went?" Derek asked from his post on the kitchen counter.

"He bought it."

"We nailed it." Marcus popped open his Guinness and dropped onto the sofa. "I was surprised how quickly he came out and offered his services."

Lily curled up in the overstuffed chair. "I'm not. He's gotten off scot-free for so long that he thinks he's untouchable. Do you think he'll be the seller?"

Derek jumped off the counter and pulled out the piano bench. Sat. "Not a chance. He'll send someone else to handle the exchange. Keep his hands clean."

"Unless he thinks Lily is still potentially part of the exchange." Marcus wagged his beer toward her. "There was definitely something there. I just couldn't tell what. Maybe we bring Lil around again and let me get another read."

She wasn't so sure about being offered up as bait. But then again, she *was* the one who'd put them in this mess to begin with. She shrugged. "I don't mind throwing it out there again. Maybe he'll bite."

"No offense, Lily, but I don't think he'll care at this point." Evelyn pursed her lips. "I think you're a thing of the past."

Marcus threw his arm around Evelyn. "I don't know, babe. You should've seen his expression when

I grabbed Lily. It was crazy. That was the *only* time I saw anything that even *resembled* emotion. Murder ripped through that man's face when I touched her."

"Yes," Derek said drily. "We were privy to that little hand grab."

"Relax, brother. We had to make it legit."

"And you did, my love. I was impressed." Evelyn kissed Marcus on the cheek. "I expect more of it for myself later."

Lily glanced between the three Morettis and smiled. It had been a long time since a family had gathered, and goofed off, in her home. Evelyn untangled herself from beneath Marcus's arm and headed for the kitchen. Marcus's gaze followed her every move as she made a beeline for the fridge.

He took a sip of his beer. "All kidding aside, I've never seen anyone so cold."

Evelyn peeked around the door of the fridge and whistled. "That's saying a lot."

"It was like staring into a black pit." Marcus set his Guinness on the coffee table. "But something flickered behind those emotionless eyes when he looked at Lily. And I didn't like it."

Derek's raised his head, looking tense. He jumped up and moved closer, never taking his eyes off Lily. What was he doing? Staking claim on her?

"Come on now, Marcus." Lily didn't want to give Derek any more ammo. "You made it pretty clear I was no longer an option. I don't think we have to worry about that aspect."

"True. But option or not, I think we should consider a protective detail. Or at the very least, you not being here alone."

"No." Lily climbed out of the chair and paced. "Not happening. That's where I draw the line."

Marcus reached for his beer. "I've read my share of faces, Lily. Rowland isn't someone to brush off."

"I'm not brushing him, or your concern, off. I'm just not taking a protective detail. I don't need it."

"Lily…" Derek chimed in. His voice held a low warning.

"This is ridiculous. Come with me." She moved to her bedroom and walked into her massive closet. All three followed.

Without a word, she yanked on the mirror frame. She stood back as it swung open, revealing row after row of weapons and ammunition tucked neatly within their hiding spots. Marcus's eyes widened. Evelyn gasped. Lily hid her smile, crossed her arms and stared at Derek. *Still think I need a protective detail?*

"Damn, Lily. You could've shared this little room of toys before." A small, tight smile played at the corners of Derek's mouth.

"Would it have made a difference?"

"No."

Lily swallowed the urge to scream. How this man could be so stubborn was beyond her. Was there nothing she could do to make him see that she didn't need to be babysat?

"This is incredible." Evelyn reached for the M4.

Lily leaned against the door frame. "Like I said, I don't need a protective detail."

"So you're armed. More than Fort Knox." Marcus nodded, then looked at Evelyn. "That doesn't take away the reality that Rowland has you in his sights."

Evelyn put the gun back. "We might need to consider pulling you out, Lily."

Lily took a deep breath. She was not being yanked from this case. She was not going into hiding. And she sure as hell was not having a protective detail following her every move. "Absolutely not."

"I get not wanting a protective detail, truly." Evelyn glanced between the two men flanking her sides.

"No protective detail." Lily pushed the frame back into place, hiding her case of weapons.

Derek's face was unreadable. "Lily."

Lily's back straightened. "No."

Derek threw up his hands. "I give up. You're the most obstinate woman I have ever had to deal with."

He turned on his heel and stalked out of the room. Lily bit her lip to keep it from trembling. She didn't want him to think she was stubborn, but she wasn't willing to let their fear of Rowland disrupt her life.

"Sorry, Lil, but I agree with him." Marcus shoved his hands into his pockets and made his way toward the living room.

Lily pressed her two pointer fingers into the corners of her eyes and sighed. "It's so not necessary."

"On the contrary." Lily squirmed beneath Evelyn's steady gaze. "Marcus came across as an equal, which we needed, but he also may have inadvertently put a bull's-eye on your back."

Lily's head spun. Again. "Not following."

"In Rowland's psychotic, sociopathic mind, if he can't have you, no one can."

EIGHT STORIES BELOW, a pair of green eyes watched Lily pace along the western wall of her loft, agitated. The binoculars lay on the passenger seat, untouched. Why use them when the lights in Lily's loft illuminated her every move? She'd made it easy, creating a fishbowl, the perfect view.

I see you...

Almost as if Lily heard the warning, she stopped pacing, looked down into the streets below. A moment later, her loft went dark.

Gloved hands lifted the heat-seeking scope and scanned the loft, searching. It picked up the outline of one human signature in the bedroom, one animal in the main living space. A dark chuckle echoed in the quiet car.

You're mine now...

CHAPTER THIRTY-TWO

Tuesday, September 30, 3:00 a.m.

LILY WOKE SUDDENLY, instincts on high alert. Something was wrong. She glanced at the clock on the nightstand beside her bed. It was black. The whole loft was dark, the shadows impenetrable. She slowed her breathing and focused her eyes, finally making out a lone silhouette in the corner. Her heart lodged in her throat.

A man sat in a chair, one leg propped on the other. Panic gripped her throat. *Was it Rowland?* She reached behind the nightstand, fingers hunting.

"Searching for this?" a familiar voice asked mockingly as the man held up her backup .32 and let it drop to the floor.

Jackson.

How had he gotten into her place? How had he gotten past Dakota? She rummaged behind her headboard next. Nothing. Damn it. How had he been within a breath of her without her knowing? Fear prickled her skin. How long had he been in her bedroom?

Watching.

Jackson laughed, the sound deep and dark. "I would've hoped you'd come up with some more creative hiding places for your firearms, Lily. Or, at the

very least, different places than when we were together."

He shifted his weight. She tensed, but didn't have
time to react before he sprang and pinned her underneath his bulk. She struggled against him.

"Hold still, damn it." He restrained her by the shoulders.

Like hell she'd hold still. She tugged an arm free,
grasped for the drawer and searched for her other gun.
Her heart sank.

It was missing, too.

Her mind raced. Her fingers landed on the lamp.
She yanked hard. It connected with the side of Jackson's head with a sickening crack. He swayed and lost
his hold. She kicked and clambered out from under
him.

Scrambling out of bed, she fell and hit her head
against the corner of the dresser. Stars exploded behind her eyes. Blood began to trickle down her face.
She wiped it away with one hand and reached under
her mattress with the other, pulling out the tiny .22. It
wasn't much, but it could still do some damage.

She climbed to her feet and pointed the barrel at
Jackson's chest. Lily blinked hard, pushed the pain
back, focused. "Where's my dog?"

He moaned and shook his head. "Relax. Dakota is
fine. He's sleeping, but fine."

"You drugged my dog?"

"Our dog, Lily. I drugged *our* dog." He glanced at
her weapon and grinned. What was so funny? She had
a gun pointed at him. "I see you sleep armed."

"Better than what I used to sleep with." She cocked
the hammer. "What are you doing in my home?"

"I told you to let me go."

"And I told you hell would freeze before I did that."

"I see some things have changed. Shame, really. The panties are cute." He motioned toward her with the gun in his right hand. "Sleeping in the nude was definitely better."

Why was he toying with her? Had he lost his mind? Maybe that was why he'd gone over to the dark side and betrayed her, their country. *Maybe.* "What are you doing in my city, Jackson?"

He lunged. Lily sidestepped, rolled and faced him.

"Nice." With a sharp flick, his foot connected with her ankle and her knees buckled. He flung her to the floor. A cry escaped Lily's lips as she hit the wooden surface.

"But not fast enough." Jackson knelt beside her. "I'm not in your city. I'm a ghost, Lily. You should have let things lie and stayed out of my files."

"What are you talking about?" She frowned. "What files?"

"I told you to forget about me. So imagine my surprise when I realized someone has been snooping into my past, searching for things better left alone."

Lily froze. She hadn't pulled his jacket—Marcus and Evelyn had requested it. *Damn it.* "If you so much as—"

"I know all about your little team."

Every muscle in her body tensed at his not-so-veiled threat. Her pulse thundered in her ears as a primal urge to protect her own surged through her. She could deal with Jackson coming after her, making her life a living hell. She could not, would not, let him lay so much as a finger on the Morettis.

Any of them.

She shoved her open palm up and connected with his face. Blood spurted over both of them. He stumbled two steps back and reached for his broken nose.

She pushed to her feet, scooped up the .22 and scrambled out of his reach. "You touch them—"

"Damn it, Lily." He glared at her. "You need to leave."

"Excuse me?"

"You have forty-eight hours to get out of Omaha, or I *will* kill you." He wiped the back of his hand across his face, spreading the crimson stain.

"I'm not leaving. This is my city. My home. You already pushed me away from one thing I loved. I won't let you do it again."

"Forty-eight hours, Lily. I'm not kidding."

She cocked the hammer back on her .22. "Neither am I."

He held his nose and glared at her over his clasped hand.

The nightmarish case that started this train wreck of her current reality flooded her senses. Her hand shook.

He took a step toward her.

She pulled the trigger.

The bullet grazed his shoulder and lodged in the wall behind him. He grabbed his arm, staring at her for a brief moment in astonishment. But he quickly recovered, tackling her to the floor and pinning her beneath his body.

Lily bucked against him. "Get off me."

He wrestled with her, grabbing her arms and yanking them above her head. "I gave you the option to join me."

"I wouldn't join you if you were the last man on the planet. I'm not a traitor."

He leaned his face close to hers. "You have no idea what you're talking about, Lily."

"Don't I, though?"

"No, you don't. Forty-eight hours. I want you gone."

He clasped his hand over her throat. Lily knew he was going for her artery. *Again.* She knew it and tore at his arms, unwilling to let it end this way.

"I won't—"

CHAPTER THIRTY-THREE

Tuesday, September 30, 3:45 a.m.

DEREK ANSWERED ON the second ring.

"I need you." Lily's voice came through the line, scared and weak.

He bolted from his bed. *Lily.* Damn it. They'd gone round and round last night until he'd just given up. He *knew* he shouldn't have left her alone.

Sliding into his jeans, he tugged on his T-shirt and darted to the door, his heart hammering in his chest. He'd never forgive himself if anything happened to her. *Please don't let anything happen to her.* "Don't hang up. Stay on the line, Lil. I'm coming."

"Please..."

He ran.

"Talk to me, Lil!"

Silence greeted him on the other end. *Shit.* He picked up the pace, rounded the corner and raced across the street.

He pulled his gun, hugged it to his side and burst into the lobby. He sailed past the graveyard shift doorman and took the stairwell. He wasn't about to wait for the elevator. Not when he didn't know what would greet him.

Not when Lily needed him now.

Derek stopped at the exit, pressed himself to the wall and slowly pushed the door open. Clearing the penthouse lobby, he made his way to her front door. Gingerly, he reached out and checked the latch.

It was closed tight.

He frowned, keyed in the code, grateful he'd talked it out of her on day one, and eased into the room. Darkness covered the loft. He tucked himself into the shadows.

"Lil."

Silence thundered in his ears. Where was she?

Derek stumbled over a mass. He crouched, reached out his hand and found fur. *Dakota*. Derek held his hand in front of the dog's nose and breathed a sigh of relief as a warm, shallow breath hit his palm.

The cold click of a hammer being cocked exploded in the silence. "Move, and I'll blow your head off."

"Wow." Derek raised his hands. "Lily, easy. It's Derek."

His eyes adjusted to the dimness. Lily stood in the middle of the living room. Her hands shook.

"Easy, babycakes. It's just me."

"You came." She dropped the gun and collapsed to her knees.

Derek holstered his gun and moved to her, scooping Lily into his arms and cradling her to his chest. "What the hell happened?"

She wrapped her arms around his neck and held tight. "Jackson."

Derek's blood turned to ice. Rogue agent or not— Derek was going to track him down and take him out. Permanently.

"Talk to me, Lil." Derek moved to the sofa, set her

down and knelt in front of her. "Walk me through what happened."

"I don't know what happened."

The vacant look descending across her face slashed at Derek. He took a deep breath and waited for Lily to continue.

"I woke up, and he was in my room." She lifted haunted eyes to his face and his heart nearly broke in two. "How could he get in without me knowing?"

Derek recognized the self-doubt in her tone and could only imagine the mental beating she was giving herself. "You didn't do anything wrong."

Her hands shook. She knotted them together in her lap.

Don't lose that fight.

"I didn't *do* anything." Her voice rose an octave. "I haven't *done* anything."

Derek laid his hands over hers. He might as well have touched icicles. "Lil."

"He gave me forty-eight hours to get out of the city. Jackson told me he'd kill me and my team if I wasn't gone in forty-eight hours." Her chin quivered. "Derek, he knows about Marcus and Evelyn."

Her eyes clouded over. Derek pulled her into his lap and cradled her close.

"If Jackson knows about them, there's no telling what he knows about you. I can't let Jackson hurt any of you. If something happened, I could never forgive myself." The last word ended in a tiny sob.

The soft sound ripped into Derek. He wrapped his arms carefully around her and tucked her close to his side as she clung to him.

Derek had wanted Lily in his arms from the moment he'd set eyes on her. But not like this. Not when she was shaken to her core by her asshole of an ex-fiancé. Derek closed his eyes and pressed his lips to the top of her head.

"I've got you, babycakes."

"He was in my house, Derek." She buried her face into the crook of his shoulder. Her tears saturated his shirt.

"I'm here now." Derek tightened his hold. "You're safe."

She didn't respond, just squeezed his neck harder. "I know I should've called Ben or George, but—"

"No, you called the right person." He gently tilted her chin up, made her look at him. "Lil, you called the right person."

She glanced down, and her eyes widened. "Your shirt…"

"It's nothing." Derek stood, scooped Lily into his arms and brought her into the bathroom, gently setting her down on the countertop. "Let's get you cleaned up. Then we can figure out our next steps."

He moved to touch her arm, waiting to see how she'd respond. She looked up at him and his heart bucked in his chest at the trust radiating in her hazel eyes. Slowly he pulled the soft tank up and over her head, dumping it on the floor. She made no move to cover herself, and Derek couldn't help but stare. The lacy white bra, now marred with crimson stains, attacked his self-control more than seeing her naked would have. It was all he could do to resist the urge to reach out and touch her soft warm skin.

"Lil—"

"I can take it from here," Lily said, a tired smile tugging at her lips.

His heart constricted. He didn't know how much more pain—emotional or physical—she could take. Most people would've already crawled into themselves and never returned. *Don't give up, Lil.*

"Right. Though, you know, I wouldn't mind helping—"

A tiny laugh escaped her, and then she cringed. Derek wanted to kick himself. He'd meant it to lighten the moment, not cause her more pain.

"Shit. Sorry. If you need anything, I'll be right outside."

He left the bathroom and pulled the door closed behind him. She may have shut him down the other day, but when it mattered most, she'd called *him*—not Ben, not George. That had to mean something, right?

He wasn't sure how she felt about him. But Derek loved that gorgeous, stubborn woman, and he wasn't about to throw in the towel on them yet.

A loud *thump* shattered the quiet room, and Lily yelped. Derek burst into the bathroom, looking around for her. "Are you okay?"

"I'm fine. Just got a little light-headed." Her voice came from inside the shower. He hadn't even realized that she'd turned on the water, so lost had he been in the newfound revelation of the depth of his feelings for her.

He stepped to just outside the shower door. Lily needed to know she could trust him, that he was safe. That she could rely on him. Derek turned his back on her mist-shrouded form, crossed his arms and waited.

"Maybe a shower isn't the best idea," he called over

his shoulder. "If you're trying to look pretty for me, I've seen you covered in blood before."

A small, soft laugh wafted up with the steam. "I'm completely—"

Derek glanced into the foggy mirror just as she swayed, then collapsed.

Shit. He yanked the shower door open. She was lying on her side. He grabbed a towel and moved to turn the water off. Then he froze at the sight of the angry purple streaks crisscrossing her back.

"What the hell?"

At first, she tried to cover herself, humiliation burning in her eyes. *Why was she acting like she'd done something wrong?* But then she pushed herself up, back toward him. Bile rose in his throat. *No wonder she always chose those high-backed dresses.* There wasn't an inch of unmarred skin left.

His blood boiled. The marks looked fairly fresh—no way they'd come from an abusive father. So who the hell had tortured her?

Lily's head hung low, and her brown hair was plastered to the side of her face. She folded her arms around herself as she turned around. "It looks worse than it feels."

Derek finally turned the water off and stepped into the shower with her. Wrapping Lily in a towel, he lifted her into his arms. She leaned into him, didn't make a sound.

He gently set her down and leaned her against the bathroom countertop.

"Who did this to you?"

She shook her head and looked down.

"Lily." Derek tipped her chin up. "Who did this to you?"

She pressed her lips together, and then sighed in defeat. "It was a parting gift from Jackson."

That wasn't in her file. "I don't understand."

"He threw me out a window," she said softly. "The glass, the fall...they're a bitch of a combo."

"He threw you out—" Derek choked on his disbelief. What the fuck was going on here? There was no doubt in his mind now that Jackson had gone rogue. You didn't throw the woman you love out of a window, no matter what cover story you were trying to keep. Derek's head spun. Too many vital pieces of intel had been left out of her file.

But on whose orders?

She frowned. "You didn't know?"

"No." His tone was murderous.

"Our last mission didn't go as smoothly as I'd hoped. Jackson asked me to join him in his little treacherous escapade. I said no." She shrugged, then winced at the movement. "He didn't like my answer, so he answered in kind."

Derek grappled for words, but came up empty. How could he even respond to something like that?

"I can still see his eyes when he let me go. I've witnessed some screwed-up things out in the field. But I've never seen such darkness before. Not like that. It was as if he wasn't there, as if he didn't see me." She looked up with haunted eyes. "He didn't see me."

The world beneath Derek gave way.

I see you.

And he wasn't going to let her go. Not now. Not

ever. He could not, would not, live his life without this woman. Somehow he'd get through her stubbornness.

"My God, Lily." Derek ran his hands over his face, feeling powerless. "I had no idea."

"Why would you? It was classified. Everything about that mission was classified. No one could know that their prize agent, their golden boy, had turned. Why the hell do you think I walked?" She pushed away from the sink. "I don't want to go round and round about something I can't change. It happened. Let's move on."

Derek took a step back and gave Lily space. He'd never had such conflicting emotions at war within himself. He wanted to take Lily in his arms and never let her go, and wanted to find Jackson and rip his throat out.

All at the same time.

She opened the cabinet door and pulled out the first-aid kit. A sad smile flickered at her lips. "Help me get cleaned up so we can track this bastard down."

Pride coursed through Derek's veins. He'd never known a more dedicated, steadfast and incredible person. Ever. This woman never ceased to amaze him.

"Yes, ma'am."

Lily leaned into the mirror and examined the bandages holding her latest gash together. Derek's throat tightened. Even with the bruising, she was stunning. The clean white towel hitched up on her thighs. His blood pounded in his ears. *Focus, man.*

"I look like Frankenstein's bride."

"No, you don't," he said, his words thick. "You're beautiful."

She slowly glanced up, catching his eyes in the mirror's reflection.

Derek didn't move. Didn't blink. His mouth went dry. There was something in her eyes that hadn't been there before.

What are you thinking, babycakes?

Without a word, she turned and stepped toward him. His stomach tightened. She put her hand against his jaw. Her warm touch sent tremors down his body.

Then she stood on her tiptoes and kissed him. Light and cautious at first, then more demanding. He froze for only a moment, then picked her up, set her down on the countertop and closed the distance between their two bodies. Every inch of his skin was on fire. She showered his face with soft kisses and pulled at his shirt.

Marcus's voice—*by the books, man*—swirled in his head.

"Wait." Derek grabbed her wrists and held her tight. He wanted her. Now. But… "Where'd this one-eighty come from? You shut the door on me, remember?"

"You scared the shit out of me." Her eyes filled with tears. "I didn't want to leave you."

"Why did you, then?"

Her face fell. Derek wanted to stop talking and pull her back into his arms, but he had to know.

"Derek, the last man I loved tried to kill me." Lily shook her head.

Did she just say "love"?

Tears brimmed in her eyes. "I never expected to love someone again, and then you dropped into my life."

Holy shit. She did say "love."

His brother's cautionary words floated through his

mind. Screw the book. Derek tipped her chin up and stared into the endless depths of her eyes. Tears glistened, then overflowed down her cheeks. He gently brushed them away with his thumbs.

"I'm not Jackson."

She caught his gaze and held it. Derek's world all but stopped. He'd never seen such transparency, such rare emotion, such raw trust, in his entire life.

Derek knew in that moment that he'd do anything for this woman. He loved her too much to ever cause her pain.

"I'm not Jackson," Derek said again, his voice husky.

"I know," Lily said, pressing her lips to his.

CHAPTER THIRTY-FOUR

Tuesday, September 30, 4:00 a.m.

LILY WAS UNDONE. Completely and irrevocably finished. The world had tipped under her when she'd looked into the mirror, saw the gentle fire burning in Derek's eyes. Clarity shot through her—he was *not* Jackson.

She loved Derek. Lily didn't think, she just went into his arms.

She hadn't realized how much she'd wanted him—needed him—until his mouth found hers, until his gentle caresses coaxed her from her hiding place. Lily let her towel fall, and with it all her inhibitions, her fear, her uncertainty.

She was his: mind, heart and soul.

"Lil," Derek said, his voice husky. He reached out, pressed two fingers to her lips, trailed them down her chin, her throat, between her breasts, until his hand rested lightly on her tiny waist.

The feathery stroke stole her breath. He cupped her face with his hand, brought his lips to hers. The kiss was soft, gentle. Inviting. Without hesitation, without pause, Lily answered its hypnotic call. She pulled him to her and wrapped her arms around his neck. His clothes were rough against her bare skin, but she didn't care.

All she cared about in this moment was Derek.

He nuzzled his lips against her throat and a small gasp escaped her. The tender touch propelled a wave of electricity through her.

Grabbing his face, she brought his lips close to hers. She wanted to taste him, feel him. His heart hammered against her chest, and his heat pressed against her. Her mouth parted, inviting him closer. His hands drew simmering lines of fire along her skin as he touched, explored.

"Take me to bed, Derek."

He hitched her up and pulled her to him. Her legs wrapped around his waist, closing any space between their two bodies. The sudden movement sent pain through her body. She winced.

He stopped moving and frowned. Reaching down, he gently touched the butterfly bandage on her stomach. "I don't want to hurt you."

"You can't hurt me." She bent her lips to his. "Take me to bed."

Hugging her naked body to him, he obliged, carefully sitting them on the edge of her bed.

He freed one hand, traced it slowly down, then up her ribs—his fingertips playing, teasing, burning. Whatever pain had zipped through her stomach vanished, replaced with a white-hot fire. Every muscle in her body tightened, responding to the desire simmering in his eyes.

"You sure?" His voice sounded hoarse, strained. "This isn't some emotional, knee-jerk reaction, is it?"

Lily loved this man and his no-nonsense, bold, honest approach to everything. His eyes searched hers. She drowned in their endless probing, *daring* her to come closer. Her heart pounded.

This was no knee-jerk reaction.

Tugging at his shirt, she yanked it over his head. He let go of her long enough to hold his arms up and aid in the process, his eyes never leaving her face.

Uneven scars—some fresh, some old—zigzagged across the tight muscles, rippling down his perfectly proportioned frame. She gasped.

He read the horrified question in her eyes and answered. "More than one mission gone wrong."

Sympathy flooded her eyes as Lily pulled her finger over the largest white scar just below his heart. She pressed her lips to raised skin.

"You understand." She looked at him.

"I understand." He kissed away the tears flowing down her cheeks.

With a featherlight touch, he trailed his fingers along her collarbone and down her arms. He reached around and traced her back. She froze. No one had ever touched her scars—no one had touched her at all, really, not since Jackson. Uncertainty gripped her heart in a tight vise and squeezed.

"You're beautiful," Derek whispered into her ear, pulling his thumb over one raised scar, then the next. "I love every inch of you."

Her throat closed with an emotion she couldn't explain. This man loved her. All of her: the good, the bad, the ugly. She relaxed, rested her forehead against his chest and closed her eyes. *He loved all of her.* He slowly drew his fingers over every scar, murmuring into Lily's ear. With each touch, each gentle caress, he stroked the desire building inside her.

She kissed him hard, tasted his sweetness and felt the softness of his tongue. He murmured her name into her mouth.

Derek lifted her up, stood and turned, gently lowering Lily onto the soft bed. He caressed her face and looked into her eyes before devouring her mouth again. He matched her passion, satisfied her need. She came up for air, breathless. Her fingers followed the muscles in his shoulders, outlined his scars, as his lips memorized every inch of her body.

He pulled away from her and grinned. Lily's heart raced. Reaching up, she pulled his head down and crushed her lips to his again. He didn't hesitate, answering hungrily. Burning, possessive lips owned hers.

He balanced his weight on one arm and brushed his fingers along her waist, back up her ribs, skimming his hand between her breasts. She wiggled, eager to feel his body against hers, skin to skin.

"Derek…"

Her insides turned molten as his lips skimmed her skin, sending a fervor through her veins. He dropped his head to her stomach and traced his fiery kisses south, down her exposed skin. Lily froze, then…

Oh, sweet Lord. She gasped and clutched the sheets with both hands. A soft moan escaped her as he found her most sensitive spot.

The tingling sensation started in her toes and grew with each soft, adoring pass of his mouth until Lily's whole body hummed. She squirmed as her body called for a sweet release.

She couldn't stand to wait any longer. "I want you now."

He looked up at her, need burning in his eyes. She

watched him step out of his jeans and forgot to breathe. She'd been around her share of perfectly sculpted men her whole life, but nothing had prepared her for what stood in front of her now. Lily crawled toward him, a ferocious desire she didn't know she possessed surging through her.

"Now, Derek."

"With pleasure." He pulled her to his chest and hauled her onto his lap. His breath hitched. "Help yourself, babycakes."

He filled her and a soft moan escaped her lips. Derek cupped Lily's breast with his hand, lowered his head. Her body arched at the sensual touch. He let go, caressed the tiny scars peppering her back with one hand.

The humming took on a feverish pitch, coiling within every single cell. Lily was fully alive. On fire. She couldn't handle it, needed the release. She pushed him onto his back.

"You set the pace, Lil."

She moved against him, took her time, fascinated with the love-drunk look spreading across Derek's face as she rode his body.

Slowly. Deliberately.

Bending low, she brushed her breasts against his bare chest. Derek groaned and grabbed her hips, pulling her closer. As they moved, heat tore through her, melting her insides. The tingling sensation returned with a vengeance. The coiling stole her breath, demanding release.

She pushed, driving against him. Harder. Faster.

The pressure built, and they rode the swell until it exploded. Lily moaned a helpless cry of release, pushed harder and fell onto his chest. Panting, she held on as if he were her lifeline.

Her blood thumped loudly in her ears as she caught her breath. *Pure ecstasy.* Derek kissed her forehead, then flopped back onto her pillows.

They lay, tangled together, and Lily listened as his heartbeat skipped, steadied, then fell in line with hers.

"Totally worth the chase," Derek murmured.

She couldn't have agreed more.

CHAPTER THIRTY-FIVE

Tuesday, September 30, 7:00 a.m.

DEREK LISTENED TO Lily's soft breathing. He'd woken with her body molded to his, her leg draped over his thigh, her face nestled against his chest. He didn't want to wake her, wanted time to stand still. Soft, warm air tickled his skin with each breath in and out. He lay there in the silence of dawn and enjoyed her closeness.

Despite his current state of bliss with the woman of his dreams cuddled to his side, naked, his damn mind refused to quiet. Something was off. Why hadn't Jackson just killed Lily? Why the forty-eight-hour ultimatum? By the looks of it, he could've easily slit her throat while she slept.

Lily stirred and nuzzled closer.

Why the hell was he thinking about Jackson with Lily in his arms? He pressed his lips to the top of her head. Then Marcus's words—*by the books, man*—shattered the fantasy forming in Derek's mind.

He slipped from Lily's embrace, slid his jeans on.

Closing the bedroom door, he made his way to the living room and grabbed his phone, keying in the numbers. It was early, but the man would be up. Derek knew his schedule like the back of his own hand.

He answered on the second ring. "Derek."

"Director, I'd like permission to speak freely."

"Go ahead, Moretti."

Derek took a deep breath. He was stepping into uncharted territory. He didn't enjoy going toe-to-toe with his commanding officer, but he had questions that demanded answers.

"Sir, I'd like to be read in on Jackson. Full disclosure."

"I'm not following."

Of course he wasn't. Derek swallowed the smart-ass response hanging on the tip of his tongue.

"You sent me here to keep an eye on him, but I'm sensing there's more to this story." Derek moved to the wall of windows, looked out as the sun danced with the horizon. Silence met him. Fine. He could play hardball, too. "She told me that Jackson was her fiancé."

The silence lengthened, and with each passing second, Derek's thin veil of patience evaporated. "Sir?"

The director cleared his throat. "That detail didn't pertain to the case, Moretti. End of story."

Derek balled his hand into a fist. *Didn't pertain to the case?* What the hell was going on with the director? It sure as hell pertained—Lily's life was at stake. "With all due respect, sir, I think it's time you read me in. I can't do my job, any of it, including protecting Lily, if I don't know what the hell is going on."

"What happened to Lily? Is she all right?"

Derek ran his hand over his hair and rubbed the back of his neck. "Jackson paid her a little visit last night."

The silence on the other end of the line was deafening. Derek bristled. *If the director knowingly put Lily in danger...* "What the hell is going on, sir?"

"Jackson was the one who first brought us Rowland."

There was a strain in the director's voice that Derek hadn't picked up on until now. He sank into the sofa. "Yes, I know Jackson had first contact with Rowland. Sir, what haven't I been told?"

"Jackson is the agent who brought Rowland to our attention, put him on our radar." The director hesitated, and it took all of Derek's willpower not to jump in with another question—because he had plenty. "Derek, this whole situation was already in motion before I pulled you into the game."

Derek had already begun to suspect as much, but he remained silent, waiting for Kennedy to continue.

"I took it up the chain of command and was instructed to kill the investigation. When I told Jackson to stand down, he refused."

"What kind of agent refuses the direct order of his commanding officer?" Derek demanded, his voice hot.

"He brought more intel to convince me—and I *am* fully convinced—that the threat Rowland presents outweighs the potential slap on the hand."

Derek couldn't believe what he was hearing. What shit storm had the director put him in? His hand curled. Forget about him. Derek could handle whatever came down the pipeline. What had the director knowingly put Lily, his own godchild, into?

Not wanting to push his luck with his commanding officer any more than he already had with this conversation, he focused on keeping his tone low and calm. "What intel? Did you authorize him to disobey your orders?"

"Yes." The director answered slowly, his voice tired. "I sent him in. Alone."

Derek's head snapped up. Alone? How was Jackson alone? Derek was here, in Omaha, with direct orders to keep an eye on the rogue agent. Who apparently wasn't a rogue agent at all.

A sinking feeling spiraled in Derek's stomach. "Alone, sir?"

The director cleared his throat. "It's completely off the books. Black. No one knows you or Jackson are in Omaha. No one *can* know. Could you imagine the type of hell that would rain down on us if any other country knew we had a black-ops mission going on in our country?"

As much as Derek wanted to reach through the phone and punch him, Kennedy had a point. It was part of the game. The game they'd all willingly signed up for.

Still...

Derek had never been on the dark side of things, not knowing every inch of an operation. And the game had never put someone Derek loved in direct danger.

That changed everything.

He got up, headed for the kitchen. He needed a drink. And given that it was barely morning, coffee would have to do. "Why Jackson?"

"Easy. He originally brought Rowland to my attention and he knows the man down to the kind of floss he uses. He asked me to send him in."

Derek reached for the coffeepot and froze. He closed his eyes and pinched the bridge of his nose and tried to keep the rage out of his voice. "So the stunt with Lily?"

"It was a staged operation. It had to look legit. And

Lily isn't an easy one to pull something over on like this." The director cleared his throat. "I admit, Jackson took it too far."

Derek's eyes popped open. "Are you shitting me right now, sir? Do you not remember that he dropped her out a three-story window?" The heat in Derek's words made his voice rise. He glanced over his shoulder, lowered his voice. "Why was he not pulled? Did no one think it prudent to yank the bastard after he tried to kill his partner?"

"We tried, Derek," Kennedy said, his voice drawn. "He went dark. You know the percentage of people we lose when they go under."

Derek knew.

He'd almost gotten lost himself.

It was his first solo mission with Unit 67. He'd been young, fearless…and stupid. He'd mentally prepped for having access to a safe house. Instead, he'd been forced to bed down within his target's compound, with no reprieve from his cover, no time to clear his head from the atrocities he'd witnessed on a daily, sometimes hourly, basis.

While it pissed him off because it directly affected Lily, Derek understood the slippery slope that may have led to Jackson's ultimate betrayal.

The number of agents who went dark was staggering. Everyone needed someone to tether to, to be reminded of the humanity hidden deep within his or her cover. Without that tie, it was easy to float away into the black pit of undercover oblivion and never return.

"Is that why I'm here?"

The director didn't respond.

Derek's shoulders tensed. Fire raced through his

bones. He spoke through clenched teeth. "Is that why I'm here?" he repeated. "To babysit an asset that should've been neutralized? Not to mention protect the agent—your agent—who unknowingly moved to the same location where her potential killer lives? With all due respect, sir, are you crazy?"

"Moretti, that's enough."

Derek sagged against the counter. He'd pushed too far, but it wasn't just his life in danger. It was his family's. *It was Lily's.* "Do we have control of our asset or not?"

"I don't know. I'm still hoping."

Derek was losing his internal battle to keep the steel out of his voice. *Hoping?* "Jackson scared the shit out of Lily, sir. He gave her a forty-eight-hour ultimatum. There's no way that bastard is under control. It's time to take him out."

"I can't authorize that, Derek," the director said quietly.

"Why the hell not?"

"If Jackson paid Lily a visit and she's still alive, we haven't lost him yet, no matter how bizarre or intense his behavior may be. Jackson can still be saved."

Derek recognized that tone. Director Kennedy believed there was hope, end of story.

"Sir…"

"Let it go, Moretti."

And the director was gone. *Son of a bitch.*

Derek walked to the bedroom door and cracked it open. Lily hadn't moved. The world shifted under his feet as he watched the slow rise and fall of her chest.

They may not have lost Jackson, but Derek was pretty sure he'd just lost her. He couldn't compete with whatever love she may still have for Jackson. How could Derek expect Lily to love him when her fiancé wasn't rogue—but was likely still one of them?

Derek shut the door and leaned his head against it. His throat tightened. He'd given Marcus so much shit when Evelyn blew into his life and turned his little brother into a teddy bear.

Derek got it now.

Lily had done the same to him—rocked his world and turned it upside down.

Only unlike his brother, Derek's world wouldn't end like the fairy tales they'd given their little sister shit about growing up. He wasn't sure how a human could experience such ecstasy in one moment and such shattering grief in the next.

If Jackson was truly still undercover, then all his actions were part of the game, most likely cloaking his true intentions. Derek knew all too well about doing one thing, but feeling the polar opposite.

Derek blinked back tears.

Lily wasn't his to have.

CHAPTER THIRTY-SIX

Tuesday, September 30, 9:00 a.m.

LILY STOPPED IN FRONT of Keystone Café, hesitated. The door to the left of the café's entrance led to Ben's upstairs apartment, the door to the right opened into Keystone's inviting café. All she wanted was to push Keystone's door open and enjoy a nice latte, forgetting about the current shit storm they were in. But she'd woken up to a nice shiner, compliments of Jackson and the corner of her dresser, and didn't think Ben would appreciate her scaring his customers.

She squared her shoulders. "Might as well get this over with. I don't know which will be worse—telling them about Jackson's ultimatum, or hearing Ben's tongue-lashing about getting hurt again."

Derek didn't respond. He pushed Ben's door open and walked up the steps toward Ben's second-floor apartment.

Lily stared after Derek, a lump forming her throat. He'd said all of three sentences to her since she woke up. She hadn't expected the about-face after last night, but here they were. A strange emptiness settled over her.

There were bigger issues to deal with than the man she'd fallen for being a jackass.

She was two for two now. *How fabulous.*

Lily knew Derek had already filled them in on her late-night visitor. That was one of the three sentences he'd spoken to her. Had he told them he'd also stayed the night? Doubtful.

Plastering on a casual expression, she followed up the stairs behind him. Pushing open the top door, three concerned faces greeted them. Evelyn's eyes widened and Marcus shot Derek a disapproving look, the muscle in his jaw clenching.

"What the hell, Lil?" Ben gently touched her face.

"It looks worse than it feels, promise." Lily shrugged. "Besides, you should've seen Jackson."

Ben's eyebrows arched and he crossed his arms over his chest. "I'm not finding any humor in this situation."

Yeah, well, neither did she.

But she needed something to defend herself from the advancing emotions threatening to take her out. She couldn't believe how many times she'd failed in the past year. And every single one of them was directly tied to Jackson. What the hell was her problem? She'd underestimated him every step of the way, and now she couldn't find her footing to move forward.

All she had was her bad humor. It was a shield. Nothing more.

Lily glanced at Derek and got caught in the intensity of his gaze. He saw through her smokescreen. She could feel it…or at least, she thought she had. She glanced away, her cheeks flushed. Her mind tumbled over itself. He was giving her emotional whiplash with his freaking mixed signals.

She didn't have time for this shit. Whatever they'd had last night—and it was beyond amazing—was apparently in the past, merely a sexy memory. If he couldn't figure out what he wanted from her, then she'd decide for him. And he wouldn't like it.

Neither of them would.

Evelyn pushed back a strand of Lily's hair and touched the angry-looking black eye. "What are you going to tell Rowland tomorrow?"

Evelyn's touch, warm and safe, melted the hardness around Lily's heart, and her chin quivered. Damn, she was going to miss Evelyn when this case wrapped. Lily had never known what female friendship was like, never even wanted it...until Evelyn.

"Nothing a little cover-up can't conceal." Lily stepped back. "Right?"

Evelyn's head tilted to one side, then the other. Pursing her lips, she tapped her fingers against them. Lily frowned. What was going on in that brain of hers? Then, almost as if in answer to Lily's silent query, Evelyn's eyes lit up.

"This is actually perfect. Jackson just gave us our ace card."

"He did?"

"He did." Evelyn smiled wickedly and pointed at Marcus. "You tell Rowland you don't tolerate business and pleasure mixing, and that you've *disposed* of the problem."

"Love it." Marcus grinned and threw Evelyn a sexy look. "Care to be my new eye candy?"

"I wouldn't miss it for the world." Evelyn went to stand next to Marcus, grinning up at Lily. "Problem solved."

Marcus wrapped his arm around Evelyn's waist. She leaned closer and draped her arm over his shoulders.

A dull ache throbbed in Lily's chest as she watched Evelyn melt into her husband's side.

"We take a few mocked-up photos of you to prove his point to Rowland. And that gets you—" Evelyn pointed to Lily "—out of the picture, and solidifies Marcus's position of power in Rowland's mind."

Derek double-tapped the table with his knuckles. "You're a freaking genius, Ev."

Evelyn rolled her eyes as a rosy sheen covered her cheeks. "Not really. I've just worked around my share of psychotic, narcissistic killers. Deep in their bones, they're all the same. They want power. They only respond to power. It's the only thing they respect."

Lily strummed her fingers against her leg and chewed on her lips. Evelyn was spot-on in her discernment of Rowland's ego. It would definitely work. And it gave Lily the out she wanted but refused to voice. She needed space to refocus and reengage.

Jackson hadn't taken her out after throwing her from a building. He wouldn't do it now with an ultimatum.

Lily nodded and smiled. "I like it."

LATE THAT NIGHT, Derek walked into Ben's home. He'd stuck to John Elsworth's side like a tick on a dog and gotten nothing. Rowland was mysteriously absent, and John had been quiet all day. Derek kicked the door closed, pulled out his .45, checked the safety and put it on the foyer table.

His firearm was the fourth in a neat row.

He glanced over his shoulder. Lily and Evelyn huddled over files spread across the dining table. Marcus stood at the stove, playing Julia Child again. The smell wafting from the pot lured a growl from Derek's stomach.

Lily looked up. Sadness washed over her face, and his throat tightened. The pain she tried to mask flickered just behind her veiled eyes, and he wanted to punch the wall.

He'd done that.

Instead of manning up and just telling Lily about Jackson, Derek had gone and taken the cowardly road.

He'd tucked tail and ran.

Without a word, he walked into the kitchen. Opening the fridge, he pulled out a Guinness and popped it open, took a deep swig. He peered over at Lily. He couldn't take his eyes off her. Her face lit up at something Evelyn said, and Lily laughed.

Derek's heart sank.

Lily fit perfectly here. With them. With him.

Or at least she would have.

"Fuck me," he muttered and turned his back.

Marcus threw Derek a sideways glance. "You going to tell her about Jackson?"

"Can't." Derek shook his head. "There's a gag order on this now. Direct from the big man himself."

Marcus stopped stirring and put the ladle down. "No shit?"

Neither one of them spoke for several minutes. Which was perfectly fine with Derek. He should've kept the line drawn with Lily. If he hadn't gotten emotionally involved, this whole thing would've been easier. For both of them.

In. Out. Done.

Only problem? He *had* gotten emotionally involved.

It was inevitable with Lily. The moment he'd spied her in Arlington, he'd known he was in trouble.

Lily was everything he wanted.

In a woman, a lover, a wife.

In. Out. Done? Yeah, no way. Derek was all in.

And now he was drowning.

"You okay?"

Derek rubbed the back of his neck. He'd expected his little brother to do his psychological thing on him and, at some point, address the elephant in the room. But he hadn't expected Marcus's simple question to shoot him through the heart.

Hanging his head, Derek leaned against the counter. "She was it, man. I'd met my match."

Marcus whistled softly. "Sorry, brother. What are you going to do?"

Derek took another swig of his beer. He shrugged. "The only thing I can do. Shut it down. Keep her safe, finish the mission and get the hell out of dodge, then go somewhere to lick my wounds."

A surprised expression flickered on Marcus's face. "That bad?"

Derek glanced over at the two women, huddled together, their heads bent over the files. The knot returned to his throat.

"She was my Evelyn, man."

CHAPTER THIRTY-SEVEN

Wednesday, October 1, 11:00 a.m.

ROOFTOP COVER WAS ESSENTIAL. Lily pressed herself against the hot roof and breathed softly, slowing her heart rate with each calculated breath. Her incision pulled, but she zoned it out. Excitement zipped through her veins. Eager tension pulled her muscles tight. She peered through her sniper scope, saw Rowland's Bentley turn the corner.

Lily reached up, pressed the button on her radio link. "Rowland's car is approaching. He appears to be with his bodyguard and driver."

"Got him." Derek's voice crackled in her ear. "Other than that gorgeous car, it's quiet on my end."

She couldn't have agreed more. The Bentley was exquisite. Lily smiled and glanced across to Derek. He was crouched behind the large HVAC system one hundred feet away.

Ass or not, he was sexy as hell and, despite her best efforts, still made her heart race.

What had happened? Why was he suddenly treating her as if they hadn't shared something mind-blowing, as if she were merely one of his male counterparts? Warmth spread through her at the memory of his body pressed against hers. There was nothing platonic about what they had shared the other night. So what was his freaking problem?

She shook her head, peered back through the scope and locked her sights on Marcus and Evelyn. "Copy that."

"Three to two aren't bad odds." Marcus winked at Evelyn.

"Make that four to two." Lily looped her finger inside the trigger and rested her finger on it. "Poor, cocky bastard. He has no idea that the odds are squarely in our favor."

Evelyn wrapped her arm around Marcus and nestled close. She looked every bit the supermodel she'd once been in her tight black pencil shirt and short jacket. And Marcus…well, he was a Moretti. Lily tapped the talk button again. "Rowland's not even going to remember me, Evelyn. I wish I had your genes."

Marcus patted Evelyn on the ass, and she smirked. Lily bit her lip to keep the smile off her face. She was going to miss those two once this mission wrapped.

"Step lightly, folks," Derek said, all business. "It's game time."

All joking ceased, and game faces went on. Lily settled into her spot on the roof behind the second HVAC and peeked through her scope again.

Rowland's car pulled up and stopped. JB came around, scanned the area and opened the door. Rowland stepped out and straightened his jacket. He looked over at Marcus and frowned.

"Where's Addison?"

"I don't take lightly to my people disobeying orders. She's no longer of importance," Marcus retorted in a sharp, biting tone. "Or any of your concern."

Lily smiled smugly. Damn, he was good. If she didn't know any better, she'd think he was a mean SOB. *Pile it on, Marcus.* She smirked and peered through the eyepiece again.

Rowland didn't move. Lily tensed, glanced between the two men. *Come on, Rowland. Take the bait. Take the bait.*

Marcus snatched his sunglasses off his face and glared at Rowland, his eyes hard. "I'm sensing hesitation, Mr. James. I'd hoped you'd take me at my word, but I refuse to let the incompetence of my hired help jeopardize this deal. If you must see proof..."

Rowland held up a hand. "No, that's not necessary."

"Very well." Marcus nodded. "Shall we proceed?"

Rowland glanced past Marcus, taking in Evelyn. Lily's skin crawled. "While I certainly enjoyed Addison's company, it certainly appears *you* don't lack companionship."

Marcus's jaw tightened. Evelyn, ever the professional, smiled.

"Are we here to discuss my companions or my business proposition?"

Rowland glanced between Marcus and Evelyn. His lips pressed together in a fine line, and his face darkened. "Before we proceed, I have someone I'd like you to meet."

He nodded to JB, who took out his phone and spoke into it.

Lily increased the pressure on her trigger. She scanned the area. Nothing. She steadied her breath, slowed her heartbeat and focused. "Derek, what do you see?"

"I've got nothing."

Marcus scowled at JB. "I never agreed to discuss anything with a third party."

"Yes, well." Rowland took off his sunglasses and cut his gaze to Marcus. Murder danced on his face. "I never agreed to having your whore sent after me, did I? If you want to do business with me, it's on my terms, not yours. And it would be in your best interest to recognize that. Quickly."

"I don't take kindly to threats, Mr. James." Marcus moved toward Rowland, his words cold, hard. Evelyn reached out, grabbed Marcus's arm.

"And I don't take kindly to being blindsided. No matter how much money is involved."

Evelyn let go of Marcus, stepped to the side and clasped her hands in front of her. Lily caught the slight twitch in Evelyn's trigger finger and smiled. Was the urge to reach for the thigh holster surging through her? If the roles were reversed, Lily sure as hell would have felt it.

"Nice restraint, Davis."

The two men squared off. Marcus fascinated Lily. Every time she thought she'd figured him out, a new aspect of his genius emerged. Did Derek have similar characteristics? Deep facets she'd yet to uncover? Sadness fell over her. The way things were looking, she might never find out.

Rein it in, Andrews.

"This is the last time you switch things up on me, Rowland. Do it again, and you won't like the consequences."

Rowland blinked hard. The vein in his neck bulged. Time stood still.

Lily held her breath. Raw unease bombarded her

nerves. Every muscle in her body tensed. The same brutal look she'd seen in Rowland's eyes before he'd stabbed her flashed in his eyes now. She had no doubt that he wanted to reach out and kill Marcus.

"Derek…"

"I see it, Lil. Marcus, I don't like this—"

Evelyn stepped close to Marcus, put her hand on his arm. "Gentlemen, I do believe we're here for a business discussion, not a measuring contest."

Rowland's eyebrows arched with a hint of amusement.

Evelyn threw him a sensual smile. "So can we all tuck it back in and continue?"

Rowland nodded and put his sunglasses back on. JB pocketed his phone. Another Bentley pulled to a stop behind Rowland's. Its windows were tinted a deep black.

Blood pounded in Lily's ear. With each frantic beat of her heart, the deep throb kicked against her eardrum. "You see this, Derek?"

"I got it. But I can't see shit. Repositioning now. Need a better angle."

Marcus reached his arm around Evelyn, his fingers sliding under her jacket, reaching for the gun. JB's face darkened. He reached for his sidearm.

Lily's heart skipped, threatened to stop. "Marcus, don't. Grab her waist. Do it now."

Marcus responded instantly, pulling Evelyn close and tucking her behind his body. JB relaxed his stance, but his eyes narrowed. He kept his hand on the butt of his gun.

The mystery car's back door opened. Lily swung

her scope and zeroed in on the passenger. Jackson sat in the back.

Holy shit. Lily's heart plummeted.

"Well, I'll be damned," Derek muttered, a strange mixture of awe and venom swirling in his voice. "Who knew this could get any more fucked?"

Lily couldn't have agreed more.

Jackson unfolded himself from the car, buttoned his sports coat and moved toward Rowland. Lily studied his face. Did he know he approached the very people who'd pulled his file? The team he'd threatened? Jackson stopped, cocked his head to the side and openly stared at the supermodel couple standing in front of him.

"I'll take him out," Lily whispered, her voice hard. "I swear, if he makes even the slightest wrong move, I'll—"

She stopped short. Wondered if her words sounded as menacing, as *ugly*, to everyone else. Or was it just her?

"Easy," Derek murmured.

And there was her answer. Lily cringed. Heat burned her face.

Rowland moved to Jackson's side. They kissed each other on the cheeks like two old Italian men. *What the hell?* Rowland spoke into Jackson's ear. He looked over Rowland's shoulder, smirked, glanced back at Rowland and shook his head.

Lily tensed.

"Mr. Young, this is Desmund De Luca." Rowland motioned to Marcus and Evelyn, then tipped his head toward Jackson. "Mr. De Luca, Jackson Young."

Why had Jackson given Rowland his real name?

She gritted her teeth. Was that even his real name, or just an alias he'd used with her…his fiancée? She took a deep, shaky breath.

Ex-fiancée.

"Easy with that trigger finger, Lily," Derek cautioned into her earpiece.

She threw him a searing look. His quiet laughter bounced loudly in her ear. *Ass.* Turning her attention back to the show playing out below her, she ignored her sexy rooftop companion.

TWO HUNDRED YARDS AWAY, hidden within the confines of an empty room, a pair of green eyes watched Rowland through the scope of the SR-25. He'd stepped over the line too many times over the past few months. He deserved what was coming to him.

Lights out for you, you bastard.

The scope aligned perfectly, and a finger twitched restlessly on the trigger. *Just a hair more…*

A flash to the sniper's right. The scope swung. Derek Moretti and Addison Moore filled its crosshairs. *Well, now, isn't this an interesting plot twist.*

Rowland James could wait. He'd get what was coming to him, but first, time to deal with the dynamic duo interrupting this moment.

The sniper recalibrated the weapon, looped a finger through the trigger. Derek and Addison had not been invited to this party. *Time to say goodbye…*

CHAPTER THIRTY-EIGHT

Wednesday, October 1, 11:45 a.m.

DAMN, HIS LITTLE brother was good. Derek rested his forehead against the hot rooftop. His shoulders relaxed, the spasms in the pit of his stomach vanished. Marcus solidified the deal: five of Rowland's weapons for half a billion dollars. The drop? Next Monday. That gave them less than a week to bring this thing home.

When Marcus and Rowland had stepped toward each other, Derek had expected bullets to fly. In that moment, he'd contemplated aborting the mission, getting his team the hell out of dodge. But then Evelyn had moved in like a pro, enchanting Rowland like a snake charmer, and gotten them all back on track. *The woman was fearless.*

She reminded Derek of the woman on the other end of the roof.

His gaze flipped from Marcus to Lily. She looked coiled, ready to spring.

He'd go into any location with her at his six without a moment's hesitation. The glowing report in her file paled in comparison to the kickass woman in a real-life combat situation.

But the longer Jackson stood in her scope, the harder her face grew.

"Until our next meet, then." Marcus's smooth voice broke through Derek's mental musing.

He peered through his binoculars. Jackson reached out, shook hands with Marcus and walked back to his car. JB and Rowland followed suit. The strain twisting in Derek's neck loosened as both Bentleys drove off.

Out of habit, Derek panned the surrounding buildings. A tiny movement, a subtle flash. *What the...? Shit!* He dropped the binoculars, sprinted and dove, grabbing Lily around the waist, taking her down with him.

Three slugs hit the ground she'd just occupied, one after the other, kicking up chunks of the rooftop.

"Sniper! We're taking fire up here!"

Lily pushed to her knees and scrambled for cover. Head down, he followed, praying Marcus and Evelyn would get the hell out of there.

"Go. Go. Go." Derek motioned Lily away from the open air.

She ran, sidestepped and pushed her back up against the HVAC at the far end of the building.

Sixty feet from the nearest exit. Damn.

It wasn't ideal, but it was all they had.

"Hold your position." Marcus's command burst into Derek's earpiece. "We're on our way up."

"No!" Derek and Lily cried in unison.

"Negative," Derek said. "You'd be walking into this blind. He's got a silencer. I can't get a read on his exact location."

Lily glanced over at Derek. "Where is he?"

Derek scanned the area, got nothing. Scanned again. Then the muzzle flashed.

"Bastard's in the building on the northwest corner,

top floor." Derek paused and quickly counted the windows. "Third or fourth in. I think."

"Copy that," Evelyn said. "We'll make our way there now and try to find him."

"Proceed with caution."

"Don't get dead, brother."

"I'll work on that," Derek muttered.

He had only one focus now: get Lily to safety.

"Where'd this joker come from?" Lily dropped her empty magazine, pulled another and reloaded. "How'd he even know we'd be here?"

Great question. The hair on the back of his neck bristled. If all their known players were in the courtyard below, who was shooting at them?

Another slug pierced the wall behind them.

Lily reached for the extra gun strapped to her thigh. He pushed her down and returned fire. She rolled onto a knee and brought both guns up. A bullet lodged into the space above her head.

"Damn it, Lily. Stay down."

"You first." She aimed at their mysterious sniper and pulled her trigger.

Fury and wonderment battled for first place within Derek's mind. God, he loved this woman. But if anything happened to her because of her stubborn warrior spirit, he'd never forgive himself.

His body jerked suddenly. A searing pain penetrated his right arm. He dropped his gun and inventoried the flayed, slightly charred flesh—nothing more than a graze. Derek scrambled, palmed the gun with his left hand and returned fire.

"He's got the vantage point," Lily called over her

shoulder. "We have to get off this roof. We're sitting ducks up here."

Derek glanced around. The next cover was thirty feet. "HVAC to stairs?"

A bullet flew past Lily's head and she ducked.

Derek pulled up both hands, returned fire. Pain ripped through his injured arm. He winced and reached for his shoulder.

Lily glanced at him. "Derek?"

He waved his gun in a quick circle as if to prove to both of them that he was fine. "Just grazed."

She left her shelter. *What the hell was she doing?* She dodged, scrambled and dove for cover next to him. Another bullet kicked up the rooftop to their right. She reached over and lifted his torn shirt. Sucking in air, she shot him a hot, pissed glare.

Even furious, she was gorgeous.

"Just grazed, my ass."

He shrugged, then flinched. "It's nothing I haven't dealt with before."

She scowled and pointed toward the door leading to the staircase. "Go. I'll cover you."

"Not happening."

"Stop being stubborn and move your ass."

The muscle in her jaw tightened. She'd stepped into the commanding role. Funny. He didn't mind it at all. The ease with which they switched roles shocked and excited him. She was his equal in every aspect of the word.

Still…equal or not, he wanted her off this roof.

First.

He grinned through clenched teeth. "Not gonna happen, babycakes. Go."

"Are you kidding me right now?"

"Nope."

She shook her head and muttered something under her breath. Finally, she glared at him. "You're such a stubborn—"

Three more bullets flew by their heads. They both slid farther down the wall, dropping as low as they could.

"Fine. We go together."

"After you." Derek winked.

She rolled her eyes, then raised both guns, took a deep breath and hauled ass with Derek right behind her.

CHAPTER THIRTY-NINE

Wednesday, October 1, 1:10 p.m.

LILY AND DEREK doubled back. Then did it again. If they'd been followed, they would've spotted someone by now, so she gradually slowed their pace. She hitched her black bag higher on her shoulder and tucked a piece of hair behind one ear. Not that that would do anything to help her appearance. They probably both looked as though they'd just walked out of a war zone.

Sirens wailed in the distance. She folded her gun close to her side. No need to get the public riled up any more than their rooftop shoot-out already had.

Lily glanced at Derek. Weren't they a pair? Between the two of them, one was always bleeding all over the place.

Without thinking, she grabbed Derek's hand and held on tight. "It's going to be okay."

He laced his fingers through hers. Electric fire zipped through her. Lily dropped his hand as though she'd been burned. "Sorry."

He gave her a small smile. "I'm not."

There go those mixed messages again. She sighed, put her arm around his waist, picked up their pace again and made her way to Ben's.

LILY OPENED THE door to Ben's house and stumbled in under Derek's weight. She glanced up and looked down the barrel of two Glocks.

"Really?" She kicked the door closed behind her. "Enough with the guns in my face."

Marcus and Evelyn holstered their guns. Marcus reached for Derek, shouldering his weight. Evelyn pulled Lily into a bear hug.

"We thought you were dead." Tears glistened in Evelyn's eyes.

"Yeah, well, we're dead no more." Lily tossed her black bag on the floor, and the spent firearms clanked together. She shot Derek a sizzling look. "Though this one is trying his hardest."

Marcus frowned. "Shit, brother, did you have to go and get yourself shot?"

"Yes, I stood up and asked to be his target," Derek said drily, joking despite the obvious pain etched into his face.

Lily swallowed the snarky remark on the tip of her tongue and pawed through her black bag, letting Marcus deal with his big brother.

She pulled out her .45, checked the magazine, chambered a round and set it on the foyer table. It wasn't her normal procedure to have a gun with a bullet in its chamber, ready to be shot at the pull of the trigger. But then again, there was nothing normal about their current situation.

Which she hated. She wasn't leaving anything up to chance. The second it took her to chamber that bullet could be the difference between life and death for all of them. No one was dying on her watch. She chambered the next gun and set it on the table.

Evelyn pointed at Derek's shirt and frowned. "That's a lot of blood, Derek."

"It's nothing." He sank into the chair closest to him, sucking in a sharp breath. "Okay, maybe it's a little more than nothing."

Derek's hot gaze dug into Lily's back, but she ignored it. If she made eye contact with that stubborn man now, she'd most definitely tell him off—not out of anger, but fear. She bent her head and pressed her eyes closed. The world had fallen out from under Lily when she'd seen him on that rooftop, bloodied. All she'd wanted to do was cover him and get the hell out of there.

True, it wasn't the first battle wound she'd seen, or the worst, really, but it was the first on Derek. A knife twisting in her gut would have been easier to deal with than seeing all that blood on him. It scared the shit out of her.

Despite her best efforts to write him off, and tuck her heart safely back in place behind an impenetrable wall, she still cared for him. *A lot.* One glance from him, and it was as if she'd stepped off a cliff and was free-falling. She reached into the bag, grabbed another .32 and repeated her process.

She couldn't decide which was worse: the fact that she still cared, or that he might not.

Unstrapping her thigh holster, she tossed it on the foyer table and glanced at Derek. The bullet had sliced through his shoulder. Not the end of the world, but still…

Lily moved to his side and gently pressed her fingers to the skin around the wound. "Evelyn, can you grab the first-aid suture kit under the sink? Marcus, there are towels in the hall closet. I'm going to need some."

"Yes, ma'am." Marcus turned and walked down the hall.

"Preferably the black ones," Lily called after him.

Evelyn headed for the kitchen and came back within seconds. She tossed the bag to Lily. Lily opened it and took out a pair of scissors.

Derek flinched. "What are those—"

"Not a word from you, buddy." She attacked the fabric keeping the shirt in place. Without touching the burned flesh, she gently tugged the shirt off and let it fall to the floor.

Vivid memories of the last time she'd seen him without a shirt flooded her mind. Heat rushed her cheeks. She froze. Her fingers itched to reach out and trace the scars.

Derek glanced up, cocked his head to the side. "What's going on in that pretty little head of yours?"

She turned her attention to the first aid kit and dug for the stitching supplies, then glared up at him. "What part of 'do not talk' do you not understand?"

"Touché." Derek gave her a weak smile.

"*Now* who needs to be stitched up?"

"Aren't we a pair?" He shut his eyes and leaned his head back against the wall.

The needle hung in midair. Yes, they were quite the pair. Lily's throat tightened. Or could've been—if he hadn't pushed her away. She shook her head and focused on stitching him up.

"Did anyone else notice how shockingly inaccurate that shooter was?" She tugged at a stitch.

Derek cringed. "Easy, tiger."

"I'm not complaining. If the shooter had been a true marksman, we'd both be dead."

Derek opened one eye. "I wondered that myself. He knew the correct location, but the bullets never even came close."

Never came close? What constituted close, a bullet through his thick head? Lily threw him a scorching look and yanked at the last stitch. "Really?"

Marcus and Evelyn glanced at each other and smiled.

"We got nothing in our sweep." Evelyn piped up. "So who was he?"

Lily shrugged. "Good question."

"You think Jackson brought him in?" Marcus leaned next to Evelyn, looped his hands together and pulled at his neck.

Did Jackson have that venomous a personality? Could he have really sent a sniper after them? Somehow Lily doubted that he'd let someone else take her out. He'd want to do that himself. Prove that she'd made the wrong choice.

"It's possible."

Ben burst through the door. Marcus straightened and reached for his gun. Evelyn jumped off the counter and pulled out her Glock in one fluid motion. Lily cringed. She'd neglected to call him. And George, come to think of it.

If Jackson didn't kill her, one of them surely would if she kept forgetting to check in.

Ben looked around and his gaze landed on Derek. The top of his bald head turned bright red. *Uh-oh.* "Did no one think it necessary to tell me you were all back, or that one of you was *shot*?"

Marcus and Evelyn holstered their weapons.

"Sorry, Ben." Lily placed the bandage over Derek's wound. "We were a little preoccupied."

"Yes, I see that." Ben crossed his arms and glared at her. "What happened out there?"

"Rowland verbally agreed to sell me five of his little bombs in a bag." Marcus tossed Ben a small recorder. "For the small sum of half a billion dollars."

Ben caught the recorder with one hand. "Was that before or after bullets started flying?"

"Before."

Turning, Ben pinned Derek with a dark, furious look. "Did you already forget about our little arrangement, Moretti?"

An arrangement? What did that mean? Lily glanced up at Derek. He averted his eyes, refusing to meet her stony face. The muscle in his jaw jumped. She double-checked the bandage, then stepped back.

"No, sir, I have not. I have no idea what happened." Derek cradled his arm to his side. "One minute I was watching Jackson and Rowland getting into their respective cars. The next, bullets were flying. If I hadn't spotted the shooter, Lily would be—"

Ben spun and glared at her. "Are you done trying to get yourself killed?"

She bristled. It wasn't as though she'd set out to land in the middle of this pile of crap. It was supposed to be easy in, easy out. Grab the necessary intel to lock Rowland up and get back to tracking Jackson.

She should have known better.

With Jackson involved, nothing was simple.

CHAPTER FORTY

Wednesday, October 1, 5:00 p.m.

LILY FELT TRAPPED. Again. She'd put in a call to Director Kennedy, only to be told that he was in an urgent, classified meeting and couldn't be disturbed. So she'd pulled out the tattered card and punched in his private number.

It went straight to voice mail.

She threw herself into the large recliner and crossed her legs. Derek lay sprawled out on the sofa next to her, softly snoring. He held his arm to his chest. Even in sleep, his face pinched in pain with each rise and fall of his torso. Ben tinkered in his garage, his way of blowing off steam, and Marcus and Evelyn had taken over the table. They pored through their files, hoping to find something, anything, that would help them figure out what the hell had gone wrong and shed some light on the identity of their mystery sniper.

Lily didn't have much hope that the files would relinquish anything new.

She glanced into the kitchen, at the clock hanging above the stove.

The forty-eight-hour deadline had passed.

She breathed a sigh of relief. Her team was still safe. Everyone she loved was safe. *Take that, you little bas-*

tard. Suddenly her blood turned to ice. *George.* Lily
snatched up her phone, dialed his cell. It went straight
to voice mail. She hung up, punched in the concierge's
number. It rang. And rang. And rang. Her hand trembled as she hit the end button.

Lily jumped up and grabbed her keys. "I need to
check something on my computer."

Marcus peered up at her over the top of the file in
his hand. "Your computer, as in at your place?"

Evelyn tipped her head to the side and quietly studied Lily. She resisted the urge to fidget. Did she dare
tell them why she really needed to go to her place?
That she feared for George? If she voiced that, if she
voiced her concern for George's safety, they wouldn't
let her leave. And she needed to go.

Right. This. Second.

She glanced at Derek. He was still asleep. *Good.
Let's keep it that way.* She didn't have a moment to
waste. She needed to go now. So she smiled softly,
shrugged. "It's important."

"It's *important*?" Marcus's brows bunched together
suspiciously.

Lily glanced away, not wanting him to use his psychological voodoo to read her.

Evelyn pushed back from the table and rose. She
kissed the top of Marcus's head. "I'll go with her."

"That's okay." Lily waved her hand in the air, playing down the urgency that ripped through every cell in
her body. "I'll be back shortly. No big deal."

Evelyn grabbed her jacket and pushed an arm
through. "I wasn't asking for permission."

"Fine." Lily reached for the door and pulled it open. It creaked slightly. She grimaced, stopped midstep and peered over her shoulder at Derek.

He had bolted upright and his gaze landed on Lily. *Great.* Shoving himself up, he moved toward the door. "Where do you think you're going?"

Lily held up a hand. "I don't need a babysitter, Derek. And you need to get more rest."

"I don't need more rest."

Look who'd woken up as a caveman?

Evelyn stepped in between Lily and Derek and put a hand on his cheek. "She's fine, Derek. I'm going with her. You stay and rest."

THEY WALKED THREE blocks in silence. Lily hadn't wanted company, but at least she wasn't under Derek's thumb.

"So why are we *really* going to your place, Lil?"

Lily shoved her hands into her jacket pocket. "How'd you know?"

"We're more similar than you might think." Evelyn stopped, turning to face Lily. "So why are we really going back?"

"George."

"You're worried about your former black-ops doorman?" Evelyn asked.

"I know it sounds absurd, but I can't shake this feeling that something is wrong. I just need to check in, see him."

"And a call wouldn't suffice?"

"He didn't answer any of my calls. He's probably in the bathroom, or something ridiculously lame." Lily scrunched her nose. "But I need to see him face-to-face, make sure he's okay."

Evelyn studied Lily's face, then shrugged. "Fair enough."

Lily chewed on her lip. "Thanks for rescuing me back there."

"I admit, sometimes the barbarian persona can get a bit annoying, even though it's done with the best of intentions."

A small laugh bubbled out of Lily's throat before she could swallow it. *Annoying* wasn't the word she would have chosen for Derek's behavior. It definitely wasn't strong enough. Derek's caveman stunt was ridiculous.

"Lil, believe me when I tell you he's only trying to keep you safe."

"Not sure why he cares," Lily groused and hunched her shoulders against the wind.

They turned the corner. Lily's building was across the street. Urgency breathed down her neck, pressing her forward. The lobby's light shone brightly against the inky evening sky.

A frown scrunched Evelyn's beautiful features. "Are you that bl—"

Lily grabbed Evelyn's arm. "Stop."

She pulled up, went quiet. Scanned the street.

Lily's eyes were trained on her building. George wasn't at the door. No one was in the lobby. She squinted.

No one was in the lobby.

She fought to breathe. Every muscle in her body coiled. Her sixth sense screamed at her. To go. To get to George. Now.

Sirens wailed in the distance.

Lily took off, sprinted across the street. Car horns screamed at her as vehicles skidded to a halt. She dodged, jumped and slid over the hood of one car. Her feet hit the ground and she pushed her body harder.

Be okay, George. Please be okay.

She burst into the lobby and slammed to a stop.

Three large red words were scrawled across the white marble wall behind the concierge desk…George's desk.

YOU WERE WARNED

Lily clasped her hand over her mouth to keep the scream from bouncing off the walls. Her legs threatened to give out.

Please, God, don't let this be happening.

She launched herself over the desk. Tears flooded her eyes. George—the man she'd always looked up to, her protector, her friend—lay in a dark puddle, his eyes open, his body riddled with crimson slashes.

Lily dropped to her knees and cradled her head in her hands, rocking back and forth. *George.* She swatted the tears away and reached for him. "George, please…"

Evelyn threw her arm out. "Don't touch him. Lily, *don't* touch him."

Lily's hand dropped to her side. She knew better. She couldn't—wouldn't—contaminate the scene. Not that the authorities would find anything. He was too perfect. He wouldn't leave anything pointing back to him.

She knew.

He'd trained her.

A sob broke through her lips. Why hadn't she

thought about George earlier? Where had her mind been? How could she have forgotten about him? He was more than just the man who'd pledged his life to protect hers.

He was family.

A crushing pressure slammed into her chest. Lily couldn't breathe. Her vision blurred. How the hell could she have forgotten about him?

The sirens wailing in the distance grew louder. Evelyn's head snapped up. She pulled Lily to her feet.

Lily stumbled, grabbed the desk. "I think I'm going to be sick."

"Swallow it," Evelyn snapped, tugging at Lily's arm. "We don't have time to get caught up in the red tape. You can give a statement later. We have to go. Now."

Lily looked over her shoulder. The image of George lying in a pool of his own blood seared itself into her mind. Her throat burned with raw emotion.

How could she leave him? Just walk away?

Evelyn pushed her out the door. "There's nothing we can do for George now, except nail the bastard who took him."

Lily blinked back hot tears. She stumbled out of the lobby and staggered away from George, her building, the life she'd known there. One block away, she broke into a run. Anger pushed at her. With each pounding footstep, the fire in her bones grew.

Evelyn raced after her. "Lil, listen to me."

Ignoring her, Lily picked up her pace. Dark emotions raged within her. Grief suffocated her. Black vengeance pulled at her, demanding to be answered. She knew who had taken George from her. To what? Spite her? To prove that he was stronger, that he was right? Right or wrong, she was going to kill Jackson.

CHAPTER FORTY-ONE

Wednesday, October 1, 5:15 p.m.

LILY RUSHED THROUGH Ben's front door and, without a word, stalked past the men and headed for the back bedroom. Yanking the closet door open, she stood on her tiptoes and reached for the top shelf. Her fingers located their target. She jerked hard, and the large black bag thumped heavily onto the floor.

She unzipped it, grabbed two Glocks and tucked them into her waistband, then grabbed the M4.

"You have a go bag?" Derek's calm voice jarred her from the dark, murderous thoughts rolling around her mind. "Here?"

"Do you have a problem with that?"

He walked into the bedroom and shut the door. Silence blanketed them. "Depends on what you're planning to do with it."

She dug through the bag. She couldn't breathe, couldn't think.

"George is gone." She gulped back a sob. "He killed George."

She'd *failed* him.

"Evelyn just filled us in. I'm so sorry, Lil." Derek reached his hand out. Lily jerked back. Sighing, he dropped his arm to his side. "What are you doing?"

"What does it look like?" She tried to step around him. He blocked her exit and she glared up at him. "Move."

"No."

"Derek."

"It looks like you're arming yourself for World War III." He leaned closer, crowding her. "You can't go after him. That isn't how we do things."

"This is different."

"How?" Derek touched her shoulder. This time, she didn't shrink back, just stood there as if she'd turned to stone. "You and I both know he probably went dark."

The warmth of his hand seeped through her jacket. Lily knew what he was doing. Trying to tether her, center her…bring her back from her homicidal intentions. They'd all been taught this move.

The makeshift wall she'd thrown up around her emotions cracked. She jerked away, couldn't afford to feel. "Don't touch me."

Derek leaned on his heels and raised his good hand in surrender. The softness in his face tore into Lily.

The crack widened.

She turned her back to him. If he wouldn't give her personal space, so be it, but she wasn't going to allow him to get inside her head.

Not this time.

"Lil." He moved so close she could feel his body heat. "Talk to me."

Lily spun around. "You want me to talk? Fine. I'm going to track Jackson down and make him suffer. And I'm going to do it in such a way that it's going to make him scream for death. But I'm not going to give it to him. I'm going to let the life seep out of him, just like he drained the life out of George. Is that what you want to hear?"

"Stop and listen to yourself for a moment. You're talking like a crazy person."

She stepped back, the words slamming into her as though he'd slapped her. Clearly, Derek had never lost someone at the hands of a lunatic. He'd never had someone ripped from his life just to be taught a lesson. If he had, he wouldn't have been arguing with her.

He wouldn't have said she was crazy for wanting justice.

She took a deep breath to pacify the fire in her blood, reminding herself that Derek wasn't the enemy, and spoke slowly, deliberately. "I am not talking crazy. I'm going to kill the bastard for taking someone I love."

Grabbing her by the shoulders, Derek twirled her to face the mirror. "Look at yourself."

Black mascara streaked down her cheeks. Wild, fierce eyes gazed back at her. Lily blinked. She didn't recognize the woman in the mirror.

"You're melting down, Lily. Start thinking like an agent, not some emotional woman."

She shook off his hands and glared up at him. "I am emotional, damn it. Any sane person would feel like their heart had just been torn out of their chest and slashed to pieces after finding a family member, someone they loved, hacked to shreds."

Derek threw up one arm. "You're right. A sane person *would* be emotional right now. But they wouldn't be strapping an M4 to their back in order to go on a fucking manhunt. They'd probably be curled up in a ball somewhere, bawling their eyes out. And rightfully so."

"I'm not that person. I'm not some weak woman—"

"Exactly my point. You're *not* just any woman, Lily Andrews. You're a 67 operative. The code we live by is different from the average person." He pointed at her chest. "You don't get to lose it."

Her lips trembled. She bit down hard. She would *not* cry in front of this man. Lily crossed her arms around her waist and hugged herself.

"I know what code I live by—"

"Do you? The code you swore to uphold and protect doesn't allow for this emotional bullshit." He stepped closer and pushed his face into hers. "You don't get to break down. You don't get to become an emotional basket case."

She didn't know what tipped her over the edge. Maybe his warm breath on her face? Or because he was so close she could see dark specks of violet floating in his aqua eyes? Maybe because he'd peeled back her stark mask of rage to the woman struggling to hold it together. Maybe because he hadn't dropped her like a hot coal.

Whatever it was, she couldn't hold her tears back any longer, and they flowed freely down her cheeks.

"Everything inside me hurts." She wiped away the moisture racing down her face.

"I know, babycakes. But you've got to bottle it up, lock it away. Don't tarnish everything George loved and gave his life for by going crazy on us." He tipped her chin up. Compassion swam in his eyes. "Be the agent he gave his life for. Be the agent he loved."

The raging fire snuffed out. Her heart broke all over again. *But not you.* She backed away, widened the space between them.

A bone-crushing sadness quickly filled the void the fire left.

But not you.

The one man she wanted to love her was the one man who no longer seemed to care, despite his confession from the other night. Her heart splintered. Life could be so cruel. Lily squeezed her eyes together. She channeled the sadness, funneled the emotion back to its rightful place, to the man who'd started this whole train wreck: Jackson.

"Jackson has to answer for what he's done." She clenched her hands into tight fists. "I need to track him down and bring him in."

"And we will. But we do it right. And somehow, I don't think parading down Main Street with an M4 strapped to your back classifies as by the book." He tipped his head to the side, pointed to the gun in her hand. "Do you?"

Lily set the gun down and shook her head. Had she really just armed herself for World War freaking III?

He gently laid his hand on her shoulder and searched her face. "Can you focus? No one will blame you if you need to sit this one out."

"I'm not sitting this one out, Derek."

"Fair enough. I'm just giving you an out, if you need it."

"I don't."

He grinned down at her, the dimple in his cheek deepening. "Okay, then. How about we go strategize our next move? The more minds on this, the better."

Lily and Derek walked into the kitchen and all talking ceased. Between her Spanish heritage and his Irish, there was nothing quiet about their heated conversation. She cringed, scrunching her nose. "Sorry about all that."

Evelyn got up, wrapped her arms around Lily and squeezed. "As far as I'm concerned, there's nothing to apologize for. You're spot-on in your assessment. Jackson needs to be brought in. He needs to pay. But… we do it right."

CHAPTER FORTY-TWO

Wednesday, October 1, 11:00 p.m.

DEREK'S HEAD HURT. They'd strategized, planned and tweaked for hours. A lump lodged into his throat, refusing to move. He swallowed hard, then scrubbed his hand over his face. They could have all the contingency plans in the world, but it would do them no good if they didn't know who they were fighting against.

Rowland. Jackson. They were known players. But this mysterious sniper threw them all into another world of chaos.

Derek hated being one step behind. This morning's fiasco had put them all on their heels. Edgy tension smothered them like a heavy blanket.

A half-dozen calls in to Director Kennedy resulted in nothing. *Nada.* The man who'd sent them into this shit storm was still unavailable. *Yeah, fucking right.* The director had washed his hands of them. Derek knew it. He recognized the signs, he'd just never been on this side of the coin before.

Ben pushed to his feet and stretched. "It's time to call it a night."

"I agree with that one." Marcus tossed his pen onto the table and leaned back in his chair. "Not sure about everyone else, but I feel like a dead man walking."

"Ditto that, brother."

"Everyone stays here tonight." Ben looked around the room. "No exceptions."

Derek cleared his throat. "Good call, Ben."

Lily's face fell. Raw emotion flashed in her eyes. She had nowhere *to* go. She bent her head and cradled it in her hands.

Derek couldn't even begin to understand the pain she was navigating through. He'd lost several team members, but never someone he loved.

Never someone like George.

Derek wanted to take her in his arms, protect her from all the pain and remind her she wasn't alone. But he couldn't. Not after tucking tail and acting like a bastard. He blew out a breath and stood.

Evelyn went to Lily and drew her into a hug. He inwardly cringed. He should be the one comforting Lily, not Evelyn.

"You can't hide behind that wall forever, sweets." Evelyn pulled back and stared at Lily. "I know. From personal experience. So when you're ready to talk, I'm here."

Lily's lips curved up into a trembling smile. "Thanks."

Ben jabbed his thumb over his shoulder. "There are two guest rooms. You're all adults. Figure out the sleeping arrangements."

He turned, ambled down the hall and shut his bedroom door. Silence filled the room.

Derek tilted his neck to one side, then the other and sighed. "I'll stay on the couch."

Evelyn and Marcus exchanged a veiled look.

Glancing between the three of them, Lily pinned Derek with her gaze. "What am I missing here?"

Marcus draped his arm over Evelyn's shoulders and tugged her close. "And this is our cue to turn in."

Derek watched Evelyn and Marcus leave. *Thanks a lot, brother.*

Lily narrowed her eyes. Even tired and pissed, she was beautiful. This was not going to go well.

"We need to talk."

"I'm listening."

"Um, I think we should go into the back guest room for privacy."

She didn't move. "Why?"

Derek's heart raced. That was *not* what he meant. Well, it was, but only in his dream world. And this clearly wasn't it.

Reality could be such an ugly bitch.

He rubbed the back of his neck and shook his head. "Let's just get this talk over with."

Without a word, Lily got up and marched down the hall.

He followed her into the back room and shut the door behind them.

Spinning around, she shoved her hands on her hips. "What is going on? Why are you being so distant? You sleep with me, and then I get this shit?"

"It's complicated."

He saw the flash in her wild eyes burn out and a dull ache filled his chest. He hated himself for boiling down whatever they'd shared into two words, but it was the truth. The whole situation *was* complicated.

"You're kidding me, right?"

"No. I'm not kidding you. I love you, but I can't be with you. And I can't tell you why." He ran his hands through his hair. "So yeah. I'd say it was complicated."

He sat on the bed and hung his head.

Hopefully that didn't sound as lame coming out of his mouth as it did to his ears. He'd been backed into a corner, and there was no getting out of it. If he stayed silent, she'd go through life thinking that he'd used her, that he was a prick. And nothing could be further from the truth.

Derek loved her. Knew he always would.

But how could he explain a situation he wasn't even sure he believed?

Hope for Jackson?

No way.

Derek didn't believe he'd killed George. Something didn't add up there, but Derek had seen what Jackson had done to Lily. Undercover or not, you didn't come back from trying to kill your partner, your ex-fiancé.

"So let me get this straight," Lily said in a hushed, furious voice. "You love me, but can't be with me *and* can't tell me why."

Derek nodded. *What a nightmare.*

"Oh, cut the spy crap. I didn't take you for a bastard." She wrapped her arms around her waist, her tone hot, livid and...excruciating.

And there it was.

He guessed that the thought had been racing around her head, but hearing it stung worse than he'd imagined. Not that Derek blamed her. She had every right to be furious with him. Shit, even he was pissed at the situation.

But his hands were tied.

"Lily, this whole thing is a complex mess."

She threw up her hands, backed further into the

corner. "No. I get it. All business, with the occasional side of skirt."

Derek's eyes snapped to her face. "Whoa, that's not—"

"You're all the same. I'm not really surprised."

Damn, she was on a roll, but he let her vent. Hopefully she'd flame out soon.

"Let's just nail the bastard, and we can both move on. Clearly, I suck at picking men. First Jackson, then you." She motioned to Derek. "Aren't I lucky? I'm two for two."

"Stop."

Derek could handle the venting, the name-calling, the words she'd probably regret tomorrow. He got all that. What he wouldn't take was being lumped in with that asshole.

He was *not* Jackson.

He reconsidered his earlier decision. If the director had written them off, Derek was no longer bound to that gag order. The woman trembling in front of him took priority. Should have always come first.

"I love you, Lily. End of story."

"Then why the silent treatment? Why the about-face?" She looked like a spooked rabbit, ready to bolt.

Pushing himself off the bed, he stepped toward her. She didn't move, almost as if daring him to come closer. He took a deep breath, steeling himself. "You want to know why I backed off?"

"Yes."

Derek hesitated. Her world had already turned upside down. He was about to put it on a spin cycle.

How are you going to react to this, babycakes?

"Jackson was sent on a mission."

Her forehead wrinkled. "I don't understand."

Derek weighed his next words, watched her face carefully. "The director knows Jackson is here in Omaha. He sent him."

"What?" The word came out in a soft whisper that dug into Derek.

"Jackson unearthed the whole Dům Hrůzy thing about two years ago. He took it to Director Kennedy, who took it to the higher-ups. The call came down that they weren't given clearance to send a team in after Rowland."

"And?"

"Jackson pressed. The director caved. He sent Jackson to Omaha, to ARME, on a deep, undercover op."

The color drained from Lily's face. She shook her head. "No. Jackson went rogue. He's a traitor. He tried to kill me."

"That was all part of the operation to make his turning appear legit."

A surprised expression flickered on Lily's face. "Legit?"

Derek rubbed his hands over his face, nodded.

"The director knew Jackson was going to throw me out that window?" Her voice rose an octave.

"He knew about the mission's outcome, yes. The window thing was a bit much."

"A bit much?" Her voice was practically a shriek, and her cheeks were flushed with rage. "I'm his goddaughter, for crying out loud. How could he be okay with Jackson tossing me out a window?"

"I don't know." The director's logic would never make sense to Derek. It was ludicrous, at best.

"I almost died." Her voice cracked. Pain flashed

across her face. She shook her head. "I almost died, Derek."

"I know. And I won't stand here and pretend that any of this makes sense. Because it doesn't. The deeper we dig, the shittier it becomes."

"How can Kennedy keep Jackson in? He tried to kill me. I don't understand…" Her voice grew thick. Bewilderment and grief warred in her eyes. "He killed George."

Derek hesitated. Could she handle any more information? Should he read her in on everything he knew, everything he suspected? If he did, if he stepped off this cliff and told her, he'd be all in.

She'd know everything.

And he could very well lose her.

He didn't know what he'd do if she freaked out now, but he trusted her with everything—including his heart. He took a deep breath. *Here goes nothing.*

"Kennedy believes Jackson can still be saved."

Her mouth dropped open. "Are you kidding me?"

"His exact words were, 'If she isn't dead, there's still hope for Jackson.'"

"No. There isn't hope." She shook her head. "He's gone. He threw me out a window, broke into my home, threatened my life and he just murdered part of my family. And to what? Prove his point? Keep his cover?"

Derek put his hand on her shoulder. "We don't know if he killed George. It could have been the sniper. We don't know yet."

She jerked away. "I know. The man I loved is gone."

"Lil…"

"No. I know it here." She pressed her hand over her heart. "He's gone."

"Director Kennedy thinks—"

"Wait." Lily's eyes flashed and she took a step toward him. "Is *that* why you backed off? Because of *Jackson*?"

Shutting things down between the two of them had seemed like a good idea at the time. Now, seeing her reaction, Derek just felt like an idiot. And an asshole.

She rammed her hands on her hips. "Is *that* why you've been so distant?"

He sank onto the bed. What could he possibly say? "It's complicated."

"No, actually, it's not."

Passion flared in her eyes. The vein in his neck throbbed, pounded. His throat went dry. A tiny smile tugged at her lips. *What the*— He didn't move, barely breathed.

"And it wasn't your decision to make. It's mine." Lily jabbed her finger into her chest. "I get to decide."

All he wanted to do was pull Lily to him and feel her soft body pressed against his. Instead, he was glued to the bed, unable to move or speak.

"Whether or not Jackson can be saved is a moot point. I can't be bound to the ghost of what was." She took another step, closing the distance between them. "That man, the man I used to love, no longer exists. The longer I allow him to haunt me, the more he wins. I'm done being bested by him. I need to move on."

This was not how he'd pictured this conversation going. Judging by the twinkle of fire in Lily's eyes, he couldn't stop it—not that he wanted to—even if he tried.

She cradled his face in her hands. "I want to move on."

The blood pounded in his ears.

"With you."

She lowered her face to his. Everything about this woman pulled Derek in: the sweetness of her mouth against his, the softness of her demanding lips, the heat of her body crowding his. He crushed his mouth to hers, all uncertainty gone.

Stepping between his legs, Lily closed the space remaining between their bodies. Derek couldn't tell where his ended and hers began. He deepened the kiss. Lily responded in kind. There was nothing hesitant in her touch.

Not anymore.

It was demanding and seeking and so hot it sizzled.

All too soon she drew back, breathless, and smiled. Derek's head swam. His heart beat wildly against his chest.

"Holy shit, Lil." Derek managed to get out before clearing his throat. "This isn't a knee-jerk—"

She put her finger against his lips. "Stupid man. What do I need to do to get it through your thick skull? I choose you."

Lily tugged off her shirt, kicked off her shoes and shimmied out of her jeans.

Derek swallowed hard.

Pushing him back onto the bed, she crawled on after him. Then she reached for his belt and chased away any shadow of doubt.

CHAPTER FORTY-THREE

Thursday, October 2, 9:00 a.m.

FOLDED CLOSE TO Derek's side, Lily listened to the rhythmic thump of his heart. Last night had been nothing she'd expected, and yet everything she wanted, needed.

She knew the bitter, painful truth. Jackson had made his choice. He'd left her without a word, gone undercover and gotten lost. It broke her heart, but it was the choice he'd made.

Now she'd made her own.

Derek.

Lily traced her finger over his broad, muscular chest. Pushing herself up on her elbow, she looked down at him. A calming sensation washed over her.

Lily had never met anyone like him.

Even Jackson hadn't come close to seeing the real her, the woman behind the disguises. But Derek did.

How she could feel the agonizing, earth-shattering grief of having George ripped from her too soon, and the tethering ecstasy of Derek's love within the same breath was beyond her.

But right here, next to this man softly snoring, was exactly where she needed—wanted—to be.

Derek's breathing changed. He stirred. "Morning, gorgeous."

"Morning." She pressed her hand to his cheek, loving the way his whiskers scratched her skin. "Shall we join the others? They've been rustling around in the kitchen for about an hour or so."

He groaned and carefully pulled his arms over his head in a long stretch. Lily stared at the sexy man beside her—like Michelangelo's *David* in the flesh, only sexier—and wondered if she'd ever get over waking up next to him. He dropped his arms and tossed back the covers. Lily glanced down and bit back a laugh, desire curling in every single cell. *Yeah, probably not.*

"You shouldn't have let me sleep so long."

"You needed it." Leaning down, she kissed him. "Especially after last night. Let's go, handsome. Our job isn't over yet."

After making themselves presentable, Derek walked into the kitchen in front of Lily. Marcus glanced up from his coffee and grinned, mischief in his eyes. "Have a nice night?"

Heat rushed Lily's cheeks. Yeah, nothing about last night had been quiet. She peeked at Ben. A smirk danced on his lips. The heat on her face grew. *How mortifying.*

"Shut up, man," Derek muttered.

Evelyn rolled her eyes at Marcus. He raised his coffee mug to his mouth and shrugged.

Lily sighed. The only way to get over the awkward moment was to address it. She grabbed a mug from the cabinet and poured herself some much-needed java before glancing over her shoulder.

"We had the time of our lives. Thank you very much."

Derek choked on his coffee.

Evelyn laughed. "Nicely played, Lil."

Shaking his head, Ben smiled. "Want some breakfast?"

THE FIVE OF THEM gathered around Ben's kitchen table. Marcus and Evelyn already knew of Derek's suspicions about Jackson, but Ben needed to be read in. His face grew stony as Derek filled him in on all the gory details. Lily knew Derek's words cut Ben deep. Jackson had been like a son to him.

Derek tugged a chair over and plopped himself down next to Lily. The warmth of his leg pressed against hers, and a soft sigh of contentment escaped her lips as he laid his hand on top of her thigh. Intense, colorful memories of last night zipped through her mind.

How ironic. In the midst of this insanity, she'd gotten the sweetest gift.

Lily sipped her coffee and glanced at Evelyn. A quick, unbreakable friendship had forged between them in the short time she'd been in Lily's world, and it still startled her how easy it had been to let down her guard with Evelyn. Lily had begun to think of her as the sister she'd never had. She took another sip of coffee and an even deeper realization swept over her, an understanding that in their dark, cutthroat undercover world went further than love could ever go: Lily trusted Evelyn with her life.

And that said everything.

"So what do we know, Ev?"

Evelyn tapped her finger on the table before answering, a faraway look in her eyes. "Well, we know Director Kennedy has gone quiet."

Lily wrapped her fingers around her coffee mug, still not believing that the director had washed his hands of her. Of all of them. He'd sworn to protect her, not feed her to the lions.

She wasn't sure which hurt worse: Jackson's betrayal or his.

"Which we all know is most likely a bad sign."

"Possibly. But it's what we have to work with." Evelyn flipped the file open. "We can also assume Rowland and Jackson are working together. But I'd even throw out the idea that Rowland is working *for* Jackson."

Derek cocked his head to the side. "Really?"

Evelyn got up, began pacing. "Did you see his body language? His whole demeanor changed when Jackson showed up. Rowland clearly took on the submissive role."

Lily's mood matched the dark liquid she swirled in her cup. Black. And hot. "And Jackson may or may not be double-crossing Rowland."

"Correct."

"Fantastic."

In perfect sync with his wife, Marcus picked up where Evelyn had left off. "Then there's our wild card, our sniper. We swept the entire floor and got nothing. It was as if he was a ghost."

Lily wanted to scream. Nothing about this operation could be easy, could it? She pushed back from the table and moved toward the coffeepot. She needed more caffeine. Pronto. "No one is a ghost."

Marcus leaned his chair back on its two back legs, nodding. "In a normal situation, I would agree. But we all know there's nothing normal about this mess we're in."

Cringing, Lily hung her head. The mess *she'd* made. "Sorry about that."

"Not following."

She looked up at four very confused faces. A lump formed in her throat. "If I'd been on my game—if Rowland hadn't made me—none of this would be happening, and you'd both be safe in San Diego."

Marcus let his chair drop back onto all fours. "Apparently, we haven't articulated ourselves well enough, Lily. The moment we met you, you became family."

Family? Lily glanced at Derek. A soft smile pulled at his lips. The lump in her throat returned, bigger this time, and she caught her lip in her teeth to keep the unexpected tears at bay.

"Granted, it took you a little while to pick up on what Derek was putting down, but you *clearly* figured that one out last night."

Derek hurled a donut at Marcus, who laughed and dodged the glazed missile. Derek got up, moved next to Lily. She didn't know what to say, how to respond. So she just stood there. Mute.

Marcus bent low, picked up the donut. "And we will do anything for family."

"Oh." The tiny word barely escaped Lily's lips. *Wow.* Smiling, Derek raised her hand to his mouth, pressing his lips to her palm.

Ben whistled and crossed his arms. "Well, there you go."

"That clear now?" Amusement pranced in Marcus's eyes.

"Crystal."

"Great." He clapped his hands together. "So we're working under the impression that Director Kennedy has gone quiet with this whole situation. Rowland and Jackson are the dynamic duo—which one is the boss man and which one is the underling is yet to be determined. And we have a mysterious sniper sniffing up our asses."

"Well, isn't this a pretty little party," Lily muttered into her cup of coffee.

Evelyn laughed, then grew serious. "Since calling in an extraction team and taking Rowland down the old-school way is not an option, we go with plan B."

Lily wanted justice so badly she could taste it. But she wasn't desperate enough to forgo the code she lived and swore by. Derek had brought her back from *that* edge last night.

She'd never go there again.

"What's plan B?"

"We send Derek back into ARME so he can ascertain the situation," Evelyn said slowly.

"Absolutely not." There was no way in hell anyone was leaving, not on her watch. And definitely not Derek.

Lily hung her head, clamped and unclamped her hands together. She knew the right response, but didn't want to voice it. What if she agreed and, in turn, signed someone's death warrant? Another person she loved.

"Lil." Derek covered her hands, stilled her movements. "It's the right call. We need eyes and ears inside."

She looked up. Four pairs of eyes stared at her. She sighed. She was outnumbered, and she knew it. *Damn it.*

Evelyn was spot-on in her assessment. Lily was confident in that, as she was in Derek's ability to get in and get out. She pinched the bridge of her nose. They needed eyes, and they needed them ASAP. Without more intel, they were screwed. Lily swallowed the frustration creeping up her throat. They'd been so close to nailing Rowland.

And now they were back at square one.

"Okay. Go. Be our eyes." She reached up and placed her hands on Derek's jaw. "But you better come back tonight. In one piece."

Leaning forward, he kissed her quickly. "Yes, ma'am."

A heavy stillness settled over the room. It was risky sending him in. They all knew it. But what choice did they have?

Evelyn reached over and gave Lily's shoulder a tight squeeze. "Okay, let's talk through this. Ben, how much gear do you have here? I don't want Derek going in alone. I want ears on him."

A grin spread across Ben's face. "Little lady, I've got it all. You think Lily had a nice setup in that little closet of hers? You ain't seen nothin' yet."

Ben's response broke the tension floating in the room.

"It's true." Lily shrugged and pointed at Ben. "Where do you think I got it from?"

"Excellent." Evelyn nodded, her eyes twinkling. "Let's get to work, then."

HOURS LATER, DEREK WALKED back into Ben's apartment. Marcus and Evelyn stopped talking. Lily looked
up and studied Derek's face. He'd called, told her he'd
be late, but she hadn't expected him to stroll in well
past eight o'clock.

"You okay?"

The muscle in his jaw tightened. "I got nothing."
He slumped into the kitchen table chair. "No Rowland.
No John. It was almost as if the place was abandoned."

"Seems strange, doesn't it?"

"Very. John hasn't responded to any of my calls
today." Derek's phone chirped. He scanned the message, the muscles in his jaw jumping. "Son of a bitch."

Lily's stomach tightened. *Now what?*

Without a word, Derek tossed her his phone. She
caught it, turned it over, read the text. "Well, that's
putting it mildly."

"What does it say?" Marcus asked.

Lily had seen her share of convoluted cases, but this
surpassed them all. With flying colors. "It's a text from
John Elsworth. He said, '9-1-1. No cops. Get my family to safety. Intruders. Home. 9-1-1.'"

Ben joined them in the kitchen, taking the phone
from Lily. "What the hell does that mean?"

Derek rubbed the back of his neck, suddenly looking very tired and worried. "With all the crazy shit
hitting the fan, I can only imagine it's the worst-case
scenario."

Evelyn's face was gray. "That said 'family.' How
many children does he have?"

"Two."

Marcus threw Evelyn a quick glance. "We get those
kids out. The dynamic duo can wait. The kids come

first. Derek, do we have any idea how many men might be involved?"

"No idea." Derek's face hardened. "But I'm guessing we'll need more than the five of us."

Ben handed Derek's phone back to him. "Got that covered."

Everyone stopped moving, stopped talking, silently stared at Ben. He leaned against the kitchen counter, his arms crossed over his chest. He didn't blink, just stared back at them.

"How?"

"After George." Ben cleared his throat and brushed his thumb at the corner of one eye. Lily's chest tightened. "I alerted my team, put them on standby, what with everything happening."

Lily slumped against the counter. "Oh."

She'd expertly compartmentalized George's death, banishing the dark, raw emotions to the depths of her soul. It was the only way she could focus on the task at hand.

One day, she'd need to address them, and she would. But she wasn't prepared for that one day to be today. At the mention of George's name, a tsunami of grief crashed into Lily. Tears sprung to her eyes. Derek laced his fingers through hers. She swallowed down the sorrow rushing her throat, locked it away.

She'd be forever indebted to him—always her protector.

Lily forced a weak smile to her face. "Good call."

"Only call to make." Ben shifted his weight.

She bit back a small laugh. She knew how much Ben hated being the center of attention. He preferred the shadows, just as she did. "How long before they can be on the move?"

"An hour." Ben shrugged. "Tops."

"Great. Then let's roll."

CHAPTER FORTY-FOUR

Thursday, October 2, 9:40 p.m.

HIDDEN WITHIN THE GRASS, Ben and his small team of men waited patiently along the front of the Elsworth estate. The whites of their eyes were the only giveaway to their exact location. Lily peered into her scope and studied each of Ben's trusted comrades.

All men he'd served with, fought by. All men *she'd* gladly die for.

Lily owed them, big time. Each man had dropped everything to fight next to her—with them—in this moment. Each responded to her apologies for the last-minute notice with, "Once an agent, always an agent."

She shook her head in astonishment. Pride surged through her veins.

"Heads down, eyes open," Ben murmured over their radio links. "Anyone have eyes on the target yet?"

They needed to get an idea of the layout before moving in. Heat signatures showed thirteen bodies. Now they just needed to verify who was friendly.

And who wasn't.

Lily and her team surrounded the Elsworth estate. Ben and his men spread out across the front. Evelyn camped out on the western corner. Derek and Marcus had positioned themselves on the east corner. Lily took the rear.

She breathed slowly, peered through the scope and scanned the yard. *Again*. She rolled her shoulders and settled in.

Going in on a dime was a bitch.

Never the kind of conditions she'd choose, but their hands had been forced. And, truth be told, they'd been in worse situations. All of them had. So while the circumstances were dicey, at best, a quiet confidence blanketed Lily.

Ben broke the silence. "Anyone?"

"I've got them." Evelyn's smooth voice sounded in Lily's ear.

Lily glanced to her left. "What do you see?"

"Three in the front room. Appears Gina's giving two brutes a piece of her mind," Evelyn reported, her voice calm. "Can't find the kiddos. Anyone got a location on them?"

Lily got up and ran low along the back perimeter of the mansion and repositioned herself. Searching through her scope, she examined the dark windows. *Bingo*. "Got 'em. They're both in the kitchen…with two heavily armed babysitters."

"Hold on." Evelyn's voice cut in. "One of the guys just hit Gina and is dragging her off. Crap. I lost visual. Anyone pick that up?"

Lily watched through her scope as Gina was hauled into view, kicking and screaming. "Got her. They just pulled her into the kitchen."

The tall man threw Gina to the floor. She looked up, glared and said something. The man backhanded her. Spitting out a mouthful of blood, she scowled at the man, but made no move to comfort the two young children cowering in the corner.

Lily studied the boys. The oldest couldn't have been more than seven, and was stick thin. Given his rumpled pj's and wild bed head, she assumed they'd been yanked from bed. He wrapped his gangly arms around his sibling. Tears streamed down his cheeks as he pulled his little brother close. The tiny boy buried his chubby baby face into his brother's shoulder and clung to him.

She didn't have to have children to feel the righteous anger burn her insides. No child should have to undergo what they were enduring.

She panned back to Gina. Incredible—the woman was yelling at the tall man again. His face darkened and he moved toward her, but Gina didn't back down.

Oh, to be a fly on the wall.

Just as she'd suspected, there was nothing soft about Gina Elsworth. But tigress or not, mouthing off to an armed intruder was ballsy. And dangerous.

"We need to get those kids out." Evelyn's voice came through the radio. "What's the game plan?"

Lily stared through the scope again. "I've got four heavily armed men in the kitchen. Three innocents, two being children. That leaves six more men roaming, possibly upstairs. Ben, can you confirm?"

"Affirmative."

Excellent. It's go time.

Lily took a deep breath. "Okay. I'll cover Gina and the kids from out here. Ben, you and your team take upstairs."

"Yes, ma'am."

"Derek, cover the front. Ev, Marcus, when it's clear, get those kids out."

"With pleasure." Evelyn's hard voice filtered through Lily's ear.

"Let's avoid bullets if we can manage it." Lily focused her scope on the children's faces. "Those kids have been traumatized enough as it is. So go in quiet. Neutralize the threat. And get the hell out of there."

Ben's voice floated into the darkness. "Old-school, boys. Let's show these young pups how it's done."

Young pups? Lily smiled into the darkness. She wasn't surprised he'd gone there. He'd given her a hard time about the new way of doing things for as long as she could remember.

"Yeah, Pops, show us how it's done."

CHAPTER FORTY-FIVE

Thursday, October 2, 9:45 p.m.

THE FEISTINESS WAS OUT in full force tonight. Lily was fully engaged, alive…and Derek loved it. He repositioned to the front and glanced at Ben. "Pops, eh?"

Ben scowled.

Derek bit back the laugh in his throat. Who knew he'd ever be on a mission with the renowned Ben Tinsdale? The man was a legend in their ranks. All newbies studied Ben's tactics while going through basic training.

It was a way to weed out the weak. Those who mastered his tactics stayed. Those who didn't washed out.

The man was a hard-ass and a true warrior.

Yet somehow, Lily had managed to get beneath the unbreakable outer layer and park herself permanently within the big man's heart. Derek would have said it was impossible, if he hadn't seen it firsthand.

Bringing his binoculars to his face, Derek scrutinized the two men pacing in the front foyer. Damn, they were huge. "Hello, boys, I got you now."

The tallest stopped moving and looked directly at Derek's position.

Derek froze. Didn't breathe.

The man scanned the area, then went back toward

his buddy. A thick, black cobra, red droplets dripping from bared fangs, rode the muscles on his arm. Derek had seen that tattoo before. Each droplet represented a hand-to-hand combat kill. He gritted his teeth.

Ben pressed the radio link around his neck, muting the connection. "What's up?"

Did nothing get by this man? Derek muted his connection, too. "I ran into this group on my last deployment."

"You know these boys?"

"Not specifically, but I know their group. Black Cobras." Derek peered through his binoculars. "What I don't understand is why they're here. Kidnapping isn't usually their forte."

Ben's face darkened. "Well, which one of us pissed off Lady Luck? She sure ain't smiling down on us tonight, is she?"

Derek couldn't have agreed more. She was all but flipping them off.

He turned his connection back on. "Heads-up, everyone. These aren't just your run-of-the-mill kidnappers for hire. They're mercenaries, known as Black Cobras, and they're mean sons of bitches."

"Fabulous," Evelyn muttered.

Evelyn's dry quip made Derek smile. He didn't know which woman had more sass: Evelyn or Lily.

They'd grown tight in the past few days. He hadn't seen Evelyn light up around another woman since her best friend, Kate, had been murdered. It was almost as if Evelyn had found another friend to let into her world. And Lily had embraced her gladly as one of her own.

A knot formed in Derek's throat. If anything happened to either of them, he'd never forgive himself.

"Proceed with extreme caution," Derek said. "I ran into this group in Afghanistan. Believe me, they won't hesitate to take you down."

"Copy that, Derek," Lily chimed in. "Ben, you and Derek cover the front. Have your team clear the second floor."

"Roger, Lil. Sam, take the team and get it done."

"Got it, boss." A deep, gravelly voice broke into the conversation.

Derek muted his radio. "I don't need a keeper."

Ben glanced over and pinned Derek with his eyes. "And I don't need Lily's heart breaking again. Stop being a pansy. She'd doing her job. Now, stay close to my side."

Derek blinked. Had Ben just called him a pansy? Ben raised his eyebrows, almost as if daring Derek to challenge him. But he couldn't. Not only did the big man staring him down scare the shit out of Derek, but if the tables were turned, he would've made the same call. He needed to get his pride under wraps if he wanted to keep this woman in his life.

He unmuted his radio. "Copy that, Lil."

CHAPTER FORTY-SIX

Thursday, October 2, 9:47 p.m.

IT WAS THE right call. Though Lily knew it rubbed Derek the wrong way. She recognized it in his voice, in the pause before he'd answered. Well, he'd have to get over it. Her team's safety was her priority. Pride didn't have a place here.

His or hers.

Lily knew about the Black Cobras. They were bad news. "Ev, hold your position until the—"

"What about the kids?"

"Hell will freeze over before anything happens to those kids on my watch. Promise. I've got my sight trained on the targets, and I will take them down if it comes to that. Hold your position."

Lily was being a hard-ass, and she knew it. Her team was good. But the Black Cobras were just as good, and much more brutal. She needed her men to neutralize as many of them as possible before they went in, and fast.

Otherwise they wouldn't come out of this alive.

Lily waited for Ben's team to do what they did best—hide within the shadows and deliver death's blow. The minutes crawled by at an excruciating pace. Lily concentrated on her breathing, not the silence.

"Second floor is clear."

The tightness in her neck lifted. She breathed a sigh of relief. *One down, two to go. Come on, Derek, talk to me.* Peering through her scope, she watched the kids, etching their faces into her memory.

"Same with the front." Derek's voice sliced through the stillness, instantly calming the racing in her chest. "All assholes accounted for, minus the monkeys in the kitchen."

And those were the words she'd been holding her breath to hear. *Excellent.* She pressed her eye to her scope. "Copy that. Evelyn, you and Marcus go get the kiddos."

"Already on the move."

Ben's deep voice cut into the quiet. "Setting up new positions within the house, Lil."

Adrenaline raced down her body, sending her nerves into overdrive. This was what she lived for, and loved. None of them had worked together before, yet they moved like a well-oiled machine. She could get used to this.

"Derek, cover the front entrance to the kitchen. Wait for my signal, then take those bastards out."

"Yes, ma'am."

Silence fell over the radio. Lily repositioned and looped her finger through the trigger.

"We're in," Evelyn's hushed voice crackled in Lily's earpiece.

"I've got you covered." Lily slowed her breath and her heart and focused on the two children. "The men have separated Gina from the kids. The kids are at the opposite end of the kitchen. Proceed with extreme caution."

The back door opened.

Hugging the shadows, Evelyn and Marcus slipped into the kitchen and closed the gap between them and the kids. Marcus inched his way toward the oldest, reached out and clamped his hand over his mouth, hauling the child into his arms. He pivoted and made a mad dash for the door.

At the same moment, Evelyn drew the youngest son to her. He yelped. Evelyn tried to quiet him. Marcus looked over his shoulder, and his face dropped.

Lily watched in horror as time crawled to a standstill. In slow motion, Gina turned, her eyes wide and brow crumpled in confusion.

With one fluid movement, the tall, bald man whirled, pulled his gun and raised his arm.

Lily didn't hesitate. She pulled her trigger.

A tiny hole appeared in the middle of the bald man's forehead.

He dropped.

Screams echoed. Gunshots blasted.

Getting up, she sprinted for the house. "Get to the back, Derek. Get those kids out."

Leaping over the boxwood plants, Lily dashed across the lawn and made her way to the kitchen. She couldn't see anyone. *Please, God, let them be okay.* She tucked herself in close to the house, gun drawn, and inched her way closer to the open back door.

"Someone talk to me." Her heart hammered in her chest. She pressed her head against the wall, swallowed the bile in her throat. "Now."

"We've got the kids," Marcus reported, an edge to his voice.

Something was off.

"Marcus?"

"The kids are safe." He repeated, his tone cold.

Lily slid through the opening and glanced at the reflection in the window. Gina pointed a gun directly at Marcus and Evelyn. Lily's thoughts stuttered to a halt. *What the hell?*

Marcus was correct in his response: the kids *were* safe. Safely huddled behind Marcus and Evelyn, their human shields.

Lily's mind tumbled over itself as she tried to make sense of it all. But the sight of that gun trained on people she loved defied all logic and sent fury coursing through her veins. Not on her fucking watch.

She didn't care who the hell Gina Elsworth was.

"Put the gun down *now*." Lily demanded and stepped into the open, her tone hard, pissed. She cocked the hammer back on her gun. "I won't ask you again."

Gina's mouth dropped open, her forehead furrowed in confusion. "Addison? What are you doing here?"

Lily glanced past Gina. Blood seeped through Evelyn's shirt. "You okay?"

Tiny droplets of sweat glistened above Evelyn's lip. Her face was pale. "It's nothing, just a scratch."

Lily caught the subtle shake of Marcus's head and the way he cast his eyes toward his watch. Just how bad a scratch was it?

She maneuvered herself, shielding those she loved as best as possible. She couldn't shelter them all, but there was no way Gina could get off two shots before Lily took her out with one.

"I'm not going to tell you again, Gina. Drop the gun."

Gina looked at her hand and relaxed her grip. The

gun tumbled to the floor. Her lips trembled. "Addison, what's going on?"

Lily stepped close enough to kick the gun aside. She glanced around. *What happened here?* All three men lay dead, swimming in pools of their own blood.

She'd only fired one shot.

"I could ask you the same thing."

Gina wrapped her arms around her waist, suddenly looking terrified, and very fragile. "I had to protect myself."

Lily glanced back at Evelyn, who cradled the younger child to her chest with one arm. The other hung limp at her side. Silent tears rolled down the boy's face. Lily tucked her gun in front of herself and eyed Gina. "Marcus, get these kids out of here."

"With pleasure." He scooped the smaller boy into his arms and moved away from the massacre. Evelyn covered the older child's eyes and guided him away.

Lily watched them leave the kitchen before she holstered her own weapon and started toward Gina. The blonde woman scrambled backward, eyes crazy. Lily raised her hands in the air, trying to calm her. "Easy. Gina, my name isn't Addison. I've been working undercover—"

"The kids are secure." Derek walked in, interrupting Lily. Ben followed behind him.

Gina's eyes widened. She glanced between the two men. Her face flamed. "What the hell is going on? Derek, why are you in my home?"

He hurried to Lily's side. "I received a distress message."

Gina stomped a foot. "From who?"

"That's classified."

Lily glanced at Derek. *Classified?* She hadn't figured he'd throw *that* card out. But there must've been a good reason for it. Lily plastered a businesslike look on her face and followed his lead.

"Classified? Are you kidding me?" Gina's eyes darkened. She jabbed a finger into her chest. "You work for me, remember?"

"Actually, I don't."

Gina looked confused. She blinked hard.

"The US government sent me in to ascertain the validity of an assumed threat against the United States of America."

Gina's mouth moved, but no words came out.

Lily swallowed her smile. *Damn, that sounded official.*

"What threat?" Gina clenched her hands into tight balls. "What the hell are you talking about?"

"Mrs. Elsworth, Rowland James has been under investigation for some time."

Her gaze flipped between Lily and Derek. "What do you mean, *under investigation*?"

"That's all we're allowed to share with you at this point, ma'am." Derek's eyes narrowed. "Where's your husband?"

"John left about four hours ago." Her voice cracked. She clenched and unclenched her hands.

"Did he tell you where he was going?"

"No. He just left. Then these monsters broke in." Gina motioned to the dead men. Her hand fluttered over her mouth, and her eyes filled with tears. "Do you think my husband is working with Rowland?"

"We don't think—"

"Did my husband hire these men to kill me? His children?" Her voice took on a hysterical edge. Her fingers pawed at her throat. "If Rowland is under investigation, is John? Oh, my god, that bastard. They're working together, aren't they?"

Moving to Ben, Gina buried her face into his chest. He peered over Gina's head at Lily, a helpless look flashing across his face as he peeled Gina off and stepped back.

"Not sure, ma'am. But you and your children are safe. We'll have some of our men here until the police arrive."

"Police?" Gina's head snapped up. "No. We can't have that kind of publicity."

Lily cast Derek a sharp glance, but his face was unreadable. "We're not too concerned with publicity at this point, Gina."

"I am."

Lily studied Gina. She'd resumed clenching and releasing her fists, and her eyelids blinked in rapid succession. Was the woman in shock? Had her mind sent her to crazy town? Why else would she refuse to let them call the police?

"Someone tried to kidnap you and your children." Lily spoke in a firm, slow voice.

Gina shook her head. "No. It'll cripple us."

Ben leaned against the counter, shrugged. "Sorry, ma'am. Protocol."

Gina's lips set into a tight line, and she crossed her arms. "So, am I now under house arrest?"

Lily tipped her head and studied the tall blonde defiantly staring Ben down. What was with her? Her emotions were all over the place, almost as if they were talking to two people. One minute she was a scared, fragile woman, the next a crazed, defiant one. Her wild gaze bounced from Lily to Ben, back to Lily. The rapid fluttering of her eyes resumed.

"We prefer to call it protection."

CHAPTER FORTY-SEVEN

Thursday, October 2, 10:15 p.m.

THE CLOCK TICKED DOWN. Each second lost could mean the difference between life or death for John Elsworth. The pressure to find him pushed at Lily, demanding her attention.

An elephant sitting on her chest would have been easier to ignore.

Ben's men would stand guard over Gina and her sons until the police arrived. Lily, Ben and Derek gathered around the hood of Derek's car. She glanced between the two men. Her lips tugged up. *Not bad for a team.*

Granted, she'd wished it wasn't so thin. But she'd pared them down to three. Evelyn needed medical attention. She'd maintained that her wound was nothing and kept a stiff upper lip when Lily bumped into her. *Intentionally.* Lily shook her head. What a freaking warrior. That woman was a total champion in her eyes, but Lily also knew better.

Nothing, my ass.

In order to stay under the radar, she'd insisted Marcus take Evelyn to Ben's to have her arm examined. It was the right decision—the only decision.

But it left them with three.

Three against what? Against how many?

She drummed her fingers against the cold metal, then rolled her head to the right and left, stretching her neck. "We need to find John. Pronto. I can't shake this feeling that this attack was meant for him, *not* his family."

"I couldn't agree more," Ben chimed in. "But where is he?"

Derek reached in his pocket and fished out his phone. "I put a tracker in his watch. Let's hope he's wearing it."

A tracker? Lily smiled. Pure genius surrounded her. He keyed in a sequence, and they all held a collective breath.

"Hang on." Ben crossed his arms over his chest and scowled at Derek. "Why are you just bringing this up now?"

What was with the glare? "Ben—"

"I know John." Derek didn't recoil from the mountain of a man, and he threw Lily a wink. *Old school and new school colliding. How was this going to pan out?* "John's priority has always been, and always will be, his family. So *that's* what we focused on. His whereabouts didn't come into play with our initial objective."

Derek put his hand on Ben's shoulder and squeezed. "Because of *your* men, they're safe, under lock and key. Now we go get the boss back."

Lily leaned against the hood of the car. Ben grunted, but that was the end of it. She breathed easier.

"So what does your gadget tell you?" Ben peered over Derek's shoulder. "Does it give you a location?"

"Yep. ARME."

Lily wasn't surprised. Everything tied back to that damn place.

Derek's jaw tightened. "Shows his vitals, too. And given his readings, he's in major distress. We need to move."

Ben whistled. "Didn't have *that* in my time."

Lily looked past Ben to the house. "Your guys okay here?"

"I'll send some of my team with you, set up eyes and ears. You're *not* going in blind."

Pulling out his keys, Derek pressed a button and the trunk opened. She followed him around the back and peeked in. He'd flipped open two large cases. Row after row of ammunition and guns stared up at her. She reached for the M4. She loved that gun. If guns could be sexy, this one would be it.

They'd be going in armed to the teeth, too.

She reached for a thigh holster, hitched her foot on the bumper and wrapped it around her leg, pulling tight. She fished around in the trunk and found a box of flash-bang grenades. They weren't lethal, but they would temporarily disorient her enemy—whoever that turned out to be. She grabbed three. Lily pushed a fresh magazine into her .45, chambered a round and shoved it into her thigh holster.

"Let's roll."

CHAPTER FORTY-EIGHT

Thursday, October 2, 10:30 p.m.

DEW SOAKED LILY'S CLOTHES. She and Derek hid within the damp grass. Peering through her scope, she studied ARME's grandiose structure. It was dark.

"You think Jackson's here?"

Derek turned his head, his eyebrows arched. "Honest?"

· "Yeah."

"I think he's hightailed it to some nonextradition country."

Lily glanced back at the shadowy building. Would Jackson really tuck tail and retreat? It didn't sound like something he'd do. But then again, she didn't know what the hell he would do anymore.

A deep sadness rolled over her. The man she'd known, the man she'd once loved, no longer existed.

"I know Jackson being in the wind will eat at you forever."

Lily cringed. Once again, Derek read her like a freaking book. Which was annoying as hell, and also endearing. But she loved him, even his profiling voodoo.

Derek turned adoring eyes on her, melting her insides. "We take down Rowland, get John to safety and I'll personally help you track Jackson. Deal?"

It was a long order, but not outside their abilities.

Jackson wasn't a priority. Not now. Not until John was safe.

"Sounds like a plan." She looked through her scope again. "All right, eagle eye, talk to us."

Ben's gruff voice cut through the air. "I see six heat signatures. Three on the executive floor. Three in sublevel one."

"Ben?" His voice was the last one she'd expected to hear wafting over the radio, but she was grateful that he'd be their eyes—nothing like family to guard your back.

"You think I'd stay with that crazy woman and miss out on this action?" Ben asked. "No chance in hell. And...I'm not the only one."

"Hey, brother." Marcus's deep voice sliced through the night.

Though Lily was grateful for the additional backup, she wanted to reach through the line and wring his throat. "Why aren't you with Evelyn?"

Marcus laughed. "Easy, tiger. Evelyn's holding down the fort at Ben's, nursing a newly stitched-up shoulder. And probably a glass of Malbec. She sends her regards and a very specific request to kick some ass."

Evelyn would say something like that. "So she's fine?"

"She's fine, but she'd be ticked if she knew we were talking about her instead of tracking down John. So what's the game plan?"

Lily could almost see Evelyn's beautiful face pinching into a stoic frown. Yeah, she would be pissed. "I'll take the executive floor. Derek will take the sublevel and bring boss man back."

"Sounds simple enough," Ben muttered through the line. "Though we all know it's not. So once you're inside, we switch to two channels. Lil, I'll be your eyes and ears on channel one and keep track of your bogies. Derek, Marcus will be on channel four."

"Copy that."

"Derek, if John ordered that hit on his family, we grossly underestimated him." Marcus voiced the concern that had been bouncing around Lily's mind from the moment she'd seen those hired guns.

"We didn't. He didn't put that hit out. Rowland's fingerprints are all over this."

Lily caught her lower lip between her teeth, contemplating Derek's thought process. "I've questioned the same thing, Marcus, but I think Derek's right. Rowland wouldn't think twice about killing those kids."

Derek yanked out his phone, checked its screen. "And John's vitals are off the charts. You can't fake that. He's not in on this."

The silence over the line dragged out for a long moment before Marcus spoke. "Fair enough. Proceed with extreme caution."

Reaching over, Derek cupped Lily's face in his hand. His heated gaze melted her insides. He pressed his lips to hers, and every nerve ending in her body exploded. He pulled back too soon, concern flashing across his face. Once again, he'd left her breathless.

"Be careful." He dropped his hand.

"Of course. I have every intention of finishing what

you just started." She leaned in, kissing him again. "Safety first."

They got up and ran toward the building, low and hugging the shadows. They flanked the entrance.

"How do we look, Ben?" Lily knew her voice was barely audible, yet she still cast a quick glance around.

"No movement. Yet."

Derek keyed in his code and the locks unlatched. He opened the doors and they slid into the foyer. Silence greeted them.

"Shit." Ben's voice echoed in their earpieces.

Derek held up his fist. They both turned to statues. Lily barely breathed.

"Talk to us."

"Our eyes are down," Ben said at last, a hard edge to his voice. "We're working on getting eyes up, but until then, it's ears only moving forward."

Lily dropped her head, fighting the urge to scream. Why could nothing go their way? Had their gear failed, or had they triggered some sort of silent alarm, some security fail-safe? "Not the best. But that'll have to do."

She glanced at Derek. "If we don't go now, John is dead. Not going to happen."

The muscle in his jaw jumped. "Ears only, then."

"Marcus." Lily didn't take her eyes off Derek.

"Yes, ma'am?"

She didn't break eye contact with Derek. "I want Derek's ass home in one piece tonight. Not a scratch on it. Got it?"

"You got it, boss lady."

"You know I'm standing right here and can hear you," Derek muttered.

She threw him a saucy look, and his eyes widened.

She muted her mic. "One piece, mister. Last night was only a prelude to the real show."

Derek sent her a hopeful grin.

Lily unmuted her mic. "Switching to channel one now. I'm out."

CHAPTER FORTY-NINE

Thursday, October 2, 10:33 p.m.

DEREK WATCHED LILY skirt the wall and disappear into the shadows. Maybe they shouldn't have split up. He started after her, stopping midstep. *Get your shit together, man.* She'd be livid if she knew what he was thinking. She wasn't just some woman with a gun.

She was the best.

Still…she was also the woman who'd captured his heart, mind and soul. His world had come alive when she'd unknowingly waltzed into it, and exploded into full color the moment she leaned in and chose him. He could still taste her and couldn't bear the idea of losing her.

Not when he'd just gotten her back.

Derek switched his radio to channel four, making his way through the empty foyer. His eyes swept the large room. Had Lily already made it to the executive level?

"She's going to be fine." Marcus's voice interrupted Derek's mental musing. "Focus, brother."

"Get out of my head, man."

"Then get into the game. You worrying about her isn't going to help anyone. And it will most likely get you killed. I made a promise to get your ass home un-scratched. So you need to focus. Now."

Marcus had a point. Damn it. Nothing like being chewed out by your younger brother in order to get your head screwed on. "Got it. Headed to the elevator."

"The elevator? Are you kidding me?"

Derek checked that his safety was off. "Nope."

"That's not ideal."

No, it wasn't. Actually, it was the worst possible scenario. He would be all but sending a calling card to whoever guarded John.

Hey, assholes, come and get me. I'll be down in T-minus however many seconds it takes for this death box to get down to your level.

"Lady Luck must really hate me," Derek grumbled.

"You sure there's no other way down?"

Pushing at the button, Derek watched the numbers flash as the elevator came closer. "If there is, I'm not privy to that information."

John Elsworth had smiled like a proud papa on graduation day when he'd mentioned that fun little fact to Derek during his tour of the facility on his first day. One way in, one way out.

The elevator chimed. Derek pressed his finger to the trigger, his senses on full alert.

No one's smiling now. Are they, Johnny Boy?

Derek sure as hell wasn't. Nothing like having se-curity protocol bite you in the ass.

Marcus sighed into Derek's ear. "Be careful, brother."

"Safety first." Derek froze. *Unreal.* He'd already picked up one of Lily's phrases. Man, he was in trou-ble, and loving every second of their crazy, wild ride.

His throat grew tight. Yeah, they definitely shouldn't have split up.

"Hey, if I don't come out of this, tell Lily—"

The elevator doors closed, and his radio went silent.

His gut tightened. He'd expected the elevator shaft to cut him off from all communication once he reached the impenetrable sublevel—not the second he boarded this death box. *Figures.*

Seconds later, the elevator doors slid back into the wall. Derek tucked himself close to the ceiling, supported his body weight and started counting. Before he'd made it to three, a wall of hot metal sprayed the box as bullets rained down their fiery fury.

His arms and legs shook with fatigue the longer he hung suspended above the blistering hell below him. He pushed against the weariness and remained in his position. One wrong move, and he was a dead man.

Two magazines later, the bullets stopped.

Derek breathed through his teeth.

A mountain of a man stepped into the elevator, glancing up. His eyes widened. He swung his AK-47.

Derek dropped, tackled the man, grabbed his head and twisted. The man went limp.

"What the hell!"

Derek instinctively hauled the dead man up and used his body as a shield. Bullets kicked and jerked the heavy mass. Dropping the dead weight, Derek aimed his weapon and pulled the trigger three times.

Two to the chest, one to the head.

The man dropped.

Adrenaline pumped through Derek's veins as his heart raced. Reloading, he raised his gun and inched his way into the expansive chamber. He hugged the wall as he scanned the massive room. It sat empty.

Heat signatures had identified three bodies down here. Two lay just over his right shoulder. So where was body number three?

Where was John Elsworth?

CHAPTER FIFTY

Thursday, October 2, 10:34 p.m.

LILY HATED WALKING AWAY from Derek. But splitting up meant more covered ground. And since time wasn't on their side, the quicker they located John, the better.

She double-checked her 9 mm Sig Sauer.

Tonight, it was one of her guns of choice. The concealability and round capacity—fifteen "plus one" in the chamber, gave her more bang for her buck. And she'd need to change her magazine less frequently, which was a definite perk. Especially considering that she had no idea what kind of mess she was walking into.

She checked her guns one final time and crept toward the emergency doors leading to the executive floor, moving from shadow to shadow. The hair on the back of her neck bristled. She froze. Pushed herself flat against the wall.

Her eyes focused on the advancing figure. Every muscle in her body coiled.

JB sauntered into view. An AK swung lazily over his back, while two .45mm guns peeked out from shoulder holsters.

Lily shrank deeper into the darkness. "I've got company."

Ben's voice sounded in her ear. "Do not fire unless fired upon."

"Copy that."

"Continue with care."

JB's radio crackled to life. He grabbed at it and listened to his earpiece squawk at him.

"Yeah, boss. There's no one here." He glanced around. "No, sir. I'm certain. I've checked the perimeters several times."

He moved closer to the shadows shielding Lily. She muted her radio and held her breath. *Keep moving, you little prick.*

Reaching for his earpiece again, he stopped just five feet from her. Lily pressed herself further into the shadows as she watched him nod his head.

"Yes, sir." He did an about-face. "I'm heading out there now."

She watched him stalk off and disappear before breathing easily again. Without a sound, she slid from the shadows and made her way toward the stairwell. She pressed her radio. "Headed up the stairs."

"Be careful, Lil. We're still blind as a bat out here. I've got nothing."

"Yeah, well, we can't wait around, Ben." She pulled the door, and it opened without sound. "I'm headed up."

Sweat gathered at the base of her neck. Tiny curls tickled her skin. She ignored the annoyance and took the stairs two at a time.

Lily rounded the first-floor landing and pushed toward the second floor. She climbed two steps. Suddenly, a hand clamped onto her ankle and jerked. Hard. She flew backward through the air and landed with a crunch, her radio shattering into pieces. She lay there, stunned. *What the hell?*

She blinked back the advancing stars right as a black boot took aim for her head. Lily rolled to her right, swallowing a scream as her stitches pulled. The boot hit the step.

Snatching up her gun, she scrambled to her feet, sucking air through clenched teeth at the fire zipping through her side. Sensing movement, she ducked. Too late. JB's fist connected with her jaw. She stumbled, steadied herself and glared at him. *Enough of this shit.* She whipped the 9 mm up and around and squeezed the trigger.

The arc was perfect. Her bullet found its mark. The brick wall of a man roared and grabbed his thigh. Blood seeped between his clutched fingers. He looked down, then slowly raised a shocked gaze to her face.

His eyes glazed over with pain and rage. "You bitch."

JB charged. Lily scrambled up the steps, but he snatched her ankle again and yanked. Covering her head, she left her body unprotected as her world flipped on end. She hit the cold granite wall, her breath escaping her lungs in a rush of air.

He reached for her. She kicked at him.

"Hold still."

She lashed out harder. He jerked her upright and threw her against the steps, the sharp edge digging deep. Hot spasms shot through her back.

Lily stretched for her ankle holster. Her fingers brushed the second metal grip frame. *Come on, baby. Come to Momma.* She spread her fingers wide.

He wrapped his massive hands around her neck.

Murder flickered in his black eyes. He squeezed, crushing her throat. Lily clawed at his steel-trap hold.

She wasn't going to die tonight. Not at this bastard's hands. Lily kicked hard, her steel-toed boot connecting with his groin.

He bellowed and doubled over.

Bringing the heel of her palm up, she smashed it against his nose. The soft cartilage cracked.

He roared and snagged both her hands, slipping them into a one-handed grip and pinning them behind her head. The other found Lily's throat. Again.

Darkness lurked at the edge of her vision, the stars in her cloudy mind beginning to dance and twirl. Lily battled it. Fought it hard, even as her body surrendered to the darkness closing in on her.

A sudden, sharp release jerked Lily back to consciousness. She coughed and gasped for breath. Pushing her badly bruised body up, she scurried away from his murderous grip.

"Yes, sir. I understand, sir."

She scrambled farther from his reach. How had he put such a beat down on her? What was he? Some freaking genetically engineered solider? Lily glanced around, spied the 9 mm and lunged for it.

The hard heel of his boot landed on her outstretched hand. She bit back the groan that rose in her throat.

"Not so fast, bitch." He grabbed a handful of her hair and jerked upward. "Rowland wants to see you."

CHAPTER FIFTY-ONE

Thursday, October 2, 10:35 p.m.

THE MAN COULDN'T have disappeared. People didn't just vanish into thin air. Derek swept the open chamber for John. Came up empty.

Where the hell are you, John?

Derek made another pass along the wall. This time, he dragged the palm of his hand over it. Maybe he'd get lucky and find something. His palm rose a fraction. He paused, then backed up. Closing his eyes, Derek focused and ran his hand over the spot once more.

His palm rose again.

He stopped and pressed hard on the wall. A door swung open, and a hallway appeared. *This* wasn't on the building schematics. Derek reached into his pants pocket, pulled out the tiny flashlight and flicked it on. The corridor sloped down and to the right.

Heart pounding, he made his way into the dark hallway, sweeping the light to the right and left. John was nowhere. Derek moved farther into the gloom. All five of his senses were on high alert.

"Well, isn't this interesting?" a soft female voice sounded behind him.

Derek spun. *Gina?*

She raised her gun and shot him point-blank.

His body jerked. His head cracked against the stone wall as he went down.

Hard.

The world tilted on its edge as Gina Elsworth walked away.

DEREK'S VISION FOCUSED, sharpened. He pushed himself up and winced. The bitch shot him. He pawed at his chest. No blood. *Thank goodness for body armor.*

A tiny light to the left spread out from under a crack and caught his attention. He moved quietly, gun drawn. He flanked the opening, pressed himself to the wall and took a deep breath.

Kicking the door open, Derek rushed into the tiny room. John sat slumped in a chair. Gina spun around, staring at Derek as if she'd seen a ghost.

He cocked his gun. "Give me one good reason not to blow your head off."

Gina tilted her head to the side. "I shot you."

"You missed."

Gina smiled. *Why the hell is she smiling? Has she lost her mind?*

"See this?" She held up a vial. It was empty. Derek's stomach tightened. He'd seen vials like that before. Nothing good ever came from them.

"It's a biochemical weapon I've been developing for the government. It was full. Do you know where it is now?"

He glanced at John. He was pale, his skin clammy. "I'm guessing you've killed him with it."

"No. He's not dead. Yet." She laughed and held up another vial. "This is the antidote. It's the only one we have. He needs it within the next four minutes."

Derek couldn't wrap his mind around the situation. He'd expected to encounter Rowland tonight. But Gina? No way in hell had he seen this one coming.

"Why are you doing this?"

"He tried to kill my children. He tried to kill me." She gave Derek a strange look. "Wouldn't you do anything to keep your loved ones from danger?"

Derek narrowed his eyes. She had a point there. No matter how fucked her logic was. "But why'd you try to kill me?"

"He tried to kill my children. He tried to kill me." Her voice trembled and she pointed at Derek. "*You* work for him. How do I know you aren't here to finish the job?"

Derek studied her and, strangely, understood her motives. Derek glanced between Gina and her husband. He hadn't seen *any* of this shit coming.

Tears streamed down her face. "He had to pay. Don't you understand that? Now, you have a choice to make, G.I. Joe."

G.I. Joe? Really?

"Save him. Kill me. Your choice." She tossed the vial into the air and ran for the door.

Derek dove for the vial as she disappeared from sight.

CHAPTER FIFTY-TWO

Thursday, October 2, 10:38 p.m.

JB OPENED THE DOORS to Rowland's office and shoved Lily into the sweeping space. "Nice knowing you, bitch."

Lily ignored the remark, focusing on the man who most likely wanted her dead. Rowland sat at his desk, the back of his chair hiding him. "I didn't expect to find your guard dogs sniffing around the place, Rowland."

"Ah, that sweet Southern accent of yours is missing. Such a shame. I rather enjoyed it." He swung his oversize leather chair around. His face was set. Darkness flicked in his green eyes. "Tell me, Lily, did you honestly think I wasn't aware of your little game?"

Her body tensed, a million needles biting into her skin. How had he discovered her real name? She went still. *Jackson.* If Jackson had sold her out, had he done the same with Marcus or Evelyn? With Derek? If he had, she was going to kill him when this was over, and not even bat an eye.

Rowland rose from his chair and walked toward Lily. She resisted the urge to back up—not that she could go anywhere with his thug breathing down her neck—and didn't break eye contact with him.

"You're good, I'll give you that. But there was just something too familiar about you for me to let it go. So after our little meeting at the Boiler Room, I did some digging into past associates that I'd…disposed of."

Lily didn't take her eyes off Rowland as he moved closer to her. *Familiar? Disposed? Where the hell was he going with this?* Her throat grew tighter with each step he took toward her.

"Imagine my surprise when I stumbled across these photos."

He held up two faded, sepia-toned photographs. Lily blinked slowly. In one, her mother's beautiful face stared back at her. Laughing. Carefree. Alive. In the other, her mother was on the floor, lying in a pool of blood, a single bullet in her forehead. The room began to spin. Lily's eyes flicked between the pictures and Rowland.

"And just like that—" he snapped his fingers "—I knew why you looked so familiar. Because I knew your mother, intimately."

"Bullshit." She lunged for him, but JB's fingers dug deeper into her arms.

"No, that's your department." Rowland pointed at her. A sick grin twisted his handsome features into something dark, evil. He stepped closer and tipped her chin up, catching her in his death gaze. "I knew both of your parents, Lily Andrews, met them in Italy at a beautiful vineyard. Should have known they were plants. But your mother…she knew just the right words to say, how to articulate them. They worked perfectly on me, until—"

Rowland faltered. A pained look flashed in his cold killer's eyes, and for a brief moment in time, the cool, detached facade lifted and humanity descended over his face, and with it grief, brokenhearted rage and unexplainable suffering. Then, just as quickly, it was gone. He cleared his throat, all humanity vanishing.

"Someone in my compound sold me out to the CIA. They killed my family." His voice was dark, murderous. "As they were the only Americans on my payroll at the time, I did what any man in my position would do. I killed them."

Lily shook her head, disbelieving. "You didn't."

"I did." He let go of her chin and pushed his face close to hers. "And I will do the same to you. How do you think I got to where I am today?"

A wave of grief crashed into Lily. *Her parents had died at this man's hands.* How many more people were going to meet the same fate? Flipping her eyes to his face, she focused the pain, the rage, the agony into a single target: Rowland James.

"Apparently by murdering your way to the top," she said in a low, I-will-kill-you tone. "But it stops here."

Within a breath, Rowland swung his powerful arm. His heavy gold knuckle ring connected with her face. Stars burst behind her eyes. Her knees buckled slightly. Spitting out blood and saliva, she focused her breathing and pushed against the advancing black.

JB jerked her upright, his fingers biting into her arm.

"You shouldn't have gone into the family business, Lily. It isn't good for you." Rowland paced, his arms tucked behind his waist. "Or for your new little makeshift family."

Realization swept over her. "George."

"Yes, I killed that old man. I'd gone there for you,

actually. Seems a bit serendipitous, don't you think?" Rowland flicked his hands in the air, as if he were swatting away a fly, and laughed. "Bad night for him, I'd say, wouldn't you? Wrong place, wrong time."

Another wave of grief crashed into Lily, followed by a tsunami of rage. *Rowland killed George.* Her beloved George. She looked up at Rowland and tightened her fists until her nails bit into the flesh of her palms.

"Just like your family," she whispered.

Anguish and rage flashed in his cold eyes. His fist connected with her face again. "You don't know anything. You don't get to say a word about my family."

She spit out a mouthful of blood and glared at him. "I'm going to kill you."

"Somehow I doubt that." The edge of his lip twitched into a cruel smile. "Now, if the family connection wasn't surprise enough, imagine my disbelief when I found out there was not one, but *two* little bitches spying on me."

Lily's heart pounded as she fought to keep her breath steady. *Evelyn. Please, God, don't let him have Evelyn.* She shook her head. No. Marcus had said Evelyn was home. Safe.

Rowland snapped his fingers. JB released his grip on Lily. Her insides shook as he stalked to the sofa, reached behind it and hauled a woman to her feet. *Please don't be Evelyn.* The woman's head hung limply to the side, and her long, dark hair concealed her face.

JB grabbed the woman's head and jerked it up.

Lily bit back a cry of relief at the same time her heart sank. Alyssa Montgomery, Rowland's assistant, stared blankly at Lily. Tears poured down Alyssa's cheeks, rolling over the tape that covered her mouth.

"Tell me, Lily. Do you know this woman?" Rowland pointed at Alyssa. "Choose your words carefully. Her life depends on it."

Lily glanced at the trembling woman. She could smell fear pouring off her body. "That's Alyssa."

"Wrong answer." Rowland's eyes darkened, and his face hardened. "I'll ask you again. Do you know this woman?"

Blood pounded in Lily's ears, and her heart thumped against her chest. She had no idea who that woman was. CIA? FBI? Interpol? *No way.* Whatever she answered, she would be wrong.

And that woman would be dead.

Lily rushed to answer. "Her name is Alyssa Montgomery. She's your assistant."

JB smirked.

"Wrong again." Rowland moved to her side and yanked Alyssa's hair, exposing her throat.

"Stop!" Lily held up her hands. She took a step toward him. "I swear to you, Rowland. I do *not* know that woman."

Rowland grabbed the knife on his desk. "And why should I believe one word that drips from your lying tongue?"

Alyssa's eyes widened. Terror mixed with tears as she struggled against his hold and shrieked behind the tape.

Lily lunged, every muscle in her body screaming at the sudden movement. JB caught her by the neck. She clawed and kicked, but he lifted her off the floor.

"She's a spy," Rowland said, his tone cold as death, his eyes wild. "I told you not to fuck with me, Lily.

This is how I deal with such treachery. This one's on you."

JB tightened his grip. Lily fought for air and watched, helpless, as Rowland reached up and, in one swift motion, pulled the knife.

Alyssa's throat opened. Blood spurted everywhere.

Bile rushed into Lily's mouth. Rowland let go of Alyssa as she fell to the floor like a rag doll. Lily's breathing came in short, shallow bursts. She dug her fingers into her palms and flipped her gaze to Rowland. He had to be stopped. Adrenaline surged through her body, numbing the pain until Lily felt nothing. Only rage.

Hot, dark rage.

She kicked with all the strength, and her foot connected with the side of JB's knee. It buckled, and his grip loosened. She wrapped her hands around his neck and twisted, waiting for the soft pop, then let go.

JB slumped, landing in a heap.

Lily turned and stared down the cold, metal barrel of Rowland's .45.

"You're going to regret the day you decided you could saunter into my house, into my life, and fuck with me."

"Yes, you've mentioned that."

Lily had no weapon. Hand-to-hand combat with a man twice her size was definitely not ideal. But she was slowly running out of options.

And time.

His knuckles connected with her lip. Her face exploded. A coppery, metallic liquid filled her mouth. She spit out the excess blood. A single drop dripped off her chin.

With a strong flick, her foot connected with his ankle. He landed on his back. She sprang, straddled him, wrapped her hands around his neck and squeezed.

He flipped her over his shoulder.

Lily landed hard. The air rushed out of her lungs. Adrenaline fueling her every movement, she scrambled and picked herself up off the floor.

With the speed of a viper, he struck her face again.

Her vision blurred. Lily rolled to the left and avoided another blow. A red river flowed down her cheekbone. Blood rushed into her eyes, making it impossible to see.

She couldn't beat him this way. She knew it. He knew it. It was only a matter of time.

Lily glanced around. JB's handgun lay two feet from her. She dove and scooped up the gun from the floor. Grasping the metal grip, she drew the gun around and pulled the trigger.

The first bullet arched and hit Rowland squarely in the gut.

He roared in pain.

The second two went wide.

"It's done, Rowland." Lily trained her gun at him. "You're finished."

"I don't think you're one to be giving me ultimatums, darling. Look at you."

He pressed his hand to his stomach and took an unsteady step toward her. Blood seeped from his fingers. He pointed at her hand. "You're trembling, and you're as white as a ghost. There's no way you can shoot me. Your arm's a mess. And I'm guessing you're clenching your teeth to stave off losing consciousness. Am I right?"

"It's just my tricep, asshole."

She cocked the trigger and pulled.

CHAPTER FIFTY-THREE

Thursday, October 2, 10:39 p.m.

DEREK YANKED OFF the needle cover, tapped the syringe twice and then looked down at his boss. "Sorry about this." He shoved the thick needle into John's chest and drove the plunger down, watched as the serum vanished.

Gasping, John's eyes bulged, and then he went limp. *Shit.* Derek pressed his fingers to the man's neck, felt a faint but steady pulse. He pulled John out of the chair and threw him over his shoulder, fireman-style, and headed for the elevator, gun up.

The elevator opened in the lobby and Derek stepped out, his radio crackling to life. "I have John. He needs a medic."

"Copy that," Marcus's steady voice confirmed. "Coming in now."

"Also, Gina isn't our victim." Derek lowered John to the floor, propping him up against the wall. "She's involved somehow in this whole thing."

"You sure?"

Derek slid his hand behind his body armor, winced. "Yeah, I'm sure."

"Well, isn't that a bitch."

Derek looked down at his boss, wondering if he'd

make it. *That was putting it mildly.* He checked his gun, crouched down next to John. "Has Lily che—"

The sharp crack of bullets being fired cut him off, the sound of his worst nightmare.

Derek took off at a run.

ROWLAND LUNGED, AND THEN his body bucked. His eyes widened. He stumbled back, dropping to his knees. He looked at Lily, his eyes glazed with surprise, and fell onto his face.

Lily tried to clear the fog in her brain. She needed to get out, find Derek. Now. She stumbled toward the door, then stopped as a subtle flutter in her peripheral vision caught her attention. She turned, the abrupt movement tilting the room on a crazy edge.

Jackson moved from the shadows and stood over Rowland's body.

The bottom fell out from under Lily. *Son of a bitch.* She scrambled to the far side of the room and shoved her back into the corner, raising her gun.

"Easy, Lil." He stepped closer, his hands up. "Take it easy."

Why was he talking to her like they were something other than enemies? "Don't tell me to take it easy. You killed my friend, you bastard. There's no way Rowland would have known where to find me, find George, unless *you* told him. George's death is on you. You may as well have held the knife yourself."

His brow wrinkled. "I didn't…"

Her hand trembled. Her heart followed suit. "Bullshit."

"Lily, I didn't compromise your location." Jackson ran both hands over his head and stared at her, confusion in his face. "Why would I do that?"

She grasped the butt of the gun with both hands. "Why would you do any of the shit you've done?"

"What I've done? I would never do anything to hurt George." Jackson's voice rose. He shook his head and his face dropped, a pained expression flashing through his eyes. "I've done nothing but try to *protect* you ever since you blew into Rowland's sights at that damn gala."

Protect her? What the hell? Lily blinked, her guard splintering. "*You* were the waiter in the hallway?"

Jackson nodded. "I tried to tell you to back off, to get out of town. I tried."

She bit her lip…to stave off the advancing blackness, help her focus. She'd seen that same look descend when they'd lost their teammate in Afghanistan. Maybe he hadn't gone rogue. *No.* She shook her head. "All lies. I should've known."

"You don't know anything," Jackson snapped, his tone harsh. "I didn't disclose your location to Rowland, and I didn't betray you."

"You didn't—" She choked on the bile that rose in her throat. "You threw me out a three-story window. I almost died. How the hell does that not constitute a betrayal?"

"I knew the Dumpster was there."

She felt like she'd been sucker punched. What was he talking about? Did he really think she'd buy that bullshit?

"There's no way you could have known that."

Jackson held his hands out in front of him, almost as if in a peace offering, and took a step toward her. "Lil, I put it there."

Her mind raced as she backed away from him.

"Move one more step, and I swear, I'll blow your head off."

"No, you won't. Despite that brilliant countermove at your loft, I know you. I trained you. And I know you won't shoot to kill."

"Don't push it."

"Listen to me. I had to disappear. Had to go silent."

Lily shook her head. The numbing effect waned, and pain fought for its rightful place once more. Her vision swam. "What are you talking about?"

His face pinched together. Regret pooled in his eyes. "I couldn't let them question your innocence."

"My *what*?" Her heart constricted. What was he trying to tell her? That he'd done all this for her? Her lips trembled. "Why'd you have to disappear? Nothing of what you're saying makes sense."

"I caught wind of ARME's secret undertaking. When I brought it to the director, he agreed we needed to make a move, but it came down the line that the government's hands were tied. If I went in alone..." He shrugged, pleading with his eyes. "The message was clear. If we wanted to bring them down, neutralize the threat, I had to go off the radar."

She blinked hard. His story matched Derek's version. *Perfectly.* Was Jackson telling her the truth? Had he really done all this out of duty? Did that mean...

Her stomach flip-flopped. Did he still love her? She shook her head. *No.* It didn't matter.

For all she knew, he'd bugged every place she loved: her home, Ben's, Keystone.

"You still left me. You still committed treason."

He tipped his head to the side. He looked ten years older now, his face drawn. "Did I?"

Lily didn't know what to believe. Truth. Lies. They all blended together to make one royal mess.

Two soft pops echoed in her ears at the same time Jackson's body bucked. Slowly, he dropped to the ground. Crimson stains spread across his chest.

Ducking behind the desk, she glanced around the room. Nothing. *Was their sniper back?* Lily kept her head low and rushed to Jackson's side. As she knelt, she pressed her fingers into his throat, searching. A thin, erratic heartbeat thumped against her skin. He was still alive.

Barely.

"Stay with me." She held her hands against the holes in his chest. Blood seeped between her fingers. "Don't die on me now."

Despite the fact that Lily wanted to take Jackson down, she didn't want it to happen this way. She didn't want him to bleed out in her hands. Warring emotions sparred within her brain, and Lily was suddenly very tired, and very freaking confused.

Jackson reached up, covered her hands with his. "Lil, I'm sorry."

"Don't talk."

He pressed his hand against her cheek. The familiar touch sent her senses reeling. Tears blurred her vision.

"I didn't betray you." His hand dropped to his side. He coughed, and a thin line of blood trickled out from the side of his mouth.

"Shhh." She cradled his head. "Don't talk."

"I didn't betray you, Lily. I love you."

Lily hung her head. Rebellious tears sprung to her eyes. All signs pointed to this man committing treason, betraying her. Could they have been wrong? Could *she* have been wrong?

"Jackson."

"I had to leave you. It destroyed me. But it was the only way to keep you safe." He laughed, and blood spilled from his lips. "I misjudged her."

Her?

Lily frowned. She stroked Jackson's face, his stubble scratching her skin. "Rowland's dead."

"Yes, but he isn't your problem," a female voice said behind them. "I am."

CHAPTER FIFTY-FOUR

Thursday, October 2, 10:43 p.m.

DEREK BOUND UP the stairs, taking two at a time, switched channels. "Ben, I need a location on Lil. Where is she?"

"We're still flying blind out here."

Shit. "Copy that. I'm headed up to the executive level, sweeping level two first. I could sure use some cover."

"Say no more. On my way."

Derek cleared the second floor, every cell in his body on high alert. Rowland. Jackson. *Gina.* Derek didn't know where the truth forged into lies.

What a fucking mess.

CONFUSION WASHED OVER Lily as she glanced over her shoulder. Gina Elsworth walked out from the shadows, her gun trained on Lily.

"Never send a man to do a woman's job."

Gina noticed Alyssa's wasted body, her throat sliced open, and clucked her tongue against the roof of her mouth, shaking her head in disgust. "What a waste of money. I sent her in to spy on Rowland for me. Clearly, she couldn't cut it." Gina laughed, high and slightly crazed, at her own twisted joke.

Lily glanced over at Alyssa, then quickly back at Gina.

Her spy? What the hell?

Lily positioned her body between Gina's gun and Jackson. She was no longer sure whether or not he was a traitor, and she wasn't about to let Gina kill him. Especially if he turned out to be innocent.

"How did you get here? The police? You're supposed to be at the house, with Ben's—"

"I called the police, told them not to come. It's amazing what powerful people like me can get away with. And those men you stashed at my house?" Gina laughed. "Well, let's just say they will no longer be of service."

"Well played, with the scared little wife act." Lily stood and raised her gun. "Clearly, I underestimated you."

Gina wasn't a victim. So was she working with Rowland? Or Jackson?

"You did. But don't kick yourself. Everyone does. How else do you think I could puppeteer all the men in my life? They think I'm weak, small-minded. Timid. When the truth is, they are." She tipped her head, made a soft clucking sound with her tongue. "Always thinking with the wrong head."

"It was my plan from the beginning. Rowland was supposed to set it up with his contacts, but he botched the timing. My poor excuse of a husband was supposed to be at home with the kids, not me. The Black Cobras weren't supposed to kidnap John. They were supposed to kill him and those brats. Apparently they couldn't deliver."

Kill them? Lily glanced between Rowland's corpse and Gina. "You put a hit out on your husband and your children?"

"ARME was supposed to be mine. Clear and free. But my father refused to let me run the company alone." Gina waved the gun in the air. "Something about him not thinking I could handle the temptation of power, or some other psychobabble bullshit."

Lily studied Gina's face, the crazy glint in her eyes. Her father had been on to something.

"So I married the son my father always wanted. And waited. I never wanted to play house with the husband and those annoying brats. But I did. I bided my time, waited for my father to die, then went to take what was rightfully mine. Only the joke was on me. The company would never be mine." Gina sat on the edge of the desk and trained her gun on Lily's chest. "That's when I sought out Rowland and invited him to join us."

"You brought Rowland in?"

"He promised to get rid of my problem. In exchange, I would give him access to our weaponry. For a price. I thought we'd come to a mutually beneficial understanding. Until he tried to sell the technology out from underneath me to that one." She motioned to Jackson with her gun.

"When I found out that he'd betrayed me and discovered his misguided plan to avenge his family using *my* company by raining hellfire down on the United States, well, did you honestly think I'd let that madman cripple the very country that's made me rich? Hardly. What do they say?" Gina tipped her head to the side, pursed her lips and looked off into the distance, almost as if she were searching for her next words. Gina's eyes refocused, and she trained the gun squarely on Lily's chest. "Ahh, yes. Don't bite the hand that feeds you."

Lily stared. *The woman's lost her mind.*

"I wanted them both dead, so I followed Rowland to his meeting." Gina laughed again, the sound harsh and wild. "Imagine my surprise to find *you* perched on the roof."

Gina was their sniper? Lily's head spun. Gina must have known who Lily was at her house. Was everything dripping from this woman's tongue a lie?

"Then the bastard had the audacity to try and double-cross me." Gina's top lip curled. "Didn't see that coming." She looked at Rowland's body. "Such a shame. He was beautiful. And incredible in bed."

Lily shuddered. His brutality could hardly be classified as incredible.

"Which you know firsthand." Gina glared at Lily. "Don't you?"

Lily's skin crawled. The woman was a lunatic.

Gina pushed off the desk. "But his usefulness ran its course. If your knight in shining armor hadn't gotten to him first, I would've enjoyed killing him." Her face darkened. "No one double-crosses me."

Gina paced. Lily peered past Gina's shoulder and prayed Derek would walk through the doors.

Keep her talking.

"So what? You kill your husband, your children, and take over the helm?"

"Exactly." Gina's face lit up. "Without John dragging his feet or pulling the morality card every fucking minute, I could usher ARME into a new era. I'd own the future."

Reaching toward her thigh, Lily searched with her fingers. They landed on the cool flash-bang grenade cylinder. She inched it out, pulled the pin, counted to two—cooking it so Gina wouldn't have time to throw it back—and tossed the grenade. Lily turned her head, covered Jackson with her body and placed her hands over his ears.

The explosion blew out parts of the window. Ceiling tiles rained down on them. If Ben hadn't found her yet, that would be a dead giveaway.

Gina dropped her gun, screamed and clawed at her eyes.

Lily shook her head, desperate to orientate herself. She knew she had five seconds, tops, before Gina's eyesight came back.

Ignoring the pounding in her ears, Lily pushed to her feet and rushed the woman.

Their bodies collided with a soft thud. She flipped Gina over her shoulder. Gina scrambled to her feet and swung her fist.

Lily sprang for the gun, ended up on one knee and pointed the gun at Gina. With the speed of a viper, Gina kicked out her foot. It connected with Lily's wrist. Pain shot up her arm. Her gun clattered to the floor.

Lily looked up.

And down the barrel of Gina's gun.

Lily's heart sank. Derek was going to be too late.

"You know what?" Gina asked, panting. "You were supposed to be on Rowland's kill list, as well."

She pushed back her hair and smiled. Dread curled around Lily's chest and squeezed. She'd seen the same darkness flicker in the eyes of the last sociopath she'd locked horns with—Rowland.

"Apparently, if I want anything done around here, I have to do it myself." Gina raised her arm and pulled the trigger.

Lily's body jerked violently. Searing pain ripped

into her shoulder and her torso. She pressed her hand against the wound and pulled it away. Blood dripped down her fingers. *That bitch had armor-piercing bullets.* Lily looked up just as Gina dropped and face-planted on the Italian tiles. Blood pooled around her body.

Lily slammed into the wall, slid down and blinked twice before the pain overcame her brain. A shadowy figure moved just off to the left. Lily searched for her weapon. She'd made it this far, damn it, she wasn't going to die now. Her fingers landed on the cool metal and pulled it into her lap. Pain tore through her shoulder.

"Easy." A familiar voice cut through the fog in her brain.

Derek? She tried to focus.

"It's going to be okay, babycakes." Derek knelt in front of her and smiled. "Sorry, my love. I was a little delayed."

CHAPTER FIFTY-FIVE

Monday, October 6, 10:00 a.m.

BLISTERING PAIN RIPPED through Lily's shoulder, jerking her from the warm darkness. She groaned and forced her eyes open. Bright light blinded her. The sterile hospital smell accosted her nose. Painful memories poured into her consciousness. Confusion and raw sorrow flooded her, choking her.

She closed her eyes. *Derek. Jackson. Derek. Jackson.* Tears streamed down her cheeks and pooled around her ears.

Jackson hadn't betrayed her.

"Lily girl." Ben's deep voice called to her. "Talk to me."

Of course Ben would be in her recovery room, waiting for her to come back to them. He was always there. But Lily didn't want to talk.

"Lil…"

"I can't," she whispered, her eyes tightly closed.

"Yes, you can. Talk to us."

Us? Lily's eyes popped open. Derek leaned against the window, arms crossed. Ben sat in the chair next to her bed. She slowly pushed herself up.

"About what? That the man I was sent in to bring down killed my parents, then George. That the man I thought betrayed me, didn't? Or that the man I trusted, my own godfather, turned his back on me?" She fought for breath. Anger ripped through her like hot lava, burning from the inside out.

"Lil. I spoke with Kennedy," Ben said, interrupting her tirade. "He didn't turn his back on you—on any of us. Kennedy was dealing with his own load of shit, right in his own backyard. Rowland had a Dům Hrůzy mole in Unit 67."

Her mouth dropped open. She glanced between both men, searching their faces.

"It's taken care of now—all the bombs were accounted for, every Dům Hrůzy mole has been taken into custody. It's been a busy five days, but like I said, Kennedy didn't turn his back on us. He was busy tackling his own hell."

Lily shook her head and the world spun. She closed her eyes, pressing the tips of her fingers against her temples. "But he knew about Jackson." Her eyes snapped open and brimmed with unshed tears. "Where is he? Where is Jackson now?"

The muscle in Derek's jaw tightened.

She clenched the sheets, fought to steady her voice. "Derek?"

Tears illuminated the blueness of his eyes. He walked over to her, gently cupped her face in his hands and kissed her softly. The he turned and, without a word, left the room. Left her.

DEREK STORMED OUT of Lily's room and glared at the tall man quietly leaning against the wall. *She'd asked for him.* Didn't that tell Derek everything he needed to know?

"She's asking for you."

Jackson nodded and pushed off the wall. Stopping in front of Derek, he extended his good hand. "Thanks for keeping her safe."

Derek reached out, shook the hand of the man who'd stolen the woman he loved. No. Jackson hadn't stolen anything. *She'd asked for him.* "Of course, man. She's one hell of a woman."

A weary smiled tugged at Jackson's mouth. "Yeah. She is."

Helpless to do anything, Derek watched Jackson walk through Lily's hospital door and back into her life.

She'd asked for him.

Derek punched the wall, turned and walked away.

HER HOSPITAL DOOR OPENED, and she swung her gaze to it, eager to see Derek, desperate for him to put his arms around her and tell her that everything was going to be okay. That they were going to be okay.

Instead, Jackson stood in the doorway. His arm hung in a sling. The remnants of an angry, fading bruise covered the right side of his face. Stitches crisscrossed from the corner of his eye to the top of his forehead.

The feebly constructed wall around Lily's heart crumbled. She grappled for words as her heart jumped inside her, and that terrified her. "You're alive."

"Hey, Lily girl."

Lily moved her lips, but couldn't get her mouth to make any sounds. Jackson wasn't dead.

Jackson looked over at Ben. "Sir, can you give us a moment?"

Taking Lily's hand in his, Ben searched her face. "Lil?"

"It's okay." She blinked and swallowed hard. "Give us a minute."

He squeezed her hands and stood, pointing at Jackson. "I could kill you for what you've put her through, what you've put all of us through."

Jackson nodded, eyes downcast.

"You have two minutes." Ben headed to the door. He stopped and glanced back at Lily. "If you need me, I'll be outside."

She waited until the door was shut before she looked at Jackson. Gray hair sporadically peppered his blond sideburns, played peekaboo in his beard. Lines etched themselves around his eyes. He seemed worn-out, old.

"Why are you here? Shouldn't you be debriefing with the director?"

"My flight leaves in an hour."

"Oh."

"I had to see you before I left, had to explain. Or at least try." He took two steps and stopped. "I couldn't leave without telling you that I love you."

His words twirled and tumbled around her head. She tried to make sense of them, of this moment. Jackson was alive. He hadn't betrayed his country. He hadn't betrayed her. He'd come back from the dead.

He was here.

Telling Lily he loved her.

Jackson moved to the side of her bed and sat down, careful not to pull at her IVs. She stared up at him, unable to respond, unable to react.

"I never stopped loving y—"

"Stop." She held up her hand, halting him midsentence. "There's nothing to explain, Jackson. You left. Without a word or an explanation, you left me. As a fellow operative, I understand what got you to your decision. I do. But it was the wrong one."

"I never stopped loving you." His voice cracked, and Lily's heart broke for him.

She pressed her hand to his cheek and carefully measured her next words. No matter how she crafted them, they were going to wound him. But that didn't change the fact that they were true. "I don't love you anymore, Jackson. You were my first love, but—"

"Derek." It wasn't a question.

At the mention of Derek's name, Lily dropped her hand and her heart nearly exploded. *Yes, Derek.* It would always be Derek. The man who'd found her, thrown her a lifeline, saved her.

The man who *saw* her.

"I love him."

"I'm so sorry, Lil." Tears pooled in Jackson's eyes. "I never meant to hurt you."

"I know." And she did. She understood how quickly an undercover assignment could go to hell.

"As always, your instincts are spot-on." Jackson got up, smiled down at her. "You couldn't have chosen a better man. He's perfect for you."

"You checked up on him?"

Jackson laughed. It was a hollow, sorrowful sound. "Of course I did. Had to make sure the man who'd stolen your heart was good enough."

"He didn't steal it, Jackson. I gave it to him."

"I know." He leaned down and pressed his lips to Lily's one last time. "Goodbye, Lily girl."

CHAPTER FIFTY-SIX

Monday, October 6, 10:10 a.m.

THE MOMENT THE door closed, Lily reached for her phone and punched in Derek's number. It went straight to voice mail.

"I don't know what the hell is going on in that sexy, stubborn head of yours, Derek Moretti, but you better get your ass back here. Please, Derek, I need you. Come back." She hung up and dialed the next number seared into her mind.

Marcus answered on the first ring.

"Where is he?" Lily asked, not even bothering to say hello. She wanted to know where Derek was, and she wanted to know now.

Her door opened and she looked up hopefully. She glanced over. *Ben.* Her heart sank. Not the man she wanted to see at the moment, but she waved him in. He moved to the chair next to her bed and sat.

She gripped the phone. "Marcus, where is he?"

"Lil, we both thought he was with you."

"Well, he's not. You tell him that if he doesn't get back here, I will track him down and kick his ass." She hung up.

Ben's eyebrows arched, but he said nothing.

She drummed her fingers against the sheets. If Ben

wasn't sitting there guarding her, she'd have yanked out her IV by now and tracked Derek down.

"You going to talk to me, or are you just going to sit there silently fuming?" Ben placed his hand over hers, halting her sporadic movements.

What was she supposed to say? That she was terrified that the man she loved had just walked out on her? Derek had become a strong, solid, unfailing fixture in just a few short weeks, and she loved him for it.

Where was he?

She squeezed her eyes tight, willing herself to be strong. Just a little longer. She was quickly losing the battle that raged in her, especially as every cell in her body sat on edge, waiting for the man she loved to come through her door.

The pain in her shoulder flared, demanding her attention. Reaching for the medicine drip button, Lily pressed down hard. At least she could take care of one source of pain. She glanced toward the door. Her eyes grew heavy.

Please come back.

DEREK'S PHONE VIBRATED. He hit End, pocketed it. Without a moment's reprieve, the vibrations started again. Loud. Demanding. Angry. He dug into his pocket, yanked it out and took the call.

"What!"

"Where the fuck are you?" Ben's hard voice demanded. "You should be here."

Derek ran a hand over his face. "She made her choice, Ben."

"You're an idiot," Ben snapped. "Jackson just left. She sent him away. She's asking for you."

Derek froze.

For me?

"All I can say, Derek, is your ass better be back here by the time she wakes up." The line went dead.

Derek turned, sprinted back toward the hospital.

HOURS LATER, LILY AWOKE. She glanced around, searching for Derek. Found him. He'd curled up in the visitor's chair, his chin resting against his chest. Her whole body gave a collective sigh of relief as her eyes soaked him up.

"You came back."

"I got your message. You okay?"

"Are you serious?" She gawked at him. *Am I okay?* "No. I'm not okay. Why did you leave?"

"Lil…"

She couldn't read him. And she hated that. Paralyzed with uncertainty, she was unable to move. Panic, agony and fear slammed into her.

All at once. Consuming her.

Why was he hesitating?

Derek looked at her, his face pinched in concern. "You asked for Jackson. I thought…"

"Yeah, well, you thought wrong." Tears brimmed in his eyes, melting Lily from the inside out. All she wanted Derek to do was take her into his arms. "Why are you sitting over there?"

Without a word, he pushed himself up, walked over and sat on the edge of her bed. She reached for him and wrapped her fingers through his. "Look at me."

Derek turned the bluest eyes she'd ever seen toward her, pain flickering across his face. He thought she still loved Jackson. She wanted to laugh, and she wanted to smack Derek, all at once. She didn't want Jackson.

She wanted *him*.

"Jackson was my first love, yes. But I'm not that girl anymore."

Derek scrubbed his hands over his face, rose to his feet. "Lily. Look. I don't expect you to—"

"Stop." She held up her hand. What was with people interrupting her today? And why was Derek acting as if she had a choice? She didn't. She belonged to him—mind, heart and soul. "What is your problem?"

"*My* problem?"

"Yes, your problem. What is it?" Lily ordered herself to calm down. The last thing they needed was for the doctors to come running if any of the freaking machines she was connected to went off. "What's going on in that sexy brain of yours?"

"Oh, I don't know. The woman I love almost died, and her fucking fiancé just sauntered back into her life…all in the same day." He kicked the dresser next to him. "So, yeah. I guess I do have a problem."

"Derek, you can be such a caveman. I love you."

He stared at her, almost as if he didn't believe a word she said.

Lily sighed. *Stubborn jackass.* "Jackson's gone. I told him I love you. He's gone."

Derek's arms fell to his side. "You did?"

"Of course I did." Lily patted the bed next to her.

Derek moved to her bed, sat lightly and pulled her onto his lap. She lowered her face to his, kissing him, losing herself in his taste, in his touch…in his desire. Breathless, Lily pulled way.

He burrowed his face into her chest. "I thought I'd lost you."

"Never." She cupped her hands under his jaw and forced him to look at her. "You could never lose me, Derek. I choose you. I'll *always* choose you."

* * * * *

ACKNOWLEDGMENTS

You'd think the second time around would have dulled the thrill. It didn't. If anything, it was an even bigger high. Without this incredible group of people, *Dead No More* wouldn't exist. I'm indebted to the following:

Jill Marsal, my agent and trusted business partner at Marsal Lyon Literary Agency. Thank you for fielding all my insane questions; I owe you!

Lauren Smulski, my editor at HQN. Your humor and critical eye is most appreciated, especially with this baby! Thank you for putting up with the countless queries, random emails and an insane timeline. Working with you has been an absolute dream.

Susan Swinwood, Margo Lipschultz, the art department and the rest of the amazing team at HQN for making this book the best it can be.

Catherine Coulter, your dedication to this craft is truly inspiring. Thank you for offering to read, for asking the hard questions, for taking time out of your busy schedule, for the invaluable advice…for paving the way for "newbies" like me. Let's be honest: I'm still pinching myself here!

J.T. Ellison, for reading, for encouraging, for pulling me onto that dance floor, for welcoming me into "the tribe." I'm forever grateful for your friendship, your wisdom and your outlook on life. Here's to another chance meet-up on the East Coast!

Karen Evans, for your friendship and for helping track down this book amongst the black hole otherwise known as the postal service.

Lynnette Labelle, for your continued advice, humor and friendship.

Jo Gunnink, thanks for seeing the vision through the fog, and for cheering me on to "finish it!"

Sarah Martini, my cheerleader, confidant and friend—"Where's the coffee?"

Lynette Ruiz, my gorgeous sister, who continues to cheer me on. Thank you.

My mom, Raenell, for taking time out of her beach vacation to hole herself up in her hotel room and read the final draft until the very last sentence. That's unconditional love!

To all the sassy, courageous, gorgeous women in my life—you know who you are. Most only have one or two such friends; I've been blessed with several across the world. And to everyone else who continues to support this dream in one fashion or another, thank you.

And saving the best for last—my incredible husband, Drew. There are not enough words to completely articulate my love for you. Thank you for championing me on like only you can do.

REQUEST YOUR FREE BOOKS!
2 FREE NOVELS PLUS 2 FREE GIFTS!

◆HARLEQUIN®
INTRIGUE®
BREATHTAKING ROMANTIC SUSPENSE

HIDIR13R

Reader Service.com

Manage your account online!

- Review your order history
- Manage your payments
- Update your address

*We've designed
the Harlequin® Reader Service
website just for you.*

Enjoy all the features!

- Reader excerpts from any series
- Respond to mailings and
  special monthly offers
- Discover new series available to you
- Browse the Bonus Bucks catalog
- Share your feedback

Visit us at:
ReaderService.com